Marc Gee has written eleven stage plays which have been performed throughout the counrty. One of his plays *Al's Lads* was made into a full feature film in 2001 and premiered by BAFTA at the Cannes Film Festival. Presently the film has been sold to over twenty two countries. Marc has lectured in screen writing at the BBC, various literary festivals, schools, universities and colleges.

AUTUMN
KILL

Marc Gee

Matador
5 Weir Road,
Kibworth Beauchamp
Leicester LE1 7FW, UK
Tel: (+44) 116 279 2299
Email: books@troubador.co.uk
Web: www.troubador.co.uk/matador

ISBN 978-1848761-537

A Cataloguing-in-Publication (CIP) catalogue record for this book
is available from the British Library.

Typeset in 11pt Times by Troubador Publishing Ltd, Leicester, UK
Printed and bound in the UK by TJ International Ltd, Padstow, Cornwall

Matador is an imprint of Troubador Publishing Ltd

For my daughters
Chloe and Molly
X

ACKNOWLEDGMENTS

In writing this book I would like to thank certain friends and family who have made it possible. Andy Jackson, Hannah Jackson, Norman Hannah, Helen Horner, Helen Barber, Cheryl Barber, Karin Gibson and all at The Keswick Book Club, Vic Gibson, Steve Duffy, Barry Pace, Principal Psychotherapist Dr Mark Stowell-Smith, Elaine Saunders, Ian Whittingham, Kevin Pritchard and Cushla Allison-Baker.

Special thanks go to Brian Hughes, Steve Barber and Peter Horner for their enthusiasm in the publication of this book. To my sister Clare who has been my sounding board and who has the patience of a saint, her belief in me is unfounded. To Angela, for her undying support and to Paul and Hazel and my dear mother whose love of books has inspired me to write this novel.

They looked away for a second, a split second, and they were gone.

Did they miss them... With every breath, of every second, of every day?

Will they get revenge? That's what brought them together.

CHAPTER ONE

A sticky Monday morning on the first day of October did nothing to quell the giggling of two teenage secretaries as they stepped inside the lift of RDT Advertising. Clutching cappuccinos in their lily white hands one of them shook the rain drops out of her long brunette ringlets sending an aroma of damp perfume around the lifts metallic walls. The pungent smell made a leather clad, despatch rider sneeze inside his battered crash helmet as a couple of trendy advertising executives, oblivious to anything, lorded-it-up over England's seven wicket victory against the West Indies at Trent Bridge that summer, a summer that had long disappeared with the warmth of the sun.

In under a minute both men would be dead.

A robotic voice indicated '*The sixth floor*' and the lift doors clicked into life. The secretaries along with the despatch rider and his crackling CB radio stepped out into the plush reception of the advertising agency as the doors of the elevator slowly shut like the curtains closing on a coffin in a crematorium.

Head buried in the latest share-index of the *Financial Times*, the tall figure of Anders Riiss had been standing inconspicuously at the back of the lift. As the lift headed upwards he removed his eyes from the small print and pulled out a gun from the inside of his suit jacket. Pointing the barrel an inch from the back of the executive's head, he pulled the trigger. Then, swinging the gun to the right fired another bullet through the back of the other man's head. The silencer cushioned the sound of the bullets, sending blood, brain and skull splattering against the lift doors. It took less than three seconds. As the men's legs buckled, their bodies trembled like an earthquake making the lift shake. One of the men's heads slammed against the silver hand-rail then crashed onto the lift's blue carpet as the other man seemed to fall in slow motion. The life taken from him; he dropped to his knees before rolling to one side in a crumpled heap; his chin slumping onto his chest. Lowering his gun Anders fired another couple of nine millimetre bullets into the men's hearts. Just to make sure. 'Two hearts beat as one. Not any more they don't!'

As the lift doors opened, Andres dropped the pink newspaper over the men, slipped the gun back inside his suit jacket and casually stepped over the bodies and onto the ninth floor. Wearing blue tinted glasses and a pinstriped suit and tie Anders waited for the lift doors to close behind him. To the left of him a wall of rain-swept windows ran the length of the deserted corridor, to his right a view of the Houses of Parliament and the London Eye, smudges on the grey landscape. Striding along the corridor he passed office doors, some open, some closed. He smelt the aroma of coffee and heard phones ringing and being answered. Somewhere a fax machine was working overtime and passing one of the open doors he overheard a heated argument in full swing. Exchanging a smile and a 'good morning' with a mini-skirted secretary who passed him, he didn't look out of place. He was straight backed, trendy, well spoken and looked like an ex-public schoolboy, British to the core.

Stopping at a water fountain, Anders leant down and helped himself to a squirt of cold water. His throat was dry, murder can be thirsty business. Running his index finger across his mouth he removed a few drops of water from his bottom lip. Over the top of his glasses, he scanned back down the corridor for any nosey-parkers; he noted he was not being watched. Putting his hand behind his back he pulled down the iron bar of the fire escape door. As an alarm blasted out, he spun around, pushed opened the door and disappeared. Anders was cool, slick.

Like a bullet out of his own gun, Anders took off down the steep stairwell. Bouncing off the concrete walls, Anders' feet left the ground as he projected himself round each turn of the stairs. Suit jacket flapping behind him like the Caped Crusader, Anders skipped step after step as he hurtled down the nine flights. Passing 'ground level', the grey haired, fit, fifty year old made it to the basement without breaking sweat. Taking in a couple of deep breaths, Anders composed himself, straightening his jacket and tie then brushing the hair off his face. Entering the underground car park with a breeze of confidence, he tried to block out the sound of the alarms rebounding off the giant pillars that supported the towering building overhead. The smell of car fumes lingered in the dark as he spotted daylight streaming down from the street onto the ramp ahead of him, his escape route. The ramp was only a few yards away, but he could feel his heart starting to race. Now he started to sweat. Reaching behind a large four-by-four, Anders retrieved a bamboo handled umbrella and started walking briskly towards the ramp. Passing a line of flashy cars, he became aware of the security cameras waiting for him. At the bottom of the ramp a middle aged woman was being ordered to evacuate the building by an irate security guard. Furious over not being able to collect her Jag, her high-pitched voice cut through the air like a knife. Putting up his umbrella Anders concealed his sharp pointed features from the cameras overhead and walked past the

3

remonstrating woman and guard. They didn't give him a second glance. At the top of the ramp he smelt the wet pavements of London's West End. Anders felt enormous relief as the rain and fresh air hit him, but although there was no remorse in his heart he wasn't about to relax, he never relaxed.

Though the rumble of heavy traffic he heard approaching sirens and lengthened his stride. His long legs took him past the occasional businessman hunched under the covering of a black umbrella. Their expressions were normal, routine, some even cheerful, unaware of the violence that had just taken place in the office block lift. Making his way round the side of the building Anders stopped at the corner of the busy road, his size eleven shoes balancing on the side of the kerb. An ambulance flashed past him and roared to a stop. For a few seconds he watched as two paramedics jumped out of the ambulance and ran through the large glass doors of the building. He knew they were wasting their time.

Darting across the busy road, Anders found refuge from the downpour under the hoarding of a Starbucks coffee shop. Conscious of the sweat running down his face and the people gathering inside the coffee shop window, he turned around. Loosening his silk tie, he unbuttoned the top of his white shirt and watched the drama unfold across the road. At the same time his mobile vibrated deep inside his jacket. Just as he was about to answer his call, he looked around to see if he was out-of-ear-shot.

'Ja, ja, the job is done. What did you expect?' His accent had changed. It was no longer the clipped British voice he'd previously spoken high up on the ninth floor of the advertising agency, now it was soft, guttural, Norwegian 'Ja I have heard of the place, ja, ja, I will find it. That will be more expensive. You understand?... No I do not want to know any details…Before we do any business, I will check to see if the money has been deposited.' Hanging up and on his guard, his long, thin fingers tapped in the numbers on his mobile. Waiting for the call to be answered, his bright blue eyes looked up at the black sky. Hoping the rain would stop soon, he threw a quick look across the road as a police car drew up. Once again his accent changed. This time he spoke in fluent German. 'Account name Anders Riiss. Number 00012567898BZA. Security code, O.L.E.F. BHY... Passwords ... F for Fishing, S for Salmon.'

As he waited, he watched as hundreds of bewildered office workers streamed out of the building and into the rain, his doing. Through a huddle of people he recognised one of the secretaries from the lift. She was being consoled by a couple of women and was sobbing uncontrollably, strands of wet ringlets stuck to her face by tears.

Suddenly a black transit van screeched to a halt outside the main entrance. As its tyres smouldered on the wet tarmac, the back doors flew open and an Armed Response Unit jumped out like Storm Troopers. Clutching sub-machine guns, the black figures hurtled into the building causing gasps of disbelief from the swelling crowd.

'Danke.' Anders hung up. He never ate before a kill and the smell of coffee and croissants from the coffee shop were making him hungry. It was time to go. Stepping onto the pavement he dodged a torrent of water that flew up from the gutter by a passing taxi and cursed under his breath, it was a near miss. As he made his way towards the hustle and bustle of a street market he suddenly stopped and turned around. Momentarily giving the chaos at the tower block one last look, a glint of satisfaction appeared in his eyes before he disappeared into the throng of Soho.

Taking the time to glance into a few sex shop windows, Anders passed the world famous Windmill Theatre and then into Shaftsbury Avenue. As usual at this time on a Wednesday, the West End was full of office workers making the most of their lunch hour.

5

Like any other major metropolis the sandwich bars, cafes and restaurants were hectic; the pavements full of the jostling tourists as the theatres geared themselves up for the afternoon's matinees, ideal for Anders to blend in. The aroma of 'Peking and Cantonese' floated around Gerrard Street as Anders manoeuvred his way through the hungry faces of Chinatown. Discreetly removing the sim-card out of the back of his mobile he knelt down and pretended to tie his shoe lace. Disposing of the card down a grid, he stood up and stared at the carcases of ducks hanging in a restaurant window. For some strange reason, it made him question his own conscience, how barbaric his life was, but it was only for a fleeting moment. There was no room for sentiment in his job.

Turning right under the Chinese Arch, Anders passed an open door advertising 'Linda' on the first floor, then back-tracked nipping down a dark side street. Finding himself in Leicester Square, he stopped at a novelty shop. Lowering his umbrella, he looked intently into the window. It was cluttered with postcards of Big Ben, key-rings of double-decker buses, Sex Pistol t-shirts along with Queen and Lady Diana mugs. Everything the tourist requires and desires. Gazing up, his eyes pierced the reflections over each shoulder, although there were many tourists milling around, he knew what to look for. If he was being 'tailed', the person would be doing something out of the ordinary. As his eyes danced in the refection of the glass, he looked for clues, someone reading a newspaper, asking directions, taking photographs of a landmark, or like him looking at the reflections in a nearby shop window. All the tell-tale-signs he'd trained his eyes to look for, all the tell-tale-signs which had now become a compulsive obsession. Looking down, he grimaced for a split second. Rain had seeped into his polished brogues. It was a minor hiccup he'd had worse moments in his life. The coast was clear. But as always Anders coldly and systematically averted his eyes and double-checked for somebody, somebody like him. He always double-checked.

As Anders waked across Leicester Square a massive advertising banner caught his attention. It was flapping in the wind high above a cinema and plugging the latest block-buster movie. The film was called *The Assassins* starring two modern day action heroes. The right hand corner of Anders' mouth slowly curled up, giving him a crooked smile across his craggy, athletic face. Squirting peppermint mouth freshener to the back of his throat, he thought back to the first time he took someone's life and started humming his favourite Walker Brothers song.

'There's no regrets.
No tears goodbye.
I don't want you back.
We'll only cry, cry again.
Say goodbye again'.

It was over thirty years ago when Anders was stationed in Germany. As a fresh-faced soldier serving in the Norwegian army, he was involved in a scrap with some English squaddies. They had been drinking heavily in a bar called 'Lucy's' a pick-up-joint in the notorious red-light district of Hamburg. When a brawl broke out over a blonde, the two sets of soldiers squared up. The fist-fight resulted in someone pulling a knife; it fell to one of the 'Brits' who didn't waste any time in stabbing Anders pal in the back. He died outright as Anders cradled him, bloody in his arms. He saw who it was, and he wasn't about to let it go lightly. A week or two later he waited for the soldier and jumped him. Dragging him down a dark alley kicking and screaming, he shut him up by wrestling him to the cobbles and gripped him from behind in a head-lock. With one strong twist and yank, he broke his neck. Anders was that pumped-up with adrenaline and revenge, it was like snapping a twig. That night changed him forever. For some perverse reason he felt elation in killing, he buzzed from the challenge, the planning, the rush of the 'hit'. For once in his life he found something that suited him, something he could make a decent living out of, but more importantly he enjoyed it. The young British soldier was to be the first of many.

Sauntering past the statue of Charlie Chaplin and a thousand different accents he paused at a mime artist complete with white face paint and wings impersonating an angel. Dropping some loose change into his hat, the mime artist instantly moved his hands and head like a robot. A group of Japanese school children wearing the same plastic see-through macs giggled and took digital photographs to show their parents back home. Anders smiled; he was pleased they were happy.

Outside Leicester Square Tube Station, Anders picked up a *Metro* newspaper. The front page informed the British public that the Chancellor was considering putting a penny on every pint of beer. A sardonic smile brushed his face. As an alien living on British soil he could never understand the English psyche. Overhead, a police helicopter flew past. It had stopped raining, and through the breaks in the black clouds he could see patches of bright blue sky. Then, like a ghost he disappeared into the bowels of the tube station. For Anders it was turning out to be a mighty fine day.

CHAPTER TWO

Brian Young sat slouched in the driver's seat of his Hackney cab. Smoking a menthol cigarette, he'd lost count of the amount of times he'd sat there in the evenings, watching, waiting. Normally he'd bring a daily newspaper with him to kill time. He'd sit there for hours mulling over the cryptic crossword. Most of the answers he knew, but he never had a pen, so he never bothered to fill it in. Some days he liked to watch the spider on the wing mirror of his cab. For hours on end, he'd try and work out how, and why, spiders spun their webs on the wing mirrors of cars and sometimes he tried to work out how many bricks it took to construct the huge prison wall opposite. A couple of million maybe, possibly three.

Brainforth Prison was built on the outskirts of Oxford by the Victorians over a hundred and sixty years ago. Now holding Category A prisoners, it once held inmates waiting for the gallows and had been earmarked for demolition by the government for over twenty years. With its razor wire and security cameras perched high on top of the walls, '*The Hanging Prison*' as it was nicknamed was an imposing sight.

As Young's cigarette smoke rolled down the inside of the windscreen, he scratched the top of his head, unaware of the dandruff that fell like snow flakes onto the shoulders of his shabby bomber jacket. Watching a stream of cars zoom past on the main road into Oxford, he compared them to the Dinky Toys he'd kept in a shoe box as a kid. Against the long prison wall the cars looked tiny, but it was just another observation, another thing to kill time.

Deep in his own world, Young yawned, running his hands over his dishwater complexion. He was oblivious to a stooped, elderly woman walking up the tree-lined road towards the cab. Santana had come onto the radio, triggering a memory. Carlos Santana had once been his favourite guitarist. As a long haired medical student he'd hitch-hiked across Europe in a Che Guevara t-shirt and duffle coat to see him play in Berlin. He was unshaven, free, no responsibilities, fresh to face the world. Now, just turned fifty five with a receding hairline, and a few extra pounds jammed under the steering wheel of his cab, his youth, Berlin and *Black Magic Woman* were distant memories.

Young stubbed out his cigarette into the overflowing ashtray and thought about lighting another. As the old woman walked past, she shot him a look from beneath her thick, cracked foundation. He wondered if she recognised him, or whether it was just a dirty look? Whatever look it was he ignored it, he was used to 'looks' of some sort or another. Coughing a smoker's cough in unison to a dog barking, Young caught sight of a milkman darting out of a garden gate. Skidding on his heels like a cartoon figure, the milkman dropped his collection money onto the pavement and barked back at the dog, bringing a wry smile to Young's haunted expression. He didn't recognise him as the regular milkman, maybe he was in bed with tonsillitis or too many beers the night before. Who knows, who cares, Young certainly didn't, he was past caring.

With the dog's bark still echoing inside the cab, Young snapped out of his daze. A few drops of rain hit the windscreen and with a furrowed brow, he looked up at the black threatening clouds circling overhead. Within minutes the rain would turn from a light shower into a heavy downpour. October was never his favourite month. Flicking on the wipers of the cab his sunken eyes looked across at Brainforth and at that precise moment he saw Tony Evans come out of the large prison gates. Watching as the prison officer skipped over the black puddles towards his car, Young started the cab. He knew Evans' car wouldn't start the first or the second time, it never did, but he was ready, ready as always. On the third time of trying Evans' car burst into life spewing out a cloud of black diesel smoke from its exhaust pipe into the damp air. As the black cab pulled away from the curb, the barrier of the prison car park lifted and Evans drove out onto the busy main road. In an instant, Young realised something was wrong and without thinking or looking flew out of the side street. Cutting across two lanes of oncoming traffic, the cab bounced over the central curb and swerved to avoid an articulated lorry. Horns blasted him from every direction. Veering in and out of the heavy traffic like a Formula One racing driver, Young swung the cab one way then the next. His knuckles turned white as he gripped the steering wheel. His face reddened as sweat started to seep out from his face and neck. Slamming on the breaks he veered to the right turning sharply and skidding back into the flow of traffic. Bringing the cab under control, he found himself bumper to bumper behind the tail lights of Evans' car. Brushing away a sweaty loose piece of hair from his forehead, Young laughed to himself, a manic laugh and heaved a sigh of relief at the same time. *Perfect timing.* Young's nicotine stained fingers shook as he lit another cigarette. He didn't know why Evans had changed direction that evening as he knew he was a creature of habit. Following for a couple of miles, Young pulled up behind him at a set of traffic lights and came to a healthy decision. Tomorrow he'd park in the country lay-by about five miles out of town. He'd had enough kamikaze driving for one day. Knowing Evans was *'usually'* a creature-of-habit, he would follow him through the winding lanes for about another ten miles. Then, when he pulled into his road, that's where he could watch him again. That would be his next move. Things had to move forward, time was running out.

Engulfed in cigarette smoke, the lights turned green and Young continued to follow. The dark night was drawing in as he flicked on his headlights. Passing a line of rundown shops, he noticed a couple of council workers hanging up a string of industrial lights in the shape of a snowman and impending thoughts of the 25th of December triggered an emotional stir. It was an escape to the past.

His mind returned, as it often did these days to one particular time as a six or seven year old on Christmas day a long, long time ago. He woke up in his bedroom to find an orange and a chocolate bar in his stocking and a bright red push-bike at the bottom of his bed. It had a shinny silver bell and gold tinsel wrapped around the crossbar and handlebars. As he took in the excitement of the day, *She Loves You* by the Beatles came booming out of a radiogram from the front room. He opened the curtains to find it had been snowing, when his mother burst in and smothered him in Christmas kisses. Closing his eyes for a split second it caused the cab to swerve, but it was the only way he could smell his mother's sweet breath on his cheek. His father who had the nickname 'Sparky' had already opened the sherry and was wearing a maroon dressing gown with a white rope trimming. Young tried to remember whether it was a smoking jacket, and then laughed quietly to himself. Being a socialist and a union man who spent most of his life working as a welder on Southampton docks he couldn't see his dad wearing a smoking jacket, but he could still see him dancing *The Twist* with his mother around the front room on that Christmas Day morning. His father's hands were big and battered, the palms covered in calluses from blister upon blister and again when he closed his eyes, he could smell the sea and the ingrained oil in his hands. One day he came home with a black eye and a bloody nose. Years later Young found out that he used to bare-knuckle fight to earn some extra cash and that he won more than he lost. He loved and missed his parents.

Cutting in front of a line of traffic, Young pulled up alongside Evans at another set of lights. Peering inside Evans' car he couldn't see his face. Glared out by a street light, he caught a glimpse of his light fingers tapping the steering wheel. He wondered what music he liked, rock, pop, reggae, jazz? But Young knew what he liked. Evans was a Motown man. Knowing where he went to on a Friday night at the end of every working month said he was a Motown man.

Before the Christmas turkey his dad lifted him onto the leather saddle of his bike at the top of the cobbled street which led down to Bindley Park. The early morning snow had vanished and only the pink glow of it remained on the sun kissed hills in the distance. His shoes barely touched the wooden peddles and the morning sherry and the stale lunchtime beer on his father's breath was ripe. With a helping hand, he was shoved hard in the back and desperately trying not to disappoint his father's shouts of encouragement, he hung on for dear life. As the bike hurtled down the steep street, the smell of beer was replaced by the smell of fear. As the sun burnt into his eyes, he remembered the choice between the cobbles or the park railings and picked the railings.

When he came to, he was laying on his side. His ankle was back to front, snapped in three places and he still bore the legacy today with a slight limp. Then he felt the warmth of his own blood as it seeped through the crotch of his brown cord trousers, flooding his thigh. His cords were brand new, a Christmas present from his grandmother. Not any more; now they would become a present for the Rag Man. A broken railing had impaled itself through his groin. For the next three weeks he didn't know whether he was going to lose one testicle or two. After that he could never remember his father being drunk around him again, not even at his wedding. In hospital, his father sat by the side of his bed and tried to cheer him up by singing a song from his old navy days. Sometimes he remembered it and sang it to himself, but only now and again.

'Hitler only had one ball.
The other is in the Albert Hall.
Himmler has something similar.
But Goebbles has no balls at all'.

Losing one ball was bad enough, but missing the Christmas turkey and never seeing his buckled red bike again was worse. Happy Christmas.

Swinging off the main road, Young followed Evans into the dark country lanes as the jingle of the evening news came over the cabs radio. He switched it of. He hated the news. But if he had continued listening he would have heard the news report on the shooting of two executives in London's West End.

14

CHAPTER THREE

Unaware he was being followed by a black cab; Tony Evans leant forward in the driver's seat and swore out loud. Straining to see through the rain-battered window screen, like the wipers of the car his temper had seen better days. It was no good moaning, until his luck changed he'd have to put up with the banger, that's if his luck ever would. Tony didn't look like the normal Prison Officer you would imagine him to look like. He wasn't big or burly, like a nightclub doorman sporting a shaven head and goatee beard; he was handsome, clean cut, sporty, lean verging on thin. With chiselled features and short blond hair when he smiled it transformed his face. It was an endearing smile, a smile that you warmed to instantly, a smile that had got him into trouble regularly as a teenager, but a smile of late that couldn't do him any favours.

The Met-Office interrupted *Pinball Wizard* on the radio. It warned of more rain and severe flooding over the South West of the Country. Oxford was Tony's patch, the place where he'd grown up. It had been raining for weeks and the farmers were desperate for it to stop. His family had lived in the area all their lives. He was the oldest son of a Conservative supporting Butcher, and had a younger sister, Vivian who lived in Scotland with her two children. They exchanged the odd phone call, birthday cards and Christmas cards but nothing else. His younger brother Alan was serving overseas in the armed forces as a mechanic in the RAF and once had trials for England Rugby Schoolboys. Out of the blue, he'd phone when he was on leave and the two brothers would go out for a few drinks, finish up getting drunk and argue, usually about why Tony never saw eye-to-eye with their sister. When his father died, the butcher's died with him. Neither of the children wanted to take on the business. 'Three generations of the family business up in smoke.' The last words he murmured on his death bed. Now and again Tony carried the guilt with him.

Tony's mother lived in a Nursing Home on the outskirts of Oxford. A school photograph of his daughter Martha sat proudly by the side of her single bed. Next to it one of his brothers proudly wearing his blue uniform standing by a Spitfire and one of his sister's graduation day in cap and gown, and completing the set, one of Tony which was taken when he was about twelve, her Sonny Jim, as she still called him. Tony visited her once a week, usually at the weekends. Sometimes he took Martha, but she didn't like the smell of the place and having to kiss the 'caterpillar' on granny's lip. Vivian only visited her once a year, another reason why Tony never spoke to his sister and another reason why the two brothers continually argued.

Tony turned on his headlights as a couple of crows flew up from a waterlogged field. The back roads of the Oxfordshire countryside were familiar to him like the back of his hand and each night he'd take a shortcut from work through the tight lanes. Some of the surrounding fields leading down to the water meadows brought back happy, childhood memories of long hot summers. Nettle stings, swigging dandelion and burdock from the bottle, the shallow, rocky stream where he fished for tiddlers with a jam jar and net. Where he swam naked for the first time as a dare and later, the corn field where he lost his virginity with Beryl, whose surname he could never remember.

As his banger hydro-foiled through the flooded winding lanes, the final bars of *The Who* came to an end. Passing 'The Highwayman' he felt like going in and having a pint to kill the taste of Brainforth in his mouth. He could smell the prisoners sweat ingrained in his uniform and the sound of cell doors slamming shut and keys turning inside locks rattled inside his headache. As a prison officer he was always looking out for danger signs. A prisoner ready to snap, two cons eyeballing each other across the prison landing, the whispers, the threats, not only between the cons inside Brainforth but from the officers as well. A blade in an officer's gut could make a prisoner feel invincible, that's until someone else tried their luck to become Brainforth's 'number one.' Then the merry-go-round of tension would start again. Constantly having to look over his shoulder had made him paranoid and working in that *God forsaken hell hole* as he called it for nearly eight years, was eight years too long, eight years out of his life.

Stopping the car an inch from the recently painted garage doors, he turned off the engine and re-tuned the car radio. The racing results from Newmarket and Doncaster were not very kind to him. Better luck next time. Slamming the car door, Tony made his way up the herringbone bricked path to number 28, Hawks' Drive, on the Birdie Estate. Every road on the Birdie Estate was named after a bird. Eagle Road, Swallow Road, Lark Road, etc, suburbia at its best. The house wasn't chocolate box, more biscuit box. A modest semi-detached, it was just over forty years old. The previous owner was eager to emmigrate to Australia. A do-it-yourself anorak he left the house half finished and needed a quick sale. Consequently Tony bought it on the cheap with his redundancy money, but spent the next year re-decorating. Eighteen years of his nearly forty years he'd worked on the belt of the local car plant, fitting hubcaps, then it shut down and the factory was re-located to Japan. Sometimes, on the night-shift he'd imagine he could see himself walking barefoot along a white, sandy beach in the Caribbean or playing the tables in Las Vegas wearing a white dinner jacket and dickie bow like 007. But more often, he could see his life mapped out before him. He knew he was no different from the next man, but it still caused waves of depression. After being made redundant from the car factory the prison service seemed a solid, secure job, but now he found himself trapped inside the four walls of Brainforth and there seemed no escape.

Tony slipped his key into the front door.

'Daddy daddy!' As Tony stepped inside the house, Martha ran out of the lounge like a banshee. Jumping into her father's arms she nearly knocked him over. Her five year old kisses were sweet, the best in the world and tasted of raspberries. Wearing pyjamas she was small for her age, with big brown eyes and long curly brown hair. She arrived out of the same mould as her mother, but when she smiled she smiled the same as her father. Both were 'cut from the same cloth' as Anne would say.

'Hello sweetheart.'

'You stink daddy!'

Tony put Martha down and tickled her ribs. 'No I don't, it's you, you little scamp.'

Martha giggled. 'I don't daddy, it's you.'

Anne's husky shout came from the kitchen. 'Tea will be on the table in half an hour!' Tony looked at his watch. 'Don't worry; you've got plenty of time before you go out.' Anne could read him like a book; there was no mistaking twenty years of marriage. Martha looked up at her father. 'Hide and seek Daddy?'

'I've just come in, let me take my coat off.'

18

'Go on Daddy, count to twenty!'

'After tea I'll play.'

'Oh please Daddy, one game before tea?' How could Tony refuse the face of an angel, his angel? 'Go on then.' He started counting. 'One, two…' As Martha ran upstairs, Tony walked into the kitchen counting. 'Three, four…' The smell of garlic and the sound of Aretha Franklin hit him. Singing along to *Say a little prayer for me,* Anne had her back to him, laying the kitchen table. Barefooted, wearing a red headscarf tied around her short black hair, her slim body hidden under flowery top and faded jeans swayed sexily to the music. She always knew what looked good on her. Her skin had lost its colour after the summer but she still looked irresistible and Tony couldn't resist. Throwing his arms around her waist he buried his unshaven face into the side of her neck. 'You smell good'. She smelt of perfume, he recognised it as the one he bought her for her birthday. Twisting around in his arms, she giggled like a teenage girl then held his face in her hands. 'Martha's right, you do stink'. Prising him away, Tony noticed a small amount of sadness in her brown eyes.

'I'm ready Daddy!'

'Eight, nine, ten, eleven, I'm coming!' Turning his attention back to Anne he smiled. 'That smells good.'

'Better than you.'

'I can't smell that bad?'

'You do, now go and have a shower.' As Tony walked out of the kitchen he reflected on the small moment of how it used to be.

Tony continued counting as he made his way down the hallway, 'Twelve, thirteen, fourteen, fifteen, sixteen, seventeen…' An overpowering studio portrait of the family met everyone at the top of the stairs. It was taken two years ago by a professional photographer in a department store in Oxford and reproduced on mock canvas. Tony hated it and said it made them look like wax work dummies. It caused endless arguments, but because Anne's mother had paid for it to be commissioned, it hung there like one of the exhibits at Madam Tussauds.

'Eighteen, nineteen, TWENTY! Coming, ready or not!'

Tony heard Martha giggling. It was coming from her bedroom, so he pretended to look around. Sliding open the wardrobe doors, he then looked under beds and banged around adding to the excitement. 'Where is she, where is she?' Sneaking into his own bedroom, he started getting undressed. 'Come out, come out wherever you are.' Taking off his prison sweater he dropped it into the wash basket. 'Where are you? Where are you?' Anne had a good eye for design, the house was tastefully decorated and the bedroom was painted in deep, dark reds and gold. A tinted picture of Venice in light blue and red hung on the far wall, the place where they spent their honeymoon and by the side of the bed next to Anne's books was a framed photograph of the happy couple in a gondola. 'Were can she be!' Tony made his way into Martha's bedroom. 'I'm coming I'm coming!' Martha's bedroom was all pink, pink carpet, pink walls typical of the modern day daughter. Barbie, Barbie, Barbie. Tony spotted Martha's feet sticking out from under the covers of her Barbie duvet. As she giggled with excitement, Tony slowly slipped his hand under the bedspread. 'Fee, fie, foe, fum, I smell the blood of…' Grabbing her ankle, he pulled Martha out from under the duvet screaming and laughing. The two of them typified the undying love of a father for his daughter and the undying love of a daughter for her father. Martha was the love of Tony's life, his world….But little did they know, that parked across the road in his black cab, Brian Young had been watching.

CHAPTER FOUR

Alistair Finch thought he heard voices, but he was always hearing voices. Lifting the shower cap from around one ear, he listened. Over the years his hearing had become sharp; it had to be, his life depended on it. The steam around the white tiled walls could play tricks with the mind as well as the eyes. Not this time. They were quiet voices, violent voices from behind the white wall.

Spinning around on the balls of his feet, he knew that at any split-second they would come. They would try and catch him by surprise, they had done it before; he knew their routine and how they worked. He had to be quick. Reaching out, he grabbed a white bath towel off a wooden hook and wiped his face and eyes dry of water. Ripping the bath cap off his head, he started soaking the towel in the jet of the shower. Tying a large knot in one end of the towel, he snapped it tight and stepped out of the shower. Wrapping the other end of the towel round his right hand, he gripped it ready. Naked, with the knot swinging down by his side he prepared himself for the inevitable. Listening, he waited. The whispers had stopped, the only sound he could hear was from the shower thundering down behind him. As the walls streamed with condensation like the inside of a steam room, the heat intensified. Turning off the shower, his eyes widened with fear. Nervously he started humming a melody. He recognised it as the *The Good Ship Lollypop,* but he couldn't be sure, but then he was, he'd sung it hundreds of times. The tune wasn't for his benefit, he hoped whoever was coming would hear him, relax and lower their guard. It was wishful thinking. The slight glint of the homemade blade was the first thing he saw. About five inches long it could easily take out an eye, slice an artery or pierce a heart. Through the steamy haze, he could just make out the frame of his assailant. He was small, heavy set with thick muscular arms. The heavy knot swung over his shoulder and whacked the guy across the side of the head. Staggering backwards the man hit the far wall with a loud grunt. Recovering he thrust out the blade again and again. Then nothing….Through the steam the two men listened for something, a breath, a heartbeat. Then from nowhere the blade cut through the steam and came at him again. As quick as the knife disappeared it drove back. One stab didn't miss. Slicing through the flesh in his side, he screamed and reared backwards. Cornered, his screams had fallen on deaf ears before but this time he prayed they would come sooner rather than later. They didn't.

Fighting for his life, Finch swung the knot blindly and missed. Swiping through fresh air, he screamed for help. Nothing, panic, and then a lucky strike. Hitting the guy on the arm the knife dropped from his grip and bounced across the floor, sliding to within an inch of his foot. Panting and scratching around blindly on the wet floor the man searched for the knife. Catching sight of a tattoo on the man's arm he kicked out with his bare foot but missed. A flash of seconds seemed a duration as the blade once again came looking for its prey. Another slash of the knife whistled passed his chest, then another. Slipping on the wet floor, he somehow regained his balance and once again kicked out with his bare foot. The momentum of the kick sent him sliding backwards. Hitting the wall, he screamed as he slid down the tiles and waited for the inevitable. Sensing his own death was imminent a prayer shot into his mind, but before he had time to start praying he heard voices. A tattoo of a 'serpent wrapped around a dagger' on the knifeman's arm was the last thing he saw as the man disappeared. At last he was alone, alive, relief for now.

Eventually help did come, his screams of terror had become impossible to ignore. Escaping with just a cut on his waist was a miracle. Although he never saw the man's face, he knew he would try again, they always did, but at least he had a certain tattoo to look out for. Struggling to his feet, his chest wheezed as he trembled with shock. He felt his blood pumping out of his side and looked down at his waist to inspect the cut. It was deeper than he first thought, more stitches. As the blood ran over his hip and down the side of his leg he watched as the trail trickled over his ankle joining the water around his feet. A couple of towels were thrown in his direction; there was no sympathy in this place.

Seven bright blue stitches were to be sewn into his side. The injection that had numbed the skin around his cut was administered by the hands of a young, spotty-faced doctor. Fresh from a year in Zambia were he had been treating war torn refugees, the doctor's surgical gloves, which smelt of condoms, repressed him of the human contact he yearned for. But 'his touch' excited him. As he lay on his back he could sense himself getting an erection. As the doctor punctured his skin with the last stitch he deflected his thoughts from sex to the amount of times he'd been sewn up.

As a young boy, aged around six he had been pushed down the stairs by his mother. Rolling down and bouncing of the wall and banister he was lucky not to have broken his neck. As his mother sucked a lipstick tipped cigarette and took a drink of Gordon's she tended to his wound. Sitting at the kitchen table, the blood which had slowly streamed down his face into his mouth was unceremoniously washed away with a wet flannel and icy water. Later in hospital, his eyebrow had to be shaved by a plump nurse so she could get to the deep cut. A white line was still evident in the hairs of his eyebrow, like the parting of the waves. The smell of gin, cigarettes and the scar in his eyebrow were always a reminder of his mother and his upbringing.

At junior school he had been in a fight with his so called best friend over a 'yellow' jibe. On waste ground left over from the war, the school egged them on as the two boys scrapped like dogs to become top-dog. Covered in dirt and sweat, he finished up with five stitches from a kick in the face. The scar ran from the top of his lip to the underside of his nose. For a year or so afterwards it gave him the appearance of having a hair-lip, but now, the scar only become visible when he hadn't shaved for a couple of days. Fighting with his best friend had left him scarred in more ways than one. It was the only friend he'd ever had and every day he shaved was another reminder of his troubled past.

More recently there were the seven stitches on the back of his shoulder from a jagged piece of crockery, a cup or a plate that ripped through his blue cotton shirt and the five at the top of his thigh from another home made instrument. He could only laugh to himself about the amount of tetanus running through his veins.

As the doctor helped him up on the hospital bed he caught a whiff of last night's aftershave on his skin. His stomach churned; he hated aftershave as it reminded him of his father, his only memory. Looking up at the flickering, white strip light he thought of the latest attempt on his life. How much longer he could run the gauntlet was anyone's guess, then his mind returned to the last words he heard from the stocky guy with the knife and tattoo. 'I'll get you next time Lollypop!'…But then, those words were nothing new to Finch, he lived with them every day.

CHAPTER FIVE

The Oxford skyline was a blur on the landscape and was vanishing quickly along with the surrounding countryside. It had been a miserable grey day. Threatening to rain all day, the clouds suddenly burst open and within seconds the light drizzle had turned into a heavy downpour. Good news for a taxi driver.

Young's cab was parked on double yellows outside a small office building on the busy High Street, its engine and heater still running. As the sky rumbled overhead he shot a glance upwards. Aware that somebody inside the office would want a cab 'quick,' he released the handbrake. Before too long a businessman flew out of the entrance, ran across the pavement and jumped into the back of the cab. Words rushed out of his mouth before he had chance to sit down. 'The Law Courts please, quick as you can!'

Rear-view mirrors can be cunning, wily objects, objects of desire. To pass more time, Young liked to scrutinise people in the back seat, their habits their looks, their posture. Without *the fare* ever knowing that they were being watched, Young would analyse their faces and their body language. It had become a fixated hobby. Man or woman, he'd try and work out their yearly salary, their private lives. The style of their suit and the cut of the cloth said volumes about them. A new shirt, fresh out of a box or a frayed shirt collar spoke volumes about their background, their family, their love life, even their sex life. A wedding ring told a thousand truths, or a thousand lies. A polka dot tie would trigger footprints of skulduggery or a trail of intrigue and depending on what mood Young was in that day and as to how far his imagination would stretch, he always painted a fairly accurate picture of *the fares* in the back of his cab. Or so he thought.

Constantly tapping and spinning his mobile on the top of his leather briefcase, Young surmised that the spiky haired man was a solicitor and extremely nervous about the outcome of a case. A baby-faced forty year old, he looked like he was a member of a gym and private golf club. He was a recent newlywed, as the gold band on the third finger of his left hand was still shiny and bright. No polka dot tie, what did that say about him? He didn't know, but his imagination would drift off into another devious theory that would pass another morsel of time, and he was happy for anything to pass the time.

'Can you put your foot down please, I'm running late!' In the rear-view Young caught the man's face. He could see he was anxious, restless and decided to ignore him. As another half minute passed the man lent forward and shouted through the glass that separated *the fares* from the cab driver.

'Hello, did you hear me? I'm running late, can you put your foot down please!' Young pointed at a thirty miles per hour road sign. 'What's that dickhead?'

Did the solicitor hear him right? 'Pardon, what did you say?' Young ignored him again. 'I will make it worth your while if you get me there ASAP?' Young was enjoying ignoring him.

'Look, I don't mean to be rude, but are you hard of hearing?' He was being rude. Enough is enough. Young slammed his foot down. The solicitor lurched forward and nearly finished in the front of the cab.

'What are you doing, this isn't the Law Courts!' Young didn't answer, he just stared ahead pan-faced his fingers strumming the steering wheel.

'I wanted the Law Courts!' As the cab's clock ticked over, Young released the locks to the back doors. The solicitor's patience snapped. Jumping out onto the wet pavements he slammed the taxi door nearly removing it from its hinges.

'I don't know what your problem is?' Ignoring the anger, Young continued staring straight ahead, and then lowering the window he struck out his palm. 'Call it a fiver.' Exasperated, the solicitor reached into the silk lining of his Saville Row suit and produced a leather wallet, Young knew an expensive suit when he saw one. Once he was measured-up for two tailor-made suits, a linen one for the summer and a woollen one for the winter. Looking in the wing mirror, he noticed a Matador and Bull embossed on the front of his wallet. It was from Spain, a cheap tourist's wallet. *Wanker.* Thrusting a twenty pound note into Young's palm, the yuppie solicitor sneered. 'I've got a good mind to report you.' Young shrugged his shoulders and lit a menthol, as if he cared. Agitated, the solicitor sighed heavily as he lingered for his change. As cigarette smoke streamed out of Young's nostrils, he saw that the rain was starting to soak into the shoulders of the solicitor's suit. Fumbling for change, he thought to himself, *let the prick wait.*

'Can you get a move on, it's raining if you haven't noticed?' Young's smirk widened.

'Didn't you hear me before, I wanted the Law Courts?'

'I heard you.'

'Why have you dropped me off here then?'

'Because I don't like the cut of your suit!'

Suddenly, Young thrust the cab into first and took off.

Gob-smacked, the solicitor stood pole-axed in the pouring rain. With his hand held out like a beggar he watched the cab disappear down the street, his twenty pound note floating in the gutter.

Flicking off the *For Hire* light, Young decided he'd had enough of wet people in the back of the cab for one day. Whistling to no particular tune, he held the cigarette between his nicotine stained index finger and thumb and took a long drag.

Stopping at traffic lights, a rain trodden couple, with bags of shopping walked up and tapped on his near-side window. In their late sixties, both their faces were long and white. They could have been ghosts. Ignoring them, Young's mind wandered once again into the past and he found himself back in the place were he was first told the news. It was red hot, 90 degrees. Wearing a light blue sleeveless shirt, the pollen count was high and his eyes had been streaming with hayfever all day. A little boy with braces on his teeth was suffering with chicken pox and he was on a house call. There was a knock at the door and the boy's father said it was for him. A police officer stood on the doorstep holding his ID in front of his face. Wearing plain clothes, he was stubby, overweight with a clipped moustache that had flecks of grey in it. He was in his late thirties, not long promoted. Next to him, shorter, was a young WPC, who could have been pretty but for a face like soil….It had been the knock on the door from Hitler's Death Squad.

An irate bus driver blasted his horn up Young's backside. Snapping back to present day, he had stalled at the lights. It was becoming a habit. A detonation of pain burnt the ends of his thumb and index-finger. His cigarette had burnt down to the filter. Flicking the ash and cigarette butt onto the cab floor, he stamped out the smouldering end with the heel of his trainer. Realising he'd only taken one single drag of the cigarette he took the last one from the packet and placed it between his lips.

As black cabs go, Young's was no different. It wasn't

plastered with an advertising slogan, although he'd been offered cash on numerous occasions to advertise for various companies, the local estate agents, a dental clinic offering teeth 'whiter than white', but he always refused. He didn't need the money. For Young, being a taxi driver was never about earning a living. It was always a means to an end. It always was and always would be.

Pinley Hospital was just off the ring road outside Oxford. It was brand spanking new, and if Young remembered rightly it was recently opened by one of the Royals, a pip-squeak of a prince with lots of blond hair and a mouth full of teeth. Turning off the main road into the hospital he found himself queuing for a parking space. He'd collected and dropped *fares* off there regularly, but not enough parking spaces for the number of hospital beds in a brand, spanking new hospital? Now that really pissed him off! Lowering the window, he shouted in the direction of a drenched security guard, who was struggling to direct the heavy traffic in and out of the hospital's overcrowded car park. 'The wanker who designed this car park should be tarred-and-feathered!' Young didn't care who heard him as long as somebody did. For a split-second the guard didn't know how to handle the spontaneous outburst from the fuming cabbie. Then, he waved and nodded in agreement as if to say, 'You're right pal.'

Young reversed into a disabled parking space directly outside the main entrance to A and E and killed the engine. Looking at the cab's digital clock, it was 3:30 PM.

Far too early.

Lighting the last cigarette that had become welded to his bottom lip, he gradually became mesmerised by the large revolving doors of the hospital entrance. Patients wearing pyjamas, dressing gowns and slippers had sneaked outside for a fag and like him they totally ignored the *No Smoking* signs. One patient even had his arm hooked up to a drip. Young laughed and blurted out to himself. 'You're just like me guys; hooked on good old nicotine and we've all got one thing in common, we all want a piece of the action from Britain's world famous National Health Service.' But at the same time there was sadness in his voice. A paramedic pushed a trolley out of the hospital and he couldn't make out whether they were male or female. They all looked the same to him in those green jump-suits, but he could see they were ready, ready for the next poor victim of a car crash or an industrial accident. Somewhere, but couldn't remember where, he read, that more workman had been killed on building sites that year than British soldiers in the Iraqi war. Waiting rooms is where he usually read things. Anyway, it was another bit of useless information, something else to slay time.

He looked at the clock again. 3:45 PM. Still too early.

As he smoked, he constantly chewed the skin round the sides of his finger nails. With barely any nails left, the ends of his fingers were like a leper's. Gnawed down to stumps, they looked disgusting, but he didn't care. An ambulance with sirens blaring, screeched to a halt. Two paramedics as thin as spindle backs jumped out of the cab and sprinted to the back. Swinging open the double doors, they sprung the trolley and its bloody patient out into the drizzle and ran him through the crowd of smokers into the hospital. From the comfort of his cab Young muttered to himself with a sarcastic scowl, 'Posers, you've all been watching too many hospital dramas on television. Got ideas of grandeur have you? Think you're the Saviours of The Universe, Angels, Super Heroes, Sex Symbols, in your bloody dreams.' Young shouted and laughed to himself at the same time. 'Lime green does nothing for you guys!' He'd hoped they'd heard him. 'Wankers!' but they didn't.

Lime green always reminded him of that other day, that other day when they came round to his house and sat there for hours,

hours on end which then turned into days. Waiting and watching as their hands fidgeted, their mumbled conversations to each other in the kitchen, his kitchen. Eating his biscuits, drinking his tea. Stirring the sugar around at the bottom of his cups, again and again and again. The sound bolted inside his head forever. He hated lime green and people who took sugar in their tea.

4:15 PM. Still too early.

Were had the last half hour gone? Were had the last eight years gone? He knew the second question was easier to answer, but not easier to fathom out. Watching the revolving door, he spat a piece of finger out of his mouth and took another drag of his cigarette. A knock on the cab window made him snap out of his daydreams. Rocking on his heels, a lanky Traffic Warden with steamed-up glasses was ready to slap a parking ticket were it hurt. Pushing his nose against the window of the cab, Young eyeballed the Warden.

'Traffic Wardens in hospitals, that sums everything up!' His voice fogged-up the window as he read the Warden's lips, through the rain streaked window. Then, he grinned and mimicked him in a voice resembling the Wicked Witch from *The Wizard of Oz*. 'You can't park there unless you are disabled. Do you hear me? Do you hear me?' Young flicked on the *For Hire* light then shouted through the glass. 'I've read your lips now you read mine. What motivates you to get up in the morning, it can't be a hard-on, because you look like you've never had one. Or maybe you did once, a long time ago when you were eight or nine when you had Sunday roast at your auntie's house. I know what you did, You went snooping around upstairs and found a soiled copy of Playboy under you favourite uncle's bed, didn't you. That's what made you into the man you are today? Is that what made you decide you wanted to become a fucking Traffic Warden? Look around you, you prick, there are no parking places! Harassing parents of children who have incurable diseases or parents who are visiting their son who has just been in a fatal car accident, and who keeps asking his mum and dad about his wife and son. Are they alive, are they dead? But being dead, they don't know how and when the right time or the wrong time is to tell him and you give them a fucking parking ticket! Where do you go to for your holidays, Traffic Warden Park? The place were all you wankers go for your summer holidays or is it winter holidays because you can give more customers tickets in the summer. Come to think of it, I don't know anyone who's ever met a traffic warden on holiday or anyone who knows a fucking traffic warden. When you clock-off at the end of a hard day, I bet you all go for a drink and complain about how your feet are killing you from too much walking don't you? I bet you exchange stories of how you shafted this person and that person; I bet there's a prize for the most *tickets* isn't there? I bet it's you isn't it? Yes you can tell. You have that face that says I'm a tosser and I don't care who knows I'm a tosser, I'm going to win *The Tosser-of-the-Year-Award* if it's the last thing I do.'

The warden had long gone.

Young looked at his watch. 4:23 PM. He'd missed his appointment.

It was the third time in a month he'd failed to turn-up. Or was it the forth time? He couldn't remember, it didn't concern him, he knew what the doctors would say, what they always said. After all, he was one, once. As Young drove off, he lowered the window and took in some fresh air. Noticing the florescent parking ticket that had been taped to his windscreen he thumped the steering wheel. It could join the rest in the glove compartment or the gutter! Looking through the side window, he noticed by the revolving doors the Traffic Warden talking to one of the paramedics. They turned and looked in his direction. Then something occurred to him. The Traffic Warden was a woman all along, as were the lime green paramedics.

CHAPTER SIX

'The huge shark flew out of the water and with its massive teeth bit off the fingers of the Sailor Prince! Help! Help! said the Princess 'That will teach you to mess with Mr Shark and me,' said the Pirate with a wooden leg, as his hook swished through the air. 'I own the seas round here, not the Sailor Prince!' 'I will return,' said the bleeding Sailor Prince, 'and when I do, you will be in big, big trouble.' The Pirate snarled and laughed. 'Ha, ha, ha, ha. In your dreams Prince,' and with that he disappeared into the thick fog that covered the sea. 'The only way we can get your fingers back is to go to 'Fairy Island'', said the Princess to the handsome Sailor Prince. 'Then my love we must go,' he said, as he looked lovingly into her big blue eyes. 'But I can't swim,' said the Princess. 'I will look after you,' said the Sailor Prince. Then taking her in his arms they both dived overboard and swam to 'Fairy Island'.'

Tony pulled the duvet up around Martha's neck. 'It's late sweetheart, I'll tell you the rest of the story tomorrow.'

'Oh please Daddy, finish the story.'

'It's getting late and you have school tomorrow.'

'Oh please Daddy, Zachariah wants to hear some more as well.'

Zachariah was Martha's invisible friend. If he was telling the story for two how could he refuse? 'Ok, close your eyes, but you must promise to go to sleep – the two of you.' Martha shut her eyes and cuddled Zachariah as well as her Teddy.

'The Sailor Prince and the Princess swam to the 'Fairy Island' and went into a dark cave. Inside were thousands of glass jars stacked up to the rocky roof. But only in one jar, was the Fairy. They only had ten guesses or the Prince's fingers would never come back and the evil Pirate and his shark would rule the seas forever. They opened one, then two, then three. Then they opened the last jar and the Fairy soared out and started flying around the cave sprinkling gold dust everywhere.'

Martha opened one eye. 'Like Tinker Bell Daddy?'

'Just like Tinker Bell sweetheart.'

'Then the Fairy sprinkled magic gold dust on the Sailor Prince's hand and his fingers came back, one-by-one. Now he could hold his sword again. The Sailor Prince said to the Princess, 'Stay here, it's too dangerous to go back to fight the Pirate and his deadly shark.'

Tony looked down at Martha, she was falling asleep another five minutes would do the trick. Continuing with the tale, he thought of his father. As a child, he'd fallen asleep to the same story many times and sometimes when he spoke to Martha he could hear his father voice. Martha's hair smelt sweet, her porcelain skin gave her the appearance of a sleeping angel. He often watched her sleep and always blessed his luck for having her in his life. 'Good night sweetheart.' Kissing her soft cheek, Tony turned off the light and quietly shut the bedroom door behind him.

Anne was standing in the kitchen doorway overlooking the overgrown garden, sipping a glass of wine. A cigarette smouldered in her left hand. Hearing Tony come into the kitchen, she took a long pull on the cigarette but didn't turn around. Her silk, bright blue Chinese dressing gown hung down over one shoulder and her wet, short, black hair had been combed back from her face. A loose lock of hair had dropped down over her left eye and cheek, complimenting her pert, slim nose which slightly turned-up at the end. It gave her a Parisian look, a look that Tony first fell in love with. She was extremely attractive, in an alluring, sexy way. Her laugh could light up a room and although she was a few years older than Tony, she kept herself fit by working out regularly at the local gym and swimming three times a week with her younger sister Jane. She loved to read and was a member of the local book club. Crime, romance, autobiographies, anything that was worth reading she would read it. Sometimes she'd read two books at a time, which always confused and frustrated Tony as he only read newspapers. They were introduced to each other at Anne's sister's wedding, over twenty years ago and were instantly attracted to each others smile. Being the best man, he took full advantage of chaperoning Anne who was the chief bridesmaid. Later, drunk, he tried to impress her like Errol Flynn by opening a bottle of champagne with the blade from an ornamental sword which he removed from the hotel wall. Slicing a large chunk out of his thumb, Anne was only too quick to tend to his wound. It was the first time they touched, but by the end of the day it wouldn't be the last. On Christmas day, usually after the Queen's speech, Anne's eighty-one year old grandmother would always suggest they watch the wedding video. For the umpteenth time, they would laugh in the same places, comment on how young they looked in the same places and go *arrrh* in the same places. Tony and Anne would always give each other a sly look across the room. At the reception and full of champagne, they had started flirting and after the sword incident she challenged him. *If you can guess where the mole is on my body, I'll let you kiss me.* He guessed, she lied, and the kiss led to them screwing in the cloakroom of The Castle Hotel. It had been their secret ever since. Six months down the line, their screwing had orbited into making love. Every possible moment of that summer had been spent in bed. She would visit him in his one bedroom basement flat near Oxford's football ground. During the long afternoons they would lay in bed making love. On match days the roar of the crowd would filter through the windows and on some afternoons they would listen to her type of music, Supertramp, Barry White, or his, The Clash or The Sex Pistols. They say opposites attract. But those long afternoons would always turn into long evenings, then long nights, and it would last with them forever. A year later Anne asked Tony to marry her on his twenty first birthday. She surprised him in a Chinese restaurant, by ordering fortune cookies. In the middle of Tony's cookie was a written proposal, she went down on 'bended knee' so how could he refuse, it was leap-year after all. And so it began.

The proposal was the centrepiece of the kitchen wall. It was surrounded by framed photographs which told of the love and history between the two of them. Martha horse riding, Anne with her sister holding up their medals at the finishing line of a fun run, Tony with his arm around George Best in an Ibiza beach bar and family holidays in Greece, Portugal and Spain. There was always Spain, romantic Spain. It was where Tony and Anne first went on holiday together. It had been special to the both of them. There, they planned a future together, a family together, innocent love. Over the years, the number of times they discussed taking up Spanish lessons together had become a long standing joke, just like they were going to take up yoga or Tai chi. Tony always made the excuses, the excuses that hid his lies. He was a master at it. They loved their holidays and were adventurous in their choice of destination. This year they had planned to go to Cuba or take

Martha to Disney Land in Florida, but for the first time in years planning a holiday was to be put on hold.

Tony and Anne were born with the same sense of humour. Constantly using each other as a sounding board, they were convinced their symbiotic relationship and the crazy laughs they had shared over the years had kept their marriage alive. Envied amongst their friends as, the perfect, happily married couple, it annoyed them intensely as they were far from it. Like most couples they had their problems and recently they had tried to move on from a major headache which was driving a wedge between the two of them.

'The garden needs doing.'

'I'll do it at the weekend.'

'The weekend's tomorrow.'

'Then I'll do it tomorrow.' Moving on, moving on, moving on.

Anne held her anger. Bringing the wine glass up to her mouth she took a sip of the chardonnay, then, pulled on the cigarette blowing smoke into the cold night air.

'Where are you meeting?' Tony put his hands around her waist and squeezed her tight sending a small gust of smoke out of her mouth.

'Same place, same time, nothing changes you should know that.' As she coughed Tony kissed the side of her neck then moved his hands up from her waist to her small breasts.

'Get off.' Anne's voice was sharp, cold. Digging him in the ribs with her elbow, she turned around in his arms. Extending her arm out to protect Tony from the burning ember of the cigarette she pushed him away.

'What's wrong?' Tony knew as soon as he asked the question. Anne stubbed out her ciggarette into a ceramic ashtray then brushed a loose piece of hair from out of her eyes.

'I said what's wrong?'

Anne gave him a challenging stare. 'Don't forget what I said.'

'I won't wake you.'

'Not that.'

'What than?'

'Piss off Tony, you know what.'

'I won't, I promise.' The word *promise* meant nothing to her and she knew the road the conversation was taking, just like it had dozens of times before. Anne's voice matched her expression.

'That's what you said last time and the time before that.' Tony tried to disguise the irritation in his voice. 'You'll be having me take a polygraph next, I said I won't.'

'We'll see.'

Tony barked back. 'What does that mean, *we'll see*?' Anne turned from the door and poured herself a sizeable glass of wine.

'We're in the shit Tony, if you hadn't forgotten.' The rim of the wine glass clinked as it hit her front teeth. 'I don't want diamonds or a big house in the country Tony, you know I'm happy with what we've got, but I can't take anymore, I'm exhausted with it all. I'm warning you.'

Tony snatched his house keys off the kitchen table and marched towards the door.

'You're smoking too much.'

'Piss off!'

'Well you are.'

'Can you blame me with having to put up with you all the time?'

For a spit second the two of them looked at each other. How the two of them yearned for that time again, for those happy days to return.

Tony slammed the front door behind him. He regretted it instantly as Anne stood alone in the kitchen, fearing the worst.

CHAPTER SEVEN

The lather from the cheap bar of soap bit into Young's green eyes. Pulling back the plastic, mould-ridden shower curtain, he reached down and grabbed a grubby towel from the side of the rust stained bath. Drying his bloodshot eyes he looked down and froze. Mesmerised by the bath water spiralling down the plughole, a couple of minutes turned into five as it brought back the stark memories of that long hot summer. Starting to shiver, he slowly realised where he was and vigorously started wiping the rest of the water from his hairy chest and back. Stepping out of the bath, his teeth chattered as he pulled on a pair of red striped boxer shorts and some oversized, threadbare jeans. After tightening a worn, thick leather belt round his waist, he placed the palm of his hand on the bathroom mirror and rubbed away a small area of condensation. It was just enough to see his face. Studying the crows-feet around his eyes, he reflected on how he was ageing more and more with every passing day. The saddle bags under his eyes were now circled with dark rings and certain teeth were heavily stained with nicotine. Around his greying temples flashes of black hair were the only reminder of his youth and of course there were those green eyes that once had set the world-alight.

Filling up the cracked washbowl with cold water; he picked up the same bar of soap and rubbed-up it around his broad chin. Then, with a disposable razor he set about the grey stubble that littered his grey face. With hardly any lather on his features he ran the blunt razor down his left cheek. Like the noise of finger nails running down a blackboard he stopped with a jolt at the bottom of his jaw. Crimson slowly appeared from a nick under his right cheekbone. He watched as the blood trickled down his face, over his chattering jaw, and down his neck. As it flowed down the side of his Adam's apple, it rested on the top of his collarbone. Drops of blood fell directly into the washbowl turning the water blood red. Rinsing out his five o'clock shadow from the razor, he placed it back on the side of the sink ready for the next time. Dabbing his face and neck, he dropped the blood stained towel back over the bath and walked barefoot into the lounge.

Stepping over faded-newspapers and take-away cartons containing mommics of rotting food, his wet footprints wandered the room looking for warmth. Through the mess, he eventually found a crumpled white vest and denim shirt and threw them on. Overhead, the silent thuds of a moth hitting the dust-covered light shade crept up into the architraves of the high, nicotine-stained ceiling. The room was cluttered with old books and discarded clothing. In one of the corners a wash basket overflowed with soiled, dirty linen and on the top of a second-hand dining table next to an empty, chipped fruit bowl a number of dusty Christmas presents remained unopened.

Young slumped down into his armchair sending up a puff of dust from the upholstery. Lighting a cigarette, he sucked in the smoke and held it in his lungs. Blowing out the smoke, he slipped into a pair of tatty trainers. No socks. Splitting a match stick with his side teeth, he started using one of the splinters like a tooth pick. Digging between his top and lower teeth, he removed a tiny piece of meat. Spitting it out, he dropped the small pieces of match stick onto the coffee and wine stained carpet. Rummaging behind his back he found the remote control stuffed behind a cushion and pressed the green button. The television sprang to life and he started to channel surf. Flick. Flick. Flick. The light from a chat-show cast a strobe of coloured images across the faded wallpaper and his insipid look. Sitting there for over an hour, smoking and flicking from one channel to another, his eyes watched but they didn't see. Oblivious to anything or anyone on the screen he switched off the TV. Pausing for a minute, to once again gauge his bearings, he stood up and pressed the pearl studs on his denim shirt together. It didn't seem to bother him that the shirt had a rip in the sleeve and two studs missing, but he might not have noticed. Sparking up the last menthol in the pack, he walked over to the large, sash-window. Pulling back the net-curtains, he released a couple of blue bottles into the room. Watching them buzz around the room then up to the light bulb, he wondered whether the moth would get the better of them.

Peering through the dirty glass onto the rain-washed-street, he blew the cigarette smoke out of his mouth and watched it circulate around the room. Once, he could blow smoke rings and do a trick by flipping the hot end of the cigarette into his mouth, after holding it inside his mouth for a few seconds he'd bring it out again still lit. It had been a party-piece at university. How he loved University, how he loved learning about medicine and the mechanics of the human body. Some memories still shone bright, some gone forever. Daydreaming, like he had done hundreds of times before, he stood at the window staring into space. He liked the way the street lights reflected off the wet surface of the road, creating oily, mosaic patterns and he liked the way the drops of rain fell onto the window ledge then splashed down onto the street below. Watching the rain gush past the wheels of his cab, he wondered how many drains there were in his road. He tried to work out who built the drains and where the rain water went to. Out to sea, vanishing for ever, evaporating and coming down as rain again. The circle of life, the process repeating itself again and again and again, like his memories. Reincarnation, he wondered what he would come back as? Something, that if provoked could fight back and defend itself, something that could kill with one strike, that's all he would need. Turning from the window, he finished the last of his smoke and dropped the butt onto a layer of mould in a fractured coffee mug. Slowly, his eyes widened as he looked across the dingy room at the far wall. Stuck in the centre of the wall was a faded newspaper cutting. It was the size of a passport photograph and bore the head and shoulders of a man. In his late thirties, he had a bland faced, with dark, slicked back hair; he wore an open necked white shirt and glasses. The cutting was surrounded by the heads of hundreds and hundreds of six inch nails which were imbedded into the wall. The light above reflected across the heads of the nails producing a magical affect, like fairy lights on a Christmas tree. Directly below the man's picture and the circle of nails was an old mahogany dresser, its top stained with numerous Olympic rings from previously hot, disregarded coffee mugs. Young slid open the bottom drawer and took out a six inch nail and claw hammer. Placing the new nail onto the periphery of all the other nails in the wall, he brought the hammer back over his shoulder and hit the nail once, then again and again. The noise made the wall shudder sending tiny particles of plaster floating down onto the top of the dresser. Admiring his handy work through a hardened glare, a number of violent thuds came back from the other side of the wall. Somebody wasn't happy. As the noise reverberated around his room, his door nearly caved in.

'Come out here, do you hear me you fucking nutter?' The muffled shouts of an angry young man meant business. Young ignored the abuse, he was used to it. Again, he brought back the hammer over his right shoulder and gave the nail one last bang into the wall. He meant this one. The thud echoed around the room and triggered another tirade of verbal abuse from behind the door. As more particles of plaster floated out of the wall, he placed the claw hammer back into the open drawer and realised he was running out of nails. Agitated, he couldn't bear the thought of running out of nails, once before it brought on an attack of asthma. As his chest tightened the man behind the door smashed it again. 'You wait pal, I'll get you!' Young heard a door slam shut. Sliding the hammer away into the darkness of the drawer, he gave the photograph another look. Breathing heavily, his eyes narrowed with spite and like laser beams his pupils dilated, zooming into the man's eyes in the photograph. It was a look of repulsion.

Picking his coat up off the floor, he checked its pockets for his cab keys and heard them jangle. To his surprise they were there, normally he would have spent an hour-or-so dragging his feet around the room trying to find them. An old carriage clock chimed out of the blackness of the bedroom across the room. 'One, two, three, four, five, six, seven, eight, nine, nine o'clock.' Young blew out a breath of frustration, the stores would be shut, the six inch nails would have to wait until tomorrow. Ready for the night ahead, he gave the room one last look. The blue bottles were in a dog-fight with the moth around the light bulb. It reminded him of the old black and white film he saw as a boy in the Royal Cinema, were the bi-planes circled and machine gunned King Kong on the top of The Empire State Building.

'Don't wait up for me.' Flicking off the light, he quietly closed the door behind him.

CHAPTER EIGHT

Guilt! When I'm drunk I always go through this self-analysis crap. Like a fairground carousel it revolves around my pissed brain and I don't share it with anybody, not anybody. I love Anne and Martha, they both know it, I tell them enough times. But I know I have let them down, but can I do anything about it? No! Drink, it plays havoc with my head, with my feelings then the paranoia kicks in. Here it comes again. The voice, I always get a voice inside my head at this time of night that says–

It's alright Tony, it's alright. Don't feel guilty.

At this time of night it never leaves my head, it's always there, it never goes away. Guilt....Sometimes I'd pretend to listen to jokes or social chit-chat, but in reality I never listen, I'm always somewhere else, in that place. Deep inside the follicles of my brain I can never work out whether the alcohol makes it better or worse. It also depends on what night I'm having, and so far tonight is going as well, as end-of-the-month Friday nights can go. But nowadays I get bored really easily, the excitement that was once there years ago has disappeared, I need excitement, a quick fix, I live for it.

It's the same every month, every end of the month pay-day. I meet the guys from work at the same time, same place. We play catch-up, work, women, families, football, and crap. The crap is always the best, the funniest. Like taking the piss out of a new haircut, 'Who cut your hair, the council?' Tonight it's Garry's new shirt, poor, poor Garry. 'Are your wearing that shirt for a bet?' 'It's amazing what you can make out of an old deckchair.' Poor, poor Garry, he's alright. He's the sort of guy, the sort of officer at Her Majesty's Prison Service that wants an easy life. He never gets embroiled in any debates or arguments at work or at play. Poor, poor Garry, but his embarrassing shirt does say 'I'm desperate for a chick, any chick will do.' What a bore, a bore that matches his featureless, nondescript face. Here they come thick and fast. Garry looks dumb-struck, the stick he's getting is unbelievable, he looks like a rabbit caught in the headlights and here's me just laughing at nothing, bored and pissed out of my tiny little skull. And then there's Billy Rogers. He loves it, the crack, always wants to be the centre of attention. He loves the sound of his own voice, loud, sun-bed Billy Rogers with his hyena laugh and permanent stare. He's alright though, he makes me laugh. Billy Rogers with that smile that's contagious. If he does his party piece, blowing up a condom on his head, I'll kill him. I'm not in the mood. Look at him the modern day man or so he thinks. He's convinced himself that he's God's gift to woman. The stories, the yarns he spins have me in stitches. Then there are the barbeques. Sometimes, some officer will throw a barbecue and the wives will grill the husbands like the hamburgers as to which slut Mr. Wonderful, the bed-hopper (as the wives have nicknamed Rogers) is bringing with him this time. Then, by the end of the barbecue all the husbands will be accused of fancying Mr Wonderful's bachelor lifestyle or his bit-of-fluff. You can never win, that's married life for you. I suppose his so-called conquests seem mild in comparison to the lives of the rest of us Brainforth screws.

What time is it? 2AM. I'm pissed. Time to go home. Here he is, like clockwork, every time I decide enough is enough, time to go, Billy Rogers arrives with another round of drinks; he's got the drinking capacity of a trout, that's if fish drink, I suppose they must do. I bet he says it, I bet he says it–

'One more for the road eh fellas!' I knew it, like bloody clockwork.

'I'm going after this one, I've had enough.' I can't believe I've just said that, you can never have enough. Don't look at me like that Rogers.

'What's up with you, drink up you boring fart.'

'Garry went home ages ago; he knows when enough is enough.'

'I'd have gone home wearing a shirt like that!' What's he doing now? Oh he's spotted an old girlfriend, now there's a surprise. 'Catch you later.' There he goes, can't keep still for a minute. On the hunt like a Great White, straight over to her, with that smile that stare. Mind you, the place is full of his old girlfriends, it should be, he's been coming here for the past twenty years. What am I doing here? Here we go again, with the self-analysis. Now it's that time again, always the biggest problem of the night. How do I fight my way through the drunks to get out of this place without Rogers seeing me and giving me a hard time?....Now is a good time, he's' dancing, any second he'll have his tongue down her throat. Right put your pint down, stand up and leave. One, two, three, go!....Whoops, slight stagger there Tony boy, past one drunk and another. Another slight stagger but I'm doing well, weaving past one drunk, then another. I'm like George Best in his hey day….The exit, the end is in sight for one of the oldest-swingers-in-town. Past the two coffin-dodgers standing at the door, the oldest bouncers in the world, down the small flight of steps, which I'm sure has seen its share of the action over the years, past the cloakroom, smile at the woman behind the desk, say goodnight. 'Good night.' Out through the main door, into the fresh air, I've made it, fresh air….Looks like there's going to be a fight over the road, ignore it, don't get involved with all that shit….Hamburgers. That smell always gets to me when I'm drunk; I always think I fancy a hamburger and then when I've had one I regret it, the hazards of being pissed I suppose. Angelo, the Hot-Dog-Man turns over cheese burgers at alarming rate. At the helm of his hotplate every Friday night, dishing and flipping buns and burgers, serving them up to every drunk who'll throw one down, then throw it up later. I've been watching him for years. I recognise him from school. He was a right bully then, burnt my football scarf and kicked my duffle-bag round the playground. The bastard never recognises me, small mercies I suppose, who wants to be known by that ugly prick. I've gone off food now, I'm not hungry; I'm just convincing myself I'm hungry. God I'm pissed. Go home. Get a cab, I need a cab. How much have I got? Fifty-five pounds and fifty pence….Don't! Don't, you prick!

Go on Tony.

Here's that voice again, The Devil's whisper. Go away. Piss off! Why do you always come into my brain this time of the night? I question you, but you never answer.

One little bet wont hurt.

One little bet wont hurt.

One little bet wont hurt.

Get out of my fucking head, get out of my head!

Go on Tony, one little bet won't hurt. One little bet wont hurt.

What am I doing? Why are my legs walking this way? You know why. Turn and go back, turn and go back. Stop, that's right stop and think before it's too late!

Friday nights! I hate bloody Friday nights. I can't remember the last time I picked-up a fare that was sober on a bloody, pissin' Friday night. I hate all nights; nights are nightmares for me, a bloody taxi driver. Whoever thought I would turn out like this, from a doctor to driving a black cab? It doesn't really matter, all days; all nights are nightmares for me. It sounds dramatic, so what if it does.

He's late, has he no consideration. What if he's not in there? Relax, he's always in there, its bloody, pissin Friday night isn't it. With those mates of his…Here comes another, another drunk another Friday night binge-drinker wanting a ride.

'Light not on, not for hire mate!' Give me that pissed off look; I've seen it a thousand times. Like I give a damn. A shit. A flying fuck, piss off.

My stomach is telling me I'm hungry that rumble from deep inside my gut. Well I think it is. When did I last eat? Yesterday? Yesterday morning, that's like, yesterday. I can't afford for him to see me though, not just yet. What did I eat yesterday? Beans on toast? No, that was the day before. Egg on toast in that café? That was last week, sometime ago, it doesn't matter.

I will have to double up tomorrow, splash out, get three, four, no five boxes of nails. Eating late at night gives people indigestion, I read it somewhere, in the doctor's surgery or did I hear it somewhere? Then again I never sleep. Sleep, what's that? Sleep, sleep, sleep, sleep, sleep, that's a joke. A laugh. A real joke. A real laugh.

Hamburger? Yes a hamburger, I fancy a hamburger. Who cares about indigestion when you're hungry?

I don't like him frowning at me, that Angelo, up there in his hamburger palace. Ok, I'm not your regular Friday night drunk I'll give you that, but treat me with a little bit of respect pal.

'Sauce and onions mate?'

'Yes.' I'm not your *mate*, but it was an easy decision sauce and onions, I like easy decisions. Saying yes to *sauce and onions,* I can feel myself nodding, nodding like a Friday night drunk. I know the nod of a Friday night drunk. I bet he thinks I'm a Friday night, pissin drunk. When I ask for the fare up front, I always get the nod, the 'yes' the vermin nod in the back of the cab. They always rummage around in their pockets, spilling coins, burping, being sick. I know the ones that can't pay, the ones who will pay, the ones who question the amount at the end of a journey, the vermin. Question me again and you'll find-out what's under my seat. I see you're wearing a crispy, brand-new overall Angelo. About time, you've even got your name monogrammed in red above the breast pocket above your heart. You're going up-market, *Angelo*; I guess you must be Italian. I wouldn't be living here if I came from sunny Italy. I believe it rains there sometimes. Like here sometimes. What was the name of that old black and white film with Gregory Peck in it? That was Italy or a place that looked like Italy. Italy looked nice; perhaps I'll go there one day. Perhaps I'll die there one day, like the poet Shelley. He was cremated on the beach. That would be a good way to go, though I doubt it. I think it was Gregory Peck who was in that film or it could have been someone called Grant, I forget his first name….Where should I eat this culinary delight? Over the road in the dark, the charity shop doorway, out of the way, where I always go.

This looks crap! Every Friday they taste like crap. Rubbery, tasteless crap. Crap, crap, crap! I should throw it back at Angelo's palace and tell him to shove his hamburger and himself back to Italy where the sun doesn't shine….What's that?' What's that sliding down inside my trainer? Tomato ketchup, sliding down the instep of my trainer, very nice, very tasty, lovely. Is it my fault for having sauce, well whose fault is it Mr Brian Young?

2.10am. He's not in there, he must have gone somewhere else, out with the wife, a family do, another nightclub, a golfing weekend? No, he doesn't like golf, well as far as I know he doesn't like golf, I don't think he does I've never followed him to a golf course. Well if hc's not in there, where is he? Hold on, there he is! That's right Tony take a deep breath. One too many is it mate, no change there then. That's right, get some fresh air into those lungs, and get it circulating up there into your thick-head, sober-up before you go home to your wife and daughter. I haven't seen that shirt before; it doesn't suit you, wrong colour. You must be freezing, dickhead. Quick hurry up, he'll be after a cab. Dump this crap, one last bite, get rid of the hamburger. Leave it to the pigeons, the rats, tomorrow's street cleaner. Come on get a move on. Cab keys, cab keys. Which pocket, which pocket? Come on, come on get across the road, put the key in the lock and open the cab door. Quick, get-in start the engine. That's right, that's right; you don't want to miss him like last time.

Ok, ok, slowly, slowly, slowly pull up behind, don't make it so obvious….That's right, you're in striking distance. Now is the time to turn round Tony, now is the time for a taxi. Don't go to Angelo's, they're crap, you know they're crap. Good lad, good lad, that's right you'll get food poisoning, what am I saying, I'll get food poisoning? Does it matter?....Hey Tony, which way are you going, wrong direction. I'm over here, come over here, over here you prick, over here, I'm coming….Where's he going? Your taxi is over here pal. If I pull up alongside him, he might think twice. It might stop him going in….Then; do I want to stop him going in? Let him go in, he's a big boy. He can tie his own shoelaces, brush his teeth, ring for a take-away. He can look after himself. Why not let him go in, he'll have a few more drinks, loosen-up like he did the last time in the back of my cab. Yes let him go in. Go in; go in, I'll be waiting. I'll wait. I'll wait for him I always wait. I'll wait for him as long as it takes on a bloody, pissin' Friday night.

That's it Tony in you go.

'Good evening sir.' That's right Mr Concierge of the Casino, immaculate in your bottle green suit and top hat, don't stop me from coming in you bastard. Do I look like I've had too much to drink, of course I do. That's right roll out the red carpet, swing open the heavy glass door, flash that gold filling and let me in because you recognise me as another loser on the loose. Think of Anne, think of Martha. You prick, you selfish, weak prick. All those hours spent sitting in that circle pouring your heart out, gone, because I'm pissed-as-a-fart! Don't use that as an excuse, just turn around and get out the place it's not too late.

It is Tony.

That voice, that fucking whisper….Neon lights, I hate neon lights, they give me a headache. The place hasn't changed. Same old faces, a lick of gold paint here and there, and my old mate, 'H' working the roulette table. Check pockets. Better leave a ten pound note in my back pocket for the taxi home. Bollocks to the taxi! I'm going to win. I always win.

That's the ticket Tony.

'Forty five pounds worth of chips please.' That smile, the cashier has been here a long time with that smile, five years, maybe eight; well she was working here the last time I came in. I recognise her pink lipstick and the look she gives you. A look that says, another mug, another mug like the last one, just another mug in the long line of mugs that have passed my way.

'Thank you sir. Good luck.' Yeah right lady, like *I bet* you really mean it, no pun intended. Ok, get out of the strait jacket, relax, you're going to win. Be positive, every man has his vices. Smoking, drugs, adultery, the booze. I don't do them. So what if I have a little flutter from time-to-time.

That's the ticket Tony.

So where do I start? What do I fancy? Where will I be lucky? The slot machine? A few pulls of the handle. Then the tables. That sounds a positive plan of action. A drink first. They're free in here. A cold beer? A coffee? To hell with the coffee, who wants to sober-up?

What about the waitress?

What about the waitress?

You're not telling me she's not pretty?

Yes, she's pretty. I haven't seen her in here before, she's new.

'Can I have drink please?' Nice eyes, amongst other things. 'A cold beer please.'

'Certainly sir.'

Nice legs, great walk.

That's the ticket Tony.

Hey cut it out, I'm a married man. Yes and a faithful one at that.

That's the ticket Tony, now concentrate.

Concentrate, that's it concentrate. Slot-machine. Win a few bob first. Then the tables. My old croupier mate 'H' will look after me. It's about time he became my good-luck-charm, my four-leaf clover.

The Las Vegas slot machine, be good to me, be lucky. There she goes. Three pulls of the handle to win. Be lucky Tony, be lucky....Two grapes and a bell, not bad for a first try....Another pull of the handle...A king, a gold bar and two cherries. Last go, pull the handle and be lucky Tony, be lucky....A king, another king and a third king! Yes get in! This is going to be my lucky, lucky night.

That's the ticket Tony.

'Your beer sir.' Give her a tip with your winnings. Start as you mean to go on. You know what they say, look after them and they'll look after you. Give her a couple of chips. Take it easy, one will do, it could be a long night.

'Thank you sir.'

The beer tastes good; it always tastes good when you win, when you're a winner. Have another go on *The Las Vegas*, why not. Pull that handle like you mean it....A cherry, a gold bar and another gold bar. Two chances left.... A king, a bar and another gold bar, nearly. You're hitting the crossbar Tony, be a winner be a winner. Give the handle a good pull Tony, a good yank; make this machine work for a living. Make me some money baby….A KING a KING and another KING… Oh you beauty! You fantastic lump of metal! If I could sleep with you I would! Happy days! Happy, happy days! Come to mother pay up, that's right *Las Vegas*, spew out MY money, MY dosh, MY spondulies These gold tokens feel like heaven in the palms of my hands, this is what it's all about; this is what life is all about. What do you say to that, voice, *you loser?*'

That's the ticket Tony, but you know it won't last.

Go away voice, go away and don't come back.

You know better than anyone Tony.

Piss off and get out of my head.

Think you're on a roll now, do you?

Why are you doing this to me, you drag me in, then you spit me out.

'Piss Off!' That was a bit loud. I hope nobody heard me, lucky. Nobody saw me talking to myself, lucky. Right let's go! Three hundred pounds 'up' in the first twenty minutes. Celebrate, have another beer.

That's the ticket Tony.

Oh, you've got a lot to answer for voice. Here I come 'H' have that table ready and whoever's up there in brain-world; trying to throw a spanner–in-my-works, forget it, this is my night!

Oh you think so do you?

Yes I do and why not?

Because you lose.

Not all the time.

Most of the time.

My luck has to change, it has changed.

When?

Now.

Don't make me laugh.
I feel it tonight.
You've been saying that for months.
You won't let me stop.
Now it's my fault?
It is.
Stop then.
I can't, you know I can't.
Then bet some more. Lose some more.
Don't tell me what to do!
Nobody can do that Tony; they've all tried and failed.
Leave me alone.
Go right ahead, the tables are waiting.

It's about time I became a bastard, a really nasty bastard.
Anyway, who gives a shit about Tony Evans; he doesn't give a
shit about me. He doesn't know me, he doesn't give a shit about
me or any of us....I could use his weakness to my advantage, let
him lose all his money then he'll come crawling to me for help.
I've got morals and pride you know, well I used to have....What
if he wins? He won't win, losers like him never win. Losers like
him don't deserve to win anyway....I'll wait for him, see what
the night brings, after all I'm going nowhere.

In for a penny, in for a pound as they say, eh Tony.
    Don't listen to the voice Tony just slot your credit card into the
Casino's cash machine. Blank him from your head.
    That's right Tony, lose some more.
    Why me, why my head? I know the answer, it's because you
think I'm weak don't you? I know I have a problem just leave me
alone.
    Why don't you stop then?
    What's it to do with you voice?

Nothing, but one little bet wont hurt.

One little bet wont hurt, one little bet.

Then, for the first time that night the voice left Tony's head. But he knew it would return, it always returned. It's amazing how losing a shit-load of money can quickly sober you up, and for Tony it was no different. As the sweat ran down the back of his shirt, he punched in his pin-number and held his breath as well as his hovering hand at the hole-in-the-wall. Ready to snatch the money out of the cash machine, he paused like a sprinter waiting for the starter's pistol. Eager to get back to the tables and win back some of his ever increasing debt he looked up and focused on his reflection in the mosaic mirrored ceiling. A hundred images of his face stared down at him, none of them complimentary and not one face could excuse him for what he was doing. Self destruction isn't easy to explain.

The cash machine held his card. OVERDRAWN. 'Shit!' The word hissed through Tony's clenched teeth. Anxiety made his fingers tremble as he fanned the cards in his thinning wallet. Slipping out another card, he repeated the procedure and waited.

'Come on, come on, please, please.' This time the cash machine regurgitated the card and released his money. Liberated, with a hand full of funds, he walked across the casino floor towards the cashier. As he walked, he spotted her waiting for him. *Come into my web said the spider to the fly.* It was the same cashier with the pink lipstick, the same cashier who smiled at him before he went on his *Las Vegas* roll, the same cashier that was happy to take his money, the same cashier who could spot a mug a mile off.

'Two hundred pounds worth of chips please.'

'Yes sir.' Would she have addressed him as 'sir' if she knew what Tony was really like? He doubted it. She smiled at him through the glass window, the same false smile she had trained herself to wear, the smile of a boaconstricta, a smile that could swallow a thousand sad faces like Tony's, a blank, distant, nervous face, an otherwise engaged face.

'H', his 'lucky-ticket' was working the roulette wheel; the casino was enjoying a good night, there seemed to be more than one loser at the busy tables. 'H' was small and round with newly whitened teeth. With ruddy cheeks he resembled a toby-jug of a drunken pirate, which Tony's mother had once cherished (it was a family heirloom that accidentally slipped out of Martha's tiny hands). A single diamond earring sat discreetly in his left earlobe, although Tony doubted it was a real gem. His hair was short, with blond tints, immaculate. He spoke in a high-pitched effeminate voice and had been the brunt of many a homophobic casino drunk over the years, although the hard calluses of skin across his knuckles told a different story. The croupier's small, manicured fingers guided the chips around the table like the pieces on a greasy chess board, as Tony watched the wheel and waited for a seat. A roar of laughter boomed up from across the table, he looked over with shallow eyes. A couple of busty hookers draped around some suited geezers with gelled hair and money to burn seemed to be losing heavily (don't play the tables if you're not prepared to lose. Good advice for Tony. Advice he never took). Another loser left the table, a big bearded man with holes in his pockets and a sunken jaw. Sighing and raising his eyebrows at the same time he offered his seat to the next pundit waiting, a bald headed guy who looked like a serious gambler. Tony could tell a serious gambler from ten-paces. They were normally alone, didn't smile or talk much and placed a bet without thinking twice. The guy with the beard raised his eyebrows again and said a despondent, 'Good luck Pal.' Sometimes for superstitious gamblers a 'good-luck-pal' could mean the kiss of death. Like seeing a policeman with a rabbit's foot on his key-ring, or crossing a nun on the stairs or mentioning 'Macbeth' to actors in the theatre. For Tony Number 22 was Anne's birthday, his lucky number; it at least gave him some solace for playing the tables. On previous visits to the casino he'd drifted around sipping beer and playing the same number all night. Number 22 had lost every time and tonight would be no different. He knew as soon as he was tempted to change numbers, that little white ivory ball would spin around the roulette wheel and stop at number 22. It was a nap, wasn't it?

3:20AM. He was running late. He hoped the ornate, gold wall clock was running fast. It wasn't. Anne would know where he'd been. Excuses that he couldn't get a cab or he didn't notice the time were wearing thin. Either way he was running the gauntlet and heading for Dodge City.

A roar went up from across the table. The geezer and his crew had finally won big-time. One of the hookers' lipstick hit his cheek, then the rim of her champagne glass, later, she would hope for a bigger tip. A large fat lady in her mid-fifties with beehive hair and a tight fitting, leopard skinned mini-skirt stood up from the table and offered Tony her seat. She had red painted finger nails and a voice like Audrey Hepburn from 'Breakfast at Tiffany's', Anne's favourite film. 'I hope you have better luck than me *darling*.' Tony saddled himself into the warm seat. Contemplating the numbers spread out before him, he slid his two hundred pounds worth of chips across the table and placed it on Anne's birthday, number 22. As he looked up he noticed his lucky charm was about to be replaced by a yawning, expressionless croupier who had hair like a scarecrow. This was 'H's' last spin of the wheel, the last spin-of-the-dice, surly it would be a lucky omen. 'H' caught Tony's gaze and sort-of smiled at him, but Tony couldn't be sure if it was meant for him or his nemesis. It was a smile like the cashier's; a smile that said, 'I've seen punters like you a million times, putting their lives on the line. Don't you know when to stop, but who am I to give advice? I only work here.' Like a smoker, an alcoholic, a drug addict, who'd given up thousands of times before, Tony promised if he won, he would never bet again. Not on the dogs. Not on the nags. Not on the internet. Not on two flies on a wall. Never, ever, again.

Tony watched as 'H's' stubby fingers spun the wheel for the last time that night. His good luck charm was his last hope. Over the years Tony had trained himself like every other compulsive gambler to listen or look out for a tip, a moment when your gut-instinct told you the time was right. Now was the moment of truth. As his eyes followed the ball round and round the wheel he prayed to himself. 'Please let it stop at 22, I will do anything to let it stop at 22.' Then the voice returned inside his head.

But will you stop gambling Tony?

I will, please, please God do this for me.

And what will you do for me?

Anything.

Anything? Anything can be dangerous in the hands of someone like me.

The ball seemed to float round the wheel like a drawn-out dream. Thoughts of Anne and Martha sleeping at home flashed into his head. What was he doing? He was playing Russian roulette with the bones of the two people's that he adored, that he would die for.

As the ball bounced and jumped from one number to the next, he felt the air being sucked from his lungs. The little air in his throat was red hot and it seemed at any second, his heart and lungs would explode out of his chest. And it did.

BLACK NUMBER 8.

BLACK NUMBER 8.

BLACK NUMBER 8.

BLACK NUMBER 8 went through Tony's heart like a dagger, like a bullet.

Falling through the swing door of the men's toilet, Tony punched a cubicle door with the side of his fist. Slumping over the sink, he vomited out the night's alcohol from the pit of his stomach. Snatching at the gold water tap, he turned it on and splashed cold water over his face.

BLACK NUMBER 8.

BLACK NUMBER 8.

BLACK NUMBER 8.

Looking at himself in the mirror that ran the length of the toilet wall, the water that trickled down his face felt like acid as the reality of a man haunted by an addiction stared back at him. One of the flash looking geezers wearing the biggest smile of a winner bounced into the toilet. Tony recognised that face; it was a long time ago, once, when he was a winner, when winning got him hooked. The geezer stood at the urinal, whistling a tune from a Hollywood Musical. Turning his head, he looked back over his shoulder and shouted. 'Good night buddy?' The ginger haired geezer spoke with an American, West Coast accent. A line of orange freckles ran over the bridge of his nose and pallid cheeks, matching the colour of his short cropped hair. 'I take it from the reluctance of your reply it's not your night buddy?' Tony swilled the sweat from his face then slowly looked up at the winner in the reflection of the mirror.

'How do you know what night I've had *buddy*?'

'Rough ride eh, you'll be alright next time.'

'What do you know about fucking next time?'

Zipping up his fly, the geezer joined Tony at the sink and started washing his hands. 'You know what they say buddy. Don't let winning cloud your judgment, don't go into the ring angry, emotional fighters make mistakes.'

'I'm not your buddy.'

'A sore loser eh?' The geezer hit the ground before the word *loser* filtered out through the gap in his front teeth. The guy could take a punch but his freckles couldn't. Crashing onto the tiles he slid across the piss ridden floor on the back of his suit jacket.

Bewildered, glassy-eyed, he tried to recover. Quick to step forward, Tony thrust out his foot hard down onto the front of the geezer's silk, purple shirt. Blood flooding his mouth, the yank grabbed Tony's ankle with both hands and tried to wrestle free. Another whack from Tony's right fist hit him across the side of the head. With a thud, the geezer slumped back down onto his shoulders as the back of his head hit the floor with a bang. As blood streamed from the American's mouth, it spilt onto the lapel of his charcoal coloured suit. Leaning down, Tony put his fist an inch from the man's face. 'Do you want some more?' The geezer's face distorted with pain and rage as his chest wheezed. Looking up at his assailant he found the inner strength to force out a defiant response through his bloody, gargling mouth.

'You fuck.'

'You're right Yank, I am a sore loser.' Noticing a bloody tooth on the Yanks bottom lip, Tony slowly removed his foot off his chest. Backing out of the toilet door like a bar-room-brawler, Tony found himself back in the bright lights of the casino. Searching the floor, it looked totally different sober, an alien world to what he was used too. He had to be quick, on top of everything else, now was not a good time to be done for GBH. Walking past the roulette-table with a throbbing right hand; he overheard the hookers negotiating terms down the ear of the Yank's friend. He hoped one knew a good dentist. At the table he noticed another pundit sitting in the same seat he'd vacated, a pile of chips staked up in front of him, 'that's about right.' Making his way past the tables and slot machines he felt the eyes of the casino were upon him. It would only be a matter of time before the geezer staggered out of the toilets, raised the alarm and caused an international incident, then he'd be in real shit. Passing the waitress he noticed the cashier pretending to laugh at a joke from a sad whippersnapper who hadn't a chance-in-hell of getting his leg-over. Tony was glad she didn't notice him, he'd had enough embarrassing, in-your-face-moments for one night. A sudden urge came across him as he passed the *Las Vegas* slot-machine. He felt like putting a sledgehammer through it, as the woman with the beehive hair yelled 'Yes!' and did a 'high-five' with a couple of other gamblers. She'd won the 'Golden Jackpot.' It wasn't easy to take. The concierge yawned then smiled flashing his gold tooth as he opened the main doors for him to leave. 'Good night sir.' He gave Tony a searching look as he hoped for a 'tip' from a winner. Tony nodded goodbye. It was a nod from a loser, the nod like a bloody, pissin' Friday night drunk.

On this pissin' Friday night, like every pissin' Friday night Young ignored drunk after drunk who banged on his window and wanted a taxi to take them home to sleep off the beer or vodka, but at last the waiting was over. As soon as he stepped out onto the street he knew who it was. He recognised the way he walked, the way he held himself. Tony Evans.

Young started the cab and like a torpedo headed straight for the stooped figure walking away from the neon lights of the Casino. Shaking his wounded hand in the cold night air, Tony tried to relieve the pain by simulating his fingers up-and-down to an imaginary silver dollar running across the back of his swelling knuckles. Looking back over his shoulder towards the entrance of the Casino, he wondered whether someone had raised the alarm or whether he'd been caught on a security camera. The first punch was a good one, the second one better, but it still didn't stop the anger of BLACK NUMBER 8. As he paced the pavements he heard the distinctive rattle of a cab's engine slowly pulling up behind him.

'Tony.' Surprised to hear his name, Tony swung around; he didn't recognise the voice or the smoking figure leaning out of the cab window.

'Do you need a ride home Tony?'

Young saw by Tony's expression he was confused, not only of the offer, but by who was offering it. 'I gave you a ride home last month.'

'Sorry pal, I've got no money.'

'It doesn't matter I'm going your way.'

'It's alright I need some air.' Tony turned a corner, disappearing down a one-way street. Young showed his venom, by spitting out the window. He couldn't follow him with the cab and he hadn't waited half the night just to be 'fucked-off' by Evans with 'it's alright I need some air.' Slamming his foot down, he drove off in the opposite direction. 'I'll give him some air!'

The one way street followed a railway line behind a large brick wall and the sound of a freight train moving nuclear-waste at a snails pace made Tony realise how late it was. As the street weaved its way around the back of some derelict warehouses Tony clenched his fists. He hoped a couple of figures would appear out of the dark shadows and wanted a scrap. The more the merrier, he was up for anything and anybody. Walking over a humped-backed-bridge he noticed the black cab waiting at the bottom of the street. Young sat inside watching, waiting as the rumble of the cab's engine puffed out smoke from the exhaust pipe into the nippy air. Young's voice tried to hide his frustration. 'Come on Tony hop in, you can't walk all the way home.' Tony was still holding a large amount of alcohol but he could sense something wasn't right. Ignoring the invitation, Tony kept on walking.

BLACK NUMBER 8.

BLACK NUMBER 8.

BLACK NUMBER 8 being called out by 'H' was like the drill from an oil rig continually pounding the inside of his head. Everything was irrelevant. Tied-in-knots, the sickness in his stomach had moved up and lodged itself at the back of his arid throat. Once again he heard the presence of the cab over his right shoulder as his fists clenched tighter.

'Jump in Tony it's a ten mile walk. It'll be dawn before you get home.' *Walk off again Evans and I'll use the fucking crow bar on you. Who do you think you are you smug prick.*

Tony spun around, malevolence sparking from his eyes and voice. 'What's your fucking game pal?'

What's my fucking game? I'll show you what my fucking game is!

'It's up to you Tony, forget it!' *And I mean it Evans this is your last chance.*

Past caring, Tony sighed deeply and took in the situation. It didn't matter who this guy was or what he wanted, if he tried anything, he would get it and he would enjoy giving it to him. It was late, his fate already sealed, screwed down with fourteen rusty screws.

Tony flopped into the back seat of the cab and ran his swollen fingers through the top of his blond crew-cut. His hair was damp with early morning dew as he stared blindly out of the window. Deserted of any nightlife the cab drove through the naked streets of Oxford. As the cab rumbled from side-to-side Tony caught a glimpse of a fox standing by the side of the road. It looked unfazed as its eyes mirrored the headlights of the passing taxi. Not a single word was exchanged between the two men, but now-and-again along with the odd sweep of a street light they caught eye contact with each other in the reflection of the rear-view mirror.

Young could see by his passenger's expression that he had a night he wanted to forget, he'd seen it before, something he recognised. Tony rubbed the knuckles of his right hand and had a delayed reaction. He felt guilty about giving 'the geezer' a belt in the casino toilets. It wasn't a good memory for the Yank to take back home to the States, his English hospitality could have been better. He tried to convince himself that he'd taught him a lesson. As a loud-mouthed-winner he had it coming, if not by him, by someone else. It was some sort of consolation but nothing else.

Fresh air, Tony needed fresh air. Lowering the window, an

early morning gust of cold wind swept over his face. The 'past caring' suddenly turned into waves of anxiety. Excuses, the aftermath of BLACK NUMBER 8 and the evening were going over and over inside his head. What was he going to tell Anne? It was no good, she'd heard it all before, every excuse, every lie. The tightrope he'd been walking for the past couple of years was now hanging by a thread, a slight thread. Young broke the silence, his voice coarse from years of smoking. 'Not a good night then Tony?' He sounded like the Yank.

'You could say that.' Tony's voice was suspicious, Young's almost friendly. 'You still working in Brainforth?'

'Yes unfortunately.' Confused by the familiarity, Tony fired a question towards the back of Young's greasy head. 'How do you know where I work?'

'You told me last time.'

'I don't remember.'

'You told me your job was pretty stressful and you needed a few beers to relax. I said if you can't have a few beers on a Friday night when can you have one?' Young pondered over his next move. 'No luck on the tables again?'

'What do you mean *again*?'

'Oh nothing, just waxing lyrical.'

'I've had enough of people waxing lyrical tonight.' Tony could feel his shoulders tightening.

'I know what you mean, I get them sometimes in the back of the cab.' Young's hooded eyes looked up at Tony in the rear-view as he lit a cigarette. 'Smoke?' For a few seconds Tony was tempted.

'We could all do with making a few extra bob. Get out of the rat race.'

'I need more than a few bob.'

Young's eyes shot back to the empty roads then back to the rear-view. The next approach would be vital. As he turned off the main road, he realised time was running out, in a couple of minutes he would be pulling into Tony's road. 'If you're interested I've got a little proposition for you, if you want to make some extra cash?'

Tony wasn't listening. 'Sorry, my mind was elsewhere, what?' Tony recognised were he was. 'Just here please.' The cab stopped a little way from his house.

'Thanks for the ride.'

'Did you hear what I said?' Young turned in his seat expecting a reply only to see the back door slam shut. *The selfish prick!* Young swung around in his seat, lowered the window and raised his voice. 'Did you hear what I said? I said if you want to make a few extra bob I can help?'

'I'll be alright thanks.'

'What do you mean, *I'll be alright thanks,* I can help you out; I'm talking about more than a few bob Tony. I'll make it worth your while; you'll thank me for it.' Young seethed as he watched Tony walk up the path to his front door. 'I know you need the money Tony, I'll be in touch.' *You can bet your fucking bottom dollar I will Tony Evans.* Fumbling for his house keys, Tony didn't catch what the cab driver had said, he had other things on his mind. Placing the key into the front door he turned and looked back at the cab. Young's eyes were still fixed on him. Tony chewed over the situation. He didn't need another confrontation, it was too early in the morning to start worrying about a nutty cab driver or a perv who'd taken a shining to him.

Cushioning his first steps in the hallway, Tony shut the door behind him and slipped off his shoes. The house was dark, cold. Using the banister as a guide he made his way upstairs to the landing. Quietly opening Martha's bedroom door he tripped over 'Harry' her toy dog in the process. Its bark was all he needed. Snatching it up from under his feet, he smothered the dogs' mouth with his hand. Martha's eyes flickered but she didn't move.

Putting the toy onto the dresser he knelt down by the side of the bed and kissed his daughter's hand. Tears pricked his eyes as he turned and saw Anne standing in the doorway. 'Where have you been?' Her voice was soft as the stillness in the room. Quiet words stumbled out of Tony's mouth. 'I'll tell you in the morning.'

'It is the morning, don't bother I can guess.' Anne tuned and walked back across the landing, closing their bedroom door behind her.

Flicking on the table light, Tony stood and looked around the spare bedroom. Christmas decorations, family photographs and old crockery spilt out of dusty boxes stacked around the walls, each one conveying family memories. In one corner an office chair and small table holding a laptop seemed out-of-place in the muddle of the dust collectors. On one of the walls held on by blue-tack was a concert poster of The Four Tops at the London Palladium. Anne loved Motown and early in their relationship she had bought tickets to see the four, silver suited harmonisers. Being a rock and punk fan, Tony reluctantly went, but was pleasantly surprised to see Marvin Gaye join them on stage. Consequently, Anne invariably ribbed him about how he danced in the aisle.

'I only danced because I fancied the arse off you.' that was his standard reply. But as much as he tried to hang on to his anarchy she had converted him.

The pink glow of the dawn had crept into the room. Flicking off the table light, he drew back the curtains and looked up at the sky. The roofs of the surrounding houses were alight with shiny pink. Covering his eyes from the radiance, he tried to work out the rhyme about 'shepherds at night' and 'the sky in the morning', but gave up as his thoughts once again flashed to BLACK NUMBER 8. The corner of a photograph sticking out of an old encyclopaedia which was lying on top of one of the boxes caught his attention. Sliding the photograph out of the pages of the book, he worked out it was taken in Spain about four years ago. Martha was a baby lying in Anne's arms, Tony the proud father with the turquoise Mediterranean behind them. Another photograph dropped out of the book and landed at his feet. Picking it up, he saw it was of their wedding. A sad smile came across his face as he ran the tips of his fingers across the snap. Anne hadn't changed, she was still beautiful, but he had, in more ways than one.

Undressing, he draped his clothes across the tops of a few boxes then pulled back the duvet off the bed. The room was slowly losing its pinkness and turning to daylight. Naked, he went to the window to close the curtains. Then he noticed Young's cab, it was parked at the end of the road, cigarette smoke floating out of the driver's window. Why was he parked there? What did he want? Think; think…Who is this bastard? Tony couldn't remember getting a lift from him before, or ever telling him his name, were he lived, or about Brainforth.

I can help you out, I'm talking about more than a few bob Tony. I'll make it worth your while, you'll thank me for it Tony. I know you need the money Tony, I'll be in touch.

Was he being stalked? Throwing on his boxers and shirt, Tony grabbed a cricket bat from one of the boxes and made his way barefooted out of the room and down the stairs. Quietly unlocking the front door he stepped out onto the cold path. At the same time Young's cab started. Wielding the cricket bat, Tony marched forward feeling the cold gravel of the road under the soles of his feet. As the cab sped away Tony started to run. Inches from the cab he swung the bat and missed. Something sharp pierced the sole of his foot, dropping the bat he winced in agony and hopped a couple of times before falling to the curb. Swinging his left foot up, he balanced it on the top of his right knee and inspected the injury. Dripping in blood, a jagged piece of green glass stuck out of his heel. On the count of three, he gritted his teeth and pulled the glass from his foot. Panting, he looking up, the cab had disappeared.

Across the road he noticed the flicker of net curtains, the neighbours were curious as to what was going on.

As he was.

Sitting at the kitchen table, Tony placed his bleeding foot into a bowl of warm salty water; it made him grimace but he was grateful for small mercies that he didn't need stitches. His hand as well as his foot throbbed as he went over the events of the night. Placing his foot onto a clean towel he dabbed the wound and put a plaster over the cut, it was a difficult place to apply the dressing. Deliberating over Young, he put it down to the drink, paranoia, deceit, anger amongst other things and the impending day which engulfed his thoughts along with BLACK NUMBER 8. The sound of the milk-float pulling-up outside and the empties being replaced by semi-skimmed on the front doorstep reiterated how late it was or how early it was…. 5:30AM. Tony's eyes were lead heavy. If he was lucky he would sleep for around three hours before Martha woke.

Climbing into the single bed, Tony pulled the duvet around his neck, it smelt of must and as soon as he closed his eyes his head started spinning. Drifting off to sleep he thought of the fox he'd seen by the side of the road and how its eyes gleamed in the cab's headlights. *As sly as a fox,* Tony rolled over and sighed. What next, Martha's money box? He really was a class-act.

Near daylight, 5.30AM. At the same time across town. Young was wide awake. Sprawled out on the couch, he kicked of his shabby trainers which fell onto the carpet with a couple of heavy thuds. As he drove off he caught a glimpse of Evans in the wing-mirror dropping his cricket bat and falling to the ground. *That will teach him to play games with me.* As he swung his legs up onto the arm of the couch he noticed congealed blood on his foot. Looking at his white, purple, veined foot, he couldn't see any injury or cut.

Picking up his trainer he smelt tomato ketchup, Angelo's tomato ketchup from his plastic hamburger. It was a relief of some sort, although it didn't bother him whether he'd lacerated his foot or not. Once, he nearly lost his thumb to a kitchen knife. While slicing some stilton, the knife slipped and severed a cut so deep it went down to the bone. Deciding he'd had enough of hospitals, he put on his doctors hat and did a quick do-it-yourself job on himself. Drinking copious amounts of whisky, he soaked his hand in the spirit and started stitching with a large sewing needle and cat-gut. With a wooden spatula gripped between his teeth, he sewed like a caveman and howled like a werewolf. Eventually he passed-out with the pain and woke to find his handy-work had done the trick, the bleeding had stopped. Bandaging the cut, he went to work as if it was just another normal day.

The pink dawn that had crept through the net curtains had disappeared over an hour ago and he was sad to see it go. Now, the bright daylight which had taken its place lit up the wall of nails. Through the cigarette smoke and void of any appetite which had deserted him months ago he looked at the small newspaper cutting circled by the nails. Leaning down he picked up a glass of scotch and slugged it down-in-one. Turning the empty glass around in his hands, his expression contorted, his eyes a cavity of any life. Gripping the glass in his right hand, he brought it back over his shoulder and threw the tumbler at the wall. As the glass shattered and flew around the room, his eyelids flickered. Drifting off to sleep was arduous, easier said than done. But he did sleep, the sleep he wished for, the sleep he yearned for, the sleep he thought would never come.

CHAPTER NINE

The long hours of Saturday and Sunday passed in a daze. Young thought he went to the shops on more than one occasion and that he watched television. He vaguely recalled watching a reality programme and that he bought more cigarettes and a bottle of scotch, but he couldn't be sure. Sometimes in-between other things, he'd stare at the blank screen of the television while eating dark chocolate and salt and vinegar crisps. As always, anything he ate was washed down with a few large whiskies. Once, he dozed off and woke up to find a fat woman winning twenty thousand pounds on a game-show. If he remembered rightly it was for answering a question about a mountain range in Spain. As to whether it was in the middle of the night, early morning or late afternoon, again he couldn't be sure. Sometimes in-between other things he would circle the armchair and the debris of food. Shuffling around the piles of clothes again and again like a junkie high on dope, he always found himself in the kitchen. There, he'd switch the strip-light on and off, on and off. For hours on end he'd stand there transfixed, switching the light on and off, on and off.

As for the rest of the time, he'd stand at the window smoking. He recollected watching a young couple kissing under the bare branches of an oak tree across the road. From the way they were kissing, he could see they were drunk. Swaying as they kissed, he worked out as he did with his passengers in the back of his cab that they most probably had been to a dinner party. They looked that sort. *Smart rich kids go to dinner parties* he thought, but then again rich kids wouldn't be seen dead around this area. The kiss lasted a couple of minutes, it was a drunken kiss, but a tender kiss, the sort of kiss Young remembered like the passing breeze in the trees. Closing his eyes he tried to taste her lips on his, but the feeling had long gone. That beautiful, tender feeling had disappeared forever and he knew it would never return.

For the rest of the night he flicked channels and trudged the room with disturbing regularity. It was as if he was lost in a maze. When Tony Evans, the prison officer did flicker into his head, he seemed for a few minutes to focus on how he would tackle him next time. He knew he had to pile on the pressure, tighten the thumbscrews, too much time and effort had gone into Tony Evans. Then, as quickly as he came into his head he vanished. That weekend he was supposed to work, but lack of sleep had caught up with him and too much whisky had dislodged any rational thinking. Closing his eyes he tried once again to forget. Then her sweet voice once again came into his head. *'Goodnight my love, goodnight.'*

Tony had a couple of hours' sleep at most. Martha startled him out of his slumber by leaping onto the bed, then jumping up-and-down like an Olympic gymnast on a trampoline. She pleaded with him to take her swimming or to the park, anywhere would do. It was the hangover cure he least wanted, but eventually, Walt Disney came to his rescue. In the dark cinema with a bucket of popcorn on his lap he rested his eyes while Martha watched ghouls and dragons fly out of the screen in 3D. For the rest of the weekend Anne had avoided him. On both mornings she left the house early, telling Martha to tell her father that she would be back late. Every second of the day, he wondered what she was thinking and what she would do. But he knew what she was thinking and who she was talking to. Anne confided with her mother and sister about everything and he could feel his ears burning. After bathing Martha and putting her to bed, he watched the clock tick away one hour then the next. Anne was late and hadn't returned home. Resigning himself to an early night in the spare room, he went to bed but couldn't sleep. Past one in the morning he heard her come through the front door. Meeting her face to face on the stairs, he made a pathetic attempt at being funny, 'We shouldn't pass on the stairs its bad luck.' She didn't laugh, if looks could kill. Her eyes were glassy from drinking, the fragrance of her hair enchanting as she brushed past him. He wanted to talk, clear the air, she didn't and closed the door of their bedroom in his face. BLACK NUMBER 8 once again whirled around inside his head. He listened to Anne going to bed, the brushing of teeth, lights off, the closing of their bedroom door. Silence, no *good nights*, a vanishing kiss.

CHAPTER TEN

Monday morning. Tony sat in his car and looked across at the large imposing gates of Brainforth. Taking in a deep breath, life couldn't get any worse. Straightening the epaulette on his crisp white, shirt, he flicked open the glove-box and took out his prison tie. Clipping on his tie he pulled-down the sun visor and started checking his appearance in the small mirror. Out the corner of his eye a large brown envelope in the glove box caught his attention. It was unfamiliar – bulky – blank front – no name – no address – sealed with sellotape. Ripping it open he peered inside. His eyes widened, the envelope contained a wad of money, fifties, twenties, a few tenners. Fanning the money, he tried to work out how much was there. At a rough guess, fifteen, maybe twenty grand. Ogling the car park, he turned sharp right and left then swivelled around in his seat and looked through the back window. Nobody, if he was being watched, they were invisible. Stuffing the money back into the envelope, he threw it back into the glove box. His hands started shaking. Battling against the perspiration that had started to trickle down his face, his mind raced. The passenger door wasn't locked, he never locked it, that's how the money arrived in the glove box, that was the easy part, but who put it there and why? A loud thump hit the nearside window.

'It's show time!' Billy Rogers stood there smiling, his hair as always groomed to perfection. Tony climbed out of the car, but this time he locked it.

'Good night Friday wasn't it?' Tony didn't answer. Rogers was his usual bouncy self as the two officers strolled across the car park towards the prison. 'I take it by the silence your weekend wasn't as good as mine? Well I'm back on with Carol, although I think she's playing hard to get. She doesn't trust me the cheeky bitch.'

At the prison gates Tony turned and looked back across the car park. He'd hoped he'd see someone, someone he'd recognise, someone who would give him a clue as to the money in the glove-box, but apart from the passing traffic on the main road there was nobody. Baffled as to where the money had come from, Tony walked through the prison oblivious to Rogers' ramblings about his sex life. Reaching the gate leading to the exercise yard, Rogers radioed for security clearance and the gate automatically opened. Hundreds of barred windows and a million rust-colour bricks looked down on the two men as they stepped out into the daylight. In the far corner of the yard a handful of cons dug at a patch of allotment, a glint of sun reflecting off the small greenhouse roof. An unmarked grave of the last prisoner to be hung in Brainforth boarded the vegetable patch. Nobody had come to collect the body, so there he lay, the evil buried with his bones, another idiosyncrasy of the prison. A patch of asphalt, marked out with a five-a-side pitch and basketball court was surrounded by a high, wire fence. Strolling across the yard, Rogers changed the subject from his love life. 'Did you finish up in the casino again?'

Tony stopped and pulled Rogers back by his arm. 'What's it got to do with you?'

Rogers was surprised by Tony's anger.

'Alright, take it easy.'

'What I do is my business, alright!' Looking up, Tony squinted at the square patch of blue sky. 'Sorry. I didn't sleep well last night and all I need is another day in this shit hole.' By the look across Roger's face he wasn't convinced. He knew Tony liked to gamble, but he wasn't aware of how serious his addiction was. Rogers had the face of a guy who peddled dodgy Rolex watches. Stocky, bald, he had a permanent suntan all year round and was pathologically vain. Muscular from years of lifting weights, his sex life was the daily topic in the locker room. Both men felt comfortable in each other's company and equally they accepted each other for who they were. They had joined the service at the same time and had trained together. Over the years their friendship had grown into a mutual respect and they had become good friends.

'So how much did you lose?' Rogers stood with his hands on his hips and raised his eyebrows like a father waiting to scold a son for pinching an apple.

'I can't remember.' Tony shrugged his shoulders. 'Not much.'

'How much is *not much*?'

'Not much.'

Rogers could only guess it was more. As a cold wind blew across the yard Rogers once again changed the subject and became serious. 'Women they don't understand me. So what do you reckon?'

'About what?'

'Haven't you been listening? I don't know whether to give it another go with Carol?' Tony smiled, Rogers was always getting back with Carol, his life was like a soap opera.

'It's about time you settled down.'

'Piss off!'

It always triggered the same response, that's what Tony liked about Rogers, his vanity was innocent and he never judged anybody for who or what they were. Across the yard they caught sight of another officer struggling to break-up a heated argument between two cons. Striding over, they asked if he needed assistance. But as soon as the quarrel had started it finished. It turned out to be no more than a dispute over the swapping of a Mars Bar for a pack of cigarettes, but *inside* little things can turn into dangerous grudges. Pent-up anger can last for weeks, months, until eventually two cons snap and explode into bloodshed. In Brainforth violence was an everyday occurrence.

Passing a number of prisoners carrying library books, Tony exchanged a few selective nods with a few selective prisoners. Officers always had to be vigilant, on their mettle. If a prisoner clocked another prisoner being overly friendly with a prison officer he would be *marked* for some *special attention*.

Skipping-up the stone steps of A-Block, the two officers entered the smallest of the prison wings. A-Block was a special unit for high-profile prisoners. It was colder inside than out, a bastard of a place, a prison within a prison. Along with Rogers, Tony had been given special training to deal with *the reviled few* as they were known. Although they were only into their second week, Tony hated it. Stepping through the metal doors of A-Block for the first time the smell of mortality had made him realise what he would be dealing with. The scum of humanity were incarcerated in tiny cells; murderers, rapists, paedophiles, along with the odd serial burglar. All locked-up inside the special unit, V.P.'s as they were known, 'vulnerable prisoners', out the way for their own protection.

Looking up at the security cameras bearing down on them they waited a few seconds before the second of the large iron gates sprang into life and opened. The gate instantly clanged shut behind them, sending a wave of echoes around the inner walls of the prison. As they made their way along the third floor landing Tony's thoughts of the money in the glove box were interrupted by Rogers' mutter. 'Here's Jennings, hold onto your shirt tails.'

Jennings' metal tipped boots could be heard in the next county. Straight backed and in his late fifties, he was a burly man with a flock of thick grey hair that swept back over his head from a widow's peak. Tufts of hair sprouted out of each ear and often his eyes would stream from the contact lenses he hated wearing. The thought of wearing glasses horrified him, he thought they made him look weak and weakness wasn't in his persona. From the old school of prison officers, a new haircut would make him feel ten feet tall. A senior officer for nearly twenty eight years, he'd paced Brainforth with those metal tipped boots every day. They were a statement of intent. Everyone knew when Jennings was coming. It was his last few days at work, retirement was on the horizon and over the past month he'd worn a permanent, pious smile, a smile he'd previously kept to himself over the past twenty-eight years. He spoke in a monotone voice and was one of these guys who thought himself funny, but was the least funny guy you could meet. Every joke came out of a Christmas cracker. When you didn't smile or laugh at one of his wise-cracks, it made him feel strangely uncomfortable and his frown would appear just for you, then you knew you were in for a bad time. He could be despairing and antagonistic at the same time and had a reputation for disliking everyone, prisoners and officers alike. If you got on the wrong side of him he could be a bad bastard. Equally, if he took a shining to you, you received some perks, the odd day off to play golf, a bogus visit to the dentist, but in the long run you paid for it. Part of the furniture, Jennings was a Brainforth legend. Tony had kept his distance, but for some absurd reason he'd taken a shinning to Rogers and treated him like a younger brother.

'Good morning guys.' Jennings' voice flowed like syrup in one octave. Tony sort of smiled back, but it was difficult. Rogers was more enthusiastic with his response.

'Good morning Mr Jennings, how are you today?'

'You scem bright and breezy today *Roy*?' 'Roy Rogers.' It was Jennings' way of being funny. 'And how's Trigger?' Rogers laughed, pathetic. Tony didn't. Jennings noticed and waited for a reaction, it never came, but his frown did. From the first day Tony worked inside Brainforth he felt oddly detached from the other officers, except for Rogers, that's the way he liked it, Jennings or no Jennings. Running his fingers through his grey hair, Jennings suddenly became serious, the ultimate professional.

'What a way for you two guys to start the week. Watch your backs in there, dealing with a basket-case can be dangerous. Lollypop's not in here for being Snow White. He likes new officers, he'll try everything to get inside your head.' With a know-it-all-smile across his face Jennings placed the key into the lock and opened cell door number A317. Jennings paused and looked over his shoulder at the two officers. 'By the way, the cheeky bastard has requested that all officers wear slippers at night. He says the noise of our boots walking down the landing keeps him awake. First time in gentlemen, let me do the talking.' Cell number A317 was watched by the minute, every minute of every hour of every day. A small security camera situated high in one corner watched whoever was in the cell and what they were doing. Long ago it was a *death cell*, a cell that held prisoners waiting for the noose of the hangman and where the ghosts of the executed still lingered in the souls of its bricks. After-a-while, category-A prisoners were allowed a few pleasures. A daily newspaper, writing material, cigarettes, chocolate, for Finch a small television perched upon a shelf in one corner of the cell was his pleasure, his only contact with the outside world. A small postcard stuck to the wall with chewing gum was the only picture in the cell. It was a faded, black and white snap of Shirley Temple, wearing a frilly dress with a large bow tied round her waist and her hair in ringlets. It resembled a publicity shot that Hollywood circulated around the press throughout the golden age of cinema, which nowadays had become an iconic image along with pictures of James Dean, Elvis and Marilyn Monroe. Underneath were the words, *The Good Ship Lollipop*.

Alistair Finch looked up from behind a copy of *The Times*. An olive, round-faced, forty-year-old, he had the look of Valentino. Wavy, slicked-back hair hung just above his shirt collar and smelt of Brylcreem. His build was slight with drooping shoulders. Both his cheek bones were scarred with marks from a bout of acne he had in his youth and his deep-set brown eyes like his deep-set voice complimented each other. Finch slowly removed his Buddy Holly glasses off his thin nose and flicked a kiss-curl off his forehead. Patting his fingers across his top lip, he grinned at the three prison officers standing in the cramped doorway of the cell.

'New faces, good morning gentlemen.' He looked at Tony. 'I would say good morning to your work colleague Mr Jennings, but on the few occasions he's accompanied anyone in here he's always been obnoxious.'

'I'm not in the mood for you today Lollypop.' Jennings huffed, his voice vibrating round the walls of the cell. Finch grinned at the two officers. 'There you go, what did I tell you.'

Jennings stepped forward. 'This is Mr Evans and Mr Rogers. You'll be seeing quite a lot of each other. They've come to take you to the exercise yard.' Rogers grasped the opportunity to gain some brownie points. 'Hurry up and get your shoes on please.' Ignoring the order, Finch looked at Tony. 'Would you like me to put on my shoes?' Finch's unnerving grin, like his question, made Tony feel uncomfortable, self conscious. 'Yes, if you would.'

Jennings picked up Finch's' shoes and dropped them at his feet. 'Come on Lollypop; just get a move on please.' Finch ignored Jennings, slipped his glasses back on and buried his head back into the newspaper. 'I was just reading an advert here for Her Majesty's Prison Service – *Because there's no such thing as*

a typical prisoner, there's no such thing as a typical prison officer,
£17,744 – £27,261 a year. Not a bad wage in today's current
climate. A tone of sarcasm had crept into his voice as he continued
reading the advert. *Prisoners aren't a certain type. They come
from all backgrounds, cultures and walks of life. To help this mix
of people rebuild their lives, step-by-step, we need an equally
diverse team of Prison Officers. You don't need academic
qualifications to understand difficult or despairing people. But
you do need a sense of empathy.'* Finch looked up at Tony. 'Well
Mr Evans you look like you have plenty of empathy.' He drew a
glance at Jennings and laughed. 'But I'm slightly confused how
you became a Prison Officer Mr Jennings, you just don't seem
the type.'

Tony caught Roger's eye as Jennings leered over the prisoner.

'I'm warning you Finch, get your shoes on or I'll confiscate
your television.' Rogers touched Jennings' arm; it was tight,
strong, and ready for a fight. 'Get the fuck off me!' Rogers reared
back, shocked. Tony tried to defuse the situation. 'Get a move on
please Alistair.'

Jennings shot a look at Tony. 'His name is Finch, Mr Evans!'
Removing his glasses, Finch slowly and meticulously folded his
newspaper, placing it onto his immaculately made bed. Tony
could feel the tension as Finch once again looked across at him.

'You look like there is something bothering you Mr Evans,
everything alright at home?'

Rogers leaned forward into Tony's ear. 'Don't let him talk to
you like that?'

'I'll give you ten seconds to get your shoes on.' Jennings was
about to snap. Finch stood up, turned his back on them, and hiding
the pain in his side, looked out through the barred windows. 'I
don't fancy any exercise today gentleman it looks like rain.'

Rogers stood rigid. 'You'll do as you're told you nonce.'

Finch cracked his knuckles and turned. 'My prerogative, isn't that right Mr Evans?' His tone was relaxed, one of total control and he knew it. Tony threw a side glance at Jennings. He watched as he took in a deep breath, then composing himself he breathed out and lowered his shoulders. 'You want to watch yourself Lollypop; we can't keep our eye on you all the time.' Jennings voice was suddenly calm, but it cut through the stale air of the cell like a teddy boy's flick-knife.

Impassive, Finch returned to his newspaper as the three officers left. Whistling and grinning at the same time Finch listened to the key locking the cell door.

Apart from when his door was left open and he saw the odd prisoner walking along the landing Finch kept himself to himself. Inside his cell he was in his own little world, it was his life for the past eight years and where he would remain for the rest of his life. As he scanned the obituaries, he could hear the muffled voices of the prison officers from behind the door. The two new officers should be easy game.

On the landing Tony had a flashback to when he was a nine year old at junior school. Bullied by three older boys who cornered him in the playground and out of view from any teachers, the lads gave him a good hiding. For weeks afterwards he ached. Black and blue from thump after thump to his body, the shins of his legs swelled-up like a mountain range from kick after kick. It was what Tony felt like as he stood outside Finch's cell cornered by Jennings glare. 'Well what a fuck-up that was. Don't ever let that prick talk to you like that again; you know what they say about fucking familiarity?'

'We were trained to….'

Jennings snapped back at Tony. 'Training manuals or rule books mean nothing in here Evans. When it comes to rules there are no fucking rules in this place concerning men like Finch.' Rogers piped-up. 'He's an animal Tony, you know that.' Tony didn't know whether Rogers' remark was for his benefit or he was trying to impress Jennings, he guessed the latter. Against the ropes, Tony needed a strong response.

'You do your jobs, I'll do mine.' In an unnerving way, Jennings once again breathed in through his nose, became calm then pointed his finger at Rogers. 'When you reacted like that in there, calling him a nonce, he knows he's got you, you're like a Christmas present to him. When I give you an order to let me do the talking I mean it's an order.' Jennings seemed to be conscious of being overheard and sneaked a look along the landing. 'A bit of advice for both of you.' Jennings leant forward smiled and started straightening Tony's tie. 'We've all learnt something in there. I know it and Finch knows it.' His eyes met Tony's. 'But once evil bastards like him start playing games with your head that's when you have to nip-it-in-the-bud, knock them down, otherwise coming to work everyday takes on a different meaning and going home at night an even bigger one.' Admiring his handy work with Tony's tie, Jennings seemed almost amused at what had taken place only minutes before. 'Now go and have a cup of coffee.'

Tony bit his lip. Jennings on one hand was professional, controlled and full of advice, a father figure in some ways, but on the other, Tony could see he was a powder-keg ready to explode. As they stood at the security gate Tony could feel Jennings eyes burning into the back of his head. 'Have you ever thought that we could end up like Jennings?'

'What do you mean?' said Rogers.

'Well, Finch could be out of here in about twenty years for good behaviour. We on the other hand could be in here for life.' As the gates opened, Tony turned and looked back along the landing. Jennings was still lingering outside Finch's cell.

CHAPTER ELEVEN

The little daylight that did cut into Finch's cell shone onto some of the marks of past prisoners. The ones that had swung from the gallows had engraved their initials into the bricks and limestone pointing, a lasting legacy to their final days on earth. Stories of ghosts and their whispers had been passed down from officer to officer, prisoner to prisoner. At night in the dark corners of the cell, the gargle from a shot of brandy to tighten a neck or voices confessing to a priest would linger in the stagnant air. As for Finch, he had requested the haunted cell, proclaiming, the voices would keep him company.

Placing the palm of his hand across the stitches in his side, Finch grimaced as he leaned on the bed for support. Kneeling down onto the stone floor, he reached under his bed and slid out a round sweet tin. Gingerly, he placed the tin onto the bed and raised himself up off the floor. Snowy scenes of Christmas ran round the sides of the tin and on the lid a number of carol singers wearing overcoats and mufflers were huddled outside a building resembling the Old Curiosity Shop. Prising open the lid, he tipped the contents of the tin out onto the bed. Rummaging through old photographs, sweets, old letters, newspaper cuttings and a small Gideon bible he picked up a sweet. Unravelling the bright blue wrapper, he removed a chocolate mint, popped it into his mouth and licked his lips it tasted good. Small pleasures.

Picking out a black and white photograph he studied it intensely. It was of a middle aged woman with shoulder length hair. Wearing a summer dress, she was sitting on a swing-chair in the back of an English garden which was in full bloom. Finch held it to his breast as onion tears appeared in his eyes. Slowly the tears spilled out bouncing off both cheeks onto his light-blue prison shirt. He kissed the photograph gently. 'God bless you mother.' Another couple of photographs in colour were of him as a young boy and his mother at the seaside. One was of him sitting on some sandstone steps leading down to the beach, another was of him tucking into candyfloss outside a Penny Arcade and another was of him perched on the top of a donkey. It must have been hot and sunny as he was wearing shorts and a stripy t-shirt and was squinting into the camera. Reminiscing at the snapshot, he remembered it being taken not long after he was made to wear round National Health glasses for the first time. On the first day back at school after the summer holidays he was teased relentlessly by the girls. It was something he tried to blank from his mind, but he couldn't, it was only the beginning.

One particular photograph intrigued him. Staring at it for almost five minutes, he stood-up and started pacing the stone floor of the cell. Dropping the photo onto the bed, he paused for a few seconds, before unbuttoning his flies and dropping his trousers around his ankles. He didn't sit down immediately on the small metal toilet, but shuffled over to the window. Closing his eyes, he tried to catch the little sunshine and warmth that shone though the window onto his sullen face. Opening his eyes, he watched the dust particles floating through the stream of daylight. They looked like flecks of snow floating inside a glass snow-ball, just like the one Citizen Kane dropped from his death bed when he groaned the immortal word, 'Rosebud'. His mother loved the movie.

Contemplating a shave, he looked at himself in the small mirror that was propped-up by the side of the sink. As he ran his fingers across the light stubble on his chin, he heard the spy-hole in the cell door slide open. In the reflection of the mirror he saw a prison officer's eye watching him from behind. He was always being watched, every second of every minute of every hour of every day. Finch liked an eye peering in at him. Then the spy-hole closed, opened then closed again, time-and-time-again, day-after-day, night-after-night. It wasn't one of the new officers, Evans' eyes were blue and the other new one with the rat face, his were green. This one he knew instantly, Jennings. *An-eye-for-an-eye, perhaps.* Finch quickly swung round, his limp penis in full view of the wide eyeball. 'Hello Mr Jennings.' The spy-hole shut and the eye disappeared. Finch laughed, that's the fifth or sixth time he'd stitched-him-up. Barefooted he giggled and crouched-down on the bowl of the toilet. It felt cold, it always felt cold. For Finch it was the worst moment of the day. Cramping his knees up around his chest, he looked across at the cell door and waited, he knew Jennings' eye or another eye would re-appear soon then disappear again, it always did. He liked blue eyes best, they seemed to blend in with his surroundings, and they were, after all, the colour of Shirley's although he could never be sure and wrestling with the dilemma he would sometimes try and self mutilate. Stretching out his arm he plucked the newspaper off the bed. Turning straight to the front page (sport meant nothing to him), he read the sub-headings and looked for some breaking news that would be of interest. New crimes, murders particularly would intrigue him and he would follow the case right through to the final days of the trial. He'd analyse the suspects; the judge who was in charge of the trial, what court the killer was being tried. Finch liked a good murder trial. There was nothing new today to get excited about, so he stopped reading and threw the newspaper back onto the bed. Then he thought of the photograph. He pulled up his trousers, he didn't need a crap, it was just a habit, like contemplating having a shave; it was just a daily routine, like trying to catch Jennings and his eye. Every morning at the same time he'd shuffle over to the window just in time for Jennings' eye to catch him with his trousers down, it amused him, it amused him no-end and today had been no different.

Picking up the photograph off the bed, he stared at it once again. His side ached as he turned the snap nervously around in his fingers. Something troubled him as he ran his hands through his hair, then he grinned as it came to him. Outside he heard the jingle of keys. Quickly, he concealed the photograph in the back-pocket of his trousers just as the cell door opened. Jennings stood in the doorway, his large frame blocking the light out from the landing. Another officer flanked-him like a private bodyguard. Finch was flattered, he liked the attention.

'Hands off cocks on socks, get a move on Finch!' Jennings' order wasn't negotiable. Jennings and the other officer watched as Finch slipped on a pair of black socks, followed by some black shoes, no laces. As he bent down he took in a deep breath as he felt the stitches stretch in his side. He took his time; he liked taking his time, little moments in the week like this broke the tedium and he found it fun having Jennings wait for him. During Finch's eight years 'inside' he'd only had one visitor, his mother. She had travelled over a hundred miles on public transport to visit him on his first day inside Brainforth after he was handed a life sentence. She brought him a tin of chocolates, some family photographs and a small Gideon bible that had been in the family for years. That had been his one and only visit; he had no friends – no family – nobody.

All in one movement, Finch gritted his teeth and lifted himself off the bed.

'Looks like your stitches are playing-up Lollypop?' Jennings smirked as he gripped his arm and guided him out of the cell door; it was Finch's one and only physical contact of the week. The last time, apart from the doctor was when another prisoner tried to stab him in the showers, the guy with the snake and dagger tattoo, that's if you could call it physical contact. Finch didn't recognise the officer who took his other arm, he was new, baby faced, and he had a different smell, his second physical contact of the week. Both officers' hands were firmly gripped around his forearms and he could feel their fingers imbedded into the previous, finger-tipped bruises that ran up both arms. Their hands felt warm and Finch was enjoying it. As they led him past the open cell doors on the landing a few prisoners gave him a look, but like him they were on A-Wing for their own protection and that's all they would give him. Through the wired, glass window in the door, Finch noticed Tony on the other side. As the door buzzed open Tony stepped back and waited for Finch and the two officers to pass. As they approached, Tony caught eye contact with Finch. Looking away, he nodded at Jennings who nodded back with an uneasy look, but he could feel his eyes being drawn back to the prisoner. The urge to look at him was hypnotic.

Evil grin, evil grin.

As they passed each other, Tony felt a gust of warm air on his cheek. Flinching, he touched his cheek and saw that Finch had leant back over Jennings' shoulder and blown in his direction. Passing through the door, Tony tried to resist the temptation to turn around as butterflies swamped his stomach. Spinning around he looked through the window of the door. Nobody. Bringing his hand up to his face, his skin crawled as his fingers hovered over his cheek. Finch's warm breath felt like a leech sucking the blood from his face. Little did he know that the photograph in the back of Finch's trouser pocket was taken at a wedding a few summers ago. The family in the photograph were smiling, dressed up to the nines. The man was in a light grey suit and tie, the woman in a summer dress and large brimmed hat. Sitting on the man's knee was a pretty young girl with flowers in her hair. The photograph was of Tony, Anne and Martha.

CHAPTER TWELVE

Fanning the bundles of money in front of him, Tony felt a bead of sweat roll down the side of his neck. Ripping off his tie, he sat back and ran his hands over his face. It was about eighty grand. EIGHTY GRAND! His mind was spinning, one second it was BLACK NUMBER 8, then it was the money, then it was Anne and Martha. The money would get him out of a hole, a giant hole. It was a matter of days before another letter arrived from the bank manager demanding payment for his ever increasing overdraft and it would stop the threats of the bookie and the Loan Shark. The money was heaven sent.

Touching the side of his clammy cheek his thoughts then ran to Finch. A wave of nausea tossed around inside his stomach. As days and nights go in Brainforth there were never really any good ones or bad ones, they were all much the same – arduous and boring. But for Tony this day had been the worst on record. It had pissed him off big-time. He hated to admit it but Jennings had pissed him off for being right about Finch and to a certain extent Rogers had pissed him off for sucking up to Jennings. But in reality, he was pissed off with himself. Up until that day, he'd never let his guard down. With cons he knew they could turn and kick you in the teeth at any second; he'd heard too many stories in the locker room to be complacent. Then there was Finch. He could still feel his warm, sweaty breath on his cheek and when he closed his eyes all he saw was that grin, it was locked inside his head, Finch had got to him big time. Tony's mind darted from one thought to the next as he looked down at the money nestled in his lap.

'*They know I've got the cash, they will want something doing, something big – I'll cross that bridge when I come to it – I've got no choice. I'll pay the bookie first, get Vine off my back. Then the Lone Sharks, put a smile back across their ugly mugs, then the bank, the good old bank. I still might have a bit left over for that winner.*

Thinking twice about putting the money back into the glove compartment, Tony shoved the envelope under the front seat. Pulling down the sun visor, he looked at a school photograph of Martha. Taken a few years earlier, she was growing up fast and recently, he'd found himself taking time-out to look at photographs of his daughter and Anne. He knew he was on the verge of losing them, but the snaps were little comfort to what was staring him in the face.

Who has given me all this money?

What do they want me to do for it?

Tony looked around the prison car park. Nobody.

Why did I say they, it could be just one person?

It could be dirty money, drug money, blood money?

Scratching through his conscience, he noticed Jennings and Rogers walk out through the prison gates.

Why had they suddenly become bosom buddies?

Hoping he wouldn't be spotted, Tony slouched down in his seat. He watched as they made their way across the car park.

I bet they're talking about me.

Plotting my downfall?

Jumping into Jennings' car, Tony could see Rogers laughing. Then they drove off. Becoming paranoid agitated him even more. More sweat, more anxiety.

One thing's for sure, whoever dropped me this money knows I'm desperate.

CHAPTER THIRTEEN

Leaving the sweeping drizzle outside, Tony stepped through the swing door of the bookie's. Like every other betting shop he'd placed a bet in before, the faces, the décor, the torn-up betting-slips that littered the floor and the smell of the so-called winners and the losers, everything was familiar to him, he felt at home.

Sliding an envelope of money across the counter he looked across at Freddy's cracked face. 'Alright Freddy, that's for Mr Vine.' Laughter was a missing commodity from Freddy's personality. Around sixty, he looked seventy. His face was lined like a walnut and his bushy, grey moustache was nicotine stained from a forty-a-day-habit. He'd been taking and off-loading bets there for years and used to call Tony by his first name, but as Tony had recently been *blackballed*, he knew the score and looked through Tony as if he wasn't there. The money wasn't the full debt, but it would help, give him some breathing space, or so he thought.

On his way out, he couldn't resist looking at the pinned-up betting pages that lined the walls. 'Mighty Friend' caught his attention. It was one of those moments, an aberration that had happened hundreds, if not thousands of times before. It was like a voice from above. 3.30 at Newton Abbot was a sure banker, a winner. Tony couldn't lose. Could he?

One little bet won't hurt.

One little bet won't hurt.

At that fleeting moment, the voice disappeared. He knew what *the voice* was doing, he was used to it. The 3.30 at Newton Abbot was going to win him plenty of money. Like the rest of the punters in the bookies, Tony picked up a small blue pen, and started chewing the end. Suddenly he started contemplating the bet. Something he'd never done before, he was always decisive. At ten-to-one, 'Mighty Friend' looked a good bet. The going was good, soft-to-firm. He was being ridden by a good Irish jockey and was wearing the silks of his favourite colour, purple. It was a sure winner, wasn't it? So why the hesitation?

That's it Tony, one little bet won't hurt, one little bet.

Tony's pen hovered over the betting slip.

Put a hundred on it. Think a grand in your back pocket.

You're back are you voice?

I never went away Tony; you should know that by now, I never go away.

Leave me alone, you always bring me bad luck, now piss off.

Don't blame me if you lose.

I won't lose, I won't lose, I won't lose.

Tony slid the betting slip with a hundred in notes across the counter. 'A hundred *'on the nose.'* Freddy viewed the betting-slip, shrugged his shoulders and sighed, a deep sigh. 'I'll have to clear this with Mr Vine first.' After a few mumbled exchanges over the phone Freddy replaced the receiver. Without giving Tony a second look Freddy took the bet. Like a thousand races before and a thousand throws of the dice, Tony's mind like all serious gamblers was racing forward to the next bet, the next race and the one after that and the one after that. He had kept some of the mysterious money he found in the glove compartment to spend on *essentials*. Come-what-may, win or lose, he was going to spend whatever money he had in his back pocket. As the race started, Tony glanced at the wide eyed, insipid faces of the other punters as they held their betting slips in vice-like grips. He wasn't alone in biting his nails.

'YES! YES! YES!' Punching the air, Tony did a little jig of celebration. He had already decided who he was backing in the next race, but he couldn't wait to feel the bank notes in his hands. As he went to cash-in his betting slip, Freddy was replacing the receiver. 'Come back later, Mr Vine's orders.' Freddy seemed to take great joy in wiping the smile off Tony's face.

'But it's my money.'

'Not according to Mr Vine.'

'But if you give me my winnings….'

'Mr Vines orders!' A callousness struck in Freddy's voice. Flushing with embarrassment, Tony could feel his cheeks turning red. Taking bets around him, Freddy wasn't about to give Tony eye contact or the time of day, never mind his winnings.

'Can you tell Mr Vine, I need a word?'

Freddy turned to his right as a door opened behind him. A squat, bald headed man wearing a black bomber jacket walked out. His short arms hung by his side, his fists permanently tight.

'Go away Tony, if you know what's good for you.'

CHAPTER FOURTEEN

At last the sun came out. Although the summer had been a wash out, the autumn evening was glorious, ideal for one final picnic at the lake. After lining Vine's pockets with his winnings Tony took a detour into another betting shop and lost heavily. He could have gambled all evening but from somewhere he found the strength and stopped. On the way home Tony called-in at a delicatessen. With some of the money that would have been slipped over the bookie's counter he bought a good bottle of red, French bread, Russian salad, lean ham and Greek olives. Anne loved Greek olives especially with garlic and fennel. Not forgetting the 'treats', he bought a good helping of chocolate profiteroles.

After picking Martha up from school, they drove home to collect Anne. Martha was so excited about going to the lake, but Anne was understandably reluctant. Tony had phoned earlier and had to persuade her to come with them. The wine and olives helped, just. The traffic was busy and the thirty minute drive was hot and clammy. Anne sat with Martha in the back listening to her i-pod;

it was her way of prolonging the torture. Tony knew she'd confront him about Friday night at some stage, she had avoided him all weekend and it was imminent. They both agreed 'they needed to talk.'

The large expanse of fresh water lake was once an old slate quarry. Surrounded by heavy woodland, it had been flooded and over the years had become a natural wildlife park. Walking along the leafy foot path, Martha held a bright orange frisbee as Tony and Anne delicately shared the handles of a cane picnic basket. On either side of them the smell of the damp pine drying out in the warm sunshine floated out of the trees into the evening air. Tony tried to make polite, happy, conversation but he could feel the tension growing as they walked. Reaching the lake, apart from a jogger running with a black, shiny coated Labrador, the picnic area was deserted. The evening sun still held a kick and twinkled across the surface of the lake which was still, like a sheet of glass.

'Come on Daddy!' Martha threw the frisbee into the air as Tony ran along the grass to retrieve it. As Anne laid out the picnic, she discovered the olives and gave Tony a token look. Would that be his 'saving grace', a plastic pot of Greek olives? He doubted it.

Anne called them over, the food was ready. As Tony opened the wine, Martha tucked into a cheese baguette, she was hungry. They watched a horse galloping lake-side, its back legs kicking-up a spray of water. Martha stood up and waved at the rider, the rider caught her wave and waved back. 'I want to go horse riding Daddy.'

'I'll take you soon.'

'When?'

'When you're a little older.'

Martha stamped her foot. 'It's always when I'm a little older.'

'You'll be old soon enough,' said Anne.

'Come and play frisbee then Daddy.' Tony stood up and threw

the frisbee as strong and as far as he could. It hovered through the air and flew across the grass as Martha took off. 'Go get it tiger!' Tony sprawled out on the rug and sipped the wine, he laughed as he watched Martha struggling to catch the frisbee as it circled back in the air. 'Jump Martha!' Martha jumped and caught the frisbee which hovered in the air like a flying saucer. 'Throw it like I showed you.' She tried to throw the frisbee into the air but it hit the grass, flipped onto its side and headed towards the lake like a coin rolling on its edge. Anne shouted after her. 'Don't go near the water darling.'

Then Tony and Anne had one of those moments, a difficult, silent moment…Tony eventually broke the ice. 'God it's hot, I'm glad I put my shorts on. I should have brought the suntan lotion.'

'You must have something else on your mind?'

Tony didn't take the bait. Wafting away a couple of midges from his bare legs, he knew where the conversation would lead too, like it had done a thousand times before.

'Not saying anything?'

'I don't want to argue.'

'We've gone past arguing Tony….So tell me, how much is it this time?'

Tony took another sip of wine then reached out towards Anne's hand. She drew it away; she was having none of it.

'I'm not gambling, its work, I hate it, you know it gets me down. And there's this guy in there that has freaked me out.'

'What, Rogers?'

'Rogers's alright.'

'Rogers's a wanker, we both know it.'

Tony shaded his eyes with his hand from the sun; it was a low, blinding light and reflected off the lake. Anne looked across at him, her black hair falling across her brow. 'I know you've been gambling again. I had a visit.'

'Who from?'

'Oh just a bailiff, he was very nice actually; he's given us a week before he takes all our belongings.'

'It won't come to that.'

'If you think my mum's going to bail us out again you can think again.'

'I will sort it out I promise you.' Anne didn't answer; she sipped her wine and looked away. Tony looked towards the lake.

'Where's Martha?'

'She's alright…Tell me how you're going to *sort it*?'

'I will.'

'How?'

Tony climbed to his feet; once again he shaded his eyes from the sun and scanned the lake side. 'I can't see her.' Anne sprung to her feet. 'She couldn't have gone far.'

'Martha!' Tony cupped his hands around his mouth and shouted again. 'Martha!'

Nothing.

Spinning around, Tony scuffed the grass underfoot. 'Martha!'

Nothing.

Tony sprinted towards the lake. 'Martha! Martha!' Looking right and left as he ran he reached the lakeside and found it deserted. He felt his chest tightening; Martha was nowhere to be seen. Anne ran along side him. 'Martha! Martha! Oh God where is she?'

'She couldn't have gone far. Martha! Martha!'

'She can't swim!'

Tony found himself aimlessly walking along the water's edge, one way then the other. Panicking, with no direction to follow, he found himself running back towards the picnic. Smashing a wine glass underfoot he called out again. 'Martha! Martha!' He heard Anne shriek from the waters edge 'God, where is she?'

'Martha! Martha!' Tony could hear the fear in his voice. Then he thought he heard her.

Silence.

The duration of lost seconds seemed a lifetime. Overhead a couple of blackbirds squawked, they sounded like a puppy yelping as another heartbeat was lost.

Then – 'I'm over here Daddy.' Martha's voice was distant but clear. 'I'm over here Daddy.' Following her voice; it came from behind a line of bushes and shrubbery that ran along the edge of the pine forest. Running, Tony shouted again. 'Martha!'

'Daddy, Daddy.' Her voice become clearer.

'I'm coming darling!'

Fighting his way through the undergrowth, Tony tripped over the trunk of a rotting tree which was infested with wood lice. Regaining his balance, he felt the cut under his heel split. Flinching with pain, he kept moving forward, pulling back and snapping branches that blocked his way. He felt the side of his bare leg sting as he brushed past nettles. 'Martha, Martha!'

'Daddy, Daddy!' She was yards away.

Eventually he found himself stumbling into a murky clearing. The stench of rotting pine and leaves underfoot floated upwards and he found it hard to readjust his eyes in the darkness. Shafts of sunshine pierced the branches high above and streamed down like laser beams casting scary black shadows everywhere.

'Daddy.'

'I'm here sweetheart?'

It was like playing blind-man's-bluff as Tony desperately tried to focus. Then, he saw her, his little girl. She was standing by the side of a man across the clearing. Hunched over, he looked slightly dishevelled, a giant shadow from a branch hiding his face.

'This man found my frisbee Daddy, I threw it into the bushes, I'm sorry.'

'Come over here sweetheart.'

Martha ran over and jumped into her father's arms.

'Are you alright darling?'

'Yes Daddy, I'm sorry.'

'It's alright.'

'Terrible feeling isn't it Tony.'

Leaning forward, Tony tried to see the man's face. 'Do I know you?'

The man stepped forward out of the shadows. Tony noticed how hot he looked; he was sweltering in his heavy coat, perspiration pouring down his face and neck. The top of his washed out tee shirt was flooded with a semi-circle sweat mark and his hands shook as he lit a cigarette that nestled between his lips. Tony suddenly registered who the man was. *The taxi driver.*

'What are you doing here?'

Young watched as his cigarette smoke floated upwards, disappearing through the branches, then, he looked across at Tony and offered him the packet. 'Smoke?'

'No.'

'I forgot, you don't smoke.'

'Martha! Tony!' Anne's voice bounced around the trees in the thick forest.

Tony shouted in the direction of her voice. 'She's ok, over here!'

Young spotted a squirrel scratching at the base of a nearby tree. 'Look Martha a squirrel. Do you think he likes chocolate?' Young took a bar of dark chocolate from out of his breast pocket, broke off a square and threw it in the squirrel's direction. Martha giggled as they watched the squirrel pick up the chocolate and scurry away up a tree. Young smiled. 'I didn't know squirrels liked chocolate, did you Tony?'

'I asked you a question, what are you doing here?'

'Martha will tell you, won't you Martha?'

'He's a 'twitcher' Daddy.'

Tony scowled across at Young. 'I don't care what you are, just because you gave me a lift home doesn't make us friends. Keep away from my family, do you hear me?'

Young turned right and noticed Anne making her way along the overgrown track into the clearing, he lowered his voice. 'Here's your better-half Tony – We need to talk, it's important.'

'Is she alright?' Anne looked terrified. 'What's going on?'

'This man found my frisbee Mummy.' Anne lifted Martha out of her father's arms and gripped her tightly, then looked at her husband. 'What's going on?'

'Nothing, this guy found her frisbee, go back to the picnic, I won't be long.'

'Leave it Tony.'

'Nothing's going to happen, Anne. It is Anne isn't it?' Young spoke through a cloud of cigarette smoke. Anne couldn't conceal her shock at Young knowing her name and looked at Tony for some sort of explanation.

'Go back, I won't be long.'

Anne leaned into Tony's ear. 'Don't do anything stupid,' then carrying Martha away she glared at Young, who stood there, still.

Like a couple of gunslingers ready to draw their six shooters, the two men stood in the clearing waiting for the other one to make the first move. Swiping away a couple of midges from his face with the back of his hand, Tony spoke.

'What do you want to talk about?'

'When the time is right I'll let you know.'

'What the fuck does that mean?'

'I will contact you when I'm ready.'

'Did you give me the money?'

'You make it sound like a gift.'

'What do you call it then?'

Young dug the sole of his trainers into the earth and disintegrated the last of his cigarette. Bending down, he plucked a weed from the ground. He blew its head once, then twice, sending its seeds floating through the air. 'You better get back to your wife and daughter.' Young turned to walk away then turned back.

'Martha's beautiful by the way; you're a very lucky man.'

'I don't want anything from you, I don't know what your game is, but you can have your money back.'

Young laughed. 'We both know you've spent *my money* Tony.'

Tony could feel himself shaking as he watched Young walk away. 'I'm warning you stay away from my family!' Then within seconds the forest swallowed up Young and he disappeared.

Tony found Anne frantically throwing the remains of the picnic back into the basket.

'How many times have I told you Martha, not to walk away?'

'I'm sorry Mummy.'

Suddenly grabbing Martha by the shoulders, Anne turned her around and bawled into her face. 'Or talk to strangers?'

Martha shook with her chin on her chest. Holding onto the frisbee like a 'comfort- blanket' that was about to be ripped out of her hands, tears rolled down her face.

'Don't think you're getting an ice cream.' Anne turned her fury on Tony. 'What was going on back there?'

'Nothing.' Tony picked up the pieces of the shattered wine glass and dropped them into a nearby bin. Pulling the rug from under his feet Anne folded it and tucked it under her arm. 'How did he know my name?'

'I shouted it out.'

'No you didn't, more bullshit.'

'What's going on? Do you owe him money?'

Tony rolled his eyes. 'No.'

'I wouldn't put it past you. What did you say to him?'

'I just asked him what he was doing, and he said he was a 'twitcher', a bird watcher.'

'I know what a bloody 'twitcher' is! If you believe that, you'll believe anything. He was a right weirdo if ever I saw one, you better report him to the police.'

'It's alright, I sorted it.'

'Like you *sort everything* eh, Tony? You're losing the plot; you think its normal do you, to wander around in the woods? Did he have any binoculars?' Tony didn't reply. 'No I didn't think so!' Anne threw the rug at Tony. As a cold gust of wind whipped-up around their ankles. Anne picked up the basket and stormed off. Tony lent down and wiped away Martha's tears. Taking hold of her hand, he felt something rough in her palm. She was holding a piece of screwed-up paper. Pulling him down by his shirt sleeve she whispered into his ear with a teary voice. 'That man told me to give it to you Daddy; he told me it was a secret. You won't tell Mummy will you?' Tony put his index finger to his lips and blew their secret. He looked up at Anne who was quickly making-tracks and discreetly put the note into the back pocket of his shorts. Wrapping the rug around Martha, he lifted her up onto his shoulders.

'Come on sweetheart, I'll buy you an ice cream.'

CHAPTER FIFTEEN

Slouching in the back pews of St Benedict's Church, Anders tried to remember when he was last in a place of worship. As the sermon flew over his head, it clicked. It was over ten years ago, at his cousin's wedding just outside Oslo. The wooden church in his home town overlooked a small lake were he used to fish and swim as a boy. It was the last time he had returned home, he had been otherwise engaged.

St Benedict's rested in the pretty country village of Farmington, north of Bedford. Gothic in structure, the church was built in the 16th century and boasted a priest who was a close friend of the Pope in Rome. Stained glass, lancet windows ran down each side of the church and its clock tower with its skeleton dials and battened numerals, looked across the countryside and the manicured lawns of Farmington Manor, now the home of a fading rock star.

Anders was cold and was suffering from a migraine. He could feel a draught whistling around the back of his neck and it was starting to annoy him. Ignoring the sermon, he listened to the rain hitting the windows and roof and looked around the church's congregation, it was two-thirds full and the average age was over sixty. The church was in desperate need of repair. Recently painted patches on the walls failed to conceal the damp and from various parts of the building and in the nearby 'lady chapel' he could hear drips of water falling into tin buckets. Flicking his shoulder length, blond hair from out of his shirt collar he caught the damp smell from the hymn books resting in a line in front of him and the breeze of manure drifting through the pews from the surrounding fields. As hard as he tried, he couldn't sit still. The hard wooden pews were playing havoc with his bony backside and he could sense the elderly woman who was sitting next to him becoming agitated by his continuous fidgeting. His migraine was becoming worse and O'Connor's voice bellowing Catholicism high-up into the clock tower only added to the aching pain.

'Mercy and faithfulness have met, justice and peace have embraced. Faithfulness shall spring from earth and justice look down from heaven.' The reply from the congregation echoed around the church. 'We love others because Christ loves us first.' Then O'Connor's voice rallied the congregation to sing. 'Hymn number 23. Praise the Lord for we are all God's children.' It was a relief for Anders to hear the organist play the first few bars of the hymn. As the parishioners stood, ready to sing, he opened a hymn book and smelt the circulating must from its pages, it made him cough slightly, causing a tickly cough. The woman next to him looked at him out the corner of her eye, he could feel her becoming more and more irritated by the stranger. Anders had no intention of singing, not because he had a bad voice, on the contrary he had once been a choir boy himself, but because he needed to concentrate on giving the priest Michael O'Connor the once-over.

O'Connor looked down from his pulpit and sang as if his life depended on it. As the tone of his Northern Irish accent bellowed over the congregation, Anders looked up from his hymn book and studied his features. Bald, with snowy white hair on each side of his head, dark crease lines ran around his ruddy complexion and a number of liver-spots scattered his cheeks. O'Connor leant to the left, was around fifty, six foot, and overweight, nothing Anders couldn't handle.

As the hymn came to an end, Anders thought it was as good a time as any to end the agony of his migraine, the wooden pews, and leave. Squeezing past the woman in her light blue summer suit, and matching light blue summer shoes, he gave her a weak smile of apology. It wasn't reciprocated.

Taking in a deep breath to relieve his cough, Anders squinted as the daylight flooded through a small lead-lined-window into the church porch. A large framed photograph of O'Connor kissing the hand of the Pope rested on an artist's easel. It was taken in the Vatican and presented in glorious Technicolor. As an atheist Anders could never understand all the pomp and ceremony that attached itself to religion, but it did intrigue him. A wasp buzzed past his ear and landed on the top of the picture's ornate wooden frame. It was dying. Anders reaction was quick and decisive. Putting it out of its misery he crushed it under his thumb. His eyes slightly flickered, as the last thing the wasp was to do before he was sentenced to death was to sting his thumb.

Stepping outside, the rain had turned to drizzle. Anders could still hear O'Connor's dulcet tones, echoing *Fire and Brimstone* around the inside of the church, he was in fine form. Slipping on small, round sunglasses, Anders discreetly rearranged the seat of his trousers, relieving the agony of his numb backside. Buttoning up his jacket, Anders walked briskly down the gravel path towards the church's wooden portico. The wind was cold and cutting and swirled around the graveyard, brushing the branches of a yew tree full of bright red berries. He caught a glimpse of the names engraved in the red ivy-clad, gravestones. The names told the story of the village's history, family names of the young and the old, Bedfordshire names.

Reaching his jet-black Land Rover, Anders climbed in, removed his sunglasses and started massaging his temples. After relieving the pain for a few minutes, Anders reached under the driver's seat and removed a Pentax camera. Bringing the camera up to his face, he focused the telescopic lens on a banner hanging from scaffolding that covered the end of the church. Fluttering in the wind it read: *£185,000 needed to help restore the church roof.* He snapped the entrance, then the clock tower.

O'Connor was the first to appear. Positioning himself outside the church entrance, his white cassock flapped in the breeze as he waited for his congregation. Slowly but surely, his loyal flock filtered out in a line. O'Connor greeted them with a Queen's handshake and smile; he was in his element. As Anders snapped away, he laughed to himself; even the woman in the light blue summer suit who shook O'Connor's hand rigorously, took a good photograph. As he snapped away he didn't need to convince himself he was doing the right thing, after all, his morals had deserted him years ago. It didn't matter to him whether any of the photographs were insignificant, that was up to his client. Then, only time would tell if his services would be required again. O'Connor watched and waved as the last of his parishioners walk away. Like himself they were unaware of being snapped by a telescopic lens through the black, tinted window of the parked-up Land Rover.

Anders scrutinized O'Connor before he disappeared back into his church. He didn't like him. Finished, he slipped the camera back under the driver's seat, started the four-by-four and drove off. The job was done for the time being. Confident the photographs would be approved by the client, he hoped he would be hired again, this was a good job and it paid well, very well.

Anders very seldom met any of his clients face-to-face. All his business was conducted over the phone, his correspondence sent to a PO Box number, which he used once and once only. He was meticulous in every detail, every fine detail. He never advertised his services, was always recommended by a previous client and prided himself in not being the normal, run-of-the-mill *Hit-Man*. When he did arrange a rendezvous with the odd client it was by his terms. No matter how lucrative the job was, the place, the time of day or night were played by his rules and if they weren't, the deal was off. If he did meet a client (there were only three occasions and all were women) he was always excited by the first and only meeting. It was planned to perfection. It would always be in a public place, a busy park being his favourite location. From a distance, he would watch the women walk to the designated bench and work out by their body language how nervous or how confident they were. How many times they looked right and left, the way they sat forward then back on the bench, the way their hands nervously held their bag. The way they dressed told of their backgrounds and the spheres of their life. All were wealthy, upper-class women and none of the three women disappointed him. It gave him that *buzz*. It was what life was all about, *that buzz* made it interesting. As if he was invisible, he sidled up alongside them and sent out an order in a firm voice, 'Don't turn around. Do not look at me.' He never wore the same coat or trousers, he'd always wear a disguise, a masquerade of some sort, and he changed his accent. He'd tried to get close enough to smell their perfume. If they were wearing a particular brand of perfume, the richer the perfume, the richer he would become. No aftershave. He was the only one who would ask the questions. Some clients who were at the end of their tether suspected their husbands of adultery. A diplomat, a gynaecologist, a judge, the headmaster of a private school, all characters from life's rich tapestry. From the tremble in their voices he knew how desperate, despondent they were. *He's a bastard you don't know what he's put me through. All I'm guilty of is loving him too much.* It all meant nothing to Anders, they were just a job no matter how modest the payment was. But it always amazed him as to why some of his clients thought they had the guts to have somebody murdered, or so they thought. But that next giant step, that desperate step in taking desperate measures to kill a person, a living soul, to callously pay for murder now that was the hard part.

This client however was different. Every transaction was done by a middle-man, the money man. It had confused him for weeks as to why he was hired in the first place. Although he liked to think he was morally bound by his conscience and the contract, he knew deep down he was a slave to the dollar and only time would tell if this job backfired.

Hitting the motorway, Anders bit into an apple and turned on the soul station. His migraine was slowly disappearing along with the numbness in his backside, but the wasp sting still lingered and throbbed deep inside his thumb. On the passenger seat next to him, were a couple of baby's milk bottles, a shoulder-length, blond wig, the sunglasses and a box of cartridges. As Anders whistled along to Stevie Wonder's harmonica he put his foot down, he had more work to do, there was no time to lose.

CHAPTER SIXTEEN

The loft of the YMCA was the regular meeting place on a Monday, Wednesday and Friday night for 'Gamblers Anonymous'. Tony hadn't been for six months and when he walked sheepishly into the room he was met by a few raised eyebrows and the odd smile. Some faces were familiar, some were not. The group was run on a voluntary basis and everyone who attended threw a couple of pounds in a session to pay for the hire of the room, some of the punters looked like they could afford it, some looked like they couldn't. The room had a single light, a wooden floor and smelt of sweaty sports kit. It was bare apart from a table tennis table leant up against the nearside wall and heap of dusty bunting that had been dumped in the far corner. From the sloped ceiling high above, a shaft of moonlight streamed through a skylight onto a circle of plastic chairs that waited for its victims. Helping himself to a cup of tea and a couple of chocolate biscuits, Tony picked up one of the pamphlets and flicked through the pages. Inside, *The 12 Step Recovery Plan*. All too familiar with the 12 steps; he'd recite them to himself as he paced the landings of Brainforth.

1. We admitted we were powerless over gambling – that our lives had become unmanageable.

2. Come to believe that a power greater than ourselves could restore us to a normal way of thinking and living.

Sitting in the circle, Tony was immediately drawn to the unfamiliar woman sitting opposite. Grey roots were starting to surface in the parting of her auburn hair and he worked out she must be in her late forties. She was pretty, but not attractive, her hair tied back in a pony tail with a red ribbon. She wore a grey, loose fitting two piece suit, the uniform synonymous with her chosen occupation as an accountant. Her complexion was lightly tanned from a recent skiing trip to Mirabel in the French Alps; he knew that from the pleasantries he overheard her exchange with someone when he first walked into the room.

3. Made a decision to turn our will and our lives over to the care of the power of our own understanding.

4. Made a searching and fearless moral and financial inventory of ourselves.

Tapping her red painted fingernails against the side of the plastic chair, she was unaware how noisy she was until the room fell silent. Volunteering to start, she stood up and addressed the circle with a false confidence in her voice. 'Hello my name's Clare and I'm a compulsive gambler. Although I haven't gambled for over a year – let's say just recently, I have fallen by the way side again. I went to the casino the other night and lost the best part of eight thousand on roulette – then lost another couple of thousand on black jack. The desperation and anxiety I am going through has made me depressed and apart from the financial loss, I have lied to myself – my family and friends. I can't look at myself in the mirror anymore and the affect it's having on my family is devastating.' With tears in her eyes, she sat down slowly to a small ripple of applause and looked humbled by the support.

As a kid Tony had come to the YMCA to play football, table tennis and the odd game of snooker. He remembered the room where he was sitting as the room you sneaked off to for a sly fag. Never did he think in a thousand years he'd be sitting back there with a gambling addiction. As Tony looked across at Clare, she crossed her legs and he caught a slight glimpse of the top of her stockings, he wondered whether it was for his benefit but then realised, she was just as vulnerable as the rest of them.

5. *Admitted to ourselves and to another human being the exact nature of our wrongs.*
6. *Were entirely ready to have these defects of character removed.*

'Hello my name's Dave and I'm a compulsive gambler.' Underneath the matted ginger beard and long straggly hair, Dave could have been aged anything between thirty and fifty. Shabbily dressed, ingrained in dirt, the right leg that dangled loosely over the other bounced nervously up and down. Scratching the psoriasis across the back of his tattooed knuckles, everyone could see he was up to his neck in quicksand and sinking fast. He was a nail-biting wreck, gagging for a cigarette or a bottle of cut-price cider. 'I get around £150 from my giro each week and it goes straight into the bookie's pocket that same day. At the moment I'm living rough and I don't really know what else to say.' Dropping down he nearly missed his chair. Being given a comforting look from everyone as well as the customary quiet ripple of encouragement, he gave a manic thumbs-up to the circle.

7. *Humbly asked God (of our understanding) to remove our shortcomings.*
8. *Made a list of all persons we had harmed and became willing to make amends to them all.*

'Hello my name is Elvis Presley and I'm alive and well and living in Oxford.' The sad figure of Alan was one of the regulars. Aged around fifty, he looked like he'd seen a few bar room brawls in his time. Leather faced with a button nose, when he smiled his eyes disappeared into his podgy face. Wearing a black leather jacket, with a penny collar that was too small for him, he'd been a policeman for over forty years. Retiring as a sergeant his pension was slowly being swallowed up on the tables and horses and the only way of coping with his addiction was to hide behind a wall of dry wit. 'I had a couple of good days last week. I lost about eighteen hundred at the Casino, a couple of grand on the dogs. The good news is that I've had *Self Exclusion* leaflets printed with my ugly-mush on them, so where I used to study mugshots for a living, now my face is on the wall of every bookie in Oxford banning them from taking a bet off me.' Garry bowed a couple of times like a sad Vaudeville clown to the ripple of applause.

Previously, Tony had one-to-one sessions from a councillor who always smelt of stale beer. He looked like he'd been doing his job too long and who just repeated things from a handbook.

'*Alcoholics get drunk to be happy, suffering depression when they're hungover. It's the same with smoking; the smoker needs nicotine, when they don't get it they can become depressed even aggressive. It could be worse Tony, people who are addicted to drugs take them to get 'high', then when they come down they're low and you know what they say about a drug dealer? They might get invited to weddings but nobody goes to their funeral. It's the same with gambling, you get 'high' from the betting, a buzz when you win, depression when you lose. The difference being it's not given a health warning like drugs, alcohol and nicotine.'*

Tony had stopped listening long after *'Alcoholics get drunk to be happy.'*

> *9. Make direct amends to such people wherever possible, except when to do so would injure them or ourselves.*
>
> *10. Continue to take personal inventory and when we are wrong promptly admit it.*

'Hello my name's Mary and I'm a compulsive gambler.' Mary lifted herself from her seat and leaned on her stick, the light reflecting in her swan shaped glasses. When she smiled, she smiled like only a grandmother could. She wore a heavy maroon overcoat, which had stains around the flowery brooches on both lapels and wore an Alice-band across her short, bright red hair. Her eyes shone through her glasses and her Marianne Faithfull mascara, her voice was silky-soft and when she spoke a tremor of a moustache moved up and down on her top lip. 'I play the scratch cards and go to the Bingo normally once, sometimes twice a day. This month has been really difficult as I've lost over five hundred pounds a week – all the money in the saving account has disappeared and I don't know where I'm going to find the money to buy my grandchildren Christmas presents. I feet ashamed with myself – what sort of person am I?' Sitting, she stared downwards, a single tear dropping to the wooden floor.

> *11. Sought through prayer and meditation to improve our conscious contact with God (as we understand him) praying only for knowledge of His will for us and the power to carry that out.*

12. Having made an effort to practise these principles in all out affairs, we tried to carry this message to other compulsive gamblers.

'Hello my name's Tony Evans, I'm a compulsive gambler…
Where do I start?'

CHAPTER SEVENTEEN

Young was anxious, his hands were hot and sweaty and he badly craved a cigarette. For the umpteenth time he looked up at the wall-clock. Crossing his arms tight across his chest, he realised he was thirty minutes early. Sometimes he was an hour early, if he had one annoying trait about himself, it was that he was always early, for everything. He was never late, never. Across the room a large print hung on the waiting room wall. It was of a young, happy Victorian couple, the man wore a top hat, the lady a long flowing dress. They were ice-skating on a frozen lake in a large park, it made him smile and for a couple of minutes he was somewhere else, happy again. Turning from the picture, the smiling face of a middle-aged woman on the front cover of a fading magazine caught his attention. A copy of Woman's Own was resting on a coffee table and, thumbing through the pages he thought, it strange that you never see anybody buying Womans Own magazine, but doctor's waiting rooms are always full of them. His eyes switched to the clock, fifteen minutes had passed. In the patterned curtains; he thought he saw images of distorted faces. Struggling to find a face, he tilted his head to one side and suddenly saw the scowl of a Mexican with a handlebar moustache. Smiling to himself, he grunted out the corner of his mouth. 'Hey amigo, give me some tequila.' Sitting alone in the waiting room he didn't care if anybody had heard him from behind the closed door opposite him. Then in the curtains he saw the face of an Aztec Prince, then a Roman Centurion. 'Hail Caesar'. Laughing to himself, he focused on the brass engraved name plate on the mahogany door. The words read, Dr. D Fowler. Looking at the clock again, he started to count along with the second hand as it made its way towards the top of the hour. 'One, two, three, four, five, six, seven, eight, nine, ten - open sez-me.' Right on cue, as the clock-chimed twelve Doctor Fowler's office door swung open. Wearing worn, cracked leather brogues, Fowler bounded through the door. He was well over sixty, thin, tall with a long face. Strands of hair the colour of sun-scorched straw flicked up and down across his bald head when he walked. Wearing a brown tweed suit, with leather patches sewn onto each elbow, the suit was too short in the legs and arms and smelt of pipe tobacco. In his left lapel was a small metal-badge with a crest, celebrating *England's Rugby Centenary Year* and his gold framed bifocal glasses which dangled around his neck on a matching gold chain swung alarmingly from side-to-side like a pendulum in a grandfather clock.

'Brian, good afternoon please come in.'

Dr Fowler thrust out his hand enthusiastically. Young hesitated then reluctantly obliged. Fowler's hands were always clammy a little like his own, and reminded him of a book he read as a young lad. The story was about a boy called Pip or David who shook hands with somebody called Uriah Heep, his hand was clammy as well, but he could never remember the novel or who wrote it.

Fowler ushered Young into his second floor office, it was a bright room with two large windows that stretched up from the wood block flooring up to the high ceiling. The view overlooked a square of ornamental gardens and the statue of a famous industrialist who had invested his time and money into preserving the historic square and its surrounding buildings. Directly opposite was the stone building of the Town Hall with its figure of Britannia perched high on the top of its clock tower. The clock, which was stuck permanently on 3:15, hadn't worked since the Second World War after a bomb had crashed through the roof and destroyed the clock's mechanism. Young liked the view of the gardens. It struck a cord of happier times when he was a doctor and had a similar office which overlooked a park. At the back of Fowler's desk stood a giant bookcase. On many occasions Young had sat there reading the titles as Fowler spoke of *recovery* and *post-traumatic-disorder*. There were books on 'Psychology of the mind', 'Freud', 'Mrs Beeton's Famous Cook Book', Fidel Castro's autobiography, 'The New English Bible', 'The Oxford English Dictionary' and many more, Fowler was extrovert in his reading as well as his personality.

'Please take a seat Brian.'

The hard backed chair was like Fowler's shoes. Made of worn, cracked, brown-leather, it had seen better days, but it was comfortable enough for the 'one-hour' patients. As Young sat down, Fowler walked to the window, produced a pen-knife from inside his jacket and started cleaning out the burnt-out tobacco from his pipe into a metal waste paper basket.

'So Brian, how are you doing?'

'Fine.'

Young placed the sole of his trainer up against the wooden desk. Fowler spun round from the window. 'Good, that's what I like to hear on a crisp Monday afternoon….Sleeping any better?'

'A little.'

Fowlers tone was sceptical, slightly pessimistic. 'Six, seven, eight hours?'

119

'About four hours, sometime five.' Young was lying, he never slept and Fowler knew it. Fowler turned slightly from the window and spoke over his shoulder. 'And you're still taking the medication?'

'Yes.' Young lied again, he was used to lying. It was easier.

'Would you like me to recommend anything to your doctor?' Young shook his head.

'So Brian tell me about your week?'

'Worked, that's all.'

'You must have done something. Did you watch the rugby on Saturday? You said you used to like watching sport.'

'I used to, but I can't remember watching the rugby, I might have done.'

'England against France, it was a good game, we won by twenty points to nineteen, a conversion in the last minute sealed it for us.' Fowler waited for a response but it wasn't forthcoming.

'If you didn't watch the rugby, try and remember something you did watch?' There was another uneasy silence as Young caught Fowler glancing at his desk clock. It was going to be a long hour for both of them.

'So come on Brian if you watched television what did you watch?'

'I can't remember.'

Fowler scratched the back of his ear, it was hard going. Gathering his thoughts Fowler turned back to look out the window and tried once again to incite a conversation. 'Brian, as I've said before, many psychologists put pressure on their clients to try and supplement their rage and anger with something positive like 'forgiveness'. I'm not one of them, I believe that you have to try and walk in the shoes of the victim, however difficult it may be and however incomprehensible it is to understand.' Fowler once again glanced over his shoulder at Young. 'I'm on your side Brian. You know that.'

Fowler thought for a few seconds, then sprung back to life with such enthusiasm he kicked over the waste paper basket.

'Ok....You told me last time a little about your upbringing, where you had gone to school, if you had any brothers or sisters, that sort of thing. Let's see if we can go back there.' Fowler took of his jacket, slung it over the back of his chair then returned to the window. 'What do you remember about your parents Brian?' Young suddenly stood-up and walked over to join Fowler at the window. Fowler became edgy and placed his pipe nervously in his mouth as Young appeared at his side. Fowler's office was his domain, his space. Patients always sat in the designated, brown-leather-chair like they had done for the past thirty years; they listened and spoke only when they were asked a question.

Looking across the gardens, Young turned and watched Fowler's mouth chewing his unlit pipe. As his pipe rattled around his teeth, he spoke but Young didn't hear, once again he had fallen into a trance. Looking out of the window Young saw a mother running after her young son, they looked so happy and thoughts of his mother floated back to him. He could see her auburn hair tied back in a light green head scarf that matched her green vibrant eyes. She liked taking him for long walks, sometimes to feed the ducks in the park, were she'd always find some loose change to buy him an ice cream. His mother was his best friend; he had no brothers or sisters and never really thought as to why all his school friends had so many. One day she took him to see a brass band playing, he liked the men's red jackets and how their polished brass instruments shone in the sunshine. Once he caught his mum crying and asked why she was so upset. She said that the piece of music reminded her of the three older brothers she lost during the war and of her father who died when she was a little girl. Years later when he was old enough, around eleven or twelve, she told him how they died. The oldest brother, Arthur was in the Royal Navy and lost his life at sea, torpedoed off the coast of Africa by a German U-boat. The second brother Mac, a soldier, lost his life at Dunkirk and the third brother Len was one of the first soldiers to liberate the Jewish victims of Belsen, where he picked up a strain of typhoid. The grandfather, who he had never known had died of a drink related illness and his mother never talked of him, just shed tears. Sometimes, when he closed his eyes, for one split second he could smell her sweet breath and see her smile and feel that kiss on that Christmas day morning.

'Sleep well my love. Sleep well.'

'Brian! Brian! Brian! Are you alright Brian?'

Young turned from the window and looked at Fowler, then smiled as tears streamed down both cheeks.

CHAPTER EIGHTEEN

The small interview room in Brainforth was cold, annulled of any life or spirit. Overhead, a strip-light made the thousands of white, porcelain tiles that lined the walls glow with sanitation. With only one door leading to a corridor of A-Block, it resembled the morgue of an Edwardian hospital. In the centre of the room two wooden chairs sat either side of a wooden table and on one of the walls a white plastic clock slowly ticked away time. High up in one corner a security camera watched and waited.

Without any airs or graces, Jennings and Rogers bundled Finch through the door. As Tony stood at the door he watched as Jennings placed both hands on Finch's shoulders and shoved him down into the hard-backed chair. Finch rolled his shoulders then calmly clasped his hands together on the table and grinned, that grin. He could feel Jennings behind him, his eyes piercing the back of his head, his warm breath down the back of his neck. Unruffled, he slouched back into the chair, crossed his arms and eye-balled Rogers across the room. Like Jennings he knew Rogers had taken an instant dislike to him, there again nobody liked him. He was used to it.

His gaze then drifted onto Tony's face. It took him back to the time he sat handcuffed in the back of the prison van. It was transporting him from the High Court after his trial to Brainforth. Outside the court a large crowd had gathered. On seeing the white prison van drive out of the back of the building a group broke through the police-cordon and attacked the van like a pack of wolves. The van was flanked by a police escort, but it couldn't stop the angry mob pounding the side of the van with their fists, shouting, 'Animal!' and 'Burn in hell Finch!' Further down the street, another horde showered the van with stones and bricks. Inside the confined space of the claustrophobic van, police sirens, mixed with the violent racket from outside boomed round the metal walls like thunder. It was hot and sticky, the taste of stale sweat and vomit lodged at the back of Finch's throat. One of the two officers turned white as the vehicle rocked violently from side to side. His face reminded him of Tony's who stood staring at him across the interview room. Finch shot his eyes across to Rogers.

'What are you looking at?' said Rogers.

Finch shrugged his shoulders as his grin widened.

'Mr Rogers has asked you a question Finch.' Although Jennings voice was firm, threatening, he smiled as Finch continued grinning at Rogers.

Suddenly the door swung open and Dr. King walked in carrying a bundle of folders under his arm. 'Hello Alistair.' Forty plus, he was small but athletic. Sporting a light grey suit and tie that matched his small grey framed glasses, his seventies rock-band ponytail looked out-of-place from his trendy appearance. Finch then directed his attention from Rogers to King, he found these little sessions fun and today he was going to have a ball.

King looked at Jennings, Tony and Rogers. 'Good morning gentlemen.'

'Good morning.'

'How are you today Alistair?'

Finch just grinned.

Spilling his folders off the side of the table, King drew breath and composed himself. Kneeling down, he started picking up the folders that were strewn across the floor. His voice shook as he talked. 'Sorry I'm running late, my dentist took more time on my crown than expected.' King stood up and dropped the folders onto the table with an enthusiastic thud.

'We'll leave you to it Mr King,' said Jennings ushering Tony and Rogers out of the room. Although King was left alone with Finch, in reality somebody would always be watching. Apart from the security camera, the door to the interview room had a reinforced mesh window and in the past Finch felt like he was in a goldfish bowl as faces would take a peek in at the monster.

'Right, where were we Alistair?' King opened a folder, shuffled a few sheets of paper around, rearranged his glasses then consulted his notes. 'On my last visit I asked whether you were still taking the anti-depressants, is that still the case?'

Just that grin.

'Are they of any help?'

Just that grin, then he looked up at the ceiling.

'Ok.' King could feel the usual perspiration forming under the rims of his glasses. 'So what we have to establish in these sessions Alistair, as I've mentioned to you on numerous occasions, is that you have a clear picture of why you offended and what we can do to stop you offending in the future.'

Just that grin, then he looked down at the floor.

Looking across the room, King saw the three officers through the window of the door. King looked back at Finch and was met once again by that grin. Finch knew he had Jennings and Rogers onboard, Tony would take a little longer, now King was very close, he'd been working on him for weeks. King's fingers nervously strummed the top of the table top. 'Is there anything you think that you need that might speed up your rehabilitation Alistair?'

Just that grin, then he looked around the walls.

Finch liked the way King called him Alistair, it was personal and he liked personal. Then he noticed a tiny freckle above his right eyebrow, he knew as soon as he saw it, it would become an obsession, his personal obsession.

King continued. 'Alistair, do you understand my questions, you're not responding?' His patience was running thin. Finch's' eyes didn't move from King's freckle. 'I think I will look into your medication, possibly *up* the dosage.'

He waited for a reaction. Nothing.

King scribbled down another note in the file. Tightening the band in his ponytail he looked-up and smiled across the table. 'I think you're playing games with me Alistair.'

Now Finch had King on board, his eyes transfixed on that freckle. Loosening his tie, King licked his index finger and flicked through a few sheets of paper in the folder. Removing a form, he brought it down onto the desk with a determined thud. 'This is a report form Alistair. When it's filled in *by me*, it is then given to the head psychologist who reads it, then makes a decision on whether I'm making any process with you. Do you understand?'

Just that bloody grin.

King removed his glasses and started wiping the lenses with the end of his tie. Finch noticed his reflection in King's eyes, they were green eyes his favourite colour after blue. As the room fell silent, King put on his glasses and removed a pen from the inside of his suit pocket. Filling in the form with a vengeance, his voice became sharp, irritated. 'Once I've handed in this form, there is no going back.' Glancing up at the wall clock, he filled in the time and date. In the whole year King had treated Finch, it was the first time Finch had seen King slightly *losing it*. Normally King was calm, courteous and caring to him, he was obviously testing his rcsolve, or possibly he'd had enough and it really was the last time he'd be seeing him. King looked down at his notes.

'I have recorded my observations. The patient shows signs of being psychopathic, behaves in an anti-social manner, has a fixated-ego, shows uncooperative behaviour and shows empathy. I sometimes wonder whether you should be institutionalised Alistair'.

King looked up for a reaction. Nothing, just that grin staring at him.

King tapped his pen on the table. 'What are you looking at?'
Finch could see the reflection of his grin in King's glasses. Running his index finger under the top of his glasses, King wiped away the beads of sweat. Then the tone of his voice changed again, he'd had enough. 'Ok Alistair, if that's how you want to play it.' Burying his head in the form, his shoulders lifted as his hand gripped the pen. 'Once again, Alistair Finch shows no response to my treatment – I now feel the time is right to try a new approach with his rehabilitation – suggesting he is now transferred to a different counsellor.' He looked up for a response. Nothing.

King continued to fill in the report. 'So it's just a matter now of crossing the 't's' and dotting the 'i's' – I feel Finch would benefit from this change – blah, blah, blah.' Defeated, King condemned the file to his past and quickly put the pen back into his suit jacket. Catching Jennings gaze through the window King nodded. As the three officers entered the room, King removed his glasses and wiped the lenses clean of sweat and condensation. Raising his voice he spoke for the benefit of everyone in the room. 'So Alistair, as we won't be seeing each other again, off the record do you mind if I speak my mind?'
There was no response, just that grin.

'I was thinking the other day on what you'll never see or do again in this wonderful world of ours. You'll never see the light of day again, you'll never take a walk along a beach or visit a zoo or go shopping or have a drink in a country pub. So I understand why you're going through a mid-life crisis or possibly you might be going mad from too much masturbation. Have you ever thought about writing your autobiography? It could be called, *Lollypop Tales, the diaries of a paedophile and retard.*

Finch continued grinning, nothing.

'I believe your mother's name is Shirley. I'm sure she's really proud of you.' Finch's eyes widened and flickered. Like a sadistic dentist, King had hit a nerve. Jennings smiled across at Rogers, he was enjoying the moment. King stood up, slipped on his glasses and leaned over the table. 'You look a bit washed out Alistair.'

King didn't give Finch the satisfaction of a final glance; flicking his ponytail off the back of his suit jacket, he picked up his paperwork and moved away from the table. At the door, he turned and looked back. 'I think we're making excellent progress don't you Alistair?' Leaning into Jennings he whispered. 'See you next week.'

Finch's grin had changed; Tony noticed it was through gritted teeth. He thought he'd won again, but his expression told a different story. As King's sweaty handprints slowly disappeared from the top of the desk, Finch looked up at Jennings. There was a spoilt firmness in his voice. 'I'm hungry.'

Jennings looked at Rogers. 'Did you hear something Mr Rogers?'

'I didn't hear a thing Mr Jennings.'

Both officers looked at Finch and smiled, both could play at this game. Finch swung his venom at Rogers. 'You look the sort.'

'Take no notice of him Mr Rogers.'

Rogers gave a huff.

'Oh I think he is. You can tell, he looks the sort who always ran with the crowd at school, the bully in the background who'd stick the final boot in when the guy was down, yes he looks the sort all right.'

Tony looked at Rogers, Finch was getting to him.

Finch continued. 'And I bet you still live with your mother, an only child, used to your home comforts are you? Yes you look the sort alright.'

Jennings stood over Finch, his voice calm. 'Up you get.'
Finch slid his chair backwards, its legs screeching and sliding across the floor. Standing mockingly to attention, Finch pierced into Rogers' eyes over Jennings' shoulder.

'Yes he looks the sort all right.'

Tony felt Finch's poison at the bottom of his stomach.

How did he know Rogers lived with his mother?

How did he know he was an only child?

He's guessing, relax.

Tony knew Rogers was sensitive, but the things Finch had said about him as a kid rang true, things he might have put to the back of his mind for years, had now been brought back to the surface by a couple of single remarks. Jennings was the only one who knew what Finch was up to, he'd witnessed many an officer's legs buckle and their nerves destroyed by Finch's tongue, but he could never fathom out how he knew private things about them. He was like a mind reader. Once he made a remark about him owning a caravan. It was true, Jennings did have a caravan. It could have been construed as a wild guess, but small details 'inside' have tendencies to be blown out of proportion and by Finch's remarks he had crept inside Rogers psyche in a big way.

Jennings led Finch towards the door. 'Are you ready Mr Rogers?'

Rogers had a delayed reaction before grabbing Finch's arm.

'Normally your grip is much tighter Mr Rogers,' said Finch grinning.

Finch looked at Tony as Rogers tightened his grip. 'That's better sunshine.'

CHAPTER NINETEEN

Anders was busy developing prints from his excursion to the village of Farmington. Partly lit by the red light bulb dangling overhead, he hummed along to the dulcet tones of Bob Dylan's album 'Blonde on Blonde'. Hidden under the blonde wig was a neatly trimmed haircut, his dark hair and grey temples now giving him the distinguished look of a Tory politician. Someone would be hard-pressed to recognise him as the same annoying person that constantly fidgeted in the wooden pews at the back of the St Benedict's church the previous day. In the makeshift dark-room, Anders removed a sheet of photographic paper from a masking-frame then placed it into a large plastic developing tray. Swilling the developing fluid around the paper, he watched as an image started to slowly appear. Anders never tired of these moments. Like magic, a person would appear before his eyes and the ones of O'Connor outside the church were no different. From the hundreds of images he'd photographed over the years these were as good as any, the client should be happy. The photograph presented a detailed image of the Priest and his parishioners congregating outside the Church. Removing the photograph from the developing tray, he placed it in a water tray to rinse away the residue of the pungent developing fluid, then, with a small peg he hung it overhead onto a string washing line to dry with the other prints.

'Mr Pearson, telephone!' Startling Anders, a woman's voice boomed from behind the door. Snapping back with a cockney accent his voice growled impatience. 'I'm busy Mrs Dovecot!'

'Aren't we all Mr Pearson?'

Anders looked at his watch under the dimness of the red light; it was 7:30AM. He'd been working non-stop through the night. Rinsing his hands under the tap, he dabbed his face with cold water. Becoming immediately suspicious as to who was ringing him so early in the morning he questioned the voice the other side of the door.

'Did they say who it was?'

'No, he said he couldn't phone you back, he'll hold.'

'Alright, tell him I'm on my way.'

'Tell him yourself Mr Pearson, you may pay rent here, but you don't pay me to be your secretary!'

'Thank you Mrs Dovecot.' Anders whipped two fingers up to the back of the door and mimed *Piss off!*

Quickly replacing the light-sensitive, photographic paper into a sealed box, Anders flicked on the light illuminating the room. The bright light stung his eyes for a few seconds as he tried to focus on his surroundings. The room was bare, depressing. A second-hand wardrobe and matching dresser filled most of the small room and a sun-faded print of Constable's 'The Haywain' hung over the single bed's light-blue, padded headboard. From the string line, which was now visible over a sink, he removed the print he had just developed. It hadn't *fixed* and was quickly turning sepia. He'd have to start again. 'Shit.'

Dropping the print into the sink, he pressed the 'off' button on the CD player and killed *'Just like a woman'* and Bob Dylan. Suddenly he felt shattered.

Unlocking his door, Anders held back a yawn and walked out into the clutter of Mrs Dovecot's living room. The room was gloomy, the only light creeping through a small round window which overlooked an overgrown front garden. Full of cheap artefacts, the clutter was only important to whoever's clutter it was. Someone obviously liked to travel and had been hoarding souvenirs from all corners of the globe. There was a carved fertility mask from Africa, statues from Peru, and around the walls hung framed posters from the Louvre in Paris. Laid out on the polished oak floor were rugs from India and the centrepiece in the far corner of the room was a large bubble pipe from Istanbul. Sitting on the couch, submerged in a book on gardening was Mrs Dovecot. Wearing sandals, with visible pop-soaks covering her white podgy legs, her long flowery dress blended her into the flowery throw-over off the couch and the sequined cushions from Italy. Now in her late-fifties, her pale, white face with long grey hair gave the impression she was still clinging to her days as a 60s wild child. As Anders strode past the dust collectors, he heard her sigh in his direction. It wasn't the first time she'd huffed-and-puffed at him, if only she knew.

Closing the lounge door behind him, Anders stepped into the hall. A Second World War poster looked at him heralding the warning that 'Careless Talk costs lives.' He didn't need reminding, he was always on his guard. Apart from the war poster the walls were covered in a number of gold, ornate framed mirrors, which led up the stairs to the first floor bedrooms, somewhere where Anders had never been. Near the front door a collection of walking sticks with metal badges from around the world rested against an old mahogany cabinet. On its top, a vase of dusty dried flowers cast shadows across a lady's bicycle with a wicker basket on the handlebars. It was hard to move around the hall without bumping into a number of large rubber plants, but over the past few weeks Anders had learned to master the manoeuvre. Using his handkerchief to pick up the phone he spoke quietly. 'Yes.' As Anders listened, he studied his face in one of the mirrors, he looked tired. Listening intensely to the person down the other end of the phone, he started doing face and neck exercises. Making the sinews protrude out of his neck, he was abrupt in his reply. 'Yes, I'm developing them now – I will have them for him when they're ready.' His voice was impatient. 'That's the only time he can do? – 'Well if I have to make it then, I will have to make it then – Yes, yes, yes, I will try, but you know the conditions – my rate, it will go up – good, as long as we understand each other.' Anders replaced the receiver and dabbed a small amount of sweat that had gathered on his forehead before neatly folding his handkerchief and putting it into his inside pocket. Shooting a glance towards the door leading into the lounge, he listened. Over the years he had trained himself to listen, but what if somebody had been eavesdropping? For a few seconds he weighed-up the situation. Then, once again he checked himself in the mirror. Hitching-up his sweater he rearranged his trouser belt, then patted his stomach and frowned at the same time. Thinking he might have put on a few pounds, he breathed in and sucked in his stomach, then convincing himself that in-fact he'd lost weight he breathed out and let out a sigh of relief at the same time. In his job you had to be fit, as the run down the steps in the London office block proved almost a week ago.

The scent of joss-sticks and the sound of a mating 'whale' from a relaxation CD, hit Anders as he walked back into the lounge. Mrs Dovecot was now sitting cross-legged on one of the Indian rugs in the lotus-position with her eyes closed. As Anders cushioned his walk across the room, she popped open one eye and hit him with another sigh that was louder that the last one. If only she knew.

'If he rings again Mr Pearson, I will tell him you're out.'
Shutting her eye, another heavy sigh sent Anders back into his room. *Bitch.* Closing the door, Anders made his way over to the sink and looked at the print. The image of O'Connor he'd previously developed had disappeared. Pissed–off, he ripped-it-up and threw it into an overflowing bin. But before starting the process again he looked back at the door. Something was playing on his mind. Had she been listening or was he just being paranoid? Since the murders in the lift he'd been having the odd panic attack, they were only slight but he was conscious he was having them. Turning back on the Bob Dylan CD, he loaded up his camera with film. Mounting the Pentax on a tri-pod he focused the lens then positioned the camera towards the blank wall. Pressing the self-timer button, he moved quickly to a chair and positioned himself. Posing for the camera he sat straight backed, rigid stony-faced as the camera flashed. Turning up the volume on his CD player he knelt down and reached under the wardrobe. With a tug, he ripped out a large brown envelope that had been duck-taped underneath.

Tipping the contents of the envelope out onto the bed, he picked up a green passport. Bearing an embossed eagle on the front, he fanned through the pages and stopped at a photograph of a man that was unrecognisable, beard, glasses, dark hair. The name was Herman Bernstein, American, occupation salesman. DOB, 1951. Disregarding it, he picked up another passport. Swedish, he once again fanned the pages to the photograph. This time the mug-shot was of the blond haired man, the same man who sat fidgeting at the back of St Benedict's Church. Underneath the face the name read, Anton Berg, born Sweden, DOB 1950. Picking out a British passport, he fanned the pages to the back. Charles Pearson, British, occupation photographer, DOB, 1953. The photograph was of how he looked now, clean cut, sophisticated. Next, he fanned the pages of a Norwegian passport; there was no photograph or name, just a blank page, it's the one he'd been looking for. Putting it to one side he put all the other passports back into the envelope and threw it back on the bed. Anders once again turned up the music and waited for the knock on the door, a response he knew would come, it came.

'Can you turn the music down please Mr Pearson!'

Anders turned down the music, then, looked at the plain door leading to the lounge. Now was as good a time as any.

Taking a squirt of breath-freshener, he turned the door handle slowly. Opening the door slightly, he peered through the gap. His landlady was sitting on the floor in the lotus position, her long grey hair that flowed down her back was rocking from side-to-side as she meditated and chanted under her breath. Slipping on a pair of black leather gloves, Anders swung open the door and crept inside the room. Sliding his leather belt from around his waist he wrapped the ends around his gloves and walked towards her. Engrossed in meditation, Mrs Dovecot had no idea that her karma was about to come to an end.

Taking-in-a-deep-breath, and all in one movement, Anders cranked-up the volume on the CD player and threw the belt over her head and around her neck. Thrusting his knee into the back of her shoulder blades he wrenched the belt upwards. Her legs sprung outwards kicking wildly. Both hands sprung to her neck, her red finger nails clawing grotesquely to get under the leather belt. Across the room Anders caught his own reflection in a full length mirror. He watched as her face slowly started to turn blue. As she fought for her life, Anders tightened this grip. Pulling harder and harder, he yanked the belt upwards. Beads of sweat dripped from his forehead onto her wriggling body. Blood appeared on her neck as she clawed at her throat. Slowly the little strength she had left disappeared as her arms went limp and dropped to her sides like lead weights. Standing strong, rigid, Anders felt the life drain from her body. As her last gasp gurgled out of her lungs, her body stopped wriggling.

For a minute or two Anders stood watching himself in the mirror. The belt still tight round her neck, his body tight with the strain of the kill, but just to make sure and being the perfectionist, he wrenched the belt sideways and upwards. The crack of her neck reverberated up through his wrists, then up his arms, reaching his shoulders, chest and heart. What heart? His body eventually relaxed and he let go. Mrs Dovecot's body slumped to the floor like a rag doll. Her face had turned from blue to purple and her vicious tongue which he'd only heard, but never seen, stuck out of her tiny mouth. Pink lipstick was smudged across her cheek and a loose sandal lay by the far wall under the window. Turning down the CD player, Anders went back into his room mumbling his favourite song.

> *'There's no regrets.*
> *No tears goodbye.*
> *I don't want you back.*
> *We'll only cry, cry again.*
> *Say goodbye again.'*

Removing his gloves, Anders threw them onto the bed next to the passports. Slipping off his shirt, he picked up a towel and started wiping his face, neck and chest clear of sweat. Checking his body in the mirror, he smiled to himself. He wasn't bad for a fifty year old. He had to keep fit, as always, murder could be a strenuous business.

CHAPTER TWENTY

For Tony, everyday in Brainforth was like rewinding a video-tape and watching it over and over again, as was his routine at home before he left for work. Clean shirt and tie, flask of coffee and a groan that sent him on his merry way.

Yawning at the first of the many security gates, Tony caught sight of a line of visitors waiting for their bags to travel through the x-ray machine. After the undignified experience of being searched they passed through the metal detector, their faces grey, drawn by a thousand nightmares of their sons' or fathers' incarceration. Eighty-per cent of Brainforth prisoners were inside for drug-related crimes. Addicted to heroin, many had stolen from the old and vulnerable to pay for their habit, the rest, who had fallen by the wayside were inside for fraud, arson, robbery or murder. Tony wasn't the only one who'd had a restless night. All night he'd tossed-and turned churning things over and over in his mind.

Stepping out into the prison yard the bright sunlight didn't help the tiredness that sat heavy on his eyes. Looking across the yard towards A-Wing he felt his energy seeping from his body as he contemplated another shift inside 'Prison World.'

The previous evening he'd watched children's television with Martha, while Anne was out swimming with her sister. They still weren't talking. All evening he'd clock-watched. He agonised over not meeting Young that night, and he'd half-expected him to arrive on his doorstep with a kitchen knife. Young seemed unbalanced and it worried him. The crumpled note that Martha had slipped into the palm of his hand at the lake read, *Devon Park Cricket Pavilion. Seven o'clock.* It was scribbled in pencil and was barely decipherable. It read nothing more, nothing less. He'd guessed the money had come from Young. But what did he want? Taking the money had put him in a precarious position, a dangerous position. Young looked the sort who wouldn't give up without a fight. He looked determined, on a mission, but what did he want?

The officers' locker room was as depressing as the rest of the prison. Void of natural daylight its grey walls matched the grey faces of the officers who used it. A line of grey metal lockers lined one wall, whilst the showers and washbasins looked like they had been left over from the war. Opening the door to his locker, Tony placed his flask of coffee inside and looked at the photograph sellotaped to the back of the door. It was a snapshot of Anne and Martha smiling on the beach. For a few seconds he could hear the sea, the warm sea and he was on holiday again. Those beautiful warm, sunny days, free of stress were a long, long way from Brainforth. The tranquillity of the moment was broken when Rogers crashed through the door, he looked washed-out, it was nothing new Tony was used to his hangovers.

'What a night. What a night! How's it going Tony me old mate, is that coffee in there?'

'No!'

'Go on pour us a quick cup. I didn't have time for breakfast if you know what I mean.'

Reluctantly, Tony opened the flask and poured him a cup. 'It's hot.'

'Cheers mate, bit of a hangover.'

'I can smell it.'

Rogers took a sip, burning his bottom lip on the ring of the aluminium cup. 'Shit!'

'You better hurry up or Jennings will slap the back of our legs if we're late.' There was sarcasm in Tony's voice. Rogers gave him an uneasy look.

'Just watch your back with Jennings; you know what he's like.'

'You're the one who should watch himself; he's taken a shining to you.'

'I want to keep on the right side of him that's all. We went for a drink after work last night – listen, I don't like him, but you want an easy life in here don't you? It's hard enough in this shit-hole without him on your back.' Tony acknowledged Rogers' logic and advice; it was advice from a friend.

Ready for the day, Rogers took another sip of coffee and threw his arm round Tony's shoulder. 'Now let me tell you about last night, with Sue and the four-poster-bed.'

'What happened about you and Carol getting back together?'

'Carol, who's Carol?'

Stripped-to-the-waist, Finch was standing at the sink shaving. Next to him, lying on the top of the smooth covers of his prison blanket was his breakfast tray. Breakfast for Finch was the same every day, of every week, of every month of the year, black coffee, cornflakes with semi-skimmed milk. Sometimes in the coffee there was an extra hidden ingredient, the cooks spit. Stepping through the open cell door, Tony and Rogers were met by Finch's lively voice. 'Good morning gentlemen.'

'Good morning.' Tony's reply was somewhat muted as Finch

ran the Bic razor blade over his stubbly cheek. Washing-out the blade into the sink, he turned slightly and addressed Rogers who was standing in the cell doorway yawning. 'Suffering from a hangover are we?' Rogers was taken-back at first then stepped inside the cell ready for an argument. 'And so what if I've got a hangover. It's better than being locked-up like you in this shit-hole!'

'Oh I don't know so much.' Unruffled, Finch continued shaving.

'Go on then, surprise me, what's good about it?' said Rogers.

'What's good about it? Where should I start, let me see. Breakfast in bed, a daily newspaper delivered to my front door, no TV licence, no daily grind of going to work, no council tax, no water, gas or electricity bills. Shall I go on?'

'Shut your mouth Finch, it's too early in the morning for this crap and anyway while you were banged-up in here last night with your dick in your hand I was with a gorgeous blonde so piss off!' Finch sniggered, Rogers was easy prey. Then, in the reflection of the small shaving mirror he caught Tony staring at his hairy back. Running across Finch's shoulders like a footballer's name on the back of a football shirt was a tattoo. The word was scripted in black and read, *Lollypop*. Finch swung round from the sink and caught Tony's gaze. Keeping eye contact with him, he picked up a small towel and dabbed his wet face. For a few seconds of silence the two men looked at each other.

'Good morning Mr Evans, Mr Rogers.' Jennings appeared in the cell doorway, his hands resting on both hips. 'Everything alright in here?'

'Yes Mr Jennings,' said Rogers, 'everything is just fine.' Jennings stepped back outside the cell and nodded for Rogers to join him. Tony picked up the breakfast tray, giving Finch an opportunity to become intimate. 'So do you like my tattoo?' Tony ignored the question as Finch's whisper entered his ear. 'Got it done in Bangkok.' Looking towards the cell door he leaned a little nearer. 'Don't let them get to you Tony.'

'What are you on about?'

'Come on, you know who I mean.' Finch nodded in the direction of Rogers and Jennings. 'Those two, you're better than them.'

'I think you should keep your opinions to yourself and don't use my first name anymore, understand?'

'So *are they* getting to you, or are you getting *to yourself*?' Finch grinned slightly.

That grin, that bloody grin.

Tony shot a glance through the open door; he didn't want Jennings to see him and Finch talking. Familiarity could be construed as a weakness as to how capable a prison officer he was and knowing Jennings, he would revel in it.

'I'm just trying to be a friend that's all.' Finch blew onto Tony's cheek. 'Don't tell me you object to a little bit of affection now and again?' Tony reared back, the breakfast tray shivering in his hands. 'I haven't finished my coffee Mr Evans.'

'Tough, it'll be cold.'

'That's how I like it, cold.' Finch pulled his tee-shirt over his head and tucked it into his trousers. 'I know what's troubling you.'

'Cut it out,' replied Tony under his breath. 'Walls have ears and in here there are plenty of them.' Tony sneaked another look at Rogers and Jennings who were once again sharing a joke. Frozen to the spot, Tony knew he was being sucked-in by Finch but felt helpless to resist. A look of admiration mixed with devotion enveloped Finch's face as his eyes shifted towards the picture on the wall. 'Do you know Shirley was only four years old when she made Little Miss Marker?' Struggling with the dilemma of the reaction to the statement or question, Tony rattled the tray. 'Hurry-up and drink your coffee.' Finch lifted the cup off the tray. 'The thing with cold coffee is you can drink it when you're ready, you don't have to drink it because of the fear of it getting cold.' Finch sipped the coffee all the time keeping eye-contact with his new friend. Placing the cup back onto the tray, Finch licked his lips seductively and whispered out the corner of his mouth. 'I know you're up to your neck in debt.' His expression was smug, confident. 'Let me guess, thirty, fifty thousand?' Tony's gaunt expression told him another story. 'Oh, I didn't realise it was that much.'

Leaning forward Finch's whispers were like daggers. 'Don't worry, I will help you. Then everything will fall into place and everything will return to normal at home. How do I know about your predicament? Let's say, it's just one of life's little mysteries.' Tony couldn't talk, the words lodged at the back of his throat. As the shock and anger started to boil inside him; he was just about to snap when Jennings intervened. 'Have you finished in here Mr Evans?' Tony's throat had dried up. 'Is everything alright Mr Evans?'

'Everything's just fine and dandy,' said Finch. 'Mr Evans is just leaving.'

'I wasn't talking to you Finch!' Jennings snapped back.

'All done in here Mr Jennings.' Tony found his voice but it was less than convincing.

'Right I'll leave you to it gentlemen.' Jennings walked away from the cell as Finch calmly picked up his newspaper and put on his glasses. 'What are you like at conundrums Tony?'

'What?' Tony stood next to Rogers holding the breakfast tray.

'Ignore him Tony,' said Rogers, but Tony couldn't.

'I know what you're trying to do Finch, playing your little games.' Finch looked over the top of his glasses. 'It's only a conundrum Tony that's all.'

'Go on then.' The bait was cast.

'Three businessmen share the bill in a restaurant for thirty pounds, splitting it three ways, ten pounds each way. Then they give the waiter a five pound tip. The waiter thinks it's too much and gives each businessman one pound back, keeping two pounds for himself. So the businessmen have paid how much Tony?' As Rogers sighed, Tony answered. 'Nine pounds each.'

'Very good Tony. Three nines are twenty seven pounds, plus the two pounds the waiter has kept, equals twenty nine pounds. What happened to the other pound?'

Finch watched the cogs turning around inside Tony's head. 'Say it again.' Finch's grin turned into a smile. 'I don't have to say it again, you were listening. You heard it the first time.' Trying to work out the conundrum, Tony looked at Finch who had returned to his newspaper.

'Say it again.' Finch ignored him and turned a page in the newspaper. 'I said say it again.' Tony's head was spinning and he felt the tray shaking in his hands. Brushing past Rogers, Tony fell out of the cell. Finch didn't look up from his newspaper.

'You better go after him Mr Rogers.'

Rogers turned and left the cell, finding Tony on the landing. Taking the breakfast tray out of his hands he looked at his pastey complexion. 'What's wrong with you?'

'Nothing.'

'We've been warned about him.'

'He knows things about me.'

'What things?'

'I don't know, just things.'

Rogers laughed. 'He tried to pull that one with me yesterday remember? Said he knows I live with my mum, so what, he just guesses. He's just messing with your head that's all; he's tried it with all the officers.'

'That conundrum about the pound...'

'What are you talking about?'

'He knows I gamble. He's set me a test, about the missing pound.' Rogers looked along the landing. His voice was calm, firm. 'Pull yourself together, remember what Jennings said, he warned us about him, he told us how he gets a 'hard-on' playing games, how he likes to get inside your head, that's what he's done and you've fallen for it.' As Tony tried to compose himself he caught eye contact with Jennings down the landing. He was talking to another prisoner, the look across his face made him feel small, uncomfortable. Rogers nudged Tony with the tray. 'Come on, Jennings is looking over.'

As the two officers walked down the landing, Tony mulled over the things Finch had said. The conundrum, he was convinced was a test of his resolve, but the gambling and the references to his home life sent a shiver through him.

Removing his glasses, Finch slowly looked up from the newspaper. Tilting his head to one side, he looked at the postcard of Shirley Temple. Each day he thought he saw something new, something different in the picture. One day, it could be the stitching on her dress, another day a new ringlet in her hair. Today he thought he saw another shadow in the background and her smile looked somewhat different, but he couldn't be sure. Humming the song, *'The Good Ship Lollipop'*, he stood up, dropped the newspaper on the bed and stepped across the cell. Taking-in her smile, he rested his forehead on the small postcard, closed his eyes and spoke affectionately. 'We're nearly there sweetheart, we're nearly there.' Then he started mumbling a song. 'I like what you like; on the account of I love you.'

CHAPTER TWENTY-ONE

Being pissed off was something Young had got used to, but being made to look like a mug, now that really pissed-him-off. A thing his mother used to say crossed his mind, although he could never be sure they were the right words. *Never be a lender or a borrower be.* He hadn't loaned the money to Tony, he'd given it to him for a reason, now he was taking the piss and he didn't like it, not one little bit. Desperate people do desperate things and he knew Tony was desperate, his weakness was what he was relying on, but the fact that he'd had the *front* not to show-up had set him into a rage. For almost three hours he'd waited for him at the cricket pavilion. He'd passed the time by reading the graffiti on the dressing room wall and smoking, while taking in the smell of stale beer that crept through the cricket pavillion's wooden walls. Now time was running out, enough was enough, the prison officer was going to be taught a lesson, a lesson he wouldn't forget.

From under the driver's seat Young slid out a crowbar. It was there as a deterrent, for his peace of mind, for trouble when he needed it, for the drunken wankers who tried their luck in trying to dodge the cost of a ride home or the wankers who argued the toss over the fare. Then they were shown the crowbar. Then they paid up. The metal felt cold in Young's hand as he held it down by his side, out of view. Walking across the large retail car park, he passed a large collection of shoppers, kids in prams, kids out of prams, husbands with paint and wood for the weekend's DIY, shoppers with new clothes for that special Saturday night-out, to a club or a restaurant, they were all in their own little world and were all far too busy to notice what Young was carrying. They never gave him a second look.

As he walked, two situations sprang to mind when the crowbar took on a life of its own. The first was on a hot summer's night when he drove a couple of young lads home to an infamous housing estate on the outskirts of the city. He thought twice about giving them a ride, but that night he was *up for it,* something he couldn't explain, then it came back like it always did. *Why me and not them?* In the back of the cab the two drunks completely ignored the *no smoking* signs and sparked up a joint. Although the cab smelt of his own cigarettes he didn't like drunks smoking in the back. They had a tendency to burn holes in the leather seats. Some of them did it on purpose. Staggering and loud, they were his last punters of the night and were conveniently going in the same direction as him, home. When he asked them to put-out the joint they laughed at him, then offered the old man a toke. He only asked the once. Slamming on the brakes, he grabbed the crowbar from under his seat and jumped out. Opening the back door, he thrust the crowbar into one of the lads' spotty cheeks. Squirming, the lad pleaded for his life as a trickle of blood started running down his cheek onto his open-necked, white shirt. Young enjoyed every second, seeing the scum of the world cower when he suddenly turned into a vigilante thug himself. Demanding the full fare and good tip for the inconvenience, they shook as they emptied their pockets. Coins and notes spilled out of their pockets onto the cab floor. They were only about eighteen and he enjoyed kicking their arses down the street. He'd taught them a lesson, and felt like Charles Bronson in the film 'Death Wish'.

The second time was surprisingly the same week; there was never a right or wrong time for Young. As soon as the couple jumped into the back they started arguing. *Why me and not them?* Within seconds the argument had turned from full on verbal abuse to a full-on fight. The women was ugly as hell, the man uglier. When she was sick over him, it caused him to give her a smack. When the man, a big burly bastard with a massive bald head and bad teeth stepped out of the cab, Young belted him across the shins with the bar. The crack echoed around the night air matching the smack he'd given the woman. As the man dropped to his knees in agony, the woman pounced on him like a vulture swooping down on a fly-ridden carcass. Kicking him again and again and again, each kick from her pointed stiletto put a hole into his body where it hurt. Young stood back and watched, he deserved it, every kick. Eventually, a few coppers dragged her off, he was lucky, she would have killed him.

Before he drove off he watched the threat of being arrested sober the couple up. As their anger turned into drunken remorse, the crying into the I love you's, the adrenaline rush hit Young and he was sick in the cab. He'd seen it all before as a young trainee doctor in A and E all those years ago on a Friday and Saturday night, when every drunk in town would stagger in wearing their blood splattered, best bib and tucker expecting him to stitch them up ready for next weekends pissed-up scrap. Now he'd become immune to violence along with his trusty crowbar.

Young brought the crow bar round his back as he passed a teenage girl wearing a pink, florescent tracksuit and matching headband. With wet hair and a sports-bag slung over her shoulder he knew he was heading in the right direction. As a boy he used to enjoy participating in physical exercise. He played prop forward at rugby and swam for the school, butterfly if he remembered rightly. He wasn't bad at cricket either, and up until 'that day' had kept wicket for his local club's third team. He liked the social life and on one occasion he got a hat-trick of catches behind the wicket. It was against the local rivals and after the match it cost him a round of drinks in the club house, it was a joyous moment. Now he didn't swim, watch rugby or play cricket.

Walking round the back of the DIY store, Young saw the grey breezeblock building of the leisure centre. From the hustle and bustle of the retail park it was fairly quiet. Looking up, he studied the position of the CCTV cameras around the building. Suddenly the crowbar slipped from his grasp and clanged to the ground. Quickly slipping a black, woollen balaclava from out of his pocket, he pulled it over his head and picked up the bar. This time the crowbar was going to hurt, this time the crowbar meant business.

CHAPTER TWENTY-TWO

Sipping a can of 'high energy', Tony and Rogers walked out through the automatic doors of the leisure centre. Running his fingers through his short, blond hair he could feel the ache in his hand from the Casino punch, a punch he still regretted. Every Tuesday night Tony and Rogers played squash, but this week Rogers had played second fiddle to the ball and Tony's anger.

'You were lucky tonight Tony.'

'Bollocks, according to you, I'm lucky every week.' Passing a couple of good looking girls heading to an aerobics class, Rogers couldn't resist a sneaky pervy look. 'Fancy a drink girls?' They ignored him. Tony smiled, 'You haven't lost your touch.'

Rogers sighed, 'They don't know what they're missing. What about you, fancy a quick one?'

'Not tonight.'

'You're not still thinking of Finch and where that bloody pound went to are you?'

'Don't be daft. I want to spend a bit of time with Martha before she goes to bed.'

'Alright misery guts, I'll catch you tomorrow.'

As Tony made his way across the dimly lit car park, he looked back at Rogers who was ogling the girls' backsides; he thought the game of squash would have helped with the stress of the past couple of days, but it hadn't. Gulping the last drop from the can, he dropped it into a bin and threw a wave at Rogers who was driving out of the car park.

Then he stopped dead in his tracks. The side panels of his car had been caved in; the back window smashed and etched into the bonnet's paintwork were the words: *Nobody fucks with me.* Spinning around, he thought he noticed a dark figure disappear from under a street light but nobody was there, his eyes must have been playing tricks. Circling the car, Tony inspected the damage. Underfoot, his trainers crunched the tiny pieces of glass from the shattered back window. Contemplating his luck he swung open the driver's door and threw his bag onto the back seat. Sliding into the driver's seat, he turned the ignition key. Amazingly the engine fired first time. Then, just as he was about to drive off, he spotted a small piece of paper flapping in the breeze. Climbing out of the car, he snatched the paper from under the windscreen wiper. It was a note, written in pencil and read: *If you think this is bad, think of the damage I'm doing to your family.*

Diving back into the car, Tony's hands and arms trembled as he gripped the steering wheel. Pressing his foot down hard on the accelerator peddle the car took off. Bouncing over a couple of speed bumps, the car skidded out of the retail park before merging into the heavy traffic on the main road. Every traffic light seemed to be against him, every junction snarled-up. Shaking, his fingers tapped his home number into his mobile. It was constantly engaged and the more he tried the more he became anxious. Weaving in and out of the heavy traffic he took chance after chance. Jumping a couple of red lights, he drove through the country lanes as all sorts of thoughts flashed through his head.

What if, what if, what if?

Screeching around the corner, Tony's heart missed a beat when he saw Young's cab parked outside his house. Skidding to a stop, he had never moved so fast in his life. Jumping out of the battered car he sprinted up the driveway and burst through the front door. The hallway was quiet. Pushing open the lounge door, he found it empty, and then noticed the light coming from under the kitchen door.

Please God, please God.

His guts churned as he swung open the door.

'Daddy!' Relieved at the sound of Martha's sweet voice, he became horrified when he found Martha and Anne sitting across the kitchen table from Young.

'Hi,' said Anne. 'Mr Young was the taxi driver who picked us up from the supermarket.' Anne gave Tony a reassuring, if not embarrassed look.

'Daddy hates shopping,' said Martha to Young. 'He was at the lake the other day, remember daddy?' Tony struggled to find the words as he watched Young sip his coffee.

'I remember sweetheart.' Tony could smell him.

Anne spoke through her cough. 'Mr Young explained what he was doing there. He's a 'twitcher', like you said.' Anne raised her eyebrows and gave Tony a savvy look; it was a look between couples who knew each other inside-out, a look that said, *Help me. I need to get out of this situation.*

'A 'twitcher' watches birds Daddy.'

'I know.'

'Did you know that magpies fly in pairs Daddy?'

'Yes darling.' After a few seconds of uncomfortable silence Young stood up and placed the mug onto the table and looked across at Anne. 'Thank you for the coffee.'

'Martha, say goodbye to Mr Young.'

'Brian – my name's Brian.'

151

'Say goodbye Martha.'

'Goodbye, Mr Twitcher.' Young once again smiled at Martha, revealing his nicotine stained teeth to her for the first time.

'Goodbye Martha.' Tony felt sick. As Anne led Young to the kitchen door, Tony blocked her way. 'I'll see him out.'

Following Young down the hall, Tony could feel the rage boiling inside him. The urge to belt Young was immense. Holding back, the two men stepped outside. Then Tony pounced. Grabbing Young's left arm he thrust it up his back, then grabbing the back of his coat collar, he shoved Young's face hard into the red bricks of the house.

'You come near my family again and I'll kill you!' Young tried to wriggle free as he spoke through his distorted mouth. 'You owe me!' Tony growled down Young's ear. 'I owe you nothing!'

'You took my money!'

'I'll pay you back!'

'I don't want the money back!' Young pushed himself away from the wall with his right hand. Releasing his arm, Tony spun Young around and pushed him back against the wall. Close-up, he could smell Young's BO mixed with tobacco, it was ripe, putrid.

'If you don't want the money back, what do you want?'

'I want you to show me some respect.'

'What are you talking about?' Young pushed Tony away. 'You kept me waiting last night.'

'After what you did to my car, you're fucking mad.'

'You meet me tomorrow or you'll know what *'fucking mad'* is.' Barging past Tony, Young strode down the path towards his cab.

'Where?' Young climbed into his cab and looked back.

'I'll let you know.'

Tony watched as Young had the audacity to blow him a kiss as he drove off.

Walking back into the kitchen, Tony found Martha sitting at

the table, lost in a Walt Disney colouring book. 'Will you colour with me Daddy?'

'In a minute love.'

'Now Daddy.'

'I said in a minute!'

Anne was standing at the sink cutting vegetables with a large kitchen knife. 'Don't shout at her like that!' Leaning down, Tony kissed Martha on the cheek. 'I'm sorry darling, I'll colour with you in a minute.'

'Has he gone?' said Anne.

'Yes, but his smell hasn't.'

'He stinks Daddy.' Anne turned from the sink. 'That's enough of that Martha…Shit!' The knife dropped out of Anne's hand and bounced across the tiled floor. Blood dripped onto the chopping board. Quickly turning on the tap, she put her thumb under the cold running water. Martha came to investigate. 'Are you alright Mummy?'

Anne looked at the cut; it was just a nick. 'I'm alright darling, go back and colour.' Tony picked up the knife and inspected her thumb. 'You'll live.' Opening a cupboard, he reached into the back and slid out a first-aid box. Removing a plaster, he attended to her wound. 'What's for tea?'

'I'm bleeding to death and you ask me what's for tea.' Normally Anne had a good sense of humour but there was a blunt, coldness in her voice.

'Why did you let him in, I thought you said he was a nutter?'

'He really stank Daddy.'

'That's enough Martha,' said Anne. 'I wasn't sure about him at first, then he apologised for freaking us out at the lake the other day and was really nice to Martha on the way home, and he helped me in with all the shopping.'

Tony snapped. 'So you just invited him in because he helped you with the shopping and you felt sorry for him?' Anne nodded at Martha colouring as if to say *that little devil invited him in.*

'No, Martha asked him in for a cup of tea.'

'Sorry Daddy, will you colour with me now? Tony didn't answer. Sitting down next to Martha, he picked up a bright yellow crayon and started colouring-in Donald Duck's beak. Anne wiped the blood from the chopping board, then laid into the rest of the vegetables. It was then that Tony noticed the phone off the hook.

'Who's been using the phone?'

Anne looked at Martha. 'Did you take the phone off the hook Martha?'

'No Mummy.'

Tony looked across at Anne, *somebody did.*

As dusk fell, Anne stood drinking a cold beer. Looking through the French windows of the lounge, she watched as her husband walked around the lawn. Reading his mood swings, she knew he was still gambling. The good-old-days when she first met him at the wedding made her sigh heavily and take another drink. The beer was cold and tasted good, killing the bitterness in her mouth. He'd always been lean, always kept fit. With blond, shoulder length hair and a beard, when she first clapped eyes on him he'd reminded her of Jesus. How things had changed, some good, some bad. Martha was the good thing; the bad thing was his gambling addiction. She had warned him, time-and-time-again, the next time he slipped up, he would be out, it would be over. Deep down she wanted it to be an idle threat, hoping he would take heed and give up, but now that idle threat and her resolve were exhausted and she was being tested to the limit. She'd made idle threats before, but the hardest thing was to walk out and walk away from everything. In the shadows of the lounge, she needed a few minutes alone before confronting him. Sitting down in one of the leather armchairs, she looked around at the memories. On the middle shelf of an oak dresser a framed photograph of their wedding day brought a tear to her eye. Everyone had said how good they looked together, how they were made for each other, the perfect couple. Now they were on the verge of throwing it all away, all those years destroyed and for what, the roll of a dice? She thought of the life she could have as a single parent. She had thought about it many times. Something appealed to her; she could sell-up and move abroad with Martha, Tony wasn't keen on the sun, she adored it. She could get a job at the airport, or sell villas, she was pretty adaptable and Martha would be bilingual before she knew it. She might even meet somebody further down the line and get married again, then, another framed photograph of another marriage would sit on another shelf, somewhere in another house. Standing next to their wedding photograph was another of the three of them at her sister's wedding. She thought she looked pretty good, slim, with long hair. She could grow it again. Tony looked dapper in his suit and Martha looked adorable with flowers in her hair. She wondered what life held, not just for her, but for the three of them.

Anne found herself sitting in the dark, her thoughts interrupted by Tony's voice.

'What are you doing?'

'Nothing.' It's funny, Anne could lie as well as her husband when she needed to.

'Do you want another beer?' Switching on the light, Tony looked like a little boy lost. He knew what was coming.

'I need more than a beer Tony.'

Tony stood at the fridge. BLACK NUMBER 8 once again flashed through his mind. If only, if only, if only, none of this would be happening. Who was he kidding? Opening the fridge, he took two bottles of beer from the bottom shelf and removed the tops. Taking a deep breath, he walked back into the lounge, like a man about to face a firing squad he tried to prepare himself for the bullets. Handing Anne the beer he watched as she took a large gulp. The beer was ice cold, like the atmosphere in the room. Stony faced, she looked up. 'How much?'

'Twenty.'

'That means thirty or forty.' She looked at his face, it said more. She took another drink.

'Don't worry, I've sorted the bailiffs.' His voice was tearful in his lying.

'How?' Anne laughed.

'I cashed in an insurance policy at work.'

'*Our insurance money you mean*! And don't tell me, you'll never do it again'. There was calmness in her voice; for years she had prepared herself for this inevitable moment. Standing up she ran her index finger down the beer bottle removing the condensation from the label. 'You don't give a shit about Martha or me do you?'

'You know I do.'

'Well you don't, otherwise you wouldn't gamble away our lives as well as your own.'

'I'm sorry, I promise….' Anne placed her index finger on his lips, it felt cold. 'Don't promise Tony, please don't promise anymore.' Picking-up their wedding photograph off the dresser, she looked at it for a few seconds then handed it to Tony, her voice wounded. 'You have till Friday, if the money isn't put back into our bank account, you're out.' She steered her beer bottle into his hand. 'You drink it; I suddenly don't feel thirsty anymore.' Turning her back on him she left the room. Tony stood in the centre of the room with a bottle of beer in each hand; it had been a pathetic attempt of a peace offering. He could feel the coldness of Anne's touch on his lips and once again he thought of BLACK NUMBER 8, if only, if only, if only.

CHAPTER TWENTY-THREE

A list of the prison rules hung on the wall of visitors' room. 'No Drugs' in large red letters made it crystal clear. But they meant nothing to certain visitors who went to extreme measures to get illegal contraband inside the prison walls. Some nights the officers could smell the aroma of dope and crack floating through the prison. In the visitors' room passing drugs through the mouth via a supposed tender kiss was common and the officers who were always watching found it impossible to detect or prove. Like exam time in the gym of a secondary school, fifty or so tables, with two chairs to each table were spread out in regimented lines across the room. In approximately two hours' time the room would be heaving with families visiting their loved ones. All of them would have news to tell their sons, fathers or husbands. Some of the news was bad, some of the news was good, some indifferent, but one thing was for sure, 'inside' the cons could only sit and listen, they could do nothing about what was happening 'outside'. Children with dead eyes would ask their fathers when they were coming home. Their wives or girlfriends would make idle chit-chat to pass the time, tittle-tattle about a gas or electricity bill. That hour of precious visiting-time could seem like a lifetime. The visitors always had to make the conversation, the prisoners tried. A cynical place to break-up or ask for a divorce was visiting-time. 'Inside', the wives and girlfriends would have the protection of the officers who lined the walls. But the biggest nightmare for the long-term cons was dealing with their constant paranoia. Throughout the long days and nights, like the shadows, their minds would play tricks on them. Why did their wives want a divorce? Were their girlfriends being screwed outside, not just by one guy, but by two or three? What some cons blocked from their consciousness was that 'outside' could be a lonely place as well. When the bad news did come, it was like being belted with a sledgehammer and they usually went crazy. For the next couple of weeks or months they would be put on suicide watch, in solitary or Rule 43 as it was once called. But for this particular hour the visitors' room had been reserved for Finch and Finch only. Sitting in the centre of the room he looked a sad and lonely individual, lost, cut off from the outside world. A bored expression was washed across his face and he yawned like a baby after feeding time. Two officers stood either side of the one and only door that lead into the room. They were unfamiliar to Finch, but like all the other officers they had been trained to look out for the prisoners who received bad news at visiting time. Brainforth couldn't afford to take any risks when it came to violent contact with visitors and in Finch's case they had to be more than vigilant as he was high profile. Category A.

Charles Munro strode in through the door breaking the staid atmosphere. Tall, with a large stomach, short back hair and large-black glasses, he wore a cream coloured, double-breasted rain coat over a navy blue pin-striped suit and a red poker-dot tie. A visitor badge was tagged to his suit lapel and he carried a black briefcase, monogrammed in gold with the initials C.M. It wasn't hard to spot Finch sitting alone and he was given the nod by one of the officers to join him. Making his way through the lines of tables, Munro seemed nervous as his briefcase banged into a number of chairs. Every little sound echoed round the empty room as an overhead florescent strip-light hummed.

'Good afternoon. I take it you're Mr Finch?' Munro spoke with a soft, alluring Scottish accent.

'And I take it you're Mr Munro.'

'Yes, Mr Munro of Lynch and Forshaw.' Munro opened his briefcase, took out a folder and sat down opposite Finch. 'If you don't mind I'll get right to the point Mr Finch.'

'And time is money, isn't that right Mr Munro?'

'Absolutely Mr Finch.'

Munro stumbled through the words. 'In order for us to present your appeal to the Appeal Board Mr. Finch, you need to know the procedure. As your legal representatives we need to present new evidence that first warrants an appeal and second we need to present new evidence or evidence to the contrary that we can prove to the panel that in your court case there was evidence that perjures the police investigation in your case in some way, and more recently we need to prove that new evidence has come to the table that warrants a new trial. I would like you to study these forms and see if there is anything that you come across that you think will hamper or progress that appeal process. Do you understand Mr.Finch?'

'Absolutely Mr Munro.' Finch grinned.

'Good, let us proceed then.' Munro placed the palm of his hand on the folder and slid it across the table. Finch flicked opened the folder, then opening his glasses case, he perched his glasses on the end of his straight nose and started studying the documents. Munro looked around the stark room and smiled at one of the officers who didn't smile back. Removing a small bottle of water from the inside of his briefcase, he unscrewed the

159

top and took a drink. 'It's warm in here today.' Running the top of his fingers around the inside of his shirt collar he then produced a handkerchief from the inside of his jacket and dabbed his forehead and bulbous nose clear of perspiration. As he waited for Finch he removed a highlight marker from inside his briefcase and slid it across the table towards Finch. Eventually, Finch looked-up from the folder, the hoods of his dark eyes rising behind his glasses, and spoke at the same time. 'It looks alright to me, just two things.'

'Use the marker pen please,' said Munro, taking another drink from the bottle of water. Finch picked up the marker and started highlighting items in the folder. Taking less than four seconds, he shut the folder, put the marker on the top of the file and slid it back over the table. Opening the folder, Munro studied the highlights on the papers then popped it back into his briefcase and stood up. 'That shouldn't be a problem Mr Finch.'

'Call me Alistair.' Finch turned to look at the two officers and grinned, that grin that said *you two are next.* Munro removed a fob-watch from his waist coat. 'Is that the time already, so would you like me to proceed?'

'Absolutely,' said Finch, with a twinkle in his eye. Finch thrust his hand across the table alarming the two officers. Munro slowly readjusted his rain coat and then reluctantly shook his hand.

'Pity you couldn't stay longer, I could have given you a tour of the place.' Finch laughed. 'And thank you for fixing that other thing for me.'

Munro smiled nervously as he discreetly wiped the palm of his right hand on the side of his rain coat. Finch had once again left his mark.

Munro didn't exchange a look or a single world with the burly officer who escorted him through the prison. His mind was elsewhere. Protecting his hair from another sudden downpour,

Munro put his briefcase above his head and made a dash across the exercise yard. Passing through the security gates he caught a couple of officers giving him the evil-eye. He was well aware that the majority of officers didn't like *briefs*, particularly those that were trying to get a reprieve for a psycho like Finch.

The fresh air cooled Munro instantly as he left Brainforth, even the warm rain that flicked across his face was refreshing. Making his way onto the main road, he turned left and walked in the same direction as the traffic. Dwarfed by the huge prison wall running along side him, Munro loosened the top button of his shirt collar and blew a sigh of relief. Waiting for a gap in the traffic, he ran across the road. Skipping a number of puddles, he gave Brainforth one last glance before nipping down a narrow pathway that cut between two sets of council houses. At the end of the littered pathway, Munro found himself in a leafy side street. Stopping by a modest black Rover, he took shelter under an oak tree and rooted inside his deep pockets for his car keys. Noticing a bird had left its mark on the bonnet he looked up and down the road before removing his raincoat and opening the car door. Throwing his briefcase and coat onto the passenger seat, he jumped in.

Sticking two index fingers up each nostril, his eyes watered as he prised out the teats from a couple of baby's milk bottles. Removing his tie, the relief was instant. Pulling down the sun visor, he checked his face in the mirror, a bead of sweat mixed with black hair die had dribbled down the side of his cheek. Clawing at his face, he removed the false bulbous nose, then, with a handkerchief he wiped his face clear of sweat, dye and prosthetics. Taking off his suit jacket, he unloosened his trouser belt and unbuttoned his shirt. Reaching inside his shirt he removed body padding from around his waist then stuffed it out of view under the front seat.

Noticing a couple of students walking towards the car, he

turned his head and waited for them to pass by. Checking the side mirror that they had gone, he double-checked all around him. Flicking open the briefcase, he took out Finch's file. Sifting through the pages, he pulled out a large black and white photograph which was concealed in the papers of the file. It was taken outside St Benedict's Church. Three men had been circled by florescent yellow marker-pen, O'Connor and two other men.

Anders Riiss, Herman Bernstein, Charles Munro or whoever next was really pleased with himself. If nothing else Anders was a master of disguise and his Scottish accent wasn't bad either.

CHAPTER TWENTY-FOUR

Ripping open a small brown envelope, Tony read the scribbled note inside. It read: *Victoria Park Café at 4*. Young had left the note for him at the prison gate. Now he had gone to *his* home, sat at *his* kitchen table drinking *his* coffee, visited *his* place of work and he knew Martha and Anne by their first names.

'Martha is beautiful by the way, you're very lucky.'

Standing outside the prison gates, Tony felt nauseous, Young was turning the screw and the pressure seemed relentless. Looking up from the note, Tony noticed a number of women making their way across the car park. All of them carried some sort of token gift, something to pass the long hours that lay ahead. A magazine tucked under an arm, a book in a bag, a letter of hope from a friend. As they passed him, he caught the look on their faces. Some looked drawn, embarrassed, frightened, some hardened by years of prison visits. Scared with the stigma of having a son behind bars for a heinous crime, many of them had lost the will to ever smile again. As the gate closed behind them he wondered what life would be like on the other side and for a split second he could see Anne holding Martha's hand as they walked through the prison gates, the sounds which would haunt them, the smell of the place, the look on Martha's face, he felt it was that close.

Slumping into his car, Tony ran his hands over his face and tried to gather his thoughts. The back window had been taped up with a plastic sheet and gaffer tape, the bonnet sprayed with black paint partially hiding the *threat.* It was ready for the scrap yard. As hard as he tried, he couldn't remove Finch's grin and that blow on his cheek from his memory.

'Don't tell me you're afraid of a little affection?'

'I know you're up to your neck in debt.'

'Don't worry I can help you.'

As he drove out of the prison car park, it suddenly dawned on him that it was Wednesday. There were only two days left for him to pay the money back into the bank; otherwise Anne's threats for him to leave would become a reality. Then there was Young. The little he knew about his motivation the more it worried him.

'When the time is right I'll let you know.'

'I will contact you when I'm ready.'

Now contact had been made and he was playing to his tune. Young seemed determined, driven, and he wanted to be paid back in blood. At whatever cost.

Tony wondered what lay ahead of him.

Victoria Park was as recognizable to Tony as the freckles on Martha's face. He'd played football there as a kid many times and had taken Martha to see the public firework display on bonfire night. Parking up, he walked past the war memorial and glanced down at the inscription. *Remember our brave men who made the supreme sacrifice in the Great War 1914-1918.* A wreath of poppies lay at the granite base as a grandmother explained the significance to her granddaughter of the memorial and the poppies. Tony followed the path that wound its way down to a large lake which was surrounded by hilly banks and rhododendron bushes. On the far side, tucked behind one of the hills was the café. Once the jewel of the area, the park was now an eyesore. Vandalised, it had fallen into disrepair over the last couple of decades and the wooden rowing boats which you could hire and take out on the lake had long disappeared. Meandering around the lake, Tony passed a couple of kids fishing and a young couple kissing on a bench. Nearby, a line of tall chestnut trees which had stood there for hundreds of years were losing their copper coloured leaves to the approaching dark winter nights and underneath the sprawling branches a father and son were collecting conkers that littered the ground. Scattering pigeons as he walked he checked the time: 4:10, he was running late. Stepping up his pace, he passed a weeping willow and a large derelict fountain that was partially hidden behind wire fencing. At the end of the path he saw the lights of the café. Young was standing in the doorway smoking, he looked nervous, agitated. As Tony approached Young spotted him, quickly stubbed out his cigarette and disappeared inside. Walking up the café steps Tony side-stepped an old boy in a flat cap carrying an overflowing bowl of water for his dog to lap-up in the warm, evening sunshine. Passing a large cut-out of a 99 ice cream in the doorway Tony entered the café and was instantly hit by the smell of burnt chip fat and damp earth. Framed photographs of how the park used to look in its heyday covered the paint peeled walls and in the far corner two boys were playing a game of table football. The large room was surprisingly busy for that time of day as Tony scanned the room looking for Young. A couple of bearded joggers were ordering bottles of water from the service counter and sitting on green, plastic seats, a number of elderly walkers, wearing boots and anoraks were enjoying a conversation about the Battle of Trafalgar. Young waved, he was sitting in the corner of the room next to a large barred window overlooking the lake. To Tony's surprise, he wasn't alone. Sitting next to him were a smartly dressed, elderly couple both in their early seventies. As Tony made his way past the walkers, whose conversation had switched to the Battle of Waterloo, he noticed Young lean over and say something to the man, who instantaneously looked-up. 'Ah, you must be Tony, thank you for coming, my name is Gordon.' Gordon thrust out his hand. Well spoken, his upper-class English accent boomed-out round the room. Two hearing aids nuzzled deep inside each ear and the white pencil-moustache which ran the length of his top lip stood out from his suntanned face. Straight backed, Tony surmised that somewhere down the line; he had been a military man. Edgy, Tony obliged and returned the handshake. Gordon's grip was firm, from the old-school.

'Please sit down, I have ordered some tea and biscuits.'

Tony refused the invitation. Weighing–up the situation he gave Young a fixed stare.

'What's going on?'

'Sit down Evans!' Young's voice came from deep inside his gut.

'Please let me introduce you, this is Helen,' said Gordon. She offered her hand upwards, across the table. It was a bony grip and Tony tried not to squeeze too hard.

'What a handsome young man. Sit down poppet.' Tony caught Young's look again.

'Please take a seat Tony,' said Gordon reassuringly.

'Manners maketh-the-man poppet, please do as Gordon says and sit down.' Helen's voice was soft but firm, it reminded him of his mother. Reluctantly, Tony lowered himself into one of the seats opposite Helen. She had a waxy, white face, void of any makeup. Her skeleton like hands, with long protruding blue veins running along the back stroked the off-white coat of an old Jack Russell that was cradled in her lap.

'Please have some tea,' said Gordon, in a parade ground voice. 'I've taken the liberty of ordering a large pot.' Locking eyes with Young, like a couple of bare-knuckle boxers taking to the ring for the first time, Tony moved uncomfortably in his seat. A large pot of tea was placed on the centre of the table by a teenage girl with black laddered tights and black, fingerless-gloves. A large tattoo of a winged vampire swept up her forearm towards her shoulder and her loose, hanging bra strap. White gothic war-paint, struggled to hide the spots across her forehead and the numerous pins and studs that ran across her broad features gave her the unfortunate appearance of a pin-cushion. The table watched in silence as the goth poured the tea. 'Thank you darling.' Said Helen. The goth's black lipstick curled upwards as she returned the old lady a smile.

'You're welcome Helen.' Tony found the goth's voice surprisingly well spoken.

'Never judge a book by its cover poppet, she's a lovely girl,' whispered Helen to Tony, as if she was reading his thoughts. As the goth walked away, Gordon waited for the right time as his watery eyes made their way across the table. 'I must apologise for all this cloak-and-dagger-stuff, but we have a proposition for you.' His voice was loud and Tony was conscious of who might overhear him.

'This was my son.' Helen removed a silver chain and locket from around her neck. She delicately opened the locket with her frail fingers and dropped it into the palm of Tony's hand. Inside was a small photograph of a young boy in his school uniform.

'Please Helen, all in good time,' said Gordon, sympathetically. Tony felt claustrophobic and extremely uncomfortable. Sliding the locket back to Helen across the table he nodded at Young, then looked at Gordon. 'I've warned him about my family, if he comes near them again, he's asking for trouble.' Tony once again shifted nervously in his seat. 'What do you want?'

Gordon sipped his tea composing himself at the same time. 'I'm sorry Tony, let me explain. It must be about seven or eight years ago that a number of our paths crossed. We met at a memorial service and then later at a support group.' For the first time, Tony heard a nervous tension growing in Gordon's voice. He watched as Gordon took another sip of tea, cleared his throat and continued. 'We found, after a few meetings that we had one major thing in common, since then we have met on a regular basis, about once a month, planning our strategy....I believe you are a prison officer Tony?'

'Yes. What of it?'

'And you have daily contact with a prisoner called Alistair Finch?' Tony watched as Helen nervously turned the tea-cup around in her hands. 'I'm not at liberty to talk about prisoners and I don't like the way this conversation is going. I think I should leave.' Tony stood up.

'Sit down Evans!' snapped Young.

Helen reached across the table and grabbed Tony's wrist; her voice was brittle, her grip firm. 'Please Mr Tony; listen to what Gordon has to say. It won't do you any harm now would it, just to listen for a few minutes?'

Looking down at her face, he could see that as a young woman she must have been extremely attractive, but now her eyes were sunken into black circles. Her frail hand steered him back down into his seat. Gordon offered the plate of biscuits. 'Let me come straight to the point. We would like to offer you a lot of money to dispose of Alistair Finch.' Tony froze at Gordon's proposition, a look of astonishment across his face. Suddenly he became self conscious and looked around the café. He thought the two off-duty firemen who were sitting in the next table could have overheard them. It made him nervous, and then the penny dropped. Now he knew what Young wanted and what the money was for. 'You look at me as if I've lost my marbles and I can understand why. It's not everyday you get a proposition to kill somebody, but believe me we're deadly serious. We have given this a lot of consideration over the years.' Gordon opened Helen's locket and once again showed Tony the photograph of the young boy. 'This was Helen's son, he was just turning six.'

Helen struggled to find her voice. 'It was taken the day after he lost his front tooth playing football.' Tony looked at Young, then at Gordon and Helen. 'You're mad all of you.'

'Madness is a matter of opinion poppet.' Said Helen under veiled eyes.

'I'm sorry but you'll have to find somebody else.'

Young spoke through gritted teeth. 'You owe me money.'

'I told you. You can have it back.'

'When, in your dreams?'

'I'll get it to you.'

Gordon interrupted the two men. 'Please Brian, perhaps I should talk to Tony alone, for a short while.'

Young huffed. 'You're welcome to him. I need a smoke anyway.' Young left the table and walked out of the café.

'I'm sorry…' said Tony.

'We don't want your sympathy, if anything we're the lucky few, we had the opportunity to go to court; many people don't. We just want closure…We're prepared to pay you handsomely.' Tony leant in towards Gordon, out of ear-shot from the surrounding tables. 'What you're asking me to do is impossible, it's madness.'

'We will pay you on top of what you've already received, another eighty-five thousand.' Gordon looked over his tea cup.

'You could do a lot of things with that type of change in your back pocket.' Tony leaned back in his seat, his eyes dancing between Gordon and Helen. Anxiety ran through his body, but most of all he could feel the anguish and the determination of the people sitting opposite him. Leaning back over the table Tony shook his head at the insanity of it all. 'Do you mind me asking why you want him killed?' Helen once again reached over the table and rested her hand on the back of his. 'Why, poppet, he has to be killed, it's the right thing to do.' Stunned, Tony glanced out of the window. He saw Young staring in at him. 'I'm sorry, but please don't come near me again.' Confused by the outcome, Helen turned and looked at Gordon, her voice offhand. 'Isn't he doing it?' As Tony shuffled out of his seat, Gordon grabbed his arm. 'You are our only hope; we thought that you would understand, being a father yourself.'

'Sit down poppet; you make me feel uncomfortable standing there.' As Tony sprung up he accidentally knocked the side of the table spilling tea everywhere. Apologising under his breath he made his way through the walkers and joggers, before brushing passed the goth at the open door.

Flying down the stone steps, he started running. Passing the fountain, he ran along the winding path towards the lake. He could feel his chest tightening and stopped to find his breath. His head was spinning, the conversation he'd just had in the café felt like a dream. As he started walking, he heard footsteps running behind him. Turning, he found Young on his shoulder. Panting, his red face ragged with hate.

'Don't fucking walk away from us!'

'Get lost Young, I've warned you!'

'I don't think your wife will be too happy when she knows what you've been up to.'

'She knows, now what are you going to do?' Tony lengthened his pace. Trying to keep up, Young's smoker's chest started to wheeze as he spoke. 'Do you know what we have gone through to get you here?'

'You'll have to find someone else.'

'We tried; we smuggled a message into the prison. Put a price on Finch's head. Someone nearly *did him* in the showers, but now he's watched twenty four hours a day, you know that. There is nobody else, you have to do it!' Young made a desperate attempt to pull him back by the arm. 'You understand, you're a father, you can get to him for us.' Tony had enough; spinning around, he shoved both palms into Young's chest, pushing him onto the lakeside's grassy bank. 'Stay away from me!'

Reaching the edge of the park, Tony turned and looked behind. Young was still coming after him. Making a dash past the war memorial he skidded on some wet leaves nearly falling over. Regaining his balance, he made it to his car as Young started shouting as he ran. 'Do you know what he did to Helen's son?' Young's screaming caught the attention of an elderly couple walking a dog and a number of other people enjoying a stroll round the lake. Firing up the engine, Tony looked out the side window and saw the manic expression strewn across Young's face as he ran towards him. Thrusting the car into reverse, Tony spun the wheel, swinging the car around backwards. Skidding in the shale car park, the back wheels spat up grit and stones into the air. Young's fists came crashing down on the bonnet.

'You can plead self defence, make it look like an accident, you can say you where trying to protect yourself after he attacked you!'

'Out the way or I'll run you over!'

'I was named as a suspect, do you know how that felt?'

'Out of the way!'

'Listen to me!'

Tony revved the engine and jolted it forward causing Young to stumble to one side. Taking off, Tony looked back into the wing mirror, he could see Young climbing to his feet and heard him shout one last thing. 'He's an animal do you know what he did to them!'

As the car sped off into the distance, Tony took another look in the rearview mirror, at last Young had disappeared from view.

Driving erratically Tony was bursting with nervous tension. His arms shook as he grinded the gears of the car and he felt at any time Young would spring up from off the back seat and grab him around the neck. His imagination was mixed with irrational thinking and he was inside the deepest of holes. Taking in deep breaths, he tried to rationalise everything. Young wasn't going to take no for an answer, he had to box clever, think on his feet. He felt like the music from Hitchcock's 'Psycho' was lodged at the bottom of his brain as Young's last words kept coming back to him over and over again.

'He's an animal do you know what he did to them?'

Now those shouts of anguish weren't just from one person, but from three.

CHAPTER TWENTY-FIVE

Flashes of orange sunshine cut through the heat haze creating scary shadows between the climbing frames. The swing park was busy, full of children's voices. Sitting at a wooden picnic table Tony looked up from his newspaper. Perching his sunglasses on the end of his nose he shaded his eyes from the glare of the sun with his hand and looked around for Martha. Like a swarm of ants she was playing with a gang of kids on a climbing frame constructed like a pirate's ship. She waved, he waved back. Returning to his newspaper he turned a page and came across a picture of Finch smiling up at him. The headline read *Finch to appeal against life sentence.'*

'Come and push me Daddy.'

Martha was sitting on the swing. 'In a minute darling.'

Slowly, from out of the page the picture came to life. Finch's mouth started moving. *'So Tony do you know where the pound went to?'* Finch then pert his lips and blew up a kiss in his direction. The smell of his sour breath hit Tony's face like it had done before in Brainforth. Finch started laughing; as the laughing intensified the surrounding newsprint blurred, turning the print to bright orange. Finch's laugh stopped as Tony shut the newspaper. Shaking, once again he shaded his eyes from the sun with his hand and looked for Martha. Swinging slowly, Tony looked at an abandoned swing, its chains creaking, creaking as it swung. Looking around everywhere was aglow with orange. Children seemed to be running and playing in slow-motion, their voices muffled, distant. Tony couldn't see or hear Martha. Moving from the picnic table his legs felt like they were treading water. Wandering aimlessly around the swing park he turned in one direction then the next. Turning back again, he found himself walking around in circles, looking, searching, praying. Everything seemed hallucinogenic, orange. The newspaper dropped from his grasp and floated to the ground. Martha had disappeared, she was nowhere to be seen.

Panic. Orange flashes ricocheted off his glasses bouncing around the metal climbing frames of the swing park. He tried to scream out her name, again and again and again but nothing would come out of his mouth. Approaching two young mothers sitting on a bench he pleaded with them to help him search for his daughter. They looked at him with vacant faces, their pupils holding his like the yellow flash in a cat's eye. A young girl aged around the same age as Martha tugged his sleeve, he looked down and she started laughing at him, her voice gravely and deep. All the time the creak of the empty swing. Then he saw the tiny figure of his daughter. She was being bundled into the back of a white van. Two men in orange overcoats held her by the arms as she kicked and screamed for her life. One of the men turned and grinned at him, the other's face hidden by a black ski-mask. Tony sprinted across the swing park knocking a toddler, in a red duffle coat and her ice cream flying onto the sponge tarmac. Reaching the gate, he found it being padlocked by Jennings, his face wearing a broad grin. Knocking him to the ground; he opened the gate and side-stepped two snarling, stud-collared pit-bulls. Suddenly, he found himself running after the van down the centre of the main road. Oblivious to the danger of the oncoming traffic, he tried to scream for the van to stop, but found the words evaporate. As the van drove further and further away he tripped and crashed to the ground. Rolling over and over on the tarmac, he eventually slid to a stop, his knees bleeding through the rips in his trousers. Panting, panic-stricken he looked and saw Martha's face. Distorted with horror it was pressed up against one of the small windows in the back of the van. Then he saw the man's face, his mouth miming the words, *One little bet won't hurt Tony, one little bet won't hurt.* Then another man appeared at her side. Wearing an orange leather ski-mask, with a zipped mouth, he covered her mouth with his leather glove and pulled her down. Ripping off the mask he looked at Tony, it was a grinning Finch. As Martha vanished, the glaring headlights and grill of a prison van hurtled towards him. Looking up at the sky, Tony wept and wept and wept.

Springing up in bed, Tony was saturated in sweat. It was the third night on the run he had the recurring nightmare. Leaving his damp pillow he swung his legs out of bed and ran his hands around the back of his soaked neck. The vision of Martha's face, Finch and the other masked man was etched inside his battered head and he could feel himself sobbing as his chest continued to pound up and down. Lifting himself off the bed, he threw on a sweat-shirt and boxers. Switching on the light, the spare bedroom looked as depressing as ever. Peeking through the curtains, he blew a sigh of relief. He'd half expected to see Young's cab hanging around outside, but it was nowhere to be seen.

Making his way across the landing, Tony went into the bathroom, pulled the light cord and drained himself of last night's beer. After leaving Young in the park, he stopped off for more than one beer. Swilling his face in warm water, he wiped himself dry of the nightmare and sweat. In the reflection of the medicine cabinet mirror, he gave himself a reality check. *You look like shit Tony, death warmed up, if the Grim Reaper was standing by my side, I wouldn't know the difference.*

Studying the crow's feet around his eyes, he tried to convince himself there were no more than yesterday or the week before, but he was deluding himself, he looked ten years older. The stress was taking its toll.

Walking out of the bathroom, he crept into Martha's bedroom the same as he had done the three previous nights. She was sound asleep with her leg dangling over the side of the bed. Tucking her-up he listened to her sleeping. Her breathing was therapeutic, like the purr of a sleeping cat. Looking at her sleeping, the love welled-up inside him and his eyes filled with tears.

Wide awake, he decided to go downstairs and make himself a strong cup of coffee. Staring into the blackness outside the kitchen window, his thoughts went back to the conversation in the park. Setting up the laptop on the kitchen table, he turned it on. Slowly it flickered to life. The screen partly illuminated the kitchen, its white screen reflecting in the blackness of the window. Programming the internet, he tapped in the words: *Newspapers. 1989. Front pages.* Scrolling the menu, he came across the month of *July*. The more he read the more he became engrossed in the newsprint. Sipping his coffee, his eyes narrowed and pierced the screen as he read the headlines:

Finch convicted of killing twins.
Police believe Finch has killed before.
Life for Twins' killer.
Monster gets Life.

Tapping the keyboard, a number of photographs of Finch slowly appeared on the screen. The first photograph was familiar to Tony; it was the face of the murderer wearing that grin which had appeared on every front page of every newspaper across the world. A couple of photographs were snapped of him being pushed into the side door of a white van by two security guards and two were of Finch as young boy wearing his school uniform, and one of him holding hands with his mother outside the front door of a terraced house. The last photograph was of a press conference. Hunched behind a long table and a bank of microphones, a mother and father's haunted expressions were flanked by senior police officers handling the case. More headlines read:

Government under pressure to bring back the death penalty.

Families will not rest until they have justice.

Families want meeting with PM.

Another article graphically told of how Finch abducted and murdered two seven year old twins. It reported on how Finch callously buried their bodies in a shallow grave in woods outside Oxford and how he was arrested by the police after they received an anonymous tip-off.

Tony felt a draught from the kitchen door as it swung open. As his eyes left the screen, Martha appeared in the open doorway clutching her teddy bear. She was half-asleep and was rubbing her eyes. Tony picked her up and sat her on his lap.

'What are you doing up sleepy head?'

'I had a bad dream Daddy.'

'We all get those from time-to-time sweetheart.'

'This monster had big eyes.'

'Well you know there is no such thing as monsters, don't you?'

'Yes, but it was horrible.'

'Well nobody will hurt you darling, because I will always be here.'

'Can I have a chocolate biscuit please Daddy?'

'It's the middle of the night sweetheart, come on back to bed.' Turning off the laptop he picked Martha up in his arms and carried her back upstairs to her bedroom. She smelt sweet as he tucked her back into bed with her teddy. Stroking her brow he watched as she slipped back into a deep sleep. She looked like an angel, his angel, his little girl. Watching Martha sleep once again his thoughts wandered back to the café and the conversation he had with Gordon and 'the proposition'. He pictured Helen's black, hollow eyes looking across at him and thought about the abduction and murder of her son and what Finch had done to the children. A shiver went through his body. It was every parent's nightmare.

Tony crept back into the spare room and into the single bed. Looking around the room, he thought, *is this what it's come down to?* Trying to sleep was pointless, his eyelids flickered with restless and unnerving thoughts, could he really be tempted to commit a murder or would he just be reaping revenge for every mother and father in the country that would happily pull the trap door or pull the trigger on a monster like Finch. Rolling over, he found himself looking up at a pencil-thin shaft of yellow light that ran across the artex-ceiling from the street light outside. How would he do it? If he was to become a murderer, he had to make it look like an accident; he had to be alone with Finch. A major problem was that Category A prisoners were wrapped in cotton wool, handled by two officers at all times, always. Then there was a security camera positioned in the corner of his cell. Every nook and cranny was taped twenty-four hours a day. It wouldn't be an easy job. Then there was the insecurity of knowing that at any time Young or Gordon could shop him to the police. He had to cover his tracks. The money would have to be in notes, avoiding a large amount of cash being deposited into his bank account was imperative.

What the fuck am I thinking about; murder?

178

The money, the money, the money, I need the money.
BLACK NUMBER EIGHT.
Finch, Young, Gordon, Helen's eyes.

Rolling over not for the first time, Tony's eyes closed then shot open again. Sitting up in bed, he found himself clawing at his face.

God help me, I'm about to lose everything.
The money.
Murder.

The money would solve most of his problems, also BLACK NUMBER 8 and the nightmares that just wouldn't disappear, but at what cost?

CHAPTER TWENTY-SIX

Anders' eyes were heavy, very heavy. The long drive through the night was hard on the energy levels and apart from forty-winks in a service station after a luke-warm Americano he'd gone without sleep for almost thirty six hours. His face distorted into a wide yawn, sending a cloud of mist around the inside of the car. Wiping away the condensation from the near-side window, the view of the King's Head suddenly became clear again. Looking at the car's digital clock it registered 11:45AM. It wouldn't be long, maybe another hour or so, Anders was used to waiting.

As the last of the remaining drunks staggered out of the pub, Anders spotted the man he was waiting for. He was tall, large, with a pot-belly and the shoulders of a Silverback. Wearing a white shirt, dickie-bow and black bomber-jacket he shivered as he lit up a cigarette in the pub doorway.

An argument turned into a cat-fight between two pissed, teenage girls on the street corner. Blowing smoke rings into the night air, the bouncer watched, unperturbed, he laughed, he'd seen it all before. Quickly removing a photograph from a brown envelope, Anders checked it in detail. Tilting the photograph towards the street light, he focused on the man in the picture. It was the photograph he'd shown Finch the previous day in Brainforth. Check, double-check. Although Anders' eyes weren't as sharp as they used to be, there was no mistaking the man circled by a fluorescent marker, outside the church. Standing next to the priest, it was the same man who was standing in the pub doorway. The bouncer flicked his cigarette onto the pavement as the fight was broken up by a couple of young policewomen. Show over, the bouncer slipped back inside the pub, slamming the large wooden doors behind him. Anders sat waiting as another yawn hit him, he had to be on his toes when the bouncer came out, he had to be ready, no mistakes. Trying to keep awake, he ran his hands over his face and rubbed his eyes. As he slapped both of his cheeks the pub door opened and the bouncer came down the steps and into the fresh, night air.

Making his way across the street, Anders found himself stiff from the long drive and tried to loosen-up as he walked. Keeping his distance, he realised the bouncer was bigger than he first thought. Hunched over, the door-man had his hands deep inside the pockets of his bomber-jacket and swaggered with an attitude as if to say, *just try your luck, I dare you.*

Turning the first corner, a young drunken couple sharing a bag of chips bumped into him. Barging through them like a bull, some of the chips spilled onto the pavement. Anders didn't catch the expletives exchanged between the three of them but he knew from the deep tones of the voices they weren't swapping phone numbers.

Anders quickened his pace after the man. Turning a corner, then another, he found himself walking down a dark High Street full of shop windows hidden behind metal shutters.

A group of imposing hoodies hung-around the dim neon light of a Greek take-away. As the bouncer shot inside, the fluorescent lights of the take-away revealed his broad features for the first time. Walking past the hoodies, Anders sneaked a look through the window at the man's face he was about to murder. At a quick glance he looked about thirty five. The photograph didn't do him any favours, he was younger, much stronger; he would be a challenge.

Walking across the road Anders ducked into a dark shop doorway. As he watched he thought to himself, *How ironic, the man I'm about to kill was having his last meal, like a prisoner waiting for the electric chair or a lethal injection on Death Row.* The man was at the back of the queue and Anders' tiredness was now running on adrenaline, hopefully, soon, he'd be in a bed sleeping away his sins.

Carrying a white plastic bag, the man turned right out of the take-away and continued walking down the dark street. Anders stepped out of the doorway running a gauntlet of abuse from the hooded lads who had nothing better to do. If only they knew.

After another couple of roads and another couple of streets, the man turned his final corner. Anders watched as he passed an elderly man walking his dog; they knew each other and Anders thought he caught his name, something he didn't want to know. It might have been Alan. Opening a small wooden gate, the bouncer took two steps up the path to the front door of his terraced house. Placing his take-away on the door step, he bent down and lifted up a flower pot that held the grey stalks of dead geraniums. Slipping the key from underneath the pot, he placed it in the door and froze. The cold presence behind him was instant. As the leather gloved hand wrapped itself over his mouth, the steel of a large serrated camping knife plunged into the base of his back. The bouncer reared back grunting. Screwing the knife deeper and deeper into his body, Anders tightened his grip round the man's mouth. He was strong and he wasn't going to die without a fight. Anders tightened his stomach muscles preparing himself for the man's elbow to swing back into his ribs, it never came. His last bit of strength went to his fingers as they dug deep into the leather glove gripping his mouth. Anders pulled the knife out of the man's body, drew it back then plunged it again into his kidneys. Just to make sure, he withdrew the knife and did it again and again.

At what seemed a snail's pace, the man's fingers finally dropped from Anders' glove and he could feel the strength and the power slowly seep from his arms. Becoming limp in Anders' grip, the man's legs buckled, his large frame dropping to his knees on the front door step with a heavy thud. Anders couldn't hold him. Slumping forward his head crashed against the panel of the stained glass door. Anders waited for a light to appear inside, it didn't come, lucky for someone. Wiping the blood off his knife onto the man's jacket, he pulled up his trouser leg and slipped the knife back into the sheath that was strapped to his leg. Rolling the man's body over to one side, Anders grabbed the heels of his boots and dragged his body round the side of the house. Leaving him hidden behind a wheelie-bin, he started singing quietly to himself.

'There's no regrets.
No tears goodbye.
I don't want you back.
We'd only cry, cry again.
Say goodbye again.'

Returning to the front of the house, Anders looked up at the first floor windows across the street. He heard a dog barking, somebody putting out empty milk bottles, laughter from a television set, a plane passing overhead. All was clear, a clean hit.

Closing the gate behind him, Anders paused, then went back and picked up the take-away off the step. Making his escape his breathing was heavy, this had been a difficult kill, the struggle of the big guy had been tough. Conscious of the street lights crossing his face, he spotted the old man with his dog walking towards him. Lowering his head, Anders started to stagger like a drunk. Whistling *Waltzing Matilda,* Anders saw the man cross over the street to avoid the drunk. Job done, no stone unturned. Anders was always on the ball.

Walking, he wondered. What went through a man's mind seconds before a knife plunged into their kidneys or a bullet hit the back of their head? He questioned whether it was necessary to fire another couple of bullets through their heart or knife them more than once, but he was a serial killer and for his peace of mind he had to make sure. Although he could describe himself as a *carpetbagger*, he had certain rules which he religiously abided by. He lived by his rules. He didn't want to know who his victim or victims were or what they did for a living, or how many children they had, that was his clients' business and no concern of his, but this job was different; he'd never been hired from a prison cell before. He knew why Finch was banged up, he'd done his research, but when someone is prepared to pay an extortionate amount of money for the hire of his services, how could he refuse, this was one job he couldn't turn down and morals didn't come into the equation.

That night Anders slept like a baby in the double bed of his hotel room. By the side of the bed was the remnant of that night's Donor Kebab.

CHAPTER TWENTY-SEVEN

Every time Tony closed his eyes he saw faces, heard voices and saw that number, his mind was in freefall. 4AM. Tony was wide awake and had stared at the ceiling long enough. Climbing out of bed, he found himself standing naked in the centre of the room. Deep in thought, he started shuffling around on the small visible space between the boxes and bed. Wrapping his arms around his body, his ice cold hands griped each muscular bicep. After a while he snapped out of his mental torture and came to a decision, a decision he knew he had to make, a decision he was forced into making. Once and for all, he was going to try and work out the connotations of becoming a murderer.

Murder, how could he live with himself, the guilt?

Every time he looked at himself in the mirror who would stare back at him?

What would his daughter see in his eyes?

What if he got caught? Prison? Public humiliation for his family. Like the visitors he'd seen going into the prison the previous day, Martha would become one herself. She would have that look, that blank face, void of a smile, of life. How could he subject her to a lifetime of visits? As an ex-screw inside, he wouldn't last five minutes in a place like Brainforth. Inconsolable in his desperation he saw the faces of the people who would congratulate him, applaud him for killing Finch, but it did nothing to deter the hopeless anxiety on the decision he had to take.

What about an internal investigation?

What about a public enquiry?

'Fuck, fuck, fuck!'

He had to be spot on, direct, determined, calculated, everything worked out to the finest detail. He would have one chance with Finch and one chance only. It would have to be quick when no one was looking, out of view from big brother, Jennings and the other officers.

Think of the money, the money.

The end of my worries, the end, the end, the end.

5:55AM. How am I going to do it? Murder.

Tony jumped when the alarm clock triggered. Shivering, he pressed the off button and realised he been standing in the centre of the room for hours. Swiftly getting dressed, last nights sweet smell of Martha on his tee-shirt was quickly replaced by the lingering odour of Brainforth that was ingrained into his prison uniform.

Outside it was still black, a layer of frost clinging to the lawn and the surrounding flower beds. Switching on the radio, Tony listened to the news headlines whilst buttering a slice of toast. Glancing at the laptop on the kitchen table he remembered the photographs and the headlines he'd read in the early hours. Suddenly he lost his appetite. Tipping the toast into the peddle-bin, his stomach felt poisoned with guilt as he thought of Anne and Martha sleeping upstairs. Quietly closing the front door behind him, Tony questioned himself one last time before setting off to work. *Am I prepared to become a news headline myself?* As from today Brainforth would take on a different meaning, a different purpose; Tony's life would never be the same again.

CHAPTER TWENTY-EIGHT

Young walked out of the doctor's surgery and nearly under the wheels of a large, people-carrier. Elsewhere, he was totally oblivious to the screech of its brakes and the obscenities screamed at him by the driver, a hefty looking skinhead wearing a wax jacket. With the word *'wanker'* ringing in his ears, he just made it across the busy road, tripping over the curb in the process. Turning around, he looked back at the driver's thunderous face and mimed back at him, *'Any time pal!'* Then he noticed two rosy-cheeked kids sitting in booster seats in the back. He felt sorry for them, what an angry dad, what an angry world they were being brought up in, God help them.

Thinking twice about turning left, he turned right and passed the graffiti strewn wall of the public toilets. Two council workers, wearing white paint-spattered bib and braces were about to start work and paint over the spray-painted obscenities until the next time. The Laurel and Hardy look-a-likes took him back to his school days and The Adventures of Tom Sawyer, the book he used to love to read as a kid and the picket fence that Tom was ordered to paint white. Walking away from the toilets, the Hardy of the two workers turned on a radio blasting out the latest 'teen' pop sensation, killing the vision of his childhood memory for a couple of seconds. Then as quickly as it disappeared he returned back to Huckleberry Finn and Indian Joe and the raft on the Mississippi River, what an adventure.

Young clinked opened the creaking gate and stepped into a large rose garden. Walking telepathically around the path he passed a hunched over green keeper racking up leaves and nodded 'hello'. Taking in the damp aroma from the flower beds and the cluster of bare rose bushes that lined the edges of the lawns he passed a sun-dial and found himself at the end of the garden next to a wooden bench which was partially shaded by the bare branches of a birch tree. For a few minutes he watched some sparrows flapping around in a nearby birdbath before sitting down. He'd sat there many times, sometimes for hours, deep in thought, staring into space. Behind his back, screwed onto the bench, was a small brass plaque. Engraved were the words: *To Dear John, love forever.* Closing his eyes he felt the warm sun breaking onto his face through the branches and circulating rain clouds. Unloosening his shirt collar, he caught a smell that took him back thirty years to a holiday in Cornwall. The smell and the swirls of the waves were instant as he walked along the long sandy beach and he could feel the sea spray on his face. Ice creams. The taste ran across his lips as he saw swimming costumes drying on the line outside a line of caravans, then fish and chips wrapped in newspaper. Good times, happy times. As a trainee doctor he'd been working twelve hour shifts in paediatrics and it was a well deserved holiday after a hard academic and practical year. Over the next thirty years the family would enjoy many holidays together. One year they went to the South of France. They loved the stone chateau they rented, swimming in the sea and dining alfresco, but that summer in Cornwall always flooded back to him when he sat on that special bench.

Slowly the slate-grey clouds moved over the sun. Young had sat there for over an hour and suddenly felt cold. It was time to go. Lifting himself up from the bench with a grunt, he pulled the collar of his coat tight around his neck and shivered. Turning, he looked at the plaque on the bench. Kissing his index finger, he touched the plaque tenderly. Seeing he'd left a finger print on the brass, he wiped it clean with the elbow of his jacket then walked away. Making his way back down the path, he looked up to the sound of the gate opening and saw a woman coming into the garden. Discreetly shooting behind a nearby oak tree, he sneaked a look at the woman. She had copper-red hair, with a small, port-wine birth mark on the side of her cheek. Aged around fifty, she was trendy for her age, wearing flared jeans, with black boots underneath a long black coat. Underfoot, he could smell the wet earth seeping up from the tangled tree roots as he followed the woman walking through the garden. Stopping at the same bench, he watched as she affectionately touched the engraved plaque before sitting down. He could see she was feeling the cold. Shivering, her shoulders were hunched forward as her gloves clung to the leather handbag on her lap. Spellbound by the woman's beauty, he watched for a short time as her hair ruffled in the breeze. Stepping out from behind the tree he headed towards the gate. With one hand on the gate he turned and looked back in her direction. She had seen him and smiled. It was a sad, tranquil smile. Her eyes recognised him and he was aware that the two of them would bump into each other again. Today she had been early, or was she late, Young couldn't remember, but like him she would always be there.

Passing the painters whistling in unison, Young removed from his inside pocket a screwed-up doctor's prescription. Just like the prescriptions he used to prescribe for his patients a long time ago he studied the recommended dose. Sighing heavily he tore-up the prescription and scoffed slightly as the bits of paper hovered in the air like confetti before floating down into the gutter. Climbing into his cab, he lit a menthol and closed his eyes for a few minutes. He felt exhausted, tired of it all.

Then thoughts of the prison officer once again came to him. Thumping the steering wheel with the side of his fist, it was time for him to get nasty, really nasty. It was time the prison officer was paid another visit. Starting the engine he noticed the woman from the garden walk across the street and go into a newsagent next to the doctor's surgery. The news stand outside read: *Polish Immigrant Murdered in Door Step Slaying.*

CHAPTER TWENTY-NINE

Strolling around the exercise yard, spots of rain fell onto Finch's face. It was cold, the heavy clouds overhead ready to break at any second. Every couple of steps, Finch would stop and do some exercises. Bending down he touched the top of his shoes with his fingers tips, then, swinging his arms around in a windmill motion he inhaled deeply and stretched some more. Now and again he would repeat the routine; it was for his benefit and whoever wanted to spy on him, from the cell windows, from the officers, from the Governor high-up in his palace. He knew when their eyes were on him, he liked performing. Using his fingers as a comb, he ran them through his hair and took a sly glance across the yard. Cracking his knuckles, he knew Tony's eyes were on him and grinned to himself, it was starting to turn him on.

Rogers came through a security gate and spotted Tony scrutinising Finch through the wire. Shaking his head he cursed under his breath and started trotting across the yard.

Sidling up alongside Tony, Roger's tone was impatient. 'He's got to you big time hasn't he?'

'What are you talking about?'

'You know what, the missing pound?'

'Don't start that crap again.' Tony felt the spots of rain and looked up. 'It looks like it's going to piss down at any minute.'

Rogers took his gaze from Tony to Finch. 'Look at him prancing around, God's gift to the Devil. It makes you wonder what turned a sweet little kid into a loon like Finch'

'We've all got a history, sometimes it's genetic.'

Rogers tapped his temple with his index finger. 'Some thing's aren't right with certain people. He for one shouldn't be allowed to walk the earth for what he did.'

Finch looked over at the two officers; Rogers tapping the side of his head had given the game away. He knew they were talking about him; apart from being watched all the time, he was used to people talking about him, the looks, the whispers of hate. Then he smiled, fame, as they say was an aphrodisiac.

Jennings walked out of A-Block and stood at the top of the stone steps readjusting his tie and shirt collar. Observing every small detail of the prison with a piercing glare, he looked down on *his patch, his prison.* His stance always meant business, hands clenched behind his back and his polished boots at ten-to-two, the only thing missing was a line of medals pinned across his chest. Clocking Rogers he nodded for him to come over.

Rogers sighed. 'Bloody hell, what does he want?'

As Rogers walked over to Jennings, Finch saw his opportunity. Taking a couple of steps towards Tony he leant on the fence and spoke out the corner of his mouth like a ventriloquist.

'How are you today?' Tony didn't answer. 'Please talk to me I've been starved of good conversation for ages.'

Tony ignored him.

'Intelligence can be frowned upon in some circles. Narrow

minded circles.' Finch shot a glance through the wire at Tony then back to the two officers across the yard. 'I know a lot about you Tony.'

A look of distain shot across Tony's face. 'Shut your mouth Finch, you know nothing about me.'

'I know more than you think. They've got to you haven't they, the ones that want me dead, the taxi driver and his friends?' Finch turned slightly and gave Tony a sarcastic look. 'I get regular fan mail from Young; the really nasty ones make interesting reading.' Tony was stunned; he couldn't believe what he was hearing. He looked across at Rogers and Jennings who were deep in conversation, out of earshot. Looking up, he glanced at the Governor's window then around at the barred windows. In Brainforth there were no hiding places. Finch continued with a relaxed, somewhat sleepy tone to his voice. 'I can't reply to Young's letters unfortunately. I would like to, just to be polite, let him know how much I appreciate them – I know they've tried to have me killed on more than one occasion, the sneaky attacks. It's flattering really having a bounty on your head. But it hasn't worked, they must be really frustrated. One of them came after me in the showers, I was naked, I didn't think that was cricket, do you? Then I worked out their next logical move, you have a lot of time in here to work things out. They would have to bribe someone who sees me regularly, someone who can get to me really easily. Someone who needs the money, it doesn't take a brain surgeon to work out who that could be. That leaves only one person I can think of, eh Tony?' Finch did a little skip of satisfaction. 'There's a little present for you in the wire?' Tony peered down, wedged into the wire of the fence was a small, rolled-up photograph. Discreetly slipping the photograph out of the wire, he concealed it in the palm of his hand. Finch wolf whistled at a prisoner passing on the other side of the wire. Suddenly a line of spit shot through the wire from the prisoner's

194

mouth hitting Finch on the side of his cheek. As the prisoner sniggered and walked away, Finch didn't baulk or react; he just calmly wiped his cheek with the cuff of his sleeve and looked up at the sky as more rain drops fell. Opening his hand, Tony looked down at the photograph. A spot of rain hit the snap, it was slightly unexposed, but he could make-out it was of himself, Martha and Anne at her sister's wedding the previous year. He was wearing a suit and Anne and Martha summer dresses. His stomach churned. Looking up he met Finch's grin. The pent up anger inside his body was at boiling point. It would have been far too easy for him to beat the living shit out of him there and then, but he had to control himself, he had to use his training, he had to deal with it. His time would come. Slipping the photo into the breast pocket of his shirt, he watched as Finch paraded himself around the yard like peacock.

'Where did you get it?'

'I've had it for a while; I thought I recognised you from somewhere when I first clapped eyes on you.'

'Where did you get it?'

'That's a long story.'

Tony could feel that right hook tightening. 'I said where did you get it?'

'Tony, I am here to help you. The photograph is irrelevant, it came from where it came from. I know that doesn't make sense at present, but it will – Do you believe in chemical castration? You see, many people want *so called* sex offenders like myself, to be castrated. I'm guilty of a number of things, but you see Tony I'm not guilty of what I'm in here for – I can see by the sarcastic expression on your face that you've heard that old-chestnut a thousand times before, but I am telling you the truth. In here I've learnt over the years to be realistic about ever being released. If, eventually they were to ever find me innocent, it wouldn't be long before they conjured up some other hideous crime to get me

195

locked-up for another life sentence and, after all, I am an evil bastard who deserves to have his balls cut off.' Tony heard his teeth grinding and rattled the wire. 'Where did you get the photograph?'

'Relax Tony, I'll tell you, if you do a little favour for me?'

Tony sneaked another glance across at Jennings and Rogers. They were engrossed in conversation and for a split second Roger's laugh broke the tension that hung in the air. 'What do you want?'

Finch sighed, a loud lingering sigh. 'About a month ago I had a vision, an angelic visitation, the whole of my cell turned bright white and standing there was an angel. She said one thing, *it's time'*, then she repeated it, *'it's time'* – It's so tiring looking over your shoulder all the time in this place, the stress some days is overwhelming. It gives you a permanent headache. I'm also bored – I've worked out how and when. You don't have to worry about a thing.'

'What are you talking about?'

'I want your help – to kill me, help me commit suicide.'

'Hey nonce your hours up!' Roger's voice came from across the yard.

Finch turned and looked through the wire with menace. 'Don't underestimate me Tony; I usually get what I want.'

As Finch was let out the gate the two officers grabbed both arms. Jennings looked at Tony with a smirk across his face. 'You want to watch him Mr Evans, he'll be having wet dreams about you.'

'Why, are you jealous Mr Jennings?' Pain shot across Finch's face as Jennings' fingers dug deep into his arm. Rogers gripped the other arm and growled down his ear. 'It's shower time.'

Then Jennings sneered down the other ear. 'And you know what can happen to you in there don't you Lollypop?'
Suddenly the clouds burst open and the rain poured down onto the rooftops of Brainforth.

CHAPTER THIRTY

Anders belched, the large English breakfast he had eaten two hours earlier in a service station kept on repeating and he could still taste it inside his mouth. The news about *The Doorstep Slaying* had been on television, on the radio and in every newspaper.

A national hunt by the police was under way to find the killer. Door-to-door enquiries around the area where the Polish immigrant, who worked as doorman, was callously murdered had begun. Either way, Anders knew his job inside-out and had left nothing to chance. Once again he went back over his tracks. Who would have seen him? The hooded youths, they looked drunk or high from sniffing glue. They wouldn't have noticed anything. Then there was the old man walking his dog. He was the only other witness; he would have described to the police a staggering, Australian drunk who he had to avoid by crossing the road. For the time being he could relax.

To help kill the boredom, Anders started manicuring his fingernails with his teeth whilst listening to a Spanish Language tape. As the gravely voice blurted out of the car's cassette payer, he repeated the words to himself in Spanish, 'Uno, dos, tres, cuatro.' then, on the count of 'cinqo' he heard the click of the latch on the churchyard's wooden gate. Switching off the tape, Anders watched as the man swung open the gate and stepped into the grounds of the church. He was later than Anders expected, but he knew he would come, human intuition can be predictable and he was a master of it. Tall, spindly with a distinctive rolling walk, Anders didn't bother to check whether it was the third man in the photograph, the way he strode conspicuously up the gravel path and passed the gravestones said everything.

As the man disappeared into the church, Anders nervously strummed his fingers on his knee. Noticing a dim yellow light appear at the bottom of the church wall he flipped open the glove compartment. Reaching inside, he removed a revolver. Screwing a silencer onto the barrel, he slipped the gun inside his raincoat. Reaching over the front seat, he removed a trilby and round, wire framed glasses from off the back seat. As always, every fine detail was observed as he placed the trilby on his head and tucked his long blond hair behind his ears. Wiping the lenses of the glasses he slipped them on. Opening the lid of a small battered tin with the words *Fisherman's Friend* indented on the lid, he removed a false moustache and fixed it across his top lip. Checking himself in the rear-view mirror, he was once again ready.

Following in the same footsteps as the man, Anders made his way up the church path and over to the side of the church. Instantly becoming aware of the noise his shoes had made on the gravel pathway he looked around the churchyard for anyone in the vicinity. All clear, he peered down into the crypt. The mottled glass of the crypts skylight was partly covered in shrubbery making it difficult to see below. But Anders could make out two dark figures moving in the dingy yellow light and hear their voices over the rumble of machinery. Shadowing the side of the church, Anders passed a stone, weather-beaten statue of St Benedict before reaching the corner of the church. Stopping, he noticed a young woman in a bright purple overcoat crouching down at an overgrown grave. Her long blonde hair hung over her face as she spoke quietly to the earth. Still mourning, she brushed away tears before laying some flowers at the headstone. Anders moved quickly. Cushioning his footsteps, he stepped off the gravel footpath onto the grassy verge. Engrossed in prayer the woman didn't notice the darting figure quietly entering through the heavy wooden door of the church.

At the same time he glided passed the framed photograph of O'Connor in Rome, the clock tower rang out. Each peal echoed inside, scattering a number of pigeons off the hammer beamed roof outside. Reunited with the smell of damp hymnbooks, Anders grimaced at the chimes of the church's bell as it sent ripples across the water in the christening font next to him. Still, like a mannequin, Anders stared like a hawk down the aisle towards the altar. Slowly the house of worship fell silent but the echo of the bells remained in Anders head. Glancing around the church, he noticed a thin yellow light creeping under the small wooden door of the vestry. Leaning forward, he straightened his right leg, keeping the sole and the heel of his foot firmly on the stone floor. Stretching, he heard his achilles crack. Then, he started revolving his right ankle, one way and then the other. Crack, then another crack and another. Never taking his eyes from the vestry door, he repeated the exercise with his left leg and ankle. Standing upright he revolved his neck then patted his coat for his gun. Slipping on a pair of leather gloves, he removed some loose change from his trouser pocket and left it on the collection plate.

Striding down the aisle past the lines of pews, Anders paused at the pulpit were O'Connor had stood pontificating the previous

Sunday morning, his rhetoric and prayers long disappeared. A few feet away from the vestry door, he noticed it was slightly open and he could hear muted voices coming from down below in the crypt. As the eyes of the Virgin Mary on a biblical tapestry looked down on him, he removed the revolver from inside his raincoat. Flicking off the safety-catch he gripped the gun in his right hand. Ready for the kill, adrenaline pumping, he slowly pushed open the creaky door, ducked under the carved, lintel and stepped inside. Swinging his gun around the vestry like a gunslinger, Anders' finger shivered on the trigger. Beams of blue and red sunshine streamed through a thin stained glass window onto a number of crisp, white, choir boy smocks which hung around the mahogany panelled walls. The smocks looked like floating ghosts and he expected at any second one would spring to life and attack him. His trigger finger relaxed. *Ghosts, get a grip Anders.* Composing himself he took a deep breath and quietly breathed out through his mouth, taking time for that crooked smile.

The voices from below had become louder and clearer; mixed with the rumble of a machine Anders overheard two men having an argument. The wooden door leading to the voices and the crypt below opened inwards. Stepping inside the door, stone steps wound down a tight stairway. Guiding himself down the stone walls with his left hand, the gun unexpectedly felt heavy and he felt himself gripping the handle tighter than he'd ever done before. His heartbeat raced across his chest as his legs felt weak, it was as if he'd been suddenly struck down with some mystery illness. Spotting a flicker of light at the bottom of the stairway his index-finger finger hovered once again with the trigger, was he ready? Wiping away the sweat from his brow, he held his breath. Placing his hand on the door, he pushed it slightly open and peered through the hinged gap. The crypt which was illuminated by a single light bulb dangling from the ceiling and from the skylight above.

Two men lingered in the dark shadows of the crypt. Once the place to lay out the dead before burial, it had been converted into a workshop. A lathe stood in the centre of the room and a workbench with hammers, saws and chisels darkened the far wall. Underneath the skylight, carved wooden angels and crosses ran the length of the room, while on the opposite wall rested old wooden pews ready for repair. He could see O'Connor working on the lathe. Wearing his dog-collar under a carpenter's apron, which hung down below his knees, he looked troubled as the other man he'd followed into the church kicked-up wood shavings and sawdust as he paced the room. He caught some of O'Connor's words. He was trying to calm the situation by continuing to work, but the other man was beside himself, gesticulating with waving arms and sprays of spittle. For a split second Anders thought of a good English expression that summed-up the two men. *O'Connor would be a good man to have in the trenches. The other wouldn't.* With that his nerve returned and he stepped inside the crypt. The timing was perfect; both men had their backs to him; Anders brought the gun up and pulled-the-trigger. *I hope you find your absolution.* One bullet entered the back of O'Connor's head the other through the tall man's temple. Both men's bodies shuddered, their legs crumpling beneath them like a couple of drunks ice skating. Stepping back, Anders watched as both men hit the stone slabs, sending up a cloud of sawdust around the workshop. Then he finished them off. Bang, one bullet thudded into O'Connor's heart. Bang, another through the tall man's heart. *Two hearts beat as one. Not any more they don't.*

Flicking off the lathe, it slowly ran-down and stopped leaving an eerie silence. O'Connor had been turning a wooden candlestick of some sort and Anders doubted if it would ever be finished. Mesmerised by the men's bodies twitching and the blood seeping out of their heads and bodies, he placed the gun back into his raincoat. He watched as the blood pumped out of their bodies and ran into the tiny cracks of the stone slabs, twisting and tuning in the channels like the canals in Amsterdam.

'There are no regrets.
No tears goodbye.
I don't want you back.
We'd only cry, cry again.
Say goodbye again.'

A shadow of a wooden cross swept across his face. For Anders the atheist it was a sign. Thoughts of his recent kills came back to him in the coldness of the room, the two advertising executives in the lift, his landlady, the Polish immigrant and now a priest and the other body which lay at his feet. Who next? A shudder shot through his body as he questioned what he'd become. Taking a step towards the door he heard a thud behind him. Spinning around he pulled the gun out and swung it round the room, nothing. Looking down at the two bodies, there was no movement, just silence. Sometimes the dead could make noises.
Then another thud.

Anders could feel the muscles in his body tightening. The thud had come from the far wall. Tightening his grip on the gun he slowly took one step back into the crypt as some loose leaves scratched the skylight.

Another thud.

Stepping over the bodies, Anders moved towards the workbench at the far wall.

Another thud came from behind the workbench.

Slipping the gun back inside his raincoat, he put his shoulder against the workbench and levered-it away from the wall. Although it was dark Anders could make out a concealed wooden door the size of a tea-chest. Anders caught a draught. Crouching down, he reached behind the workbench and slid open a metal bolt and unlocked the small door. The smell of urine hit him like a slap across the face. Rearing back, he brought the sleeve of his coat up to his face to combat the stench and coughed violently. Eyes watering, he peered into the dark space and tried to focus on what was inside. Shafts of tiny light and air came from the ventilation holes in one of the bricks. On the sooty floor a disregarded, soiled tartan rug lay next to a cracked bowl of stagnant water. Dabbing his eyes, a breeze came through the holes in the brick and brushed his face, causing another thud. Dangling from above, two rusty shackles swayed on chains in the draught.

Sweeping up the stone steps, Anders made his way through the door into the vestry. Coughing, he was about to walk back into the church when he heard voices. They were young voices.

Peering through the gap in the door, he saw a number of choir boys milling around the altar. It took Anders less than a second to react. Turning up the collar of his raincoat, he picked up a couple of hymn books and tucked them under his arm. Stooping, he coughed and limped out of the vestry door. The boys chatter stopped as they turned and looked at the unfamiliar figure limping towards them. Silence is golden and for a split second Anders thought about shooting all of them, *far too many witnesses*.

Passing the altar he cut the stillness and addressed the boys in a broad, Northern Irish accent. 'Top of the mornin' to ye' lads, the voices of Angels is in the stars, sing up now do ye hear?'

CHAPTER THIRTY-ONE

Walking out of the swirling wind and through the front door, Tony prayed they would be there, but he knew instantly. It was dark, silent. All he could hear was the hum of the refrigerator from the kitchen. The sound of his daughter's laughter was missing and Anne's warming smile had deserted him and their home. Friday, D-Day had suddenly become a reality, he was alone. Like a ship listing in a storm, Tony dropped to one side as he made his way into the kitchen. Anne had opened his mail and read the bank statement. It was left for his benefit in plain view on the kitchen table. *£19,000 deposited (cash).* Then in large red letters: *Balance £83, 000 overdrawn. Account withdrawn. Legal proceedings will start unless the money owing has been repaid in full in seven working days.* Another statement read: *Further to your recent re-mortgage of your property for £18,000 we would like to offer you further banking details of our new savings account.* He laughed at the absurdity of it all. Anne hadn't a clue about the re-mortgage, and opening the letter of further deceit would have been the final straw, that was it. Pouring himself a cold beer, he flopped into the arm chair. Short of breath, he unclipped the prison tie from around his neck. It was like a noose. Sitting in silence he felt like the life had been sucked out of his whole body. He tried ringing Anne on her mobile, no answer and he surmised she had gone to stay with her mother, at least he knew there she and Martha would be safe. It gave him peace of mind if nothing else.

His mobile rang. He didn't recognise the number. He let it ring, another missed call. Dodging missed calls was his forte, particularly from people like the bank manager. Opening the fridge door, he leant down and removed another cold beer from the bottom shelf. Something floated out of his shirt pocket and landed onto the kitchen floor, it was the photograph Finch had slipped him earlier. Placing it behind a fridge magnet of Rome, last year's romantic weekend, he took a long hard look at it. Taking a swig of beer, he wondered how Finch had got his grubby hands on the photograph and he felt his world had been violated.

'I want your help – to kill me, to help me commit suicide.'

That voice, the smell of his breath had lodged itself inside his head and put a lump in this throat. It was another major problem to deal with, it was all he needed, questions, questions, questions. If Finch had enough of living, why hadn't he tried to commit suicide before? He seems intelligent enough. Being on twenty-four hour surveillance, he knew he couldn't have any shoe laces or a belt, there was no conceivable place or way he could hang himself, even the bars on his cell window had been covered so that he couldn't wrap a sheet around them. Sitting at the kitchen table he stared at the photograph, his mind was spiralling. *Does he want to get a kick out of somebody taking his life? Get a real kick, sexual pleasure out of looking into his killer's eyes, MY EYES just before his last heartbeat disappears from his body?*

Looking at the bank statement, Tony's mobile rang again, another missed call.

£83,000 overdrawn, £83,000 overdrawn, plus the rest, there was no way out. Then there's the bookies and the Loan-Shark, it wouldn't be long before they came knocking at the door, hunting me down. If Finch wants to die, let it happen, make it happen. It could be tomorrow or the next day as long as I keep my nerve. If I'm to commit murder, how do I know I will be paid by Young and his friends? There's no guarantee, but the money in the envelope proves they mean business.

Tony needed another drink; he needed to get his shit together. The beer was the only thing that tasted good in his mouth and he knew that before the end of the evening the remaining half dozen beers from inside the fridge would flow down his neck.

£83,000 overdrawn. Would wiping out the debt get Anne back? There would be endless questions; Anne would want to know how I obtained the money? I could say I won it on the tables or say I was left a shitload of money in an old aunt's will, an aunt I never knew I had.'

Wiping the debt would solve one problem but Tony could see it creating another major one.

£83,000 overdrawn. BLACK NUMBER 8.

Tony thought of the prayer the group would recite at the end of every session at Gamblers Anonymous.

'God grant me the serenity
to accept the things I cannot change…
Courage to change the things I can…
And the Wisdom to know the difference.'

If ever he needed God's help it was now.

'Oh God please help me.'

Opening another bottle of beer, he knew he had to reverse the tables. He had to speak to Young. He needed to tell him about Finch, he was his only hope, a very dangerous hope. His mind raced with uncertainty, irrational confusion. Flicking through the

Yellow Pages, he picked up the phone and dialled... 'Capital Cabs? I'm trying to track down a taxi driver who works a black cab; his name is Young, Brian Young.'

CHAPTER THIRTY-TWO

Young's mobile sprang into life. Nobody rang him, ever, unless it was Gordon. Fumbling inside his coat pocket, he took out his mobile. It wasn't Gordon's number flashing on the screen and as his was the only number stored in his phone he paused for a few seconds before answering.

'Hello.'

'Brian?'

'Who is it?'

'It's Alf from Capital Cabs.'

'What do you want?'

'There's a pick-up for you.'

'I don't do pick-ups, I've told you before.'

'I know, but this guy only wants you. 34, Hawk's Drive, on the Birdie Estate. You must have made an impression on somebody Brian, he was adamant....'

Young threw the mobile onto the floor of the cab and swung a sharp right. He felt euphoric, the excitement racing through his body. Putting his foot down, he ripped the wrapper off a new pack of menthol with his teeth and headed for the county lanes.

Hold-on, it might be Evans' wife? No, it can't be, I watched her leave with the little girl earlier in the day, along with a couple of heavy suitcases. It could only be Tony Evans. This was it, at last. So this is what it feels like to be happy, I remember now. No it wasn't this good, but I do remember.

Watching Evans day to day had become a habit, an exhausting obsession. Young was ecstatic; he knew Evans had finally cracked. Although he felt some sort of sympathy for him, now was not the time for him to become weak. The hypnotic sound of the rain beating down on the cab's roof put Young into auto-pilot state as he drove. Wondering how the conversation would develop, he tried to put two-and-two together, he gathered it must be something to do with Evans' wife leaving; perhaps she had left him for good, perhaps he didn't care, perhaps she didn't care, perhaps they both didn't care. After he killed Finch what would Evans do? Would he skip the country? Then as he drove he remembered the casino, that night almost a week ago when he enticed Evans into the back of his cab. The most logical conclusion was that he was hooked on gambling and that he'd lost a fortune.

Of course the visits to the casino, the bookies, they all fit into place.

Turning off the dual carriageway, the cab pulled into a long, tree-lined truckstop. Driving past a couple of articulated trucks, Young was oblivious to their drivers tucking into bacon and eggs outside a mobile café. Pulling-up alongside a phone box, he killed the engine. Leaning across the luggage space of the cab he picked his mobile up off the floor. Knowing he had little credit in his phone he decided to double-check anyway, having never rung anybody he then questioned himself as to why he had a mobile in-the-first-place. Perhaps it was for company, just to know that there

209

was contact with the outside world if he needed it. Sometimes he liked to watch the pictures on the phone, some were pretty, colourful, his favourite being a scene of a bright yellow sunset, but it was only another way of passing the time. On many occasions he'd sit in his armchair drinking whisky and smoking with the phone on his lap as it charged. He'd watch the screen until it changed from 'charging' to 'fully charged', again it passed the time. Slipping the phone into the inside of his coat pocket, he lit a cigarette. Trying to gather his thoughts, he watched a traveller changing the wheel on his mud-splashed caravan. As the rain bounced off the back of his donkey-jacket a woman appeared at the caravan window and berated him over something. She sounded like she had tourettes. The man ignored her.

The phone box stank of fresh urine and the windows were covered in fuzzy lines of blue spray paint. Slotting some loose change into the box, Young checked Gordon's number on his mobile and tapped in the number. As cigarette smoke drifted out of a cracked window a business card jammed behind the back of the phone caught his attention. On the card was a cartoon of a partially dressed vixen advertising *Delicious Dianne.* Appearing stoned, he took another drag of his cigarette, lost in his own thoughts. 'Remember, remember the fifth of November.' He couldn't remember the last time he had female company, the feel of a woman's body against his, the feel of her sweet breath, a tender kiss. It might have been in the month of November, or was it?

'Hello Gordon, it's me, Tony Evans wants to see me – Yes I know it's good news, but he'll want some guarantees.' Young heard voices and looked down; a couple of young scallywags wearing black hooded coats had their noses pressed up against the cracked glass of the phone box. Suddenly he became irritated, his voice hardening. 'I thought we agreed to take one step at a time?' As he pulled on his cigarette, the kids started kicking the glass at the bottom of the phone box. 'I'll cover all our options – ok, ok, I will phone you later.' Agitated, he replaced the receiver, swung open the door and stepped outside into the heavy downpour.

'Hey mister will you give us some money?'

The taller of the two lads had an intimidating voice. 'Why don't you say *please* to the gentleman Shaun?'

The bad-cop, good-cop approach, they'd been taught well.

'Please mister give us some money?'

'Leave the fuckin' man alone boys!' Their dad had taken the skin off his knuckles while fixing the wheel of the caravan. Jumping to his feet, he grimaced as he shook his bleeding hand and cursed into the damp air. 'Give them a little change there mister, a little won't harm you now will it, shut the little bastards up.' His camouflaged trousers and jacket were drenched, his face mixed with rain and sweat. Picking up the flat tyre, he chucked it off the road, dumping it into some thorn bushes.

'Go on mister give us some money?'

Hanging onto Young's shirt tails, the smaller kid blocked Young's way to the cab.

'Go on, please mister. Oliver can get really angry at times.'

Young looked at them, their faces holding the dirt. In ten seconds flat, both their arses were going to be kicked all around the lay-by. He was going to enjoy this one, they'd trodden on his toes, and if their dad wanted some he'd get it as well.

'For crying out loud lads, leave the fuckin' man alone.' The dad, with the mouth of a drain, gave Young an apologetic look. 'I'm sorry about the little fuckers, a little change will get rid of them.' Young ignored the kids' voices, but not the voice of their dad, his voice was familiar, he'd heard it before. Trying to remember, the brassy looking woman, wearing a leopard skin overcoat appeared in the caravan doorway. The couple started arguing, the vulgarity of their voices as high pitched as their kids.

Trying to out-do-each-other, their swearing intensified, bouncing back and forth like a couple of jousters. Then he remembered that argument, that night, that couple, when Young had been her knight-in-shining-armour. You never forget a prick who you give a good whack to, especially across the shins with a crowbar. The two lads ran over and started to prise their ranting parents apart. Old men dressed as little boys.

Leaving the family from hell, Young had to get back-on-track, concentrate on matters-in-hand. The demise of Tony Evans was about to take another turn, in more ways than one.

CHAPTER THIRTY-THREE

Jumping into the back of the cab, Tony was instantly hit by cigarette smoke and the damp smell of Young's putrid body odour. For a spit second both men caught eye contact with each other in the rear-view mirror. As Tony shook the rain out of his blond hair like a Border collie he was jerked back into his seat as the cab took-off. If the two men had one thing in common, it was that they were both conscious of being spotted together. When Tony had been in the back of Young's cab before, he knew where he was going. This time he didn't, this night was blacker than black.

Climbing out the back of the cab, Tony paused for a few moments before looking up at the imposing, yellow bricked building in front of him. To the left of the building was a patch of waste land and to the right, three women stood in a darkened doorway smoking. One shouted something, the others laughed, the men oblivious to what was said. Across the road a number of boarded up houses looked like they were ready for demolition. Young motioned for Tony to follow him. As they passed under the shadows of a leaning oak tree, Tony noticed Young walked with a slight limp and climbing the stone steps to the front door, he wondered where Young had found the strength to come after him in the park. Broken glass shimmered across the doorstep as they stopped at the boarded-up front door. Finding the time to light a cigarette, Young didn't bother with a front door key. Putting his shoulder against the door he shoved it open.

Inside the hallway, what little light there was shone down from a cracked skylight high up in the stairwell. Damp patches seeped through the thirty year old wallpaper and water could be heard pouring from a broken gutter outside. The noise of a game show and a wild life programme mixed with the aroma of different greasy foods sneaked from beneath a line of bed-sit doors that faced them. At the bottom of the stairs, a junkie sat slumped against the paint peeled banister like a ghost, a disregarded syringe, tin foil and heroin pipe his only friends. Side-stepping the drug addict, the two men trod the creaking boards of the stairs. Making their way along the first floor landing, Tony caught Young take a glance over his shoulder as if to say, *are you still with me?* From behind one of doors a fight broke out. It sounded like a young man and woman fighting. A baby started crying. Tony had found himself in hell.

Stopping at the last door on the landing, Young unlocked two mortice-locks, either side of a Yale lock and pushed the door. Pale light spilt onto the landing as the door swung open. Stepping inside, there was no going back.

Young flicked on the light. The dingy, bleak flat reminded Tony of the squalor from a Dickens novel and smelt like a dog kennel. Removing some old tea-stained newspapers from a chair, Young nodded. 'Take a seat, enjoy the ambiance.'

If Young hadn't been such a sad figure Tony would have laughed out loud at his dry wit. Sitting down, Tony took in the room and caught the smell of black fungus that clung to the mustard painted walls. Voices and someone washing pans came from behind the walls. Young didn't offer, he just poured two large glasses of whisky and handed one to his new house guest. The two clinked glasses, to the death of a thousand sailors.

'Cheers, it's about time you and I had a little chat,' said Young.

Tony sniffed the scotch as if he was connoisseur. Taking a mouthful he grimaced at the sharpness of the spirit.

'So you're going to do it?' There was a slight irritation in Young's voice as Tony coughed slightly as the scotch slid down his throat. 'That depends.'

The flippancy of the remark angered Young. 'When are you going to do it?'

'I said that depends.'

'On what, if it depended on something you wouldn't be here.' Over the top of his whisky glass, Tony noticed how the wall across the room sparkled.

'You haven't answered me.'

'What?'

'I said if it depended on something you wouldn't be here.' Taking a large gulp of whisky, Tony felt like a rat caught in a corner. Young noticed him looking at the wall and deflected his attention. 'How much are you paid Tony, eighteen, twenty, twenty-five thousand a year?'

'About that.'

'Bullshit, don't piss me about, I'm not in the mood. You know it will take you years to pay off your debts – I want to know when you're going to do it?'

Tony took a deep breath. 'For the third time, I said that depends.'

'On what for Christ's sake?'

'On whether I can plan it properly, on whether I can be guaranteed to get away with it, on whether I get the money?' Tony held out his empty glass.

Young poured him a large one. 'Oh you'll get your money, but how do I know you will do the job properly?'

'I guarantee it. I can't afford to get caught.'

'Not good enough.' Both men looked at each other over the rim of their glass as they sipped the whisky. Weighing up the situation, Young pulled back the curtains and peered down into the street below. Eventually he broke the silence. 'You'll get your money when the job is done.'

'I'll want to see it first.'

Young scoffed. 'You've seen my money already, or have you forgotten?'

'I haven't forgotten,' said Tony quietly.

'Good, as long as we're singing from the same song sheet.' Tony couldn't be further away from *singing from the same fucking song sheet.*

Slugging the whisky down in one, Young paid a visit. Lifting himself out of the chair, Tony looked towards the open door of the bathroom and could see Young urinating. Stepping over the debris that littered the floor, he made his way across the room. Standing back, Tony gasped at the sparkling wall strewn with the heads of hundreds of nails. In the centre of the nails was a small faded newspaper cutting bearing the picture of a man. Leaning forward over the dresser, he studied the chiselled features of the man. The light was poor and at first he didn't recognise the face. Then it suddenly became clear. It was Finch.

Zipping up his flies, Young coughed as he shuffled back into the room. Turning from the wall, Tony was met by an unexpected sadness in Young's voice. 'Every nail is a nail in Finch's coffin, one for each day, since he killed my little girl and little boy.'

Tony looked at Young's face and then it came to him, who he was.

'The twins were in the garden. It was hot and they were playing in the paddling pool, we used to live in the country then.' Young fell into a trancelike state. 'Their older brother John was

216

looking after them, he was only sixteen. He was in the kitchen talking to his girlfriend on the phone. When he looked out the window they were gone.' Young poured them both another whisky. 'The gate to the side of the house was open, that's how Finch got in. He used chloroform apparently. All they had on was their costumes. The only witness was our neighbour, Mrs Dolowitz; she was a nice woman, a Polish refugee from the Second World War. She said she saw a white van drive off. It was only a week after they disappeared she remembered seeing a picture of Shirley Temple taped onto the back window. John was questioned by the police. Like me he became a suspect, until they could *eliminate us from their enquiries* as they told us. He killed himself six months later, he couldn't handle the guilt. He was a good looking lad, took after his mother. Good cricketer, a wicket keeper, had junior trials for the county. Better than me. He loved animals, kept a grass snake. He used to watch television with it wrapped around his wrist. Use to freak his mother out. We just drifted apart, engrossed in our own grief I suppose. I bump into her occasionally in a rose garden. There's a bench there for John. We used to talk, go on holidays together, but not anymore.'

Young slugged the scotch and poured another. 'You know what Finch did to my kids don't you?' Tony nodded; he couldn't find his voice, a lump stuck in his throat. Young stared into the abyss of the nailed wall. 'Before he buried their bodies in the woods, he did a lot of damage to them after he killed them. When the police investigated him they thought it was possible that he could have abducted and killed Helen's son. Her son had been missing for over five years. He cut him up. Put some of his body parts in bin liners and dumped them into builders' skips. Some parts were never found. The police had no evidence, they couldn't prove it, but all the signs were there.'

Tony downed the scotch. Young lit another cigarette, blowing acrid smoke around the room and continued catching Tony's gaze.

'I've thought why me, out of all the people put on this earth why me? What have I done? I thought about suicide on many occasions. I bought some pills once.' A wry smile came across his face. 'I already had the whisky. Once I found myself standing on a bridge looking down on motorway traffic. I thought that might be a good way to go.' Young looked down at the bottom of his empty glass. 'Believe me; you have nothing if you don't have your family. Life becomes meaningless.' Picking up a weathered, leather-backed bible from the table, he flicked through the pages and removed a small photograph from inside. For a few seconds he looked at it then handed it to Tony. 'It was taken the week before they were abducted.' Tony looked at the photograph it was of Young and his family taken in the back garden of their home. They were all smiling apart from the twins who were pulling tongues into the camera. Innocence personified.

'Once the sun used to shine in our house.' As Tony put the empty glass and the photograph onto the dresser he could feel Young's tears. 'Do you know what it's like to be a celebrity?' Tony looked puzzled by the remark. 'You can't imagine the whispers. In the street, shopping, everywhere I went – there goes the dad of the twins. – I often wonder what they would have been like when they'd grown older, whether they would have got married, had children of their own?'

Tony started to panic, walked to the door and reached for the handle. 'I'm sorry I have to go.'

'Your daughter has beautiful eyes, imagine never seeing them sparkle again.'

'That's emotional blackmail.'

'What if it is – you've felt undying love haven't you Tony?'

'Yes.'

'But what you've never felt is undying hate.'

Tony felt himself trembling. 'Why have you asked 'me' to kill Finch?'

'I followed and watched a few of you from the prison for a long time. I knew the only person who could get to Finch was someone who had daily contact with him. You fitted the bill and you seemed the most interesting. The bookies, the bank and then the casino. Every time you came out, you looked like you lost more than you won. You had more to lose being a family man.' As Tony turned back to the door, Young poured himself another whisky then held up his glass as if giving himself a toast. 'They call this The Water of Life....Have another drink.'

'I have to go.'

'I've got cancer.'

Turning again into the room, Tony watched as Young slid opened the draw of the dresser. 'The doctors have given me three to six months at the most. I won't see the next equinox.' Young sipped the scotch. 'The whisky helps with the pain – I went to Barcelona once and I remember a Catalonian saying, *eat well, shit well and you'll have no fear of dying.*' Young scoffed and took a drink.

There was a moment, a silent, tranquil moment between the two men that seemed to last forever. Young removed a claw hammer and a single six-inch nail from the draw then offered them like a peace offering to Tony. Looking into Young's dead eyes, Tony could see he'd once again disappeared into his own dark void. Feeling uncomfortable, but obligated, Tony took the hammer and nail out of Young's hand. Placing the nail against the wall, he brought the hammer back over his shoulder and banged the nail into the wall.

Young smiled a sad smile. 'My guardian angel deserted me a long time ago, but something tells me yours never will.'

Suddenly, the door leading to the landing caved in tracked-by a deep, angry, Mediterranean voice. 'I've warned you, now you're going to get it!'

Knocking Tony behind the door, a stocky built man in his late twenties lunged for Young. Tony didn't hesitate. Swinging the hammer around the front of the man's neck, he grabbed the head of the hammer with the other hand and gripped both ends. Pulling the wooden shaft hard into the man's windpipe, Tony swung the man's body around, smashing his head against the wall. An elbow thrust into Tony's stomach. Buckling, Tony just held onto his grip with the hammer. The man gasped for breath sending spit up the wall. Tony grunted his face nestled into the back of the man's stubby, bald head. 'Take it easy pal!' Blood was smeared across the wall as the man wheezed through his clenched teeth.

'OK. OK.' The man's body relaxed.

Swinging the hammer back into Young's hand, Tony released the man, who swung round in one movement and pointed a poisonous finger in Young's direction. 'Stop the banging!'

Staggering, the man held his throat and slumped backwards against the door. A red scorch-mark ran across his neck and blood oozed from his right nostril. 'Next time, you crank, next time!' Catching his breath, the man lifted himself off the door and holding his throat with both hands, stumbled out of the room and back into his bed-sit.

Young shrugged his shoulders and smiled at Tony, his eyes still pricked with tears. 'Last week one of the nails went through the Greek's wall and hit his electrics.'

Hanging over the banister of the first floor landing, Young watched Tony as he made his way down the stairwell. A tear spilt from his eye.

'Tony!' Stoping Tony looked up and saw Young silhouetted against the broken skylight. 'As there is breath in my body I want that bastard dead. Remember there's more than one way to skin a cat!'

As the front door slammed shut, Young heard the Greek choking and spluttering from behind his door. A smile mixed with his tears. *He won't be doing that again in a hurry.*

Staring at the nailed wall, Young's body shuddered as he coughed up phlegm into his hand. Looking down, his palm was swimming with blood. Picking up an old shirt he wiped the blood from his hand and mouth. Taking a couple of prescribed pills out of a medicine bottle, he washed them down with a gulp of scotch. *Revenge is sweet, an eye for an eye*. Like his impending death, it was that close. Removing the rest of the blood from his hand onto the hip of his jeans he took his mobile out of his coat pocket. Weeping, he longed for company. It would be his last time and the first time in years. Dialling a number from a business card his hand shook. He didn't have to wait long before someone answered. *'Hello, this is Delicious Dianne?'*

Crying his heart out, Tony walked in a daze. Oblivious to the stinging rain, he could hear himself sobbing as he turned another corner of another street. Sheltering from the rain he fell into a dark doorway and ran his hands through his soaked hair. Young's manifestation and his ghostly voice wouldn't leave him. High above, the black sky was whipping up a gale as he searched for guidance. Then Finch's proposition came back to him.

Realising the he was standing in a pub doorway he turned and went in.

CHAPTER THIRTY-FOUR

Anne's ring-tone startled her out of a deep sleep. Leaning over the bedside table, she fumbled for her mobile. Through the slits in her eyes she looked at the illuminated number. It was Tony. Bringing the phone up to her ear, she muffled her voice into the snugness of the pillow.

'Tony it's 3:30 in the morning.' Martha was lying asleep next to her and she wanted to scream. 'You're drunk – I always know when you're drunk – I'll speak to you tomorrow.'

She hung up.

Within seconds, her mobile rang again. Slipping the phone under her pillow, she felt the mobile click automatically into the messaging service. After a minute or two it rang again. Again it clicked into her voice messages. Sliding the mobile from under her pillow, she turned it off. After checking on Martha she put her head back down on the pillow and closed her eyes. As hard as she tried to get back to sleep, the harder it became. Her mind was working overtime. Rolling over she looked at Martha sleeping, a picture of innocence. Lying there, Anne thought about the life changing decision she was about to make, the decision she had to make. She needed to be strong, not just for herself but for Martha.

Wide awake, Anne tied the belt of her towelling dressing gown before opening the small bathroom window. Dropping the lid of the toilet seat, she sat down and sparked up a cigarette. Inhaling, she swivelled around and blew the stark smoke out of the open window. A cold draught brushed the back of her neck and she rolled her shoulders. Switching on her mobile, she took another pull on the cigarette and listened to the four voice messages as they clicked.

'Anne it's me. I'm looking at the photograph of the three of us taken in Spain, the one on the kitchen wall when Martha was about two. I think the kitchen needs another coat of paint, perhaps not, what do you think? Anyway, do you remember the guy who took the picture? He was German, aged about a hundred and eighty and dropped the camera. (Slurring) We saw him the following day in the flea market with his wife and we made a joke about him not taking another photograph and his wife, thought we were English nutters as we took imaginary photographs of each other. His wife dragged him away, we nicknamed him....'

Anne pulled on the cigarette as the next message clicked-in.

'It's me again. You're not going to believe this. You know we thought cats were digging up the plants. Well guess what, it's a family of hedgehogs. Martha would love this. We'll have to get Spring Watch in. There are four of them. Mum, Dad, two kids, not that I'm an expert on hedgehogs, but I might take up hedgehog lessons after this. Their eyes light up, weird little bastards they are...Hold on one is going...'

Once again the garbled massage was cut off -

'Hello, where was I? Oh yes, our friends the hedgehogs. One squeezed under the shed door that's what the smell is in there, hedgehog crap... (Tony's voice lowered into a whisper). They're going now...'

A couple of clicks, then a recorded voice, followed by –

'Just to say pleasant dreams – I'm sorry – Kiss Martha for me – I love you.'

Switching off the phone, Anne turned her wedding ring around on the third finger of her left hand. It was made out of white gold and inscribed on the inside were the tiny words: *To Anne, now and forever, Tony x.*

Taking another smoke, tears streamed down both cheeks like wax spilling down the side of a candle. She told herself she wasn't going to cry, and thumped the side of the wall.

'You bastard Tony.'

A knock on the door startled her out of her sadness. 'Are you alright in there?'

Anne ran the back of her index finger across her tears and tried to waft the smoke out of the window at the same time. 'Yes Mum.'

'Are you sure darling?'

'Yes Mum, go back to bed.'

'Alright darling, see you in the morning.'

'Good night Mum. I love you.'

Then a pause, followed by 'I love you too darling.'

As Anne continued to wipe away the tears, she looked around the confined space of the bathroom. With its dripping bath tap, that had dripped as long as she could remember (her father had promised to fix-it thousands of times and never did. Her mother never had it repaired, it was like a strange legacy to him after he died) and its print of 'Sunflowers' hanging from its light blue walls, it was a stark reminder of separation. This wasn't her or Martha's home. She wanted her home back. She wanted to sleep in her own bed, watch her own television, make a cup of tea from her own kettle. Anne kept asking herself the same questions over and over again and kept on coming back with the same answers. It was simple, the answer was simple, and she'd known the answer for the past five years. She was on the brink of losing everything. The drip, drip, drip of the bath tap had intensified inside her head, it was like Japanese torture and she could feel herself getting a headache. Flicking the cigarette stub out through the open window she looked up at the constellation of stars. Where had Tony gone? What world did he live in? Where had his carnival spirit disappeared to, the one she fell in love with, the one she had made love to in that basement flat all those years ago? Turning at the door she looked back at the dripping tap and could hear her father's voice. *Are those tears just for you sweetheart or someone else?*

CHAPTER THIRTY-FIVE

Sounding like a nuclear explosion inside his head, Tony reached over and thumped the top of the alarm clock. Sunshine streamed through the small gap in the curtains and he could feel the warmth on his naked back. Stretching across the cotton sheets of the double bed, he spread his fingers out like a fan and searched. For a split second he could feel Anne lying next to him, then, as soon as she was there she was gone. Only the sweet smell of her fragrance remained, another wake-up call. Groaning, he remembered ringing her in the early hours and leaving those garbled messages which made him feel worse. One of his eyes flickered open. Trying to focus on the red numbers of the digital clock he ran his tongue across his sandpaper lips. Dehydration rocked between both temples and as he gulped it set a jack hammer off inside his head. *10:14AM. What day was it? Friday? No, Saturday? Saturday.* Saturday was a good day; any day was a good day when he didn't have to go to work inside that poxy prison. Rolling over onto his back, the sun pierced his eyes like an interrogator's lamp. For a few seconds his tongue stuck to the top of his parched mouth. Ravenous, he could hear his stomach crying out for food. It was a long time since he'd last eaten and a hangover cure was the order of the day, coffee and a good fry-up.

Taking *one-small-step-for-man-and-one–giant-step-for-mankind,* Tony swung his legs over the side of the bed. With the heel of his hands he lifted himself up off the bed and felt the coldness underfoot of the loose change strewn across the bedroom carpet. Slipping on a pair of tracksuit bottoms and white v-necked tee-shirt he could feel the pulse of his heartbeat matching the banging inside his head. Like a zombie he shuffled across the landing to the bathroom. Squeezing a good helping of toothpaste onto his toothbrush, he brushed away last night's whisky from the back of his teeth as his immediate thoughts flashed back to Young. Swilling his face with water, he looked at someone else staring back at him in the mirror. He looked like a train-wreck and promised himself he would never drink again. *Ha, how many times have I said that?*

Sliding his hand down the banister, Tony made his way gingerly down stairs. Reaching the bottom step a newspaper flew through the letterbox. Tucking it under his arm he made his way into the kitchen and was instantly drawn to the photograph on the fridge that Finch had given him. Young's whisky wasn't good enough to kill the images of what Finch had done to Young's kids and slowly, all the memories from last night seeped back into his thunderous brain. How he nearly throttled the Greek guy with a hammer and the nails surrounding the face of a serial killer which looked like a voodoo shrine he'd once seen in a movie. Playing the fruit machine in that pub and knocking over his beer. How he got home was anyone's guess. But one image, one single image wouldn't disappear; it was of Young's ghostlike face and how he described his children's abductions and murders. He had painted a picture in his mind.

Sipping a strong mug of decaffeinated coffee he saw a note

propped up against the toaster. Unfolding the note, it read: *Gone to mum's, don't phone. I need time to think. If you want to see Martha, pick her up at three tomorrow.* The coldness of the note made him angry.

'You can have all the time in the world you want.'

Screwing-up the note, he chucked it across the kitchen, then spreading the newspaper out in front of him he thumbed the pages with a vengeance. Passing a double-page-spread of b-list celebrities flashing their knickers as they stumbled out of various limousines, the next page announced to the world that: *Children, who tie their shoe laces quickly, turn out to be scientists or doctors, and children who tie their shoe laces slowly, will become footballers or pole dancers.* Tony made it to the back of the newspaper in less than a minute. '*Tabloid crap!*'

As a couple of eggs sizzled away on the stove, he took another sip of coffee and read the front page. *Priest Murdered in Church Shooting.* Delving further into the article; it described how two men had been found murdered.

Shot dead in the crypt of the church as only yards away, angelic faced choirboys rehearsed for their Christmas recital.

Two photographs of the murdered men looked up at him.

The Priest was named as Father O'Connor.

The other victim William Pearce a local photographer.

Turning off the gas, Tony was drawn back to the newspaper, he couldn't explain what gnawed at him but something did. Picking up the newspaper his heart suddenly accelerated. Another photograph in the newspaper was of the church were the murders took place. His eyes shot to the photograph on the fridge door as the hairs on the back of his neck stood on end. It was St Benedict's church, the same church in the background of the photograph taken of Anne, Martha and himself. The same photograph Finch had slipped him through the wire in Brainforth. If Tony needed a hangover cure, he'd got one.

CHAPTER THIRTY-SIX

On-the-dot at three, Tony arrived with a lingering hangover to collect Martha. Sitting in the car he looked at the thatched cottage and dreaded the reception that waited him. The first time he was introduced to Anne's parents was on Boxing Day over twenty years ago. They were having one of those, after Christmas Day gatherings of the family. Anne had met him at the front door and kissed him on the cheek; she was nervous and excited at the same time and told him to relax. It was the wrong thing to say, how could he? He felt nauseous, intimidated by meeting her parents for the first time and the atmosphere of the wealth that met him. Upstairs, he could hear the sound of Glen Miller mixed with emptying bath water and the ticking grandfather clock which stood in the corner of the hallway, with its swinging pendulum made him feel like he was being hypnotised. Rodney came bounding downstairs and greeted him with a firm handshake.

'Hello you must be Tony?' His cotton-top hair was still wet and his red striped shirt smelt of Old Spice aftershave. A silver sixpence could have passed through the gap in his front teeth that were slightly stained from smoking a lifetime of small cigars. Tony could see his piercing blue eyes giving him the once over, a smile across his square face that said, *I hope my daughter never has to marry someone like you sunshine.* Rodney had always wanted his daughter to marry someone with 'prospects'. A bloke who worked in a car factory wasn't his idea of a success story. When Anne broadcast to the family that *she had an announcement to make,* Rodney knew what was coming. Squirming in his leather armchair, he plucked a chocolate from the Christmas tree and popped it into his mouth. Disguising his revulsion, he chewed away on the chocolate, his eyes transfixed on his daughter, not his future son-in-law. And that was how it was for the years that followed. Anne's mother Pat had carried on 'the looks' after her husband died. She had a gift for making everyone think the world revolved just around her. Tony always felt uncomfortable in her presence and now both her and her late husband's prophecies about him were coming true. As he walked up the pebbled path towards the heavy wooden door of the cottage he felt like a dead man walking. Ringing the bell, Tony followed it with a nervous knock and looked up at the sky. Although a strong wind blew, it had stopped raining and the sun was trying to break through the clouds, good conditions for flying a kite. The look that greeted him gave him another weather forecast to think about. With a face of thunder Pat turned and shouted Martha's name before disappearing into the dark house. The frosty reception was to be expected, but not being invited inside for the first time in over twenty years spoke volumes. As he waited on the doorstep he thought of doing a Reginald Perrin, stripping-off his clothes and disappearing into the sea, but unlike Perrin when he thought of his mother-in-law he didn't think of a hippopotamus, he thought of the 'cold truth.' When Pat brought Martha to the door she told him Anne was out, he knew she was upstairs. Later that day Martha would innocently spill the beans.

Under orders to have Martha back no later than six; it was enough time for them to enjoy the afternoon together. 'Ted's Farm' was a place where kids had the opportunity to hold the animals. Martha loved it and Tony took photographs of her cradling a lamb. It was too cold for ice creams, but they shared one anyway. Her questions were endless. He tried to explain to her how some grown-ups eat lambs for Sunday lunch and how some grown-ups are vegetarians. Explaining things to her wasn't a chore, he loved her questions, he loved being a father, and he loved being in charge of all the kisses. Later, they went to the park where they flew the kite, nicknaming it, 'Star Drop'. Underfoot the sodden grass was muddy and when he ran with the kite his legs went from under him. Skidding and sliding through the wet leaves and mud Martha's laughing could be heard all over Oxfordshire. Then the wind dropped along with Tony's heart. It was time to take Martha home, although it wasn't home for the two of them anymore.

'Why are Mummy and I staying at Gran's Daddy?'

'It's only for a little while sweetheart.'

'Why aren't you staying there with us?'

'All will work out.'

'Are you staying for tea?' Questions, questions, questions, but there were no answers.

Hugging each other on the doorstep, Tony fought back the tears.

'I love you sweetheart.'

'I love you too Daddy.'

As Martha disappeared inside, Pat couldn't close the door quick enough. The sound of it being shut in his face and the rattle of the letterbox reminded him of the cell doors slamming in Brainforth. It also felt like an arrow through his heart.

As he reached the car he looked back and saw Martha at the

bedroom window. Waving, he blew her a kiss. Then, as she waved back she was pulled away. It reminded him of his orange nightmare and sent a cold shiver down his back. Welling up, he climbed into the car and drove off, giving the bedroom window one last look. At the end of the street he turned the corner and slammed on the brakes. Sobbing uncontrollably, he put his head in his hands. He felt empty and he pined to be with his daughter, to read to her a bedtime story, to watch cartoons together, to swing her around in a towel after bath time. He wanted to smell her hair, hear her laugh and see her smile, her smile that had been taken away from him.

Driving home, Tony felt destroyed. Self-inflicted pain mixed with self-pity weighed heavy as he thought of the uncontrollable damage he was causing. But something else irritated his consciousness, deep inside he felt different, strange. Then it hit him. All afternoon, he'd never taken his eyes off Martha. Not for one instant. Not one split second. Young had changed him. When he saw Martha being pulled away from the window it brought back the nightmare of his recurring dream, but thinking of Young and how he lost his children had etched further into his mind. Wherever he looked, he could see his haunted expression, his dead eyes and whenever he saw him he thought of Martha.

That night Tony sat watching a news report on the church murders. His mind was once again in freefall, trapped in a maze of connotations and formulas. On one occasion he found himself wandering the abandoned house looking for answers. Walking into bedrooms, empty of any life, drained of any laughter, he found himself standing in the spare-room. Staring at the computer, the voice returned.

Go on Tony, one little flick of a switch, turn it on.
'Please, please go away, I beg you.'
One little bet won't hurt Tony. One little bet won't hurt.

Slumping onto the bed Tony put his hands over his ears.

Another move of the mouse and click, the Gambling Channel.

Go on, one little bet wont hurt, one little bet, blackjack, poker, roulette, the slots.

Tony looked around the spare room, if ever he needed a deterrent not to gamble it was all around him.

One little bet won't hurt. One little bet wont hurt.

Tony screamed through convulsing sobs. 'Not this time, go away, not this fucking time, please, please!'

Go on one little bet wont hurt, one little bet wont hurt.

Tony stood up and looked at the computer; thoughts of getting his family back and how to get away with murder were put on hold as he flicked on the computer.

CHAPTER THIRTY-SEVEN

Engrossed inside a book, Finch stood in the penalty box of the five-a-side pitch. For a short time in his long days, novels took him outside the walls of Brainforth and into another world, a world that was changing by the day. Turning another chilling page of Stephen King, the final chapter would have to wait, it was trying to rain. Folding down the corner of the page he closed the book and looked up at a rainbow disappearing over the grey slates of the prison roof. With their backs to the pot-of-gold, Jennings and Rogers stood watching, chatting like a couple of housewives hanging over the garden fence.

'How did you get the photograph?'

Finch didn't turn around. He knew who it was on the other side of the fence. 'Good morning Tony.'

'It might be for you.'

'The tables not being kind to you again?'

'I don't know what you're talking about.'

'One of the things that has always frustrated me Tony is that someone as intelligent as you sees the necessity to lie.'

'Go to hell Finch!'

A smug expression drifted across Finch's face. 'Well I'm sure I won't be going to heaven.' Tony looked over at the two officers. Rogers gave him a friendly nod, Jennings a thousand yard stare. Turning his attention back to Finch, Tony gritted his teeth. 'How did you get the photograph?'

'Our deal was for you to help me, in my request for fulfilment' A weird snigger followed his grin.

'What deal? We have no deal.'

'We will have.'

Opening his book he sighed and pretended to read. 'I used to own a large haulage company, over eighty trucks. We delivered all over Europe. Italy, Spain, Greece, I was one of the biggest around, built the business up from nothing. When I was arrested, the police seized my assets but they didn't seize my little nest egg. It was banked in a lucrative off-shore account. The guy who handles my money would be very useful to the police. I know a few things about him that would lock him up for a very long time. We have a business arrangement, a mutual understanding. I know for sure he would like to see the back of me as well.'

'Where's this leading to?'

'Well, I can't spend all the money in here can I Tony, it's got to go somewhere.' Turning another page, he glanced up from the book and checked on the two officers.

'Did you work out were the missing pound went to?'

'You seem intent in trying to wind me up.'

'I try not to; but you seem to be doing a better job of it than me.' Then his voice changed, it was chilling. 'I warn you, get on the wrong side of me and it'll be the last thing you do….So what about my little proposition, I can't do it all by myself?'

'Don't threaten me. You tell me where you got that photograph and I'll get you some help.'

Finch laughed. 'I've had everything they can throw at me in

here, medication, psychiatrists, enhanced thinking schemes. I haven't had electronic treatment, that would be interesting. Did you catch the news yesterday?'

'What about it?'

'Read anything familiar?'

Tony spat through the wire. 'How did you get the photograph you prick?'

'So you read about the murdered priest, O'Connor and the other one, Pearce?'

'I read the paper saw the news and bought the tee-shirt and I know it's the same church as in the photograph you gave me. So you're not as smart as you think you are.' Finch shut the book and slid his back down the fence. Crouching on the ground with his knees tucked up to his chest, he grinned and looked up at the rainbow. He was relaxed and loved being in control. 'The priest and the other man, Willy Pearce, who were murdered at the church, they used to be very good friends of mine, well not friends as such, more…business acquaintances. The photograph, it came via them. O'Connor, the priest, used to suggest to happy couples who were getting married in his church, that a local photographer, Pearce, took their wedding snaps. Little did they know that the photographs he was taking had a hidden agenda. Everything was above board. The couple received their wedding day album, complete with them super-imposed in a champagne glass on the cover. But they didn't get them all. The smiling Pearce, all-suited-and-booted, complete with carnation in his suit lapel would listen to the family's accents. The ones from outside the area were 'ear-marked'. He approached the families who had travelled from around the country and say things like, 'Would you like a photograph taken, one of you and the kids?' Then he would take down their addresses and forward on the snaps. We would meet, normally in the church; it was as good a place as any. There we would, lets say, drool over the snaps. The kids were marked, then we'd travel, have them watched and follow them... It was at the church that O'Connor and Pearce became obsessed with Young's twins.'

Tony felt his stomach turn; his thoughts went back to Young and his description of how his children were abducted and murdered.

'When the time was right, hey presto they were snatched. Nobody would suspect us because the families were scattered all over the country and we'd come from out of the area.'

Tony's voice shook. 'I remember him; he took that photograph and our address. You could have murdered my daughter. – What sort of perverse bastard are you?'

'The best.'

Finch shrugged his shoulders. 'The thing is another guy got involved, a Polish immigrant called Lech. He worked as a doorman and had contacts all around Europe. Then O'Connor and Pearce paniced, we'd all agreed for the Pole to sell the kids on to a couple of rich fuckers from London who had contacts to ship them out of the country. They were front page news as well, they got shot in a London lift, ring any bells?' Tony shook his head as Finch happily continued. 'Then, without my knowledge they thought the Pole might turn and they changed their minds. Deciding to get rid of the evidence, they used me as their safety net. They set-me-up, just in case they were investigated and got caught with their trousers down. They put spots of the kid's blood and fibres from their clothes in the back of my van which was used to grab the kids, but forensics found particles of wood shavings and red berries from a yew tree which they never used as evidence in my defence in court. They came from St Benedict's.' Finch looked up from the book again and saw Jennings and Rogers strolling towards him. 'I can't help liking children's company, but O'Connor, Pearce and the Pole went one step too far.

Tony spoke through the gulped-up vomit that was trapped at the bottom of his throat.

'Why didn't you tell the police about them?'

'I did, they paid them a visit. They had been planning it for weeks, covered their tracks, there was no evidence against them.'

'I like children you see Tony. I wouldn't hurt them and certainly wouldn't kill them, but they set me up.' The clink of the gate cut the conversation dead.

'Up you get Finch, before it pisses down!' Looking down on Finch, Jennings kicked his ankles.

'Why don't you join me down here Mr Jennings we could count the colours in the rainbow together.'

'I wouldn't do anything with you Finch.' Bending down, Jennings grabbed Finch by the arm and yanked him up to his feet. Finch was quick to respond. 'Easy, easy, Mr Jennings, you'll do yourself an injury, we don't want you getting all hot under the collar do we?'

'Shut up Finch!' Rogers steered him gently towards the gate. Jennings noticed the look on Tony's face then spoke to Rogers in a loud voice for Tony's benefit. 'Mr Evans doesn't seem to be his normal self Mr Rogers.' Jennings then clocked Finch grinning. 'What are you smirking at?'

'Oh I was just thinking how stupid you are Mr Jennings. Why it seems the only head I've pitched my tent in is yours.' As Jennings and Rogers frog-marched Finch across the yard towards A-Wing Tony caught Finch's gaze followed by that grin and a sly wink.

As the rainbow disappeared over the prison roof, Tony noticed Finch's rain splattered book lying on the ground. It was Stephen King's The Green Mile and it was a book Finch would never finish.

CHAPTER THIRTY-EIGHT

Slumped over the toilet bowl, Tony wretched. The veins in his neck felt like they were about to explode as his body took on a life of its own. Through watery eyes, he looked up at a line of graffiti scrawled on the toilet wall. *Don't let the bastards get you down.* Irony has a way of kicking you in the teeth. Wiping his mouth free of vomit he reached up and removed a pack of cigarettes and lighter hidden behind the toilet. Placing a dog-end between his teeth he lit up. It was the first time he'd taken a smoke for over eight months. Coughing up his guts, smoke streamed out of his nostrils and mouth. Light headed, he slightly lost his sense of balance as he flushed away the butt and vomit, before falling out of the cubical door and stumbling over to the sink. Ashen faced, he cupped his palms and filled them with cold water. Splashing his face, he looked up into the cracked mirror; all he could see was Finch's grin.

Clipping on his tie, Tony walked briskly along the prison landing. The smell of prison food mixed with the taste of stale tobacco inside his mouth made him nauseous again and fighting a losing battle, he slipped inside an empty cell and was sick again. Disorientated he sneaked back onto the landing and bumped into one of the lifers.

'Hello Mr Evans, how are you on this a beautiful day?' George Rose spoke with a light, Glaswegian accent, had an engaging smile and bounced with all the joys of spring.

'I'm fine George.'

'That's good news Mr Evans, very good news.' Fresh from the showers with wet, thinning grey hair, George Rose was in his late sixties. Small, round, he dabbed water from his podgy face with the end of a towel that was slung over his shoulders. Hitching his trousers up over his fat stomach, it gave him the appearance of Tweedledum. But far from being 'dumb', Rose was an intellectual. Having spent half of his adulthood behind bars, he had re-educated himself inside, gaining Masters degrees with distinction in Mathematics, Science and English. Starting off as a petty criminal in the late sixties with a notorious gang from the west side of Glasgow, he progressed to forging bank notes, then drug running off the Shetland coast. He could spin a yarn for every day of the week and had the nickname 'The Grass Cutter.' If anyone *grassed to the police*, he'd have the job of knocking-them-off. There was a rumour that he'd murdered over twenty people all by the same method, a piano-wire garrotte. Nice. Tony had a soft spot for him. He liked him because he was from the old school of criminals, when there was honour amongst thieves and not the modern day hard-hitter who'd knife you in the back for the old shilling. Like every con inside he pleaded his innocence, but it was always tongue in cheek innocence with George Rose. He was on A-Wing for depression, two failed suicide attempts had made him vulnerable, not only to himself but those with a long memory. Over the years he'd become indoctrinated in the system, prison was his home of homes.

George leant on the wall and ogled Tony's washed out complexion with a sympathetic face. As he spoke tiny bits of bloody tissue-paper moved up and down on his Adam's apple where he had cut himself shaving. 'If you don't mind me saying Mr Evans you look like you could do with a holiday.'

'Where do you suggest George?'

'Anywhere would be nice, preferably abroad somewhere, the damp gets into your bones in this place. You couldn't arrange a little trip for me could you?'

'I'll look in the window of a travel agent, they might have something for you.' As the two of them shared the joke, Tony noticed Rogers standing outside Finch's cell; he looked conspicuous, on edge. George could see Tony was distracted by something and followed his gaze with a puzzled look.

'I wouldn't like your job Mr Evans, dealing with nonces like Lollypop.'

Rogers then disappeared into Finch's cell. George whispered. 'I'm, thinking of digging an escape tunnel, then you and I can break out of here. We can go on that holiday. What do you think?'

George could see Tony was elsewhere. 'So what do you think Mr Evans?'

'Let me think about it George.'

Tony left George's wit and baffled expression and walked down the landing. Clocking off couldn't come quick enough.

The door to Finch's cell was slightly open, Tony placed the palm of his hand on the door and pushed, but it wouldn't open.

Rogers' voice growled from behind the iron door. 'Piss off!'

'It's me, Tony.'

'Go away.'

'What's going on?'

Then, like a kid playing hide-and-seek, Rogers' face appeared through the gap in the cell door. 'Go away Tony.'

'What's going on?'

Jennings' voice interrupted them from inside cell. 'Let him in!'
Rogers slammed the cell door.

The three officers stood with their backs to the door. Wide-eyed, they looked across the cell at Finch's body. Slumped against the brick wall, he was jammed in between his bed and the toilet. Covered in blood, his legs and arms were spread eagled out in front of him, his head dropped to one side resting on his right shoulder. His wrists were sliced open and blood pumped out from both arteries. The stone floor was awash in blood and slowly flooding its way around a discarded razor blade. Finch was barely recognisable. Drained of blood, drained of life, strands of greasy black hair fell down over his grey face. The men stood in silence. Tony could feel Rogers trembling next to him when he spoke. 'We found him like this.'

Tony found his voice. 'He needs a doctor.'

Jennings sprang him a look. 'He doesn't. I know dead when I see it.'

Apart from his father, Tony had never seen a dead body before. 'We need to press the emergency button.' But there was no conviction in Tony's voice. This was a way out, he didn't have to commit murder, this was a stroke of luck. The money was his.

Jennings turned and faced the men. 'We don't have to do anything.'

Rogers was shaking. 'What do you mean, press the button.'

Jennings stood his ground, blocking his way.

Rogers shot a look at Tony. 'Tony, tell him!'

Tony stood transfixed, his eyes glued on Finch.

'Tony, tell him to hit the fucking button.'

Martha's face flashed before Tony's eyes. Guilt, guilt, guilt. Following the wave of guilt a bolt of conscience hit him. *What am I doing?*

Turning, Tony went for the emergency button. Jennings was

quick. Stepping in front of him he grabbed his arm and threw him backwards against the cell door.

'He wanted to die,' said Jennings. 'What goes around comes around.'

'This isn't right and you know it!'

'Right?' Jennings leaned into Tony's face, his voice cutting deep. 'What do you mean it doesn't make it *right*? This guy makes Jack the Ripper look like a saint.' Tony could smell Jennings' stale breath on his face. 'The beast wanted to die; we're just giving him a little help, turning a blind eye so to speak.'

Suddenly Finch started gargling, a spray of blood shot out of his mouth. Rogers started waving his arms in Finch's direction. 'He's still alive!'

Barely conscious, Finch's head tilted backwards his mouth full of blood, overflowing down his chin. Seeing Tony, he smiled as his eyes rolled up inside his head then back down again.

Rogers's face was awash in sweat. 'He needs a doctor!' His plea fell on deaf ears. 'Didn't you hear me, he needs a doctor!'

Jennings didn't move. 'By the time a doctor gets here he'll be dead.' Then his voice became calm and clear. 'What do you think will happen to *us* when they find out that he's killed himself? We're supposed to be babysitting him don't forget. He's the most high profile prisoner in here. We'll be suspended, pending an enquiry and if you two hadn't forgotten, I'm retiring at the end of the week.'

Rogers looked up at the camera in the corner of the cell. 'What about the camera?'

Jennings voice was chilling, controlled. 'Leave it to me – we lock up, clock off, say our goodbyes and go home, everything as normal. Then when he's checked on later, they'll find him and it will be reported as a suicide. We don't breathe a word to anyone. As far as everyone's concerned we're not involved.'

Rogers pointed at the camera. 'We're on camera!'

'*I said leave it to me.*'

The three officers looked at Finch as he tried to speak. Tony pushed Jennings to one side and crouched down in front of Finch. Eyes empty of any life, Finch tried to focus and talk again.

'What's he saying?' Said Rogers.

Tony listened. Apart from Finch's wheezing lungs filling up with blood, the only sound in the cell filtered from outside as prisoners kicked a ball around the exercise yard. A faint grin washed across Finch's face. 'The missing pound, you've got it Tony.' Then, slowly his eyes rolled upwards inside his head as the last gasp of breath oozed from his body.

'What did he say?' said Rogers.

'I, I don't know.' Tony lied.

The three men stood over the body, silent, mesmerized by the death of the serial killer.

'I'm going to be sick.' Rogers shot both hands up to his mouth. Jennings opened the cell door and pushed him out. 'Go to the locker room you wanker!'

Jennings voice was like ice. 'As I said Evans, a doctor would have been too late... So we're agreed, we don't say a word. As far as we're all concerned, he was fine and dandy when we left him.'

'What about the camera?' Jennings shot his hand under Tony's throat and thrust him up against the wall. 'For the last fucking time, I said I would sort it.'

Tony grappled free as a spray of spittle sprayed out of Jennings mouth. 'I'm warning you, don't fuck this up, if anyone finds out we were in here when he snuffed it we'll be put on a charge. Nothing will happen if we keep our mouths shut.'

As Tony walked down the landing, he felt every set of eyes in Brainforth were upon him. This was what it felt like being inside; this was what it felt like to be someone like Finch.

Following a trail of Rogers' vomit along the landing, Tony

found George Rose on his shoulder. 'So what about it Mr Evans?'

As George followed him towards the security gate, Tony tried to act normal, but he was in a world of his own.

Think of it Mr Evans, you and me like Steve McQueen jumping the wire, in the film the Great Escape.' George looked perplexed as Tony ignored him. 'You alright Mr Evans? You look like you've seen a ghost!'

CHAPTER THIRTY-NINE

As Tony drank the last drop of Californian red he closed his eyes and went through the story over and over again. In the locker room, his mind was spinning and under duress, Rogers and himself had agreed to a pact with Jennings. The three officers had gone over their stories half a dozen times and agreed that everything they did should be as normal as possible. Jennings was adamant they'd done the right thing. Ridding the world of Finch was something they could be proud of. But there was trouble in his voice as he warned them that they would be called into the Governor's office for questioning and that there would be a full blown enquiry. *Don't panic, stay cool.* But Tony couldn't stay cool, as he felt the energy seeping from his body. It was like he was signing his own death certificate. He would be known in certain circles as a murderer, someone who had taken a bribe to kill Finch.

At home, Tony ran the complexities of the story over and over in his head when the phone rang again. He knew it was Rogers. He was drunk somewhere in a city centre pub and he had been phoning all evening. Hysterical over *the security tape* being discovered, he didn't believe Jennings would, in his words *sort it*.

Earlier that evening Tony had called Anne and they talked for about two minutes, that's all. She wasn't coming home, not for the foreseeable future and the longer she stayed away the more he could hear her mother warning her with every passing minute. *He's no good. He's never been any good. I warned you about marrying him, your father was right. He's a loser. He'll always be a loser.* She was right. The house was cold, naked. It wasn't home without Anne and Martha. *You've got nothing, if you haven't got your family.* Young's words were ringing true.

Rogers fell through the front door. Bouncing off the walls, he staggered into the lounge and collapsed into one of the leather armchairs.

'What are you doing here?'

'Have you got a drink?'

'No!'

'Well I have.' Rogers reached inside his purple coloured bomber jacket and removed a half bottle of brandy.

'You shouldn't be here. We agreed everything should be as normal.'

'We have to tell the truth.' Rogers unscrewed the top of the brandy bottle and took a slug. Grimacing he leant forward shamefaced. 'I keep seeing Finch's face looking up at us, his body just laying there. Jennings is mad, what if he doesn't get that tape? I can't go to prison.'

Tony's mind was swimming, on one hand he wanted to come clean, the guilt was driving him insane, but then there was the money, the end of all his worries. 'You won't go to prison you've done nothing have you, unless you're not telling me everything?'

'What are you talking about?'

'What happened before I came into Finch's cell?'

'Nothing, Jennings found him like that.'

'What do you mean *Jennings* found him like that. I thought the two of you were in there at the same time?'

'I was a minute or two behind him.' Taking another drink, he ran his hands across his face. 'I've tried to get Finch out of my head, but he's in there all the time. Have you washed your uniform like we said?'

'Yes.'

'And your shoes?'

'Yes.'

'What if they find our DNA on the razor blade?'

'What are you talking about?' Tony was losing his patience.

'Nothing, I don't know what I'm talking about, I'm drunk.'

'How did Finch get the blade?'

'I don't know.'

Tony stood over Rogers. 'Was it Jennings?'

'You know what Finch was like. He kept on winding Jennings up, day after day.'

'Did Jennings give him the blade?'

'I don't know.'

'You were there.'

'I told you, not at first.'

Tony needed a few seconds to think. 'I'll make some coffee. I can see this is going to be a long night.' Rogers shouted after Tony as he made his way out of the room. 'I don't want coffee, I've got a drink!'

Lingering doubts remained about Jennings. Was this a set-up, and if so, why? Stirring a hole in the bottom of the coffee cup, he went over the facts. The biggest question was if he was an accessory to murder, what would happen?

'Here get this down you.' Walking into the lounge holding a mug of coffee, Tony found Rogers sparked-out. Sitting upright in the armchair, his chin rested on his chest. Spilling the coffee, Tony just caught the brandy bottle as it slipped out of Rogers' hand. Trying to wake him with a few shakes, he gave up. It was a hopeless task. Walking back into the kitchen, he poured himself a large nightcap from the brandy bottle. It tasted sharp, and did nothing to convince him that he could have prevented Finch from killing himself. But the more he tried to convince himself, the more he saw Jennings hand Finch the razor blade. Watching him bleed to death answered his own question.

A knock at the front door startled him. He looked at the wall clock, 12.20A.M. Making his way into the hall he noticed a shadow move across the small glass panels in the front door. Moving into the lounge he took a sneaky look through the curtains. Nobody stood on the doorstep, making him question whether he was hearing or seeing things. A cold gust of air cut into the back of his neck. Swinging round, he heard the kitchen door click shut cutting the flow of air. Stepping away from the window, he lent forward and peeked through the lounge door catching another shadow in the refection of the hallway mirror. Spinning around, he searched for an object, something to grab, something to protect himself with. Nothing. As Rogers snored in the armchair, Tony brought his fists up to chest. Ready, he inched his way out of the lounge. He never saw the punch coming as it landed squarely on the side of his jaw. Staggering backwards towards the front door a second man grabbed him round the neck punching him hard in the kidneys. Lurching forward, a knee thrust upwards, cracking him under the chin. Crashing onto the carpet, a size eleven boot came from nowhere and kicked him in the ribs. Not once, not twice, but three, four times. As Tony lay curled up in agony a voice boomed down his ear. 'That's from Mr. Vine!' Another kick thundered into his guts. 'Mr Vine is a bookie not a bank. He would like his money within two days; otherwise we won't be so friendly next time.' Leaving Tony with a final calling card a tattooed fist smashed him across the side of his face. The house shuddered as the two thugs slammed the front door behind them. After the blood and thunder of the beating came the tranquillity of silence. Feeling his mouth filling up with blood, Tony ran his tongue across his front teeth to feel if any were missing. Wheezing with pain, he slowly recovered, dragging himself to his feet with the help of the banister. Staggering along the hall towards the kitchen he fell against a framed photograph of Anne and Martha and shattered the glass.

Blood dripped from his nose and mouth leaving a trail of drops across the kitchen floor. Supporting himself on the marble worktop, he leant over the sink and turned on the cold water tap. Disorientated, his arm caught a number of plates on the draining board sending them crashing across the floor. Spitting blood out of his mouth into the sink of unwashed plates and pots, he filled the palm of one hand with water and rinsed out his mouth. There was more blood than he realised and he could feel throbbing on the side of his face. Dabbing his mouth and nose with a tea towel he reached across and grabbed the brandy bottle off the table. Taking a swig, he swilled the spirit round his bleeding mouth and gums. Spitting the mixture of brandy and blood back into the sink he started to tremble with shock. His whole body felt like it was on meltdown. Gripping the side of the kitchen table, he regained his balance and equanimity and took another shot of brandy. Assessing the damage to himself, he heard Rogers' snoring. The absurdity of him sleeping through the whole fracas made him chuckle, causing another shudder of pain to dart through his body. Washing down a couple of pain killers, his ribs and back throbbed. All of a sudden his mobile rang. Before picking it up he watched it vibrate around in a circle on the kitchen table.

'Hello…how did you get my number? What do you mean it doesn't matter? Yes, yes, he's here…I know he's going to fuck things up – I tried telling him but he's pissed out of his head – His car, hold on…' Holding his side, Tony delicately made his way into the hall. Leaving the brandy bottle on the bottom of the stairs he opened the front door and took in the fresh air. Stepping outside in his bare feet, he could still feel the cut under his foot. Looking around he spotted Rogers' car under a streetlight. Half of it was on a grass verge, half of it was parked on the road. Tony shook his head in disbelief, then brought the mobile up to his ear and spoke quietly. 'He drove here the stupid bastard – good idea – you know the address? How long will you be? OK.'

Hanging-up, Tony made his way back indoors.

Kicking Rogers' feet, Tony could hear his own voice boom inside his head. 'Wake up, Jennings is on his way over.' Wincing with pain, his ribs felt like shattered glass inside his body. Kicking Rogers' feet again, he strained to raise his voice. 'Wake up, Rogers wake up.' Dropping onto the couch, Tony gave-up. Rogers was dead-to-the-world, Jennings could take over the babysitting when he arrived.

What seemed like hours were only minutes, when Jennings appeared on the doorstep. It was the first time Tony had seen him out of uniform. Wearing brown elephant cords tucked into green wellies and a wax jacket, he looked more like a country squire than a prison officer.

'Where is the prick?' Storming into the lounge, Jennings slapped Rogers across the face. 'Wake up!' Fleecing Rogers' pockets for his car keys, there were no pleasantries, Jennings didn't intend to hang around. 'This prick is a liability; he phoned me from some pub and said he was coming round to you.' Jennings turned and slapped Rogers across the face again. The slap was meant to hurt.

Rogers came to; his head lurching backwards as his eyes rolled open.

Tony tried to defuse the situation. 'He'll be alright.'

Jennings looked at Tony. 'If you think I'm going to take a chance on losing my pension for this prick you can think again. Some of the officers were talking about him, asking questions, as to why he was sick today.' Then he noticed the bruising and cuts around Tony's face along with the congealed blood that was forming under his nostrils. 'What happened to you?'

'Nothing.'

'Have you two been fighting?'

'Does it look like we've been fighting?'

Jennings voice was firm, inquisitive. 'What then?'

'That's my business.'

'If it affects me, *it's my business*.'

'It doesn't.'

'It better hadn't! Who knows he's here?'

'Nobody, as far as I know.'

'Let's keep it that way. If anybody asks you, he came round pissed, you tried to persuade him not to drive but when you turned your back to go for a slash or something, he walked out and disappeared. Let's get him out of here.'

Tony didn't reply, then, with great difficulty he helped Jennings lift Rogers to his feet. Holding back at the front door, Jennings surveyed the closed curtains of the surrounding houses for any prying eyes. Satisfied, he gave the nod for the two of them to leave the house. Bundling Rogers onto the back seat, Tony grabbed his shoulders and dragged his dead weight further into the car. Rogers' eyes flickered open and he mumbled something. 'Inch, e bayed inch du bayed.'

Tony gave him a reassuring ruffle of the hair. 'You'll be alright in the morning mate.' Rogers reached out and mumbled some more. Tony tried to catch what he said as Jennings leant over the front seat. 'Close the fucking door.'

As Jennings drove off, Tony made his way back indoors, with Rogers' voice playing on his mind. Tony tried to decipher what he said. It worried him. *Bayed, bayed*, *du, inch* or something, but it meant nothing. Reaching for the brandy bottle he'd left at the bottom of the stairs, his hand grabbed at fresh air. It puzzled him, he looked around. It had vanished. Then it came to him, *bayed – blade*. Then the name. *Inch – Finch*. Rogers had said, *Finch, He gave Finch the blade*.

CHAPTER FORTY

Amongst the cluster of cedar trees overlooking the sprawling Oxfordshire countryside a coverlet of mist hovered above the wet grass. Along the back of the trees, tags of sheep's wool swayed in the wind on the barbed wire fence. Although it was early morning, it was still black as night. Buttercup Hill was waiting for the sun to rise and expose the last of its fading, yellow buttercups to the world. In the dark shadows of the car park, a single red Volvo with steamed up windows rocked from side to side. A short distance away on the road that wound its way up from the dual carriageway, another car watched and waited, its windows also steamed up, but for another reason.

Eventually the passion stopped inside the Volvo and the demister kicked-in. The back door swung open and a red faced man in his forties with a wing collared shirt and loose dickie bow stumbled out. With a broad grin across his face he started rearranging his loose shirt into his open trousers. Reaching into the car he took out his badly creased dinner jacket and threw it on. As he jumped into the driver's seat the other back door opened and another man wearing a dinner jacket fell out laughing. Holding a champagne bottle, he brought it up to his mouth and toasted the dawn. Wiping his dribbling mouth with the back of his hand he threw the champagne bottle over the fence and took a piss. Zipping up his fly, he turned and collapsed into the passenger seat. The car's engine roared into life, disturbing the birds from their slumber. Reversing, the car swung around. One of the men in the Volvo shot a glance into the parked-up car as they drove past. The car was empty and blowing a sigh of relief, he made a wise-crack to the other man about his wife having him followed by a private detective.

All quiet, Jennings didn't waste a second. Springing up from the driver's seat he started the engine and drove up to the deserted car park. Leaping out of the car, he opened the back door and reached in gripping Rogers' jacket. Lifting him up, he pulled him along the back seat and out of the car. Locking both arms under Rogers armpits and struggling to support his weight, he dragged him to the nearside door, lifted him into the car, propping him up into the driver's seat. Then, swinging his legs into the car he positioned his right foot onto the accelerator pedal and jammed his left foot in-between the brake and clutch pedal. From the inside of his wax jacket, Jennings snatched out the stolen brandy bottle and unscrewed the top. Pouring the brandy over Rogers' shirt and trousers, he then gripped his jaw with his fingers, forced open his mouth and poured the last of the brandy down Rogers' throat. Rogers came to life. Spluttering and choking, he failed to regain full consciousness as his head rocked backwards then forwards. Dropping the bottle onto the passenger seat, Jennings lent over Roger's lap and released the hand brake. Instantly, the car jerked forward lifting Jennings off his feet. Regaining his balance, his shoes cut up the gravel as he gave the car a hard, strong push. As it slowly gathered momentum, Jennings quickly removed a box of matches from inside his jacket, lit a match, then threw it into Rogers lap and slammed the car door shut. Just.

Crashing through the small fence, the car took the barbed wire with it as it ploughed into the field of buttercups. Standing at the top of the hill Jennings watched as the car hurtled down the hillside. Scattering bleating sheep in its wake, the car rolled over and over, then flipped into the air. Crashing down onto its roof, the car exploded into a huge fireball. Jennings reared back at the ferocity of the blast. Snapping a branch off a nearby tree he used it as a brush, sweeping over the scuff marks made in the gravel by the back of Rogers' heels when he'd pulled him along the side of the car.

Looking back at the burning wreck, Jennings could feel the heat on his face. The explosion was immense, sending up a plume of black smoke like a small atom bomb. It had lit up the whole countryside and, hearing police sirens in the distance, he knew he had to disappear fast. Giving the burning wreck and rising sun one last look; he threw the branch over his shoulder and disappeared into the cedar trees and the early morning mist.

CHAPTER FORTY-ONE

5.30AM. Tony was awake long before he heard the alarm go off upstairs. Finding it impossible to sleep with the pain of his beating, he'd wandered downstairs in the early hours and stretched out on the couch. Considering his mouth, ribs and back ached from the previous night's uninvited guests, the couch had been a good refuge, a trusty friend. Feeling stiff, he winced as he lifted himself up onto one elbow, leant over and switched on the table lamp. Running his hand across the stubble of his face he felt the swelling around his jaw and under his chin. It would be impossible to hide and he wondered what questions awaited him at Brainforth. Going underground wasn't an option and not going into work would instigate suspicion. Lifting himself up from the couch, the top of his eyelids itched as he noticed an indentation of Rogers in the leather armchair. Scuffing his feet across the lounge carpet he picked up the phone and dialled Rogers' number. No answer. Parched, he picked up a glass of water and took a long drink. He didn't have a hangover, but he knew he'd had a drink the night before and although he could taste the dried blood in his mouth the water tasted good.

Stepping out of the shower, Tony looked in the bathroom mirror and inspected the bruising around his face. It wasn't as bad as he first thought, but an explanation into the grazing across his cheek and temple would have to sound convincing. Moving his toothbrush around a couple of wobbly teeth he heard this mobile ring from the bedroom. Thinking twice he decided to let it ring. Then he heard the land line ringing downstairs in the kitchen. Both phones stopped, than rang again. Wrapping a bath towel around his slim waist he inspected the bruising on his back in the landing mirror before stepping inside the bedroom. Picking the mobile off the bed he read the missed call. Brainforth. The jolt of the ring tone shot through his body as the mobile burst into life in his hand. Brainforth again. Taking a deep breath he pressed the symbol of the green phone. 'Hello… What – When? Last night – what time? Everything was ok when we left him… Ok, I'll be in as quick as I can.' Cutting the voice off, he sat on the bed and pondered whether he'd sounded convincing. Through the bedroom door he caught Anne's eyes looking at him from the family portrait. Lying to her about his gambling and covering his tracks over the years had become routine, but now he had to think about lying for his life. Picking up the remote control he flicked on the television. The news was being read by an attractive newsreader wearing a white blouse and far too much make-up. Sitting down on the bed he waited for the inevitable bulletin on Finch's death. But it never came. *The Church Murders* (as the national press had christened them) were headline news. Turning up the volume on the small plasma, Tony watched as he threw on his prison shirt. Numerous images of St Benedict's cordoned off by police and white suited pathologists searching for evidence flashed across the screen. Wearing his dog collar, the face of O'Connor appeared, then an interview with one of the parishioners, a distraught middle-aged lady wearing a light blue jacket and hat. She was in tears as she conveyed *the shock of the community*. Followed by a charcoal sketch of the wanted assailant, the mug-shot presented an old, stooped man with glasses. Then a reporter enlightened the general public that, the police were looking for a man with a Northern Ireland accent aged around sixty. Another of Finch's dying wishes had been granted.

Tony stood in the centre of the bedroom and stared at the television. He wondered whether the authorities would connect Finch to the murders at the church, if so, who could prove it. Finch was dead after all.

CHAPTER FORTY-TWO

Anders poured petrol then developing fluid over Mrs Dovecot's decomposing body. Her legs and arms had been snapped like twigs, her body squeezed inside the boot of the Land Rover. Stuffed around her body was Fowler's pinstriped suit, the raincoat, blonde and black wigs, camera equipment, photographs and various other bits of clothing and disguises. Pulling off his black leather gloves, he dropped them onto her body. Lighting a match, he stepped back and threw it into the boot. As the back of the Rover burst into flames he back-tracked. He'd stripped his room clean. Wearing surgical gloves he had wiped clear every possible fingerprint from the flat. Obsessive, he'd cleaned and disinfected everywhere. Like a phantom he avoided the neighbours by removing the body of his landlady in the blackness of the night. Not satisfied he went back and cleaned again, then again and again until his fingers bled. Unscrewing the u-bend under the sink he searched for strands of his hair. Tortured by paranoia, he bleached his mattress and every nook and cranny of his room. Putting himself inside the mind of a forensic officer; he knew a minuscule amount of fibre might reveal his identity. He couldn't take that chance, so he torched the place. Everything went up in flames including the dust collectors from all round the world. No chance taken, every fine detail meticulously worked out.

Digging inside his green, cord jacket, Anders took out a bundle of money and handed it over to a beer-bellied scruff in an oily boiler suit. Sweeping his long grey hair out of his eyes, the scruff started counting the money as the dog end of a roll up clung to his broad, bottom lip. Satisfied, he scratched his arse before pressing a large red button on a control panel sending the Land Rover down into the scrap yard's crusher.

Skipping a number of oily puddles, Anders made his way across the cobbled yard before stopping at a Jag that was parked up by a stack of wrecked vehicles. Ignoring a snarling Alsatian that was tied-up to a metal chain he looked back across the yard. In seconds his old Land Rover would be the size of a television set, another part of his past gone forever. Or was it? Something kept on nagging.

As the Jag sped out of the wooden gates of 'Turner's Scrap Yard' it headed towards the setting sun. As he drove, Anders constantly checked the rear-view. Old habits died hard. His latest kill wasn't easy. An iron bar across the back of the scruff's scull had sent him crashing to the cobbles, but like the Polish doorman he wouldn't die without a fight and had to be whacked again and again. Making sure blood didn't splash onto his clothes, he stripped-down to his boxers. After slitting the Alsatian's throat he hit the red button of the crusher and within seconds the scruff's body had joined man's best friend.

'There's no regrets,
No tears goodbye,
I don't want you back,
We'd only cry, cry again,
Say goodbye again.'

Although he'd used the scruff before, this time he noticed he was surly, evasive, he couldn't take the chance.

After an hour on the motorway Anders was satisfied he wasn't being followed and turned off a slip road. A mile into the countryside, he swung into a muddy lane which led along a heavy wooded dirt track. Turning off the Jag's engine he lowered the window and listened. Overhead, a ghostly breeze rustled through the branches of the trees and apart from a few birds the only noise he could hear was from the rumble of the traffic on the nearby motorway. Suddenly a dog barked and he heard voices. Opening the glove compartment he reached inside for his gun. Then the shout of a woman crackled through the air. Through the side window and overhanging branches he watched as an elderly couple came into view at the turn of the track. Wearing matching red anoraks they started to make their way up the track in his direction. Too busy arguing, they were oblivious to the Jag concealed in the thicket of the trees. Calling out to their dog, they suddenly changed direction and disappeared.

Jumping out of the Jag, Anders started dismantling a pile of branches next to the car. The smell of rotting foliage rose into the air as slowly a Silver BMW was uncovered. Stripping off the vinyl, false number plates, Anders disposed of them through the window of the Jag. Suddenly from out of the thicket a Jack Russell appeared and started scurrying around his ankles. Growling and sniffing, Anders tried to kick it away. But the dog came back for more and started barking. He could hear the shouts of the woman. Reaching through the open window of the Jag, he picked up his gun off the passenger seat. Kicking out at the dog again, Anders heard the woman's voice joined by the man's, they were getting nearer. Anders' finger hovered on the trigger, he could feel his heart beating and he had started to sweat. Catching the dog under the jaw with the toe of his shoe, the dog yelped and ran off down the track. Lucky for him and its owners.

Back on the motorway Anders tapped a number into his mobile phone then pressed 'send'. In the woods the Jag exploded into a million pieces sending up a large mushroom cloud of black smoke.

Anders' shoulders dropped as he sat back in the BMW, for the first time in days he could relax. Switching on a CD of The Swinging Sixties, he went straight for the track by the Walker Brothers, then thought twice, that song was for special occasions. The Tears of a Clown by Smokey Robison and the Miricles would do nicely. It was getting dark as the robotic voice of the sat-nav gave him his next direction. *Turn off at the next junction.* It had been set to an address just outside Oxford.

CHAPTER FORTY-THREE

Outside the prison gates, a swarm of journalists and photographers had been arriving since dawn. Finch was big news, international news and it hadn't taken long for the jungle drums to find their way to Fleet Street. Some screw would be a few grand richer for the tip-off. The police had erected metal barriers in front of the gates and were marshalling the media frenzy behind it. Brainforth hadn't witnessed anything like it since the last public hanging.

Tony sat watching the crowd through the side window of his car and tried to collate his story, his alibi, the lies he was about to spin. A couple of loud knocks rattled the window. Like a Jack-in-a-box Jennings had appeared from nowhere. With an aggressive look across his face, he gestured for Tony to lower the window. Appearing agitated and nervy he surveyed the milling crowd outside the prison gates, his fingers strumming the roof of the car.

'You look like your car, shit.'

'I feel like shit.'

'What are you going to say happened to you?'

'I'll say Rogers accidentally hit me with a squash racket.'

'Then you'll have to think of something else.'

'Why?'

'Because Rogers is dead.'

'What?' Tony's heart missed a beat.

'His car was found burnt out, up at Buttercup Hill. A copper mate of mine rang me this morning. He thought I should know before the press got hold of it.'

As Tony tried to get out of the car Jennings threw his weight behind the door. 'Take it easy.'

'I want to get out!' Putting his shoulder against the car door, Tony pulled down the door handle and pushed. Pain shot through his ribs, the agony shuddering through his body. Jennings leant down to the open window, the tone of his voice, soft, composed. 'I said take it easy.'

'What was he doing up at Buttercup Hill? He could hardly walk never mind drive.' Jennings leered down on him. 'Keep your voice down – most of the officers in Brainforth know you don't like me and visa-versa, if they spot us talking it'll look suspicious and the way your hands are flashing in and out of the window like a tic-tac man you'll make the fucking situation worse.' Tony had no option but to sit tight as the pain in his side intensified.

'The police will question us. The way I look at it we have no choice. We have to say that Rogers came to your house last night. He was drunk, pissed out of his head. Tell them he'd been drinking brandy all night. When he arrived in his car you told him he was mad driving, but he took nothing in, he was that drunk. Tell them he looked worried, you had never seen him act that way before, then he told you he wanted to go somewhere quiet, somewhere to think. You never saw me, understand, you never saw me. Again, when he left, you pleaded with him not to drive. He left about one in the morning. Where's your mobile?'

'Why?'

'Just give it me!' Confused, Tony removed the mobile from inside his jacket.

Snatching the phone out of Tony's hand, Jennings removed the sim-card, dropped it to ground and stamped on it. 'When the police ask you questions about Rogers and what happened yesterday, you know what to say…'

'It doesn't make sense; you were the one that was driving.'

Jennings tossed the hollow phone through the window on to Tony's lap. 'Anyone asks for your phone tell them you lost it'

'What happened after you left me?'

'I drove him home and left him in his car to sleep it off. He was a dead weight, I couldn't move him. He must have driven up there by himself – Listen, he would have sent us both down with him. He was obsessed with the security tape. I said I would fix it and I have done.' Their conversation halted when a young woman, wearing a baseball cap and wrapped up in a puffer-jacket walked past. She was carrying a tray of take-away coffees and looked like she was preparing herself for a couple of long arduous days outside the prison. She diverted their attention for a minute, giving Tony time to think. 'Where is the tape?'

'It doesn't matter.'

Jennings stepped away from the car and opened the door. Tony struggled to climb out. 'What if the police question us individually?'

'They will do.'

Tony looked Jennings directly in the eye. 'What did you do to him?'

A look of madness appeared in Jennings eyes. 'I didn't do anything to him.'

'I don't believe you.'

Jennings scanned the car park to see if anybody was watching, then, with a sly dig he punched Tony in the ribs. Buckling over, Tony wheezed in agony. Instinctively his fist clenched, his immediate reaction was to strike, but he held back. 'You're crazy.'

Unruffled, Jennings took hold of Tony's arm, then nodded towards Brainforth. 'Crazy? Blame it on that place.' Cool-as-you-like, Jennings continued. 'A word of advice Tony, get out of the prison service quick as you can, you don't want to spend the rest of your life behind bars do you?'

The two officers started walking across the car park, as a cold gust cut into the side of their faces.

The young girl was leaning against a large van with the words 'BBC Outside Broadcast' on the side. As she sipped her coffee, she smiled at the two men as they walked past and brought a walkie-talkie up to her mouth. Jennings was alert, his eyes everywhere.

'The police will at some time connect Rogers and Finch. If we tell them Rogers looked continually agitated in Finch's company. If we say Finch kept on winding him up. We thought Rogers could take it, but obviously he couldn't.' Jennings turned into Tony's ear. 'You fuck things up and it will be the last thing you do. I know everyone. Inside and outside.' Then once again he became unnervingly calm, collective. 'Listen Tony, if there was any other way out of this I would take it. Stick to the story and everything will work out fine. Trust me.' Jennings spoke out the corner of his mouth. 'They will estimate the time of death and put two-and-two-together. If they thought we were involved in any way the police would have called by now. That's how they operate. We've covered our tracks, now take it easy. By the way, that copper friend of mine is a Chief Inspector. He has given me an alibi. We played cards at his house all night – What's yours?'

Jennings wore a smile as they waded through the crowd of journalists. Tony followed, his head down, his mind everywhere. With Finch he was desperate for the money, with him dying it was a way out, but with Rogers it was different, he was his friend. Now he was planning more lies, to cover Jennings' back as well as his own, he felt like he'd made a pact with the devil. Pushing his way through the note books and cameras, Tony felt the pain in his ribs as he was jostled by a couple of reporters. Panic rushed through him. Jennings had covered his tracks, he had the night to arrange an alibi and with a copper. He didn't.

'Hey pal, do you have any news from inside, about Finch?' A microphone was thrust into Jennings' face. 'Sorry I'm not at liberty to comment.' The journalist was young, aggressive, with a spotty complexion. A few cameras flashed. 'Did Finch kill himself or did someone get to him first?' As the press buffeted each other to get to Jennings, one of the journalists spilt coffee over the back of his knuckles. After swearing at himself his cockney tongue fired another question in Tony's direction.

'What will they do with the body? I can make it worth your while!' A frenzy of questions followed Tony and Jennings as they were guided through the metal barriers by two policemen. At the prison gates Jennings turned towards Tony. 'Stick to the story.'

For all the wrong reasons, the buzz inside Brainforth was electric. The officer on the gate raised his eyebrows and nodded in the direction of the Governor's office. Enough said.

Humidity was a thing a prison officer had to get used to inside Brainforth or any other prison; it was part of the job, but today the air was different, everyone could taste it. The previous day Tony felt like the eyes of the prison were upon him, today they were.

In the small office an ageing computer sat on a single desk along with a framed photograph of two, toothless infants, a small tray of paperclips and a few ballpoints. The little light that did creep through the window cast shadows from a cast-iron fire escape outside, making the room darker than it should have been. Standing on a grey filing cabinet a glass vase full of drooping red carnations brought the only colour to the drabness in the room.

As Tony sat on a bench seat that ran the far wall he caught his reflection in the blackness of the computer screen. Apart from the bruising around his cheeks and forehead, the colour had drained from his face. Running his hand across his face he looked at Jennings standing at the window. Turning briefly he gave Tony a look over his shoulder. *Stick to the story.*

It was a look obsessed with control. Tony was living on his nerves, his eyes became fixed on the imposing door to the Governors office, it was like a trap door and he wondered how he was going to survive the grilling that was imminent. Glancing down, he noticed Jennings' highly polished Doc-martins. He looked immaculate. Clean shaven, with a line perfectly creased down the front and back of his trousers, his shirt, whiter than white. In his familiar stance like a sergeant major, with his hands clasped behind his back; his recent trip to the hairdressers had left a white track-mark that ran around the side of his head to a perfect square-neck. Unruffled, he looked the pinnacle of respectability.

Hearing muffled voices behind the Governor's office door it swung open and a middle aged secretary walked out.

'The Governor is ready to see you gentlemen.' Her voice was gravely and she wore a plain grey trouser suit which was as plain as her expression and as grey as her office. Tony caught the fragrance of her perfume. He thought of Rogers and how his eyes would have flashed towards her large breasts concealed under her white blouse and jacket. Tightness lodged in his throat as he followed Jennings through the doorway into the Governor's office.

Seeing the large round room for the first time, Tony became overwhelmed by the power of the establishment. Nostalgic black and white photographs of the prison filled one wall, reminding Tony of the photographs he'd seen in the park café when he'd gone to meet Young. In the far corner of the room a coffee percolator bubbled away next to an opened pack of chocolate digestives. In the other corner a set of golf clubs rested next to a dusty display cabinet holding a single, silver cup with the inscribed words, 'HMP Athletics Club 1965.'

Sitting behind a large leather-topped desk Governor Morris' head was submerged in a thick file which he was studying meticulously. Like his secretary he wore a grey double breasted suit to match his grey personality. Taking a peek over the top of his bifocals he acknowledged the two officers as they entered his office. 'Good morning gentlemen, there's only two of you?'

'Yes sir, Rogers hasn't reported in today.'

Morris gestured for the men to sit. 'I won't be a minute, please take a seat.'

The formality and interrogative tone in Morris' voice added to the tension, the only thing missing was a black cloud hanging over his head. Tony sat to the left of Jennings, to the right of him an empty chair reserved for Rogers. One minute turned into two then three, as the officers waited to be addressed by Morris or scolded, either way Tony knew Morris had no intention of being the fall-guy.

Heartburn caused Tony to fidget and he could sense the anxiety coming at him from Jennings' direction. Trying to compose himself, he started to hypothesize about Morris. Looking across the desk, he noticed the silver tie and matching silver hankie sticking-out of his breast pocket like a pyramid. He surmised it as a box-set, that was most probably given to him at Christmas. A present given to him by his equally grey wife.

A number of thin strips of hair were combed from the front of his tanned, bald head, to the back, giving the impression of railway lines disappearing into the distance. It was a cruel twist of fate as to why Morris became a prison Governor. After graduating from Oxford University, just, Morris applied for a position in Highways construction. After a clerical mixed-up by the local council he found himself being interviewed for a job as a prison Governor. A distant uncle, who owed the family a big favour, persuaded him that he would be 'made for the job'. Fast-tracking him through the prison service and after a year strolling the landings and indoctrinated into prison protocol he was offered the top job inside Brainforth. It was a job he loathed. In the past eighteen months, Tony recollected seeing Morris on the shop floor on no more than three occasions. The first time was when an entourage of government ministers were reviewing prison reform. The second, he was orchestrating a good-will gesture for a group of humanitarians who were visiting British prisons from Brazil; on both occasions he acted like a buffoon and talked down his nose to the prison officers like children. Then of course there was the traditional Christmas walk-about. Like a politician with his sights set on Prime Minister, he walked around *his prison* shaking hands with everyone. If there had been a baby to be kissed for a publicity photograph he would have posed for that as well.

The Governor's office overlooked the prison yard. Like past Governors, Tony wondered about the number of times a prisoner would have looked up and caught eye contact with the Governor who was looking down on them. In the past they would have been feeling the sunshine or the rain on their faces for the last time before the hangman put the hood over their heads. How many times had Morris looked out of his window and down on Finch wandering around the yard reading? How many times had they caught eye contact with each other? Did Morris ever catch that grin?

With a constipated expression across his face Morris looked up from his file and ogled the officers like a Head Master who was about to tick-off two naughty school boys. Picking up a pencil, he started tapping the leather on the desktop. He was as nervous as them and hesitated before he spoke. 'So gentleman *we have a problem* as Huston once said.'

'Sir, if I may talk first?'

'You're the most senior officer Mr Jennings, is that right?'

'Yes sir.'

'I thought so.' Morris' tone tried to convince himself of his competence if nothing else.

'When we left Finch he was his usual self. As far as I could make out he was under no distress whatsoever and he gave us no reason to believe he would take his own life.'

'Well he did Mr Jennings.'

Jennings stuttered, lost for words. Then, at the last second he found his voice again. 'Yes sir, we can only surmise that he was slipped the razor blade when we finished our shift.'

Morris pondered the statement rearranging the crease in his trousers. Then he swung his attention at Tony. 'And you Mr Evans?'

'I have no idea what happened sir.'

Tony didn't know were the words had come from and why the lies didn't stick in his throat.

'What's happened to your face?'

'It's embarrassing sir, I tripped on the bottom of my dressing gown and fell down the stairs.' Another lie, Tony sounded convincing.

'Have you been looked at?'

'No need sir, it looks worse than it really is.'

Morris took his gaze to the empty seat then to his secretary who was hovering by the window. 'Helen will you try ringing Mr Rogers for me please. Helen left the office as Marsh continued tapping his pencil on the desk. 'I suppose you have no idea how he obtained the razor blade?'

'No sir.' Jennings' voice was strong, direct.

Morris sighed. 'You're sure nobody is passing the buck Mr Jennings?'

'No sir.'

'You know what I'm worried the press will see gentlemen?' Morris pointed the pencil first at Jennings then at Tony, then at the empty chair. 'The three wise monkeys. See no evil. Hear no evil. Speak no evil.' It seems Marsh had a sense of humour. 'They will ask questions as to why three officers couldn't prevent this from happening and of course the press will have a field day. *Prison cover-up, white wash.* Not to mention I've had to cancel golf in the Algarve this weekend.' Morris looked across at the two men for some sort of response, it wasn't forthcoming. 'I'm the one on the front line, I'm the one who has to face the press. As you are well aware, this incident will be on the front pages of every newspaper in the morning. Finch has always been front page news. I will ask you this once only, is there anything I should be made aware of, before I put myself, Brainforth and all our reputations on the line?'

'No sir.' The words were in unison. *All for one, one for all,* except for Rogers, who would never utter another word. 'I need a full report from all three of you on my desk by first thing tomorrow morning and of course you'll be witnesses at the coroner's court. Are your logs up to date?'

Jennings answered for the two of them again. 'Yes sir.'

'Good. We're all held accountable in here.'

For a second Morris returned to his file then looked up again, his voice candid with the next question. 'We also have the little problem as to why the security tape of the incident didn't record properly.' Tony felt sick. He could feel himself wanting to look at Jennings, see his reaction. A silent sigh of relief blew through the prison from the two officers as Morris continued.

'Normally somebody would contact the prison to claim the body. But nobody will. A corporation funeral, that's all Finch will get. I suppose that's all he deserved.'

Morris' secretary came back through the door. 'Mr Rogers isn't answering his phone sir.'

'Keep trying please Helen.'

'Yes sir.' Closing the door behind her, the smell of her perfume hung in the room. Morris looked across at Jennings. 'Have you cleared out his cell?'

'No sir, not yet, it won't take long, Finch had few possessions.'

'Good. If nothing else we need the space. I think that's all for now gentlemen.'

As the two officers stood to leave, Morris spoke. 'I believe it's your last day tomorrow Mr Jennings?'

'Yes sir, thirty two years.'

'Congratulations, the prison service will miss conscientious officers like yourself.'

'Thank you sir, you're welcome to join us for a drink tonight.'

'I might just do that.' But he had no intention.

Helen was sitting behind her desk on the phone. She looked bored and Tony spotted her clock-watching, he wanted to tell her she was wasting her time in phoning Rogers. It was a phone call that would never be answered. Jennings smiled at her and she returned the smile, if you could call them smiles. They were secret smiles that had been nurtured between the two of them over the years. Rumour had it that Jennings and Helen had been having an affair and from the look the two of them gave each other it only enhanced the gossip. Now he knew how Jennings had got hold of his phone number and obtained his address the night he came to collect Rogers.

For the rest of the day the two officers ran the gauntlet of questions from prisoners and officers alike.

'What did Morris say?'

'How did Finch die?'

'Did someone kill the bastard?'

'Did he commit suicide?'

Avoiding Jennings all day, Tony had spotted him on the landing. He seemed relaxed and walked with his usual swagger, whereas Tony was on edge. Thoughts of covering up Finch's suicide had now been overtaken by Rogers' death. He knew at any time the police would come calling and he could feel the stress throughout his body tightening with every passing second.

'We need a little chat.' Jennings was waiting for Tony outside the locker room. Looking both ways down the corridor, Jennings ushered him in through the door. Unusual for the time of day the room was dark. Closing the door behind them Jennings flicked on the light. 'Surprise!' Strewn across the back wall was a banner with the words *Congratulations on your retirement.* The locker room was full of officers; some uniformed some ready to paint the town red. Jennings faced the celebrations head-on and took all the handshakes and back slapping in his usual style. Blending into the background, Tony headed for his locker. Watching the centre of attention smile and soak up the adulation of the officers; the more he looked at Jennings the more the rage burnt-up inside him. As the men filtered out, Tony overheard Jennings saying he was going to get changed and meet them at 'The Lock Up' the pub hidden away in a cul-de-sac at the back of the prison. The small function room upstairs was a convenient place hired by officers and over the years it had seen its share of retirement parties, wetting the baby's head and strip-a-grams. If anything was worth celebrating it was celebrated in that small room, it was the customary venue and the walls could tell a thousand stories. Rogers had his 30th birthday party there and organised his own stripper. That was Rogers.

Jennings waited for the last officer to leave. 'What did I tell you, a piece of cake.' Jennings was smug as ever.

'What are you talking about? We'll be interviewed by Morris again and questioned by the police.'

'And?'

'What do you mean, *and*? You know what coppers are like, they'll try and catch us out.'

'Well they won't if we stick to the story.' Jennings unlocked his locker and to Tony's surprise removed Finch's sweet tin.

'What are you doing with that?'

'We need to check the contents, just in case there's anything in here that might...' Jennings smiled with an air of sarcasm in his voice. 'Incriminate us.'

'What if someone comes in?'

'They're all gone to *my retirement party* if you hadn't noticed.' With every passing minute Jennings was drawing Tony into his web of deceit and murder. He was using words like *us* and *we* and the more he used them the weaker Tony seemed to become. For a few seconds he tried to step back and analyse the situation, but there wasn't a split second to think. Every second, every minute, seemed to unearth more and more about Jennings. Prising opened the lid of the tin, Jennings laughed as he took out the postcard of Shirley Temple. 'We could sell this on eBay, make a few bob.'

Jennings laughed again. Tipping out the contents of the tin onto the table, Jennings sifted through a number of photographs and passed them on. Half-expecting to find another one of himself, Tony paused at a black and white snap of Finch as a young boy with his mother. The photograph was taken at the seaside and they were holding ice creams. It was a picture of innocence. Another more recent one was of him and his elderly mother sitting on a swing chair in a back garden. She was wearing a flowery dress and he was wearing a maroon sweater with snow flakes running across the chest. His flock of black hair rested on her shoulder and mirrored the image of him slumped between the toilet bowl and his bed, the blood flowing from his wrists. As Jennings filtered through the pages of Finch's bible, Tony spotted a hand-written address on an envelope, he recognised the writing instantly and opened it. It was from Young and dated six months ago.

Finch,

As you can see I've left off the Mr, which is reserved for a man, a human being which you are not. In my previous letters, which I know you have received I have asked, why you are still here, breathing on this earth? I have asked you to do the decent thing and dispose of yourself. Then decency is a thing you would know nothing about. Therefore I have taken the matter into my own hands. This is the last time you will receive a letter from me, because as from today my energy will be to get to you in a manner that you will only be too familiar with.

Hopefully your days are numbered.

Brian Young.

Suddenly the letter was snatched out of his hand. Jennings' eyes went straight to the name at the bottom of the letter. 'Brian Young, you know who he is, don't you?'

'Yes.'

'Poor bastard.' Smiling, Jennings picked a sweet out of the tin, unravelled a mint and popped it into his mouth. 'Nothing to worry about in here.' Satisfied, Jennings rummaged around in the bottom of the tin and took out the remainder of the sweets. Holding them in the palm of his hand, he held them out to Tony as if it was some sort of peace offering. Tony shook his head.

Jennings popped another one into his mouth. 'Suit yourself.'

Opening his locker, Jennings removed a sport bag and threw the reminder of the sweets inside, then mumbled something as the sweet travelled around the inside of his mouth. Tony hoped he would choke on it. Putting the photographs, postcard and letters back into the sweet tin, Jennings put on the lid then placed it back inside his locker. It was then that Tony caught a glimpse of a VHS tape.

Turning into Tony's face, Jennings picked at the mint between his teeth 'You want to liven up, because sooner or later it will get us both into fucking serious trouble. I've warned you sonny.'

Tony stood his ground. 'I know you murdered Rogers.'

Jennings swung around and shoved Tony up against the lockers. 'Shut your mouth Evans, You've already lied about Finch to Morris and you've lied about not knowing where Rogers was last night. You never raised the alarm yesterday. You're up to your neck in this.'

'Is that the tape in your locker?'

'What tape? Jennings slammed his locker door shut. 'One push of a button and it was wiped clean along with all the other tapes in the prison. A technical problem apparently. So there goes the suspicion of any cover-ups.' Unruffled, Jennings turned the key in the door of his locker. 'Forget Rogers, he was a waste of time, a loser, why don't you come and have a drink?' As Jennings turned to walk to the door, Tony hesitated, then spoke. 'You know when you give your farewell speech tonight? Explain this!'

The punch that had decked the Yank in the Casino the previous week appeared from nowhere, but on this occasion it came from the heart. Reeling backwards, Jennings tottered on his heels before smashing against the locker room door, blood dripping from his nose before he hit the ground. It only needed one punch, that was enough. Whereas the Yank could take a punch, Jennings couldn't. Sprawled against the bottom of the door, the shine had been removed from his polished boots as well as his ego. His fist once again throbbed, his side felt like a knife had gone through it, but it was worth it. Looking down on the scrunched up figure, he didn't feel guilty or any remorse about hitting an older man, the punch was well overdue. Jennings was out cold. Bending down, Tony removed the locker key from a bunch of keys that were inside Jennings' pocket. Opening the locker, Tony removed the VHS tape and tucked it under his belt and inside the back of his shirt. Tossing the key into Jennings lap he grabbed the heels of his boots and pulled him away from the door. As he slid him across the floor on his back he could feel the tacks on the bottom of his boots cutting into the heels of his hands. With his legs in the air Jennings came-to. Slowly realising what was happening he looked up at the silhouetted figure pulling him across the floor.

'I'll get you for this.' Dropping his legs to the floor with a thud, Tony lent over Jennings. 'That one was for Rogers!'

Tony left the room.

Running his index finger and thumb under the bottom of his nose Jennings inspected the blood, then looking up he noticed the door to his locker was wide open.

Stepping outside A-Block, Tony tried to ignore the cacophony of excitement bouncing from one prison window to the next.

'Lollypop is on the telly!'

'About time someone got that nonce!'

'I heard he hung himself!'

'With his own dick!'

Laughter floated down from the cell windows as Tony made his way across the yard. As he approached the security gate he was surprised at see the rotund figure of George Rose being escorted through by two officers. For a prisoner, passing through that particular security gate it meant only one thing. He was being taken up to the Governor's office. George spotted him and smiled. 'Our holiday will have to wait for the time being Mr Evans.'

Tony looked inquisitively at one of the officers. 'What's he done?'

'He's owned up to the attack on Finch, the one in the showers.'

The other officer looked at him off-handedly. 'At least Finch and George have livened up the place.' It was then that Tony noticed the tattoo on George's arm. It was of a serpent wrapped round a dagger. George mimed a throat cutting motion. 'I slipped up with Finch I'm no good with a knife, but it's difficult getting piano wire in here.' George smiled and laughed at the same time, a gleam of evil in his eyes. Smelling and tasting his own sweat, Tony looked up and caught Morris looking down on him from the office window of his Ivory Tower. Morris didn't move, a golf club slung over one shoulder, his face insipid.

Outside the prison the crowd had swelled. The snarl-up of heavy traffic mixed with the chit-chat of journalists and onlookers rattled through the misty rain. Scaffolding had been erected in one part of the car park and a smartly dressed woman holding a microphone was being filmed transmitting a live broadcast to the nation. Tony recognised her from Breakfast TV, the one in the white blouse and heavy make-up. Pushing through the camera men and stepping over discarded coffee cups, Tony caught another news reporter applying his own make-up by the side of a truck. He was being directed by an irritated young man wearing headphones, that he was 'on-the-air-in-three.'

Even in hell, Finch was still making headlines.

CHAPTER FORTY-FOUR

Tony knew Jennings would come after him. If he had murdered Rogers and if he'd instigated Finch's death he was capable of anything. For some unknown reason he'd driven the wrong way out of the prison car park and found himself parked-up outside his mother's Nursing Home. He couldn't remember getting there. Looking at the security tape on the passenger seat, his thoughts were interrupted by a young woman struggling to manoeuvre a wheelchair through the home's double doors. Recognising the skeletal figure in the wheelchair as the old man who lived in the next room to his mother, he smiled to himself. 'Old Arthur' as his mum called him was off to the pub for his weekly constitution of beer and scotch. Every time he visited his mother he knew what to expect. If she wasn't complaining about the cold coffee, she was moaning about having to take her prescribed medication. '*Tablets fit for an elephant*' as she referred to them. Refusing to swallow the tablets, she would hide them under her tongue, and then spit them out afterwards, just like Jack Nicholson in One Flew over the Cuckoo's Nest. She drove the nurses mad with her stubbornness. It was a family trait.

There wasn't a good or bad time to visit his mother. Some days were better than others. Like all eighty year olds she was never free from aches and pains and when her arthritis kicked-in his mother was no different. She had strong opinions on everything, religion, politics, particularly the morals of politicians. She liked to read and rattled off a book a week. Over the years she had won everything by entering crossword competitions, winning televisions, cameras, tea-sets and on one occasion a shopping weekend in New York. She could fly through any cryptic crossword that was put in front of her and her mind was still sharp as a knife.

The security at the nursing home reminded him of Brainforth. To enter through the double doors and into the building you had to ring a bell. It was more often answered by an incoherent voice through an intercom. After being questioned and grilled as to whom he was visiting, a male nurse called Henry would usually buzz him in, reminding him of the nursing home rules. 'Please sign in.' Name, who he was visiting, car registration, date, time. Wondering what all the security was about, he often shared a joke with his mother about whether she was at risk of being abducted by aliens or she was a spy with MI5. Henry always addressed Tony as 'Tonnneeey'. With blond tinted hair and two silver earrings in his left ear he spoke with a soft, effeminate, Welsh accent. Whenever he spoke he laughed nervously. At first Tony thought it was just in his company and Anne used to tease him about whether he was *really going to see his mother or Henry?* The manner of his high-pitched laugh made certain people feel uneasy in his company, but Tony liked him as he was kind to his mother. Pleading with Tony to have words with his mother over taking her *elephant tablets,* Tony said he would do his best but couldn't guarantee a result. Henry laughed nervously then told him that his mother was in the conservatory playing scrabble.

Outside the last remains of daylight had disappeared along with the view of the large garden with its award-winning rose bushes. The windows in the conservatory were pitch-black reflecting the bright lights of the nursing home and everyone inside. Tony spotted his mother slumped forward over the scrabble board by the far window. She was asleep in a hard backed chair and wrapped around her shoulders was the woollen shawl he'd given her as a present for her 80th birthday. A woman about the same age as his mother, with recently blue rinsed hair sat opposite and turned a piece of scrabble around in her frail fingers. Approaching the ladies to the sound of Frank Sinatra crackling from a CD player he spoke softy. 'Hello I'm Elsie's son.'

The old lady looked up, her green eyes focusing on his face. 'Who?'

Tony spoke a little louder. 'I'm Elsie's son.'

'Oh hello, she's been asleep for about half an hour, she didn't have a very good night last night. I said it might have been the milk in the tea, it didn't taste right.' The piece of scrabble fell out of her hands and bounced around the plain grey carpet.

'Oh dear, could you pick that up for me please deary' Tony knelt down and picked up the letter Z. 'You'll have a tough job getting rid of that letter.'

She smiled, an endearing smile. 'Oh I have something up my sleeve, your mother plays a tough game you know.' Tony drew up a chair and sat down. With that, Elsie stirred and slowly came to terms with her surroundings and the brightness in the conservatory.

'Hello Mum.'

Elsie rocked backwards and focused on the face in front of her. 'Hello son.'

'Are you alright Mum?'

'Yes I'm fine. Is Martha with you?'

'No, I'll bring her next time. I'm just paying a quick visit.'

'What happened to your face?'

'Playing squash.' He tried to recollect whether he'd ever lied to his mother before. He reckoned he must have done, as a young boy growing up. A white lie here, a white lie there, but this white lie was blacker than black. 'Henry says you're not taking your tablets?'

'I don't need to take them. Do you want me to grow big ears and a trunk?'

'Mum please, you have to take them.'

'We'll see.' She looked at the lady opposite, smiled and shrugged.

Looking at the board, Tony pondered the conundrums of the letters. 'So who's winning?'

'I can't remember.' His mother chuckled.

'It's my go Elsie.' With that, the lady placed the Z onto the board. 'Zoologist. I think that's a few points to me.' With a broad smile across her face she picked up a pen and scribbled down the score. Tony watched his mother, her eyes flashing from her letters in front of her to the words on the board. Concentrating, her delicate fingers finally picked up three pieces and moved them up to her thin lips. Contemplating her move, her hand crossed the board with the conviction of a chess master placing the letters Q, U and I on top of Zoologist to make the word 'Quiz'. Elsie turned and gave Tony a sly wink. That's what he loved about her; she was a smart-cookie. Scribbling down the numbers, her opponent added up the score. After double checking she conceded defeat.

'That's five games to three to you Elsie.'

'It was a good game though wasn't it Shirley?'

Elsie was always diplomatic in victory. Knowing she only had a limited number of opponents in the home she occasionally let them win so they didn't become too disillusioned by defeat. That was Tony's mother, she was also gracious.

Henry came into the room, placed both hands on his hips and made an announcement in the manner of a camp, game show host.

'Stew and dumplings are now being served in the dining room.'

Both women looked at each other and grimaced. Henry walked over to where they were sitting. 'Have you had a word with Elsie Tonnneeey?'

'Yes, she said she'll take them.'

'Good girl Elsie.' He raised his eyebrows, he didn't seem convinced. As Henry walked away, his mum leant over and whispered to her son. 'He's as daft as a brush you know.'

Tony laughed and stood up. 'Alright mum, I'll leave you to your stew and dumplings. I'll see you next week.'

'Will you bring Martha with you?'

'Yes, I'll bring her straight from school.' Tony met Shirley's eyes; they were bright sparkling and focused. 'Nice to meet you.'

'I wish I had a son like you.'

Flattered by the remark, Tony held her gaze for a few moments before kissing his mother on the cheek and leaving. Passing a number of old-timers shuffling on their zimmers he made his way out of the conservatory and into reception. A framed picture of Lord Mountbatten looked down on him as he picked up the pen to sign-out. A puzzled expression swept across his face, something had irritated him and played on his mind, but he didn't know what.

'Come on Elsie.' Henry's high pitched voice echoed round the conservatory. Turning around, Tony looked back through the door. Henry was helping his mother into a wheel chair. It gave him peace of mind, she was in good hands. Then to his surprise he watched as Henry shot a stern, cold, remark towards Shirley.

'You'll have to wait your turn Shirley, understand!' It perplexed him. How could someone be so caring to his mother and abrupt and uncompassionate to another old lady? Although it wasn't any of his business, it made him feel uncomfortable.

'Shirley! I've told you, you'll have to bloody wait!' Taking a step back towards the conservatory door, Tony became transfixed by the situation. As he watched Henry wheel his mother through the adjoining door into the dinning room, his eyes moved back towards Shirley. Studying the old lady's face, he watched as she dabbed away a tear on her gaunt face with the rags of a tissue. Then it hit him, suddenly everything became clear. His mind flashed back to the contents in Finch's sweet tin and the photograph of Finch resting his head on his mother's shoulder. The woman, who minutes earlier had been sitting opposite his mother playing scrabble, was Finch's mother.

CHAPTER FORTY-FIVE

Tony felt suffocated as he drove home. Inside Brainforth, Finch's fixation with his mother was common knowledge. But he questioned why, of all the nursing homes in Oxfordshire, in which there were hundreds, why was she in the same nursing home as his mother? If Finch had gone to such bizarre extremes as to organise it from inside his cell, it could only be for only one reason, emotional blackmail. In helping him to commit suicide, Tony would have to look after the welfare of Finch's mother as well as his own mother. Finch would have the self gratification, the peace of mind knowing that she would always have a visitor who had a guilty conscience. Then he wondered why he'd turned the wrong way out of the prison and visited that particular evening, surely someone would have informed the old lady that her son was dead. Or would they?

Flashing past 'The Highwayman', his mobile rang. It was Jennings. He ignored the call. It was the third time he'd rung in the past hour. Skidding to a stop, he did a U-turn and swung the car around. He needed a drink, time to think.

A swirl of gold and silver coloured leaves followed Tony through the low, creaking wooden door of the 'The Highwayman.' The pub boasted being the oldest pub in Oxfordshire and was his and Anne's regular drinking hole before Martha had come along. Behind the bar in an old wooden cabinet was a leather highwayman's boot. Supposedly belonging to 'Dick Turpin', the locals had always been cynical to the myth, but turned a blind eye to it bringing in the odd American or Japanese tourist. Ducking under the low wooden beams that lined the ceiling he leaned on the bar and looked around for a familiar face. The bar was empty, the only sound coming from the crackling and spitting of an open fire at the far end of the room. Suddenly Joan, the smiley, smiley landlady who had pulled pints there for years appeared behind the bar and poured him his usual. For a minute or two they made small talk about the weather. Oblivious to her chatter, all he needed was a quiet corner. Deciding on the window seat by the open fire he walked across the stone floor and sat down. As he took his first sip of beer, he looked up and found Joan standing over him. Wiping down his table with a cloth that smelt of strong bleach, she smiled again. Resisting the temptation to look down her cleavage, he thought once again of his friend Rogers. He would have loved the moment. Her smile, which was starting to annoy him, reminded him of someone. Someone in his past, but he couldn't think who. Recently his life was full of surprises.

Alone at last, he stared into the embers of the fire. He thought of Martha's smile and how it could light up a room and for a couple of minutes his worries disappeared. Closing his eyes, it was good to feel the warmth of the flames on his face and the beer tasted good. But with every drop of beer, another problem came into his head. There was another reason why he stopped at the 'The Highwayman.' Sipping his pint, he looked across the room at the fruit machine. Its flashing lights flickered around the brass ornaments like a seventies disco ball and he couldn't resist.

One little bet won't hurt.

One little bet won't hurt.

Pulling some loose change out of his pocket he ploughed the coins into the machine. The jackpot was £50, nowhere near as inviting as the Las Vegas machine in the casino, but it didn't concern him, a-bet-was-a-bet. If somebody had put an empty shoebox in front of him with a slot in the top, he would have lost money in that as well.

Looking at the coins in the palm of his hand Tony had an option, another pint or the rest of his money in the machine.

One little bet won't hurt.

Go on Tony, one little bet won't hurt.

The side of his fist thumped the fruit machine, he was used to losing, but his thump meant something else, it was meant to hurt.

Slumping onto a seat nearer the fire he heard the pub door open behind him. It sent a cold gust whistling around the pub, the bite of the wind making him roll his shoulders. He didn't bother to turn around, just moved closer to the fire. Whoever walked in held no interest for him, the last thing he wanted was company. Overhearing the landlady once again wax lyrical about the weather, the sound of her voice grated on him. Rubbing the heat of the fire through his hands, he moved back to his previous seat and picked up his pint. Over the top of his beer glass he watched as a man pulled up a stool and sat down in front of the fire. Wearing a pink golfing sweater under a navy blue jacket, his baggy grey trousers hung loosely around his waist. Stealing the heat from the room the man took a mouthful from a large brandy. Untying his shoelace, he removed his shoe and started massaging the cold out of his toes. Tony was drawn to his unusually bright orange socks which looked out of character with the rest of his conservative clothes. Swilling the brandy around in the glass he held it up to the fire then took a gulp.

'Excuse me, you're blocking the heat.'

The man ignored him and continued massaging his toes.

'Did you hear me, you're blocking out the heat.'

The man leant down, slipped on his shoe and started tying his lace. Knocking back the brandy in one, he stood up and without acknowledging Tony's existence walked out of the bar. Following the man with her eyes the landlady looked back across the room at Tony and shrugged.

Pockets empty of cash, Tony finished his beer and placed the empty pint glass on the bar, smiling a *goodbye* as he walked out.

The sky was black and somewhere a number of cows wanted milking. The air was fresh, mixed with the taste of manure. *'A good healthy smell'* as his dad used to say. He could have stayed in the pub all night, the beer tasted sweet and for a while he'd tried to forget about all the shit in his life, but he'd used up all his hangovers and tonight he needed his wits about him.

A couple of packed suitcases met Tony as he stepped in through the front door. His heart plummeted. They used to be holiday suitcases, not any more.

Anne was sitting at the kitchen table. She was wearing her coat and turned a photograph in her slight hands. Overhead the spotlights reflected the tears around her smudged mascara, her eyes swollen from crying. Shaking her head at the sight of the bruising around his face, a quiver broke in her voice. 'I want a divorce.' No airs or graces, straight to the point. Anne had always been straight to the point, that's what attracted him to her in the first place.

Over the last bottle of red in the house, the two of them argued, slammed a few doors, talked and cried into the early hours. Long patches of silence were followed by more long patches of silence. In the short term, they both agreed for him to pick Martha up after school on Wednesdays, as long as he had her back by seven and all day Saturday. These were the rules, the rules he had to get used to; then, she left a parting shot.

'We'll have to think about selling the house.' No airs or graces, straight to the point. As the photograph dropped from her fingers she gave him one last look and added quickly. 'We had it all.'

That photograph. That photograph Finch had given him.

It was well after three when Anne left. Loading the cases into the back of her mother's car, Tony made a joke about her taking *the kitchen sink*. He thought he saw a glimmer of a smile, the smile he'd fallen in love with, but he was mistaken. Watching her drive off, he could hear her mother's voice. *'Don't look back, don't feel sorry for him, he's had it coming for years, be strong.'*

Sitting at the bottom at the stairs, Tony felt like a ghost in his own house. Inside, his heart was torn apart as he sobbed uncontrollably. His chest wheezed with self-destruction and self-pity as he felt himself heading over a cliff. Time passed, it could have been an hour, maybe two before Tony noticed through the little tears he had left, a crumpled piece of paper sticking out of the letterbox. The note was scribbled in pencil and read: *'Thank you from all the mothers and father's of the world. As promised, it's in your garage.'* Again, the handwriting was instantly recognisable. The tears had dried on his cheeks but he knew in the following months there would be more to come.

Quietly opening the front door, Tony looked through bloodshot eyes into the dark. It was still, quiet, the sky full of stars. Making as little noise as possible, Tony turned the handle on the garage door. Lifting the door over his head, he took a step inside. Flicking a switch, the dingy garage became partially flooded with shadowy light. At the far wall, a number of boxes and a pile of half empty paint tins were squashed in by a stack of unused wood flooring. Resting alongside some garden furniture was Martha's bike. He noticed it had been moved. Crouching down he spotted through the spokes of the wheel an unfamiliar tartan wash bag from a launderette. Reaching between the bike and the paint tins he yanked out the bag and slid it across the concrete floor towards him. Unzipping the top of the bag he peered inside. The light was poor so he switched on a battered desk lamp and shone the blue light onto the contents. The wash bag was packed with bank notes. The wind rattled the garage door. Spinning around, Tony looked behind him. He was alone, but at any second he thought someone would spring out of the darkness and snatch the money from his grasp. His hands trembled as he dug deep into the bag. Removing bundles of bank notes, his eyes gleamed. There were fifties, twenties and tens. A bead of sweat dripped off his nose and dropped onto one of the banknotes, hitting the Queen's face. Tony laughed, trying to control his excitement he stared at the bundles of cash. There was sixty, eighty grand, possibly more. Young had kept his word, his promise.

Stuffing the money back into the wash bag he felt himself having an adrenaline rush. It was just like the ones he had when he won on the horses, just like the ones he had when he won on the tables. This is how it felt to be a winner. Concealing the bag behind the back of the garden furniture, he moved Martha's bike back in front, then switched off the garage light.

Standing in the hallway, his prison shirt stuck to his back with sweat. Trembling all over, Tony ran his hands over his sweaty face and counted the money over and over again in his head. *Eighty grand possibly more.* The money would pay off most of his debts; it would give him a second chance. Tomorrow he would pay off Vine the bookie, then he'd put a smile back on the bank manager's fat face. Short-lived, the adrenaline drained from his body. His thoughts reversed back to Anne and Martha, Finch, Rogers then Jennings. Then he remembered the security tape. It was still sitting on the passenger seat of his car.

Slotting the tape into the video recorder, Tony resisted to temptation and poured himself a neat vodka. Pressing the 'play' button he sat back and prepared himself. On a few occasions he turned away from the television, the images on the screen too disturbing to watch.

After watching the tape, Tony continued drinking vodka in the silent darkness. His body and mind felt numb.

'Please let me sleep. Please take me into your arms sweet Morpheus.' But the voice inside his head never answered him back. Frightened to close his eyes with the thought that he might never wake up again, he eventually dozed off.

Tony found himself waking up on the couch. Focusing through the gap in the curtains he looked up at the strip of stars in the blue black sky. Rolling to one side, he tried to work out what time it was. 4, 5, 6, in the morning? Rubbing his bruised ribs, he grunted as he sat up. Sitting in the dark he could feel the stiffness throughout his body. Stretching his legs, his bare foot kicked over the empty vodka glass. Although his head throbbed with vodka the swelling in his face had gone down. He was grateful his nightmare hadn't returned as his thoughts drifted to the images on the security tape.

He thought about BLACK NUMBER 8.

He thought about the money, blood money.

He thought about Finch and his mother's gaunt, whitewashed face looking up at him.

He thought about Young and his children. He heard their cries for help.

He thought about Rogers' smile.

He thought about Jennings. His bullet-proof face.

He thought about Anne, the divorce.

He thought about Martha's sweet smile.

He thought about his debt.

Leaning over the arm of the couch, he reached for the switch of the table lamp.

'Leave the light off!'

The voice sounded like it was threaded through a mouth organ. Tony squinted in the direction of the voice. A silhouetted figure sat in the far corner of the room.

'I warn you, I have a gun in my hand and I won't hesitate to use it, do you understand?'

Then the click of the gun's safety catch. 'Yes.'

'Good we understand each other.'

The figure lifted himself up from the armchair and pulled back the curtains sending a shaft of street light into Tony's eyes. For a few seconds he was blinded as a CD of Bob Dylan landed in his lap. 'You have good taste in music.'

Tony brought his hand up over his brow and tried to shield his eyes from the bright light. 'Who are you?'

'I'm the friend of winters past.'

'What do you want?'

'A favour, a request, an order. It all depends on how you look at things.'

'You've made a mistake I…'

'I don't think so Tony.'

'Do I know you?'

'It doesn't matter who I am.'

'Are you going to kill me?'

'That depends on you.' The figure took a deep breath and moved away from the window. 'I have a client who has very generously paid off all your debts.'

'What client? What are you talking about?'

Ignoring the questions, the figure continued. 'My client has asked you to do something for him, but apparently you're reluctant to help him?'

Confused, Young flashed through Tony's head. Tension tightened his shoulders and chest. 'Who are you talking about?'

'Somebody I can't get to unfortunately. You seem an intelligent man, work it out.'

Then it clicked.

'I don't like loose ends, and he's a loose end for me.'

Tony had to think quickly, Finch was dead, his life was at stake. 'You have no say in the matter, it's me who you're dealing with now.' Tony caught a glint of a gun.

'You need to kill Finch for me, for his sake as well as your own. Then everyone will be happy. Let me explain something to you. I kill people for a living, I also organise things that need organising. Like having Finch's mother moved to a certain nursing home you're familiar with. You have a nice family. I will kill you and them and sleep easy at night. There are no ifs, no buts. All my client wants in return is that you be nice to his mother. Take her a box of chocolates on her birthday; she was born on Christmas day, that's not easy to forget is it.'

Tony could feel his heart pounding as the figure hovered behind him.

'You will kill Finch sooner rather than later.'

Cold metal tickled the back of Tony's neck. 'This gun has killed about twenty people. Follow me, and it will kill you.' Tony pissed himself. As the figure moved towards the door, Tony caught a flash of his orange socks. Seconds later he heard the front door shut quietly. Rigid, with wet trousers, Tony sat motionless, terrified to move. Six or seven minutes passed, when eventually he found the nerve to walk out of the lounge and into the hall.

Shivering, he thought about the man with the mouthorgan voice. He obviously hadn't read or listened to the news that day and as for the tape sitting in the video recorder, if he'd watched that he would have found out he'd been wasting his time.

CHAPTER FORTY-SIX

Winter was finally starting to creep in, the country was glad to see the back of the worst autumn on record, including Tony, who no longer knew or recognised himself. At times when he rattled around in his house he felt like a child, too young to understand what was happening too frightened of what the future would hold. On Saturdays he had Martha for the whole day. They'd go to the park or go to a movie. She would stay overnight and they would watch a video and order pizza, he cherished every moment. But one Saturday Martha had a Halloween party. Lost, Tony found himself in the bookies, courtesy of Young's cash. He knew what he was doing, what he was about to do, but the place was like a magnet and he didn't know why, he never knew why. Unexpectedly that voice would creep up behind him when he was least expecting it.

One little bet won't hurt Tony.

One little bet won't hurt.

Around ten in the morning he went into the bookies and it was well after six in the evening when he came out. He'd missed the rain, the sunshine, and had drunk over ten free cups of coffee. Starting with the cartoon races he moved onto placing bets across ten race meetings, winners, doubles, and place-pots. Next the football, score draws, first goal scorer, half time, full time. He lost count of how much he bet on the dogs, but the money came out of his pocket as quick as the greyhounds came out of the traps. In his pocket was a wad of more than two hundred betting slips and was worth over £1,500 in winnings, but he'd spent over three grand in bets. It wasn't the buzz of winning or losing, he didn't know what it was that kept on dragging him down into the world of gambling, but he knew one thing, *money was the root of all evil*, another saying he remembered from his upbringing, another bit of advice he ignored.

Looking across the road he could see through the brightly lit window of the terraced house that the Halloween party was still in full swing. Checking the time on his wrist watch, Tony recalled the time when Anne had bought it for him. It was a first anniversary present. On numerous occasions he'd come an inch-close to pawning it off, when he had holes in his pockets, when he considered taking the money in Martha's money box.

Three weeks had passed since the man with the mouth organ voice and the orange socks had paid him a visit. '*I have a client who has very generously paid off your debts.*' The following morning he had made a few phone calls and to his amazement, the man who had threatened his life had been telling the truth. His first call had been to Vine the bookie. According to Freddy, a snotty-nosed kid slid a brown envelope across the counter and said it was *from Mr Tony Evans for Mr Vine*. The debt collectors in contrast, had been paid off by an unknown source straight into their bank account and another donation into the bank had returned the smile to the bank manger's fat face. At last the weight of the world had been lifted from Tony's shoulders. Finch and the man with the orange socks had known a lot more about him than he first thought. The financial relief had been enormous, but as hard as he fought, the gambling continued. On the same day he made the phone calls, he watched breakfast TV foggy headed. Governor Morris' appearance on television headlined the BBC News. Standing outside Brainforth, Morris read out a statement, pontificating to small crowd of journalists and flashing cameras,

'At seven thirty yesterday morning on the 23rd of October Mr Alistair Finch who is serving two life sentences for murder was found dead in his cell. On the discovery of his body, the conclusion was that he was beyond resuscitation. As is the custom with Her Majesty's Prison Service a full, official, internal enquiry will take place. Regarding the death in Brianforth Prison of Alistair Finch a full report will be released into the public domain when the enquiry is completed.'

From behind a microphone a reporter shouted out a question. 'Is the death of one of your officers found up on Buttercup Hill connected in any way to the death of Alistair Finch?'

'No.'

'Isn't he one of the officers who found Finch?'

'No.'

A number of other questions were thrown in Morris' direction which he answered in his usual dour manner before finishing with, 'Thank you, I have nothing else to say at this present time.'

The three weeks since Rogers' and Finch's deaths seemed like three years.

Tony's mobile rang, it was Jennings. He let it click onto recorded message. Jennings was in the pub and he wanted him to meet him for a supposedly friendly drink. After Jennings had retired, they had spoken and met only the once and Tony had called the shots. Jennings was still sweating over the security tape, *let the bastard sweat.*

Minutes after Morris' broadcast the police had called at Tony's house. Their questions were relentless about Rogers. Why was he so drunk? What was his state of mind? Why did he let him drive? Did he know why he would take his own life? Reluctantly he stuck to the story, Jennings' story.

Rogers' burnt out car had been discovered up by Buttercup Hill and Morris had been given the job of telling Tony and Jennings the bad news on the day Jennings had cleared out his locker for the last time. '*I'm sorry. I knew he was a good friend of yours. Expect a knock at the door from the police. They will think the two incidents are connected. Put them straight; think of the reputation of Brainforth.*'

After Rogers, Tony knew that for him, being a prison officer would never be the same again. There were many officers inside Brainforth like Jennings; he'd left his legacy. Seeing him in his true light, dangerous, full of bravado the insanity in his eyes, on reflection he should have seen it coming. He'd made him feel uncomfortable on the first day he met him, small, how he manipulated Rogers, but more than anything it had now made him question his own morals. There would always be the lingering whispers around the prison walls about Finch's death. It was to be expected, but things had changed and Tony knew whatever the outcome his days at Brainforth were numbered. It was too early to put in a transfer request, but it would be on Morris' desk before too long. Knowing how the prison service worked, Finch's name would be swept away like the autumn leaves and never mentioned again. Finch was a monster, but the guilt over Rogers was self-inflicted and it was something that would haunt him for the rest of his life.

On the second day the police paid him a visit, the first of the 'divorce papers' shot through the letterbox. Anne's solicitor had made it clear in bold, red letters citing 'Unreasonable Behaviour'. It never entered his head to contest. The house would be on the market by the end of that week. Sad as it was, it was time to move on. As for the police, he stuck to the story, the story that Jennings had worked out in his sick head, the story that wouldn't be questioned. But there was one thing he could do.

Tony wrote the address on the front of the envelope.

For the personal attention of,
Mr Morris,
Governor of Brainforth Prison.

Slipping the security tape inside the jiffy bag, Tony thought of the repercussions. The tape showed Jennings and Finch having a heated argument in the cell. Then Jennings snapped. Shoving the prisoner to the ground, Finch snarled up at Jennings and grinned, that evil grin. More words were exchanged, before Jennings bent down and from nowhere produced the razor blade. Moving forward he sliced through one of Finch's wrists. Then grabbing his other arm he sliced through his other wrist. Finch fell backwards and smashing the back of his head against the brick wall, became wedged between the toilet and his bed. Wiping the blade clean of fingerprints Jennings dropped it to the floor. Then Rogers entered the cell. He looked distraught and went to help Finch. Jennings held him back, his face distorted with rage. Then, Tony forced his way through the door. Arguing with Rogers and Jennings the tape crackled, sending lines of interference across the screen. Clearing, it showed Tony bending down by the side of Finch. Obstructed by the angle of the camera, it looked like Tony was trying to help. When Tony stood up he reached for the emergency button. The tape showed him being thrown against the cell door by Jennings, then, once again he was held back from trying to get to the emergency button. If the police came calling again, he would tell them the truth. Confession was good for the soul.

Wearing a witch's costume, Martha ran out of the house and dived into her father's arms. Spinning her around and around, he kissed her on the cheek, once, twice, three times.

'Can I have an ice cream Daddy?'

'It's freezing, you'll ice up like the Snow Queen.'

'Oh please Daddy, I didn't have ice cream at the party.'

'Come on then.'

As they walked towards the car Martha waved to someone across the road. Tony turned to see who she was waving at. Parked under a streetlight, leaning out of his cab window, Young was smoking his customary menthol cigarette. Acknowledging Tony with a smile and a nod, the two men held each other's gaze before Young started the cab's engine. Taking Martha's hand Tony smiled back. In a strange sort of way, Young and Tony were lost souls who had rescued each other. In different circumstances he would have liked to have known him better. Martha tugged the sleeve of his jacket. 'Can I have an ice cream Daddy?'

'Daddy can I have an ice cream?'

Picking Martha up in his arms, he held her close, his eyes pricked with tears. 'Promise me something darling, you'll always stay close to Mummy and Daddy?'

'I promise Daddy.'

'Promise me again darling?'

'I promise Daddy. Stop squeezing me, put me down.'

Tony relaxed and lowered Martha to the ground, holding her face in his hands he kissed her again.

'Can I have an ice cream now?'

'Of course you can sweetheart.'

Tony looked up and watched Young's cab disappear into the darkness. He would never see or hear from him again.

CHAPTER FORTY-SEVEN

Anders cast his line out onto the large expanse of lake. The surrounding tall trees, packed with heavy snow sent out an aroma of pine that was intoxicating, at this time of year. Early December in Norway was spectacular.

Sneaking out of Oxford two months earlier, he drove his BMW out of the country via the ports of Dover and Calais. The photo-fit of his face which was across every front page and circulated at every port and airport in Europe bore no likeness to him what so ever. The choir boys who watched the old Irishman limping out of St Benedict's and the man who identified a drunken Australian had done a good job.

Finding himself on the top deck of the Cross Channel Ferry he looked back at the White Cliffs. It was windy, icy cold as he stood alone. Hearing about Finch's death on the car radio, his thoughts then strayed to the prison officer, but only for a fleeting moment. Feeling the sea air on his face, he looked down and caught sight of an orange glow, his socks. A crooked smile brushed his face. What a giveaway, he hadn't given them a second's thought. Now, sitting by the side of the lake he was totally unrecognisable. Head shaved to the bone, he had grown a bushy, handlebar moustache like a Hell's Angel and lost weight. Interpol and Scotland Yard had been after him for over a decade but he'd meticulously covered his tracks. Leaving no ticket-chase, it had become a game of cat and mouse, a game he'd won. They would have a hard job rooting him out now. With false papers, a false identity, he had finally retired. Finch had been his last employer. It was the end of the road.

A slight tug at the end of his line sent ripples shooting across the fresh water. He was tempted to jerk the rod upwards and go for the catch, but reconsidered, like his previous profession, fishing was a game of patience. It had been a successful day; so far, the three trout he had caught would provide him with a hearty dinner that night.

A heron swooped down and settled on a nearby rock, it was totally oblivious to Anders, who sat there admiring its beauty. Another tug came on the line. Suddenly a couple of birds shot out of a cluster of bushes behind him breaking the tranquillity of the lakeside. The heron took off from the rock; its back legs skimming the lake as its long wings flapped, gaining momentum as it flew into the air. Anders watched as it circled the lake like a seaplane before it disappeared over the tops of the tall trees. All was quiet again.

Thin layers of ice were starting to form across the water and by tomorrow the lake would be frozen over, putting an end to his fishing for the next six months. In the summer he would dive off the wooden jetty and swim in the lake, the same lake he'd once swam as a boy, a boy who nobody knew as the man sitting there today. Between a gap in the branches of the trees Anders could see the weather vane of the local Sten church. Like many of the buildings in Norway it was built out of wood by the local tradesmen and crafted to perfection. Earlier that day, as he made his way towards the lake he passed the entrance to the church and looked up at the carved faces looking down on him. One carved face was of a snarling devil, with flaming eyes and fanged teeth. It reminded him of St Benedict's and the smell of death. Anders never dreamt of his past, he trained himself not to have a conscience, but he knew that possibly one day his conscience would catch up with him. And it did. The night before, the small cramped space with its trapped light and dangling shackle came into his dream. Hearing children crying out for help, he could smell the stench of the concealed cupboard. When he woke his chest thundered with palpitations and he prayed the dream was a one-off, time would tell.

Anders tightened his grip on the rod, it was time. Whipping the rod backwards the fish took the bait and the hook. Anders reeled in his catch. From the fight the trout was giving him, he knew it was the catch of the day and he was right, it was a beauty. Lowering the silver scaled fish into the net, it flapped for its life, its mouth gasping for air. Anders grinned; *this is the one, the one that will finish up on my dinner plate tonight.* Then he froze. From behind him, Anders heard the *click* of a gun's safety catch. *What goes around comes around.*

> *There's no regrets.*
> *No tears goodbye.*
> *I don't want you back.*
> *We'd only cry, cry again.*
> *Say goodbye…*

CHAPTER FORTY-EIGHT

Crunchy white snow as vibrant as the setting orange sun enveloped the large graveyard. Lyndon Cemetery was the burial place for thousands. Sprawled across a hillside, some of the graves were marked with giant obelisks. Gaelic crosses along with winged angels decorated the tombs crafted in granite. It had been the final resting place of the rich cotton owners, whose mills had littered the surrounding countryside in the age of industrial Britain, now long forgotten.

The wreaths and flowers that rested by the side of the open grave brought a flash of colour across the bleak landscape. Some cards read: *In loving memory to Brian.* Another read: *To Brian, you will always be remembered. From the group.* Wearing a heavy black overcoat over his prison uniform, Tony stood huddled amongst the pinched faced mourners. Rubbing his cold hands together, a couple of snow flakes floated down the back of his shirt collar. It caused him to shiver, sending out a stream of grey fog from his chattering teeth into the icy air. Pulling up his collar around his neck he mulled some more. He'd read about Brain Young by accident. His name had appeared in the obituaries column of the local rag and he wrestled over attending the funeral for days. In the end his conscience had got the better of him.

Oblivious to the mundane tones of the vicar's voice reciting the *last-rights,* he could only look downwards into the grave and onto the coffin lid with its inscribed brass plaque. Memories of his father's funeral came back to him. The things he wanted to say, the things he wanted to forget. He wished he'd spent more time with him, now those wishes were lost forever. He missed him dearly.

Anne and Martha had moved back into the house, which was now off the market. They both agreed over a few glasses of wine that it was best for Martha. It was a civilised break-up. Renting a small two-bedroom flat not far away from the family home and Brainforth, Tony was reasonably content. Anne had started Spanish and yoga lessons. Recently, he'd noticed her wearing different make-up and she'd had golden tints put in her black hair, the hair he'd always loved, the hair he longed to smell next to him again. He'd come-to-terms that a new man would come into her life at sometime, but he never in a thousand years thought he would become another government marital statistic. Bring on the violins, everything was self-inflicted. Martha took everything in her stride and stayed with him at the weekends and one night in the week. He wasn't as good a father as he had first thought. She had her own pink bedroom but had grown out of the bedtime stories. Attending the meetings at Gamblers Anonymous, he always questioned the 'do's and don'ts'. Every week there was new a face, every week an old face had disappeared. Deep inside his coat pocket, a number of leaflets bearing his picture were about to be distributed around every bookie in Oxfordshire. They were *Self Exclusion* leaflets which Tony had taken out himself. It banned every bookmaker in Oxford from taking a bet off him, no matter how big or how small. Although it was wishful thinking, he hoped that at some stage in the future, Anne might come back to him. Hope he clung to daily.

On learning the security tape had found its way onto Morris' desk, Jennings committed suicide. He was found swinging from a branch in the woods behind his semi-detached. Hanging himself with his own prison belt, his wife, who found him, was oblivious to his ten-year affair with Helen, Morris' secretary. He left behind two grown up sons who were studying law at university and a daughter who was planning her wedding that summer. Jennings' retirement would have been spent behind the same iron bars he'd patrolled for years and he would have become a prize-catch for a young con that was out to make a name for himself.

Morris had called Tony into his office in the early hours of the morning – out of the way. Explaining that *'In the best interest of everyone connected with Brainforth, the tape would be destroyed.'* Morris also made it crystal-clear that as Tony had been seen trying to help Finch on the tape that it would be *'In his best interest if the whole incident was forgotten.'* – brushed under the carpet. Their conversation would remain strictly confidential.

Tony felt the resentment from some of the officers as he walked the landings of Brainforth. Every time he turned his back he could hear the gossip of the locker room. After Finch, one officer dying was bad enough but two in such a short time gave him the tag of a being a 'Jonah.' For his own protection he was relieved of duties on the prison landings and on A-Wing. Transferred to 'The Gate.', he watched the daily comings and goings and it bored him rigid. Some days he was met with smiles, some days he had scowls, he had learned to live with it.

'Certain hope of the resurrection to eternal life. Thanks be to God who give us the victory through Jesus Christ our Lord. Amen.'

306

As Tony looked up, the Vicar closed his bible and brought the proceedings of the funeral to a blunt end. A woman with striking-red-hair stepped forward and looked down into the open grave. She kissed a single red rose then let it drop from her trembling hands onto the coffin lid. Looking around at the mourners' faces, Tony thought everyone's eyes were on her, but he was mistaken. Slowly he realised he was the focus of everyone's attention. Their tearful eyes, their gazes were transfixed on him. He noticed Gordon and Helen from the park, her dog still nestled in her arms. They acknowledged him with their eyes and a slight downward frown.

Joining the line of mourners, Tony waited his turn as one-by-one they scooped-up a hand full of soil, and dropped it into the grave. The soil felt moist and cold in his hand as it filtered through his fingers onto the coffin lid. The woman with striking red-hair touched his arm as he passed and said thank you. With a tear sodden handkerchief she wiped away the water lines that had cut through the blusher on her cheeks. She tried to smile, her eyes past grieving, entombed, lifeless, her beauty snatched away from her. Then the goth who he recognised as the waitress from the café in the park stepped forward.

'Thank you.' Her voice was broken, teary.

Then more familiar faces, acknowledged him with a sad smile and a nod. Then he remembered. They were all in the café the same day he went to meet Young, the same day he was propositioned by Gordon. The two firemen, the bearded joggers, the elderly walkers. All of them shook his hand as they passed him by the graveside as if he was some sort of dignitary, as if he was one of them. Some of the faces he didn't recognise but all of them carried an invisible weight. Self-conscious, he wanted to disappear, never set eyes on them again, but for some strange reason he couldn't move, it felt like his legs had been bolted to the ground, he felt humbled by the attention.

Gordon had lingered behind. Thrusting out his hand in

Tony's direction, he cuffed his other hand around his arm and the two men shook hands. 'A sad day Tony, Brian was a good man.' They had only met the once, that day in that café, but the firmness of the handshake and the over familiarity of the greeting added to the confusion running around Tony's head. Filtering away from the grave, Tony turned to Gordon. 'Who are all these people?'

'We never said we were working alone.'

Helen was a few yards away with the goth supporting her arm. Her terrier was sniffing around the base of a large oak tree, its white coat merging into the snowy ground.

'Everyone here was brought together by grief. We've all been affected by murderers like Finch in some sort of way. Not just the parents. Grandfathers, grandmothers, brothers, sisters, cousins, close friends.' Gordon's spidery fingers unbuttoned his woollen overcoat. Reaching inside he took out a hipflask and unscrewed the silver ornate top. Bringing the flask up to his mouth he took a hearty slug then offered the flask to Tony.

'No thanks.'

'Go on poppet, it'll put hairs on your chest.' Helen smiled at Tony as her dog cocked its leg up against the tree. 'About time Charlie, you silly dog.' Her voice scratched through the icy air. Gordon smiled and raised his eyebrows, the wrinkles around his eyes adding to his age. Tony took the flask from Gordon and took a stiff drink. He felt the brandy warming its way down his throat. It made him cough, making his eyes water. Gordon slapped him lightly on the back. 'It's strong stuff, I should have warned you.' Slightly embarrassed, Tony handed the flask back to Gordon, who took another drink and licked his lips. 'Only the best for this occasion.' Turning it around in his leather glove, Gordon admired the silver flask. It was antique silver and bore the inscription around the glass base: *To Dad on your 40th birthday. Love John.*

'This was Brian's – his oldest son John gave it to him. He

was only sixteen when he killed himself. He blamed himself for being on the phone when the twins were taken. For weeks afterwards his girlfriend was found sleeping by the side of his grave. His death had killed her. Brian's wife gave me the flask after he died, said he wanted me to have it. That's her, Lila, the one with the beautiful red hair. Tony looked over at Young's wife. A fair distance away, she was standing alone, by a line of graves.

'Poor Brian, he fought against the cancer. Treated himself the best he could. At least he had some solace in death, thanks to you. Are you coming for a drink?'

'I can't, I have to go back to work.'

'Pity, you could have met the rest of our little group.'

'We're having cake, poppet,' said Helen. Tony caught the goth's smile. It was as a polite smile hidden behind black lipstick if nothing else. With quite some effort, Helen bent down and picked-up her dog. Brushing some loose snow off its coat she sounded exasperated, her breath loose. 'Come on Charlie you little rat, we'll catch our deaths.' She took hold of the goth's arm and they started to walk down the icy path that snaked its way towards the large iron gates of the cemetery.

Following a few steps behind, Gordon continued.

'When Brian lost his family, it destroyed his marriage. They both suffered nervous breakdowns, you can understand it. Losing one child was bad enough but losing three, it's just unthinkable what they went through. Did you know he was a well respected physician?'

'I didn't know.' Tony was surprised, sad.

'Oh yes, very well respected. He was struck-off, for supposed malpractice. He started drinking you see, sold his house. It was beautiful; he showed me a photograph of it once. Out in the country. The sale of his house, that's where the money came from to pay you – that's the one thing we all have in common, all of us

309

would somehow raise the money to pay for things to get done – we know it's an expensive business we're in. Money not only gets things done, it buys silence.'

'Are you asking for the money back?'

Taken back by the remark, Gordon stopped and brushed Tony's elbow. 'Why no, Tony, that's for you, a job well done.' Tapping his nose with the index finger of his leather glove he winked slightly like a dodgy second-hand car dealer 'Our little secret.' Underestimating how cold it was, Tony blew into his hands sending out another cloud of grey mist into the cold air. The sun was slowly disappearing, its tangerine glow now resting on the branches of the bare trees. As they continued walking Tony contemplated telling the truth. He felt wrenched, having sold his soul he felt like a charlatan. Gordon sneezed then buried his nose into his monogrammed handkerchief. 'Bloody cold, I've had it for weeks.' Helen and the goth were talking to a small group of mourners that had congregated at the gate.

'They've come from all over the country you know. See the tall couple; their son went to help an old lady being robbed by a gang of youths. They turned on him, then beat and stabbed him to death. Two of them pleaded guilty and were sentenced to thirteen years. They'll be out by the time they're forty to kill again. See the firemen, the one on the right, that's his daughter next to him. They've come all down from Scotland. Last year they had plans to celebrate his wife's fiftieth birthday by going to New York. All the family were going. The day before they were leaving she was abducted and murdered. The man who killed her cut up her body and set it alight. They knew at the funeral that the coffin was empty. His daughter now takes so much medication that she has dropped out of everything. She wanted to be a vet like her mother. The guy who murdered her mother had his sentence reduced from twenty three years to eighteen on appeal.' Another shot of brandy did its best to kill the cold. Tony looked across the graveyard at Lila. She hadn't moved, surrounded by gravestones, she looked like a ghost. A black ghost.

'You see the young girl with Helen.' Gordon was referring to the goth with the sad, snow-white smile. 'If it wasn't for Helen.' A wheeze, followed by a long sigh locked into Gordon's chest. 'I don't think she would have made it. Her grandfather came out of his house in the middle of the night to stop his campervan being stolen. They ran him down and just to make sure he was dead, they reversed and drove over him again and again. They arrested two men in their forties who had a track record for car theft and had lengthy criminal records. The inquest has been adjourned three times and they still haven't been convicted. There's a good chance they'll be set free to amble the streets again. She's attended every court hearing and has said that the two men show no remorse and just glare and snigger at her across the courtroom. Nobody knows what she's been through – do you know she's on first name terms with the gravediggers here, that's not right for a young woman is it? What we've all been through – it's devastated all or lives.'

Tony looked across his shoulder at Gordon's face. It looked haggard from when he'd first met him. 'What about you?'

Gordon contemplated the question. Lifting the hip-flask up to his broad lips he took another swig. 'Who is the politician you most admire Tony?'

Frown lines ran across Tony's forehead as he tried to fathom out the strange question.

Gordon passed him the flask and answered for him. 'I'm no different from the majority of people who say Nelson Mandela. Why is that you think?'

Tony shook his head.

'Because he forgave his perpetrators, the men who murdered his people. That is why we admire him. All of us want to believe we could be as strong as him and forgive. It's alright thinking you might have the strength to forgive and forget, but unless you have ever been affected by the horror of having someone close to you who has been murdered, then you can never know how it feels. Believe me some of us have tried to forgive.'

Gordon looked across the graveyard then closed his eyes feeling the last of the sun's warmth on his face. Taking a deep breath the words fell from his quivering mouth. 'My only granddaughter was murdered with an eight and a half inch kitchen knife. My family fell apart, ten years later it's still not back together, I doubt if it ever will be. Outside we may give the impression that we're all fine, but inside you're shattered. The slightest thing can trigger a memory too painful to endure. To never hear her laugh or see her smile, to never smell or hug her again is insufferable. In the end nobody's accountable. Apart from us fighting our own grief, we have to fight the Criminal Justice System as well – but you know that, being in your line of business.' Gordon wiped away a tear then guided the flask back inside his overcoat. 'They used to say an eye-for-a-eye, not any more.'

As the mourners left the graveyard, Lila walked up to Gordon and kissed him on the cheek. She had snowflakes in her hair, the port wine mark on her white face more evident. Her eyes were naked of life as she looked at Tony. 'Thank you.'

Two middle aged women clutching bunches of flowers passed through the gates and recognised Lila instantly. Whispering behind the back of their hands, Lila knew what they were saying. As Young had once said, they would always be known as the mother and father of the twins.

As Lila left, Tony offered his hand to Graham, who refused and gave him another wink. 'Before you go Tony, Helen would like a little word.'

Lowering her dog onto the path, Helen left the security of

the goth's side and tottered forward. Tony offered his arm for her to hold onto, she was happy to take it.

Steering him off the main path, she guided him between two lines of gravestones that stretched up the hillside. Her thin, frail fingers dug into his arm and he could feel himself holding her weight as she lent against him. As the snow crunched underfoot, he caught the aroma of her perfume, it smelt of lavender and he thought of Martha and how sweet she smelt. Conscious of the snow and patches of black ice he was surprised how confidently she walked although her breathing was heavy. He noticed they where following a trail of small footprints in the snow. Passing twenty or more gravestones, two crows flew overhead and landed on the top of some nearby branches, stark black against the white landscape. As they continued walking, he was becoming more and more intrigued as to what Helen wanted to talk to him about when suddenly she tugged his arm; it was a signal for them to stop. Looking around, he realised they were in the exact place were Young's wife had been standing alone. Looking down, he saw the footprints in the snow had come to an end. Waiting for Helen to talk, he felt a cold, unspoken breeze thread its way through the graveyard. Then he noticed their names, etched in white onto three black marble gravestones.

John Young, aged 16, loving son of Brian and Lila Young.
Kevin Young aged 7, loving son of Brian and Lila Young.
Sally Young aged 7, loving daughter of Brian and Lila Young.

Crestfallen, Tony looked back across the graveyard and saw two gravediggers shovelling soil back into Young's grave. Helen felt his body quiver. Clinging to his arm, she looked-up and saw tears flooding his eyes. One tear spilt and rolled down his cheek before dropping to the snow. It was a giant tear that joined the thousands of other tears that had fallen onto the summer's grass and the winter's earth.

The sky was slate grey; it had started snowing again. Finding her voice, Helen looked at Tony with black watery eyes, his face forlorn.

'How would you like to do another little job for us Poppet?'

If you have enjoyed reading *Autumn Kill* you are now invited to read the first Chapter of Marc Gee's next novel *Declaration of Guilt*. It will be published by Troubador Publishing in 2010.

Declaration of Guilt

Murder, that's how it all started.

I suppose I should start by introducing myself. My name is James Jacob or 'Jake' as I'm known to a handful of cons incarcerated inside these brick walls of Brainforth Prison. (Inside, I keep myself to myself, I have no choice) I'm writing this book on lined paper on a small table inside my cell, I can honestly say that I don't pretend to be any different from any other prisoner who has written their life story; it's up to you, the reader to pass your own judgment. I know already it won't win the Booker Prize or any other prize for that matter, don't' think of me as a defeatist, but it has never been my intention to create a literary masterpiece. 'Obligated' is the wrong word to use, I feel 'duty-bound' to write down what has happened to me as a legacy to the other prisoners, the other prisoners waiting their turn.

If this manuscript is ever miraculously published, I have visions of it disregarded in a waste paper bin in some Spanish hotel room with a sun faded cover and Ambre Solare thumb prints littering it's dog-eared pages.

If so. So be it.

Well, where do I begin, to tell you the story of murder? Not one, not two, but possibly three by the time I've finished this book and how I ended up in this shit-hole of a jail serving ten years with every villain that has pleaded their heart rendering innocence whilst being 'put-down' by an open mouthed, judge and jury. Insignificant me, a name and prison number scribbled inside a prison log-book, that sleeps deep-inside a dark, bottom draw which never sees the daylight, a name so insignificant that it runs off the bottom of page 132 and continues onto the top of page 133. So why bother? Why spend all these hours sweating over the right sentence and pronunciation, working through the night on full stops, inverted commas, where a paragraph begins and ends, re-write after re-write, because what happened to me on my first night inside 'Cell Number 43' a month ago today, almost cost me my mind and soul. What you are about to read you can dismiss as total fabrication, or a hallucination, lies at its most sinister, I don't really care.

So were did it all begin?

It began on a winter's night in November 1947, just after the Second World War.

Why start here?

Because up until yesterday morning, I didn't know that my fate had subsequently been sealed all those years ago.

Does my fate scare me? It never used too, but now it haunts me. Am I telling the truth? Read on; make your own mind up, but one thing's for sure. What I'm telling you is the truth, the whole truth and nothing but the truth. So help me God.

And so it began, on that winters night on November 1947.

CHAPTER ONE

The drunks who propped-up the bar of the Blazing Stump were a mixture of granite faced Dockers, prostitutes past their sell-by-date and lost souls who had survived Hitler's Luftwaffe and The Blitz. Stale sweat mixed with cheap perfume cut through the haze of cigarette smoke that floated around the walls and scratched the surface of the sawdust floor, which over the years had seen its fair share of spit, broken glass and spilt blood. In the shadow of the docks, rows of brick warehouses and flour mills ran either side of the ale house, opposite silhouetted against a full moon and black sky the giant cranes of the shipyards. 'The Stump' was the natives home-from-home and on this Friday night it was no different from the thousands of other Friday nights when they had got pissed, thrown a few punches, or hitched up their skirts down a back alley for a few extra bob.

Through the pub window, a flickering street light cut lines across Len Hutton's craggy face. Heavy-set, he sat alone on a bar stool sipping his pint, his eighth of the night. Watching the alcohol take hold around him he pulled on a Woodbine and coughed a chesty cough, a smoker's cough. Approaching sixty he'd seen it all. An ex-merchant seaman, with a button nose, receding grey hair swept back over his head and nestled on the shoulders of his leather jacket. Crooked yellow teeth, stained from years of nicotine, matched his yellow shirt and his baby-blue eyes could convey a thousand sea-faring stories, from fist fights in Hong Kong through to feeding basking sharks in the Straits of Gibraltar.

As the calluses on his large hands wrapped around his pint, something caught his attention out the corner of his eye. Swivelling around on his bar stool, he leant forward and wiped the condensation from the pub window with the palm of his hand. Squinting into the blackness of the glass he struggled to focus through the reflections on the window and the glare of the streetlight. Outside, in the shadowy cobbled street he saw a streak of light, it looked unnatural, surreal. Then, the realisation of what it was hit him like a thunderbolt - as the hairs stood up on the back of his neck his eyes widened, a look of horror sweeping across his face. "Jesus!" Springing to his feet, the pint slipped from his grasp sending an explosion of beer and shattering glass across the wooden floor. Crunching the glass under the soles of his leather boots, he barged through the drunks spilling beer in his wake. Someone shouted "fight!"

Usually, but not this time.

Crashing through the double doors of the pub, Len was hit by the smell of the sea and a vision that would haunt him forever. A few hard hitters looking for a piece of the action staggered after him and froze in disbelief. What seemed like a young teenage girl was engulfed in flames. Staggering across the road one of her shoes skidded across the polished cobbles, her high-pitched screams cutting through the air like a knife. More drunks fell out of the pub and watched as Len ripped off his jacket and stepped towards the human fireball. A trail of flames clung to the girl as she spun around in circles before smashing into a warehouse door. Crashing to the ground, her skull smacked the curb with a tortuous crack. Dropping his leather jacket over the burning girl, Len fell to his knees and started beating his hands on the epileptic body as it bounced violently up and down. A woman screamed, the smell of paraffin and flesh poisoning the air. The palms of Len's hands started to burn as he frantically thrashed his jacket from the girl's head to her back, then down to her thighs and legs. What seemed a lifetime, the flames were eventully smothered. Len choked, his face smudged with black smoke, his eyebrows and eyelashes singed by the intensity of the fire. Defeated, his hands shook as he benevolently placed the jacket over the girl's head. Some of the women turned away, horrified by the sight of the girl's body, her screams which had now died along with her young life.

Exhausted, Len climbed to his feet and looked down on the twitching body. The palms of his hands were arid and strands of hair were entangled in his burnt fingers. Feeling dizzy, he could hear his chest wheezing as the air fought against the smoke in his lungs. Len was suddenly nudged to one side as the beer bellied Landlord tipped a bucket of water over the blackened, charcoaled figure. He was too late. The water brought hissing and a cloud of steam up into the cold night air. All that was recognisable was the girl's shoe lying in the gutter, a small black lace-up and the hem of her smouldering flowery dress. The shrill from a policeman's whistle zipped into the ears of the huddled crowd. A babyfaced copper, with short blond hair and acne barged his way through the silent onlookers. "Police! Out of the way there, let me through!" Looking down on the corpse, he whisked his hand across his mouth and nose as the smell of death drifted upwards. Turning white, his stomach churned. Spinning on the heels of his polished boots, he pushed his way back through the spectators. Falling against the pub door, his legs buckled as he curled forward and wrenched up his guts. He wasn't the only one. Overhead, the pub sign of The Blazing Stump swung and creaked as a cutting wind blew. Paint peeled, the sign showed an old sea-dog slumped drunk in an armchair, a pewter mug of ale spilling out of one hand, his wooden leg in flames in the hearth of the open fire. Ironical.

A comforting hand patted the back of the policeman's shoulder as the heavy voice of the Landlord came from behind him. "You alright son?"

Wiping his mouth with the back of his hand, the policeman slowly recovered, his eyes bloodshot and watery. Turning to a scruffy kid wearing a peak cap that shadowed his eyes, the Landlord spoke in an unyielding voice. "Go to the station as quick as your legs will take you lad and ask for the Desk Sergeant, tell him what's happened." The kid whisked off, the tail of his coat flapping after him, his clumpy boots thumping across the cobbles.

"Come with me." The Landlord escorted the ashen faced policeman into the deserted pub; macabrely a couple of drunks, oblivious to anything were still slumped at the bar singing an out-of-key sea shanty. As the Landlord stepped behind the bar, the policeman felt beads of sweat trickling down his brow. Running his hand across his forehead, he caught his reflection in the mirror at the back of the bar and noticed a splatter of vomit across the shinny, silver buttons of his police tunic. As he brushed his hand down the front of his uniform, a shot of brandy was slid across the bar in his direction; he nodded a *thank you* at the Landlord's fat, ruddy face and knocked the spirit back in one. The brandy was harsh and made him swallow a sharp intake of breath. One by one, the drunks filed back into the pub, sober, mortified, lifeless eyes, some of the women sobbing uncontrollably. Catching Len's gaze, the policeman turned his back as embarrassment turned into pent up emotion and shuddered through his body. Gulping hard on the acid at the back of his throat he gripped the bar for support and suddenly found himself sobbing uncontrollably.

According to police records a child goes missing every five minutes, thankfully the majority are found but for some anguished parents some are not. As a father myself I could not imagine what it would be like to lose a child in such horrendous circumstances. In researching certain elements of this book I have avoided the sensitive issue of interviewing any parent or any relative who has lost a loved one, but this book is dedicated to all of them.

A donation from the proceeds of this book will be offered in support of Claire House Children's Hospice.

Claire House
CHILDREN'S HOSPICE
WHERE QUALITY OF LIFE IS PRECIOUS

The old fashioned meaning of the word hospice was 'a place to rest on your journey'. At Claire House Children's Hospice we don't have the power to change the end of the story but we can make a significant difference along the way.

Claire House charity number: 1004058